About the Author

Robert Potok holds an Sc.D. (Doctor of Science) degree from M.I.T. in Nuclear Engineering, and has spent his career as a data scientist and research director both in the physical and marketing sciences. He and his wife, Penny, were both foster and adoptive parents with the State of New Jersey, and deacons with the Presbyterian Church USA. Widowed and remarried, Robert is now semi-retired and lives with his wife, Bolaji, in Mountainside, NJ.

Author's note: One of the great enjoyments of creative writing for me is exploring the possible evolution of both technology and morality. I have kept the sci-fi in this novel "hard" to the best of my ability, tying it to actual physics and technology where possible (my foundation for wild extrapolations!). I am especially fascinated by what's currently a missing science, the physical basis for consciousness. On this topic, sincere thanks to physicist Roger Penrose for his groundbreaking observations and conjectures.

Robert E Potok

TRIAL BY FUSION

Robert E. Potok

TRIAL BY FUSION

Vanguard Press

Vanguard Press is an imprint of
Pegasus Elliot Mackenzie Publishers Ltd.
www.pegasuspublishers.com

First Published in 2024

Vanguard Press
Sheraton House Castle Park
Cambridge England

Printed & Bound in Great Britain

I dedicate this work with much appreciation and love to all the people who taught me how to understand, how to trust, and how to doubt.

Chapter 1

Time: Tuesday, December 22, 2099 01:31 U.T.

Location: 80 degrees 16' South, 156 degrees 30' East, 1800 meters altitude in the Darwin Mountains, 1085 kilometers from the South Pole

"What do you think, Jorani? Now?"

My walking companion tilted her head towards me, pulled back a flap on an enormous glove and glanced at her wrist assistant. "Yeah, or maybe another minute. What the heck. Call it now."

I nodded and we turned to stand side by side, putting our backs to a brilliant sun and gazing at the tall granite marker before us, our shadows touching its base. We were commemorating both the solstice and an event that had occurred at this site four thousand five hundred days previously, exactly to the moment.

Such dichotomy! We were in a frozen world filled with dazzling white light, and right at this moment, the sun's azimuth was due north with an annual high noontime altitude of thirty-three degrees. Jorani and I and all the other finalists had been at Pic station for nine days now, occasionally catching glimpses of the never-setting sun as it made its grand oval loop in the sky. But we never had time to wander about and appreciate the stark and awesome beauty around us, not until now.

Jorani seemed to echo my thoughts. "What a contrast, Steve. A part of my mind is telling me everything I'm seeing is what I should expect. But another part of me just wants to freak."

I sympathized with her. I had grown up in the Commonwealth of Yukon, but as I learned when we shared adjacent seats on the Pic transport, this was Jorani's first trip outside southwest Cambodia. "Really? I thought you had mountains in Koh Kong."

Jorani laughed. "Nothing like this!" She waved expansively with her arms and added, "I'm so glad it's over, the testing, I mean. Not just here. I mean the years of insanity."

I grunted an affirmative in reply. Our final evaluations had ended a few hours ago. The only part left now was to blow off some steam and wait for the results. And I mean blow off some steam literally. Jorani suggested we take a break from the festive parties going on in the residential areas, so, after asking permission from base personnel, we donned parkas from one of the storage lockers and came outside to the stone pillar that marked the center of Pic territory. I idly thought we had the same shape as the marker, walking cylinders in what was for the area a balmy day. The current temperature was minus twenty-seven C, and the air super dry and unusually still, making our steamy exhales interesting to watch, especially for Jorani. My eyes fell to our shadows, watching them stretch towards the Pole.

I felt Jorani's glove bump against mine, and for a moment we held hands through centimeters of insulation. "Want to go for a hike?" she asked.

"Hmm? What do you have in mind?"

"Oh, nothing crazy, just to the perimeter and back." As I studied the sky, Jorani added, "We can keep an eye on the weather. First sign of the katabatic, we head for the nearest building and come back through the tunnels. Come on!"

What Jorani was suggesting was a four-or-five-kilometer walk, and as candidates we had access to just about everything except the transport. "Okay." From the center marker position, the terrain slopes gently up to the north, south, and east, and down to the west. Without further discussion, we both started to follow our shadows, walking south across the hard ice. The South Pole is magnetic in more ways than one, I guess.

We were walking on sovereign Pic territory. Two weeks ago, only a handful of people had ever done it, and now the number was close to a thousand. After two years of worldwide competition and international horse-trading for the slots, nine hundred and sixty finalists plus a small team of U.N. observers had arrived here for the last selection process. And later today, the observers and at least half the candidates would board the Pic transport and return to Canterbury, New Zealand, the first leg on their way home. But for the others…

The Pic. It all began the year I was born, on a mundane Friday morning in early 2081. On January tenth around 06:00 U.T., unusual blips of static began mixing with the L4 carrier wave used by global positioning satellites. It was nothing the error-correction codes couldn't handle, but the periodic nature of the blips drew an immediate investigation, and results from the first analysis didn't make sense.

The source of the spurious signal seemed distant but locked in a helio-synchronous orbit with the Earth-moon system, in the plane of Earth's ecliptic with a direction perpendicular to the Earth-sun axis. The attributes should have been mutually exclusive. Close to Earth, a body would have to orbit the Earth too, and far from Earth, the object would have a solar orbit very different from Earth's. Yet day after day, the signal source maintained its position, drifting with us against the stellar background at a rate precisely one revolution per year.

For a while the only conceivable explanation was a completely unknown resonance phenomenon between the solar wind and the far fringe of Earth's magnetic field, though how such an interaction could generate periodic pulses in the GHz range was unfathomable. Ground-based receivers soon determined, however, that the signal source was nowhere near Earth, then additional measurements from the solar orbiters caused a second wave of shock. The parallax displacements were huge, more than two minutes of arc and implying a distance of 9.25 light-days, much closer than interstellar. Could this be some ancient deep-space probe run amuck?

But no, the whole situation was preposterous. How could any object 9.25 light-days away orbit the sun in one year? It would have to be under an acceleration of… of what? A simple calculation predicted an object travelling approximately sixteen percent of light speed, maintaining a circular orbit with a radially inward acceleration between 9 and 10 m/s^2.

So a person on the object would be experiencing an Earthlike gravity. For several days, the world was in chaos. Some countries made it a capital offense to attempt contact with the mystery source, but people tried anyway, and with messages so crazy that the United Nations finally got their act together and sent a unified response. A common message was sent from multiple stations, basically asking one simple question: *Are you for real?*

Nineteen days later on February ninth, we got an answer schoolchildren now recite verbatim. "Yes. We are an exploration vessel. We are peaceful creatures. If you want us to come and visit, we will visit. If you want us to go away and not come back, we will go away and not come back. If you want something else, what is it?" The signal wasn't hard to translate. It used the same coding scheme as the messages sent from Earth, and the text was in plain English. And the simple words changed the universe. After a brief and tumultuous session, the United Nations beamed a welcome invitation.

The years 2081 through 2087 were times of soaring expectations. The vessel maintained its helio-synchronous alignment with Earth's orbit, but also began a slightly modified Bernoulli spiral down into the sun's gravity well, maintaining its right-angle position relative to the Earth-sun axis but also dropping a factor of pi in distance to the sun every year. This was no Hohmann transfer orbit! The amount of thrust needed to execute such a maneuver was mind boggling. Even an ultimately efficient light-burner drive would be woefully insufficient to the task, especially considering the vessel's payload had to support a live crew.

Or did it? Were we conversing with an automated system? It didn't seem so, and as the long years of waiting dragged by, the wisdom behind the super-slow descent became clear. Our visitors were giving us time to get used to their presence. Year after year, communications became more conversational as the round-trip time delays dropped annually from 18.5 days to 5.9 days to 1.9 days and so on, down to twenty-eight minutes by the beginning of 2087. And all the while, we were doing our best to get the planet presentable. Worldwide warfare and terrorism dropped to unprecedented lows in what are now called the Approach Years. There was also new determination to tackle longstanding environmental problems. At the time, it was just too embarrassing to do otherwise. Visitors were coming!

Back in 2081, one of the first questions Earth asked the visitors was what they called themselves. They replied their native language used sounds and frequencies outside of human expression, and they asked what name we would be comfortable with for their species. The various

Earth governments were unable to agree on a reply, and a few months later the visitors announced their name as Pic. Someone made a comparison to their earlier communication. "Pick a name for us" had become "Pic, a name for us." It was our first exposure to the Pic sense of humor.

Personally, I kind of like it. Pic technology, Pic transport, it's distinctive and easy to say. And I have clear memories of the live satellite imagery as a young child, seeing the great ship enter Earth polar orbit at the end of July and then land in the Darwin Mountains four weeks later on August 27, 2087, a few minutes after 01:30 U.T. After much negotiation, the U.N. had granted the Pic sovereign rights on a circular plot of land two kilometers in radius, as requested at a site as isolated as possible. And the Pic had chosen a poetic moment for their landing. It was the first day in more than four months that the sun had shone upon their landing site. At the precise moment of touchdown, the very top disk of the sun was a thin sliver of brilliant orange light touching the northern horizon.

In spite of the politeness of the conversations, there were monumental fears whether this was the first phase of an Earth invasion. The Pic had revealed almost nothing about themselves in the years it took to descend into the sun's gravity-well. And in the final year of their approach to Earth, our best space telescopes and several fly-bys by reconnaissance probes revealed indisputable evidence of construction. The Pic ship, what is now called the Pic transport, appeared to be building itself in deep space, a great eggshell surrounding a small core that was never quite visible. Doing this after an interstellar journey, and during an acceleration maneuver? How was this possible? And there were no visible means of propulsion. The Pic would politely refuse comment, giving their classic answer, "We have not yet decided to respond."

The ten years after the landing are referred to as the Quiet Years, though 2088 was anything but. After much prodding, which probably had nothing to do with their decision, the Pic answered a few questions about their technology, and it had Earth's scientists howling in dismay.

The Pic claimed they had portals inside their vessel, manufactured structures they called "entangled spacetime," that provided instant access to their home planet. They also said their ship was propelled through portal momentum exchange with a gas giant in their home star system. And no, they wouldn't give another demonstration for a while. Wasn't their ship's observed history demo enough? And no, they had no intention (at least currently) of sharing the technology.

And so began a decade of limited contact and small amounts of trade, mostly in intellectual property of an entertainment nature, music and literature, very little science except for a brief period in the early 2090s in molecular biology. The Pic helped Earth make medical advances against bacterial and fungal infections, but then stopped the program due to concerns about technology transfer. And except for hints from their literature, they told us very little about their culture and government, saying they were still debating the ethics of potentially changing Earth's political structures.

I'm ashamed of my species to admit it, but the mid-2090s had some of the nastiest wars imaginable. The planet was filled with groups of people committing ethnically driven and religiously justified genocide, with other groups screaming at the Pic for not using their technology to stop it. It was one incredible global mess, and as a boy growing up as a citizen of the sixty-three States of the USNA, I often wondered what war my country would send me to someday.

In the midst of this insanity, the Pic kept negotiating and quietly struck a few more trade deals. They began making trips with their transport, and in return for a wide assortment of Earth's fruits, nuts, and vegetables, they used their transport to remove dangerous space-junk from Earth orbit and to place spectacularly massive and capable U.N. satellites throughout the inner solar system. They also gave us physiological information on their species.

Centaur is a really bad description. Yes, Pic are both hexapods and quadrupeds, with four legs plus two arms, but there is no vertical torso, just a breathtaking shoulder design and a graceful horse-like neck supporting a head that looks remarkably like a dolphin's. And they whistle somewhat like dolphins too. But they're definitely land animals, and except for their heads and hands, Pic bodies are covered in short feathery fur. They have lips that can mimic human speech, and like humans, Pic have a majority of their bones in their hands and feet. We share remarkably similar structures in our wrists and fingers, though Pic hands are more slender. I suspect a blindfolded human wearing a glove could shake hands with a Pic and never realize it.

A Pic has five clawed toes per foot on the front pair of legs, and four clawed toes per foot on powerful rear legs. The bidirectional nature of a Pic front shoulder is a biological marvel. It supports both an arm and a leg. Years ago, my first reaction to seeing their body image was to be a bit shocked, and it wasn't just the arms. It's their eyes, larger in proportion to their heads than a human would expect, and having a W-shape similar to the eyes of a cuttlefish. But during my time here in Antarctica, I've learned that Pic are very expressive with their eyes, perhaps even more so than humans. I've come to see Pic as beautiful and very graceful creatures.

Regarding body size, their mass is about the same as a human. The typical adult range is seventy to ninety kilograms, depending on gender, and by that I mean all six genders. Yes, six genders, with each gender fertile with two others. What a bombshell! Humans and Pic share many proteins and amino acids in their genomes, but evolution, and in particular sexual reproduction, took a very different path on the Pic home world.

Pic genders form a 3 x 2 grid, three types by two modes. The mode is what we humans normally think of as gender, male and female. Three Pic genders are female mode. After insemination by the male genders, females give birth and nourish their children through suckling, just like Earth mammals. But the Pic also have the fascinating division of type, described in their own language by multi-tone whistles, but for us simply called alpha, beta, and gamma.

No gender type is fertile with its mode counterpart. For example, alpha males are fertile only with beta and gamma females, while gamma females are fertile only with alpha and beta males. And there is a grand oscillating expression of gender type across the generations in the Pic DNA. Alpha-beta mates will produce only gamma-type children (both boys and girls), alpha-gamma pairing produces beta children, and beta-gamma pairing produces alpha children. The three alpha-beta-gamma gender types are thus entwined genetically just as tightly as the two male-female gender modes.

There are distinct physical characteristics for each gender, and it is in the type direction that personality differences are the most apparent. From Earth documentaries on Pic and also my own experience with the testing, the alphas are crisp, polite, very energetic, and they'll get very annoyed with you if you aren't completely honest with them. Oh, you can withhold commenting about something, that's okay, and you can joke around with them too, but when you do say something seriously, you better speak your true feelings. Feather-fur for the alphas is a motley pattern of black and brown, and their bodies seem harder and more athletic than the other types. A human really doesn't want to get into a fight with an alpha Pic, male or female.

Betas also abhor dishonesty, but they're much more nuanced in expressing their displeasure. They're the most sociable creatures imaginable, and perhaps the prettiest to look at, soft pastel pink and gold zebra striping in their feather-fur. In spite of the grueling pace of the exams, I hope all of us candidates enjoyed our interviews with the betas. My feelings afterwards were of having pleasant conversations that ended too soon.

And then there are the gammas, feather-fur a solid white for the males and tinged with blue for the females. Not much is known about the gammas, at least not until this final round of competition. Previous to our testing, Earth contact with the Pic has been almost exclusively with alphas and betas, but we candidates were interviewed by gammas extensively. I often found the conversations embarrassing. Nothing degrading was ever said, but gammas showed an uncanny knack of pointing out contradictions in my thinking. I never knew my understanding of reality had so many holes in it.

Pic language is as complex as the Pic described it during the Approach Years. They normally talk in simultaneous frequencies, multiple sets of vocal cords producing modulated registers in a high whistling range they call "over" and a single low register called "under" that's in the middle of the human voice range. Humans cannot talk in native Pic, but fortunately Pic can speak human language by using their lips and low-register vocal cords and talking in pure "under". The creatures are also very expressive with their hands, and they have chromatophores on their muzzles to add emotional context. After my days of testing, I have a private conjecture that chromatophore communication might be more advanced than we realize. During one of our rare breaks, I think I saw a pair of betas carry an entire conversation with just their snouts.

The last couple of years are referred to as the Preparation Years. In August of 2097, the Pic were invited to Brussels to attend a U.N. event celebrating the tenth anniversary of their arrival. It was during this event that the Pic suggested a trial testing whether our two species could merge socially. After a decade of acting as quiet visitors and small-time traders, the Pic decided to change the game.

Their proposal was spectacular. They would accept a group of humans on their home world, a group of young men and women eighteen years of age at the start of the trial. The Pic would accept at most four hundred and eighty candidates, and we would be treated as an incoming undergraduate class. We would be taught by Pic instructors for six years at a specially constructed island University — nothing of their advanced technologies, just a normal Earth education in math and sciences and lots of immersion courses on Pic culture. And if things went well, after graduation, they hoped we would have the freedom to move about their home world, finding jobs and living as closely as possible as normal citizens within their society. The trial would end thirty years after graduation, thirty-six years in all.

Earth was astonished. Thirty-six years? And the restrictions on the trial were severe. The Pic would allow only one-way communication during the trial. Candidates could receive personal messages, care packages, and general news from Earth, but nothing would flow in the other direction, not even news of death. And the trial was not without danger. If the Pic suspected a breach in their security concerning portal or other critical technology, the affected candidates would likely be isolated from the others and never allowed to return.

The Pic also revealed that procreation rights were regulated in their society. Humans in the trial (both before and after graduation) would have to petition for each child desired. The worst-case scenario would be the Pic judging the trial a failure but not wanting to send us back. In that case, the Pic would try to give our lives meaning and enjoyment, but no further procreation permits would be issued, and in time the small human population on Pic would age out of existence.

And without much more detail, that's the proposal the Pic laid on the table. They suggested beginning the trial before the end of the century. And oh yes, a Pic year was about two-thirds of an Earth year, so the trial would end in the mid-2120s in Earth years, though the Pic wouldn't get more specific with a date.

Jorani and I reached the southernmost point of Pic territory, designated by an elevated hut boldly labeled with the number 180. It was one of seventy-two perimeter entrances to the tunnel network. Just beyond the hut was a great arc of alternating black and yellow markers, and the terrain beyond that appeared very similar to what we were standing on. Jorani climbed the short steps on the southern side of the hut and on a whim held her wrist assistant near the reader. A large pocket-door slid back and interior lights came on.

I joined her and saw a long flight of stairs descending to a landing and another door. "I remember from orientation there's another flight of stairs beyond the door. Want to go back this way?"

Jorani studied the clear skies around us and shook her head. "I'd rather stay outside, if that's okay with you. Today might be our last view of Earth." She gazed down the stairwell. "This is extremely well built; what a contrast with the wilderness here."

"Well sure, the portal, an infinite resource just a few minutes away. It's the death of distance."

"Yeah, I suppose..." We closed the door and started walking east counterclockwise along the markers, slowly drifting back north. The next hut was labeled 175, then 170. Jorani waved her arms, getting the circulation going, and said to me, "Did they ask you, Steve, what you would miss the most?"

During the testing, we were on our honor not to discuss our interviews, but the testing was over. "I guess I gave a common answer. I talked about my family and friends, stuff like that. I told Ellie I'd miss playing with my dog."

"Ellie?" asked Jorani. "You were asked that question by an alpha?"

"Uh huh. Who asked you?"

"A beta. Do you know Russell?"

"I think so. Enough to say hello to him. He never interviewed me."

"Ah…"

I looked at Jorani curiously. "Ah, what?"

Jorani frowned. "Oh, I was just comparing your answer with mine. I talked about everything from Earth weather to having twenty-four hours in a day. I told Russell I'd miss it all, from Earth units to the colors of the Bonn Pchum Ben, and furthermore,"

"Huh?" I interrupted. "Colors of the what?"

Jorani gave me a sheepish look. "Oh, sorry. It's the Buddhist festival where we bless the souls of our ancestors. So I talked about missing that, and furthermore, what the hell happens if I get pregnant without a procreation permit? At the time, I was so comfortable with Russell that I thought I was just being open. But looking back, I wonder if I was blabbering."

I shrugged my shoulders and then realized that through the thick insulation Jorani couldn't see the gesture. "I'm wondering about the daily issue too," I mumbled as I tried to take in everything Jorani had said.

Who wouldn't be worried about permanent jetlag? The Pic had revealed their planet's daily rotation was somewhat longer than Earth's, but they didn't say by how much. I thought for a moment and added, "That last part though, that's not really about missing something. What did Russell say about the pregnancy question?"

Jorani shook her head. "Just the book response that it would depend on circumstances and he wasn't authorized to discuss the matter further. His eyes though, I think he was asking me to trust that Pic are not monsters. And uh… Actually, I guess he did say something that might be related."

"Oh yeah?"

"Russell said that in Pic culture, morality is more of an individual responsibility, compared to human cultures where governments and religious organizations bundle morality into obligations and punishments." Jorani turned and stared south towards the Pole. "He said something else too. He cautioned me not to think of Pic as godlike or superior to humans. He said the Pic have suffered through social problems we humans have avoided."

"Wow. That's a hell of an interesting comment. Have you told anybody?"

"No, just you."

Our conversation ended for a moment. We continued hiking. As we passed hut 155, Jorani returned to our earlier topic. "So how did Ellie react to you talking about your dog?"

"Oh, she was okay, sympathetic… Of course, alpha sympathy never seems to last very long."

Jorani laughed. "No, it sure doesn't! They're very project-oriented creatures, so different than the betas. It's amazing to think of the two as the same species."

And yet, I had sensed a friendliness with my alpha interviewer and I felt compelled to defend her. "Yeah, but alphas aren't all business. Ellie whistled and translated something at the end of our talk. She said it's a Pic truism: Nobody laughs like an alpha…" I was about to say more when I saw a Pic galloping towards us. *Boy, they sure can move when they want to.*

From my time of testing, I thought there were four distinct Pic work groups at the Antarctic station. The first three groups were adults, several hundred each of base personnel, transport crew, and interviewers. The fourth group seemed a much younger crowd, adolescents, and they acted as friendly guides and escorts for the human candidates. The alpha Pic approaching us now was Albert, one of the base personnel I was chatting with at the party. I called his name in greeting as he stopped before us.

He gave a curt nod of recognition in return. "Steven and Jorani, you are requested and required to come to Pavilion-B." It was obvious he meant right now. "Do you remember the location?"

I felt a lump in my throat. So soon! The decisions had been made. There were two assembly halls at Pic station, each capable of holding five hundred humans easily, and the departure schedule stipulated that the accepted and non-accepted candidates would congregate separately. Pavilion-A was very comfortable, one of the nicest places on the base. Pavilion-B was strictly utilitarian.

Trust an alpha Pic to be polite and issue the summons personally, when he could have just called us on our wrist assistants. "Sure," I replied. "East of the transport, above the cafeteria area. We will comply."

On a whim, I extended my arm and through a thick glove tried to give a hand gesture a beta taught me, left-hand fingers stiff and horizontal, palm to the outside with thumb pointing down, a polite way for a non-alpha to say goodbye to an alpha, and I was certainly a non-alpha.

Through his heated goggles, I could see Albert's large W-eyes blink, and then he did something unexpected. He splayed his arms and forelegs and bowed his neck to us both. It was a gesture of deep respect.

"Wow, Albert," said Jorani. "Thanks. What was that all about?"

"You are my fellow citizens now. Excuse me. There are others I must notify." And so saying, Albert pivoted and galloped back north. Jorani and I turned to each other as recognition set in.

A half day later.
Time: December 22, 2099, 13:32 U.T.

My Antarctic dorm room was cozy, three long comfortable cots taking up most of the floor space, with one tiny multi-paned window through a thick wall pointing directly towards the Pole. I was somewhat surprised when the sun woke me, bright white light coming in almost horizontally. The sun was at the low point of its loop, just fourteen degrees above the southern horizon.

So I had managed to fall asleep, and for seven hours too. Well, that was unexpected but welcome. I felt relaxed and refreshed and had absolutely nothing to do until 14:00. I threw off my covers and cancelled the alarm on my personal assistant. As expected, the room was very cool. With the transport gone, the Pic complex was running on pure battery and hydrogen fuel-cell power. Though the backup systems here are vast, as a rule the Pic are frugal when using them. Inside room temperature would have to drop to around six C before the heat would come on.

Feeling a bit lazy and enjoying the free time, I pulled my warm comforter back on and just snuggled in bed for a while. I was alone in the room. Neither of my two roommates had passed the exams. I had seen them off as they boarded their return flight to Christchurch International Airport. The Pic transport had departed 06:20 U.T. and should have made the 4144 kilometer journey in fifty minutes, landing about an hour before local sunset. The return journey would be just as fast, though the vessel wasn't due back until 14:00 U.T. The United Nations had an evening ceremony scheduled to welcome back the finalists who didn't make the cutoff, and of course the Pic were invited.

My mind went back to my own trip in the transport. Such an amazing way to travel! With effectively infinite thrust at its disposal, the only constraint on the transport was to get above most of the atmosphere before going supersonic. It rose vertically sixty kilometers in six minutes and then took a great-circle suborbital route through the mesosphere, flying in a space too low for satellites but well above human air traffic.

Last chance to back out, I thought to myself. By design, candidates were not allowed outside communication privileges after arriving in Antarctica. The Pic wanted to give us a preview of what the isolation from Earth would be like, to give us one last chance to ask ourselves, *Am I really okay with this?* But if I did resign now, I would not be replaced. The human freshman class on the Pic home world would start with one less student. I thought for a moment and chuckled. One less USNA student... wouldn't my government just be thrilled about that?

My schedule for today was both simple and profound. As soon as the transport was back and re-established main-power connection with the base, the graduates in both the men's and women's dorms would shower and have a light buffet breakfast then work with the Pic to return the residential areas to pristine condition, cleaning and doing the wash in the common facilities rooms and packing everything into storage. It was expected the work would be finished before 18:00 U.T., then we would congregate in Pavilion-B again. From there we would hike a short hundred meters to the transport, entering a central area that had never been seen by humans.

That last short hike across the ice would be absolutely the last moment to change our minds. Once we entered the transport, we would be given additional information on portal operation, knowledge the Pic had no intention of releasing to Earth, at least not for many years. We had all agreed the Pic had the right to drag us physically through the portal if necessary, once we had entered the transport.

The bright white light from my dorm window faded to a dull gray as quickly as if someone had flipped a switch. I got up, looked out and blinked. Something huge was building on the southern horizon. Maybe we would be using the tunnels today. Except for technology, whiteout conditions here could be absolute and dangerous. I remembered my orientation day, practicing setting my wrist assistant to distress mode. It would automatically give me visual and audio cues to the nearest building.

Pavilion-B last night... I'd never forget the excitement. Jorani and I might have been among the last people to arrive, but we were the first candidates to know we were the accepted group. I don't know why, but I never got around to telling Jorani Ellie's full translation of the Pic truism: Nobody laughs like an alpha; nobody shows loyalty like an alpha; nobody breaks the rules like an alpha. Albert wasn't supposed to tell us that we had passed.

Shortly after the U.N. observers announced the news to us, they posted summary results on a large display. We were a class of two hundred and forty men and two hundred and forty women. The Pic had accepted their stated maximum, which was very encouraging, and had evenly balanced the men and women, which was nice. The country breakout gave me pause, however. The USNA was extremely fortunate to have twenty of its thirty-nine candidates selected. Otherwise the Pic had chosen a representation heavily biased towards Earth's smaller countries and cultures, and right now many of those cultures were at war with each other. Would we continue those wars on the Pic home-world? God, I hoped not. At least we all spoke a common language, English. It was something the Pic had insisted on, and their point was very reasonable. Our university instructors had been learning English for years.

Back in 2097, some countries had grumbled a bit over the language requirement. But the two countries with the largest English-speaking populations, China and India, gave their approval, and of course the USNA and the British Commonwealth countries were happy about it. Other countries, I think, were a little miffed, not that they didn't compete just as fiercely for the slots. Many thought it was amazing the U.N. had managed to keep the selection process organized. From the Pic perspective, perhaps that was the first phase of the trial.

I took a deep breath and stretched in my cool dorm, feeling very relaxed. Earth thought the Pic might have given a hint about the spin time of their home planet about its axis. The Pic scheduled the time of final exams here at the Darwin Mountains to run on a twenty-five-hour daily cycle. With the sun always above the horizon, I didn't find it hard to adapt to the longer rhythm. It was kind of nice, actually. It took the edge off what otherwise was a very grueling schedule.

The lights in my dorm brightened and I heard the heating system turn on. The transport must have returned a few minutes early. Relieved that the ship was back before the storm hit and eager for the day and some company, I grabbed a towel and walked barefoot across cold floors, heading deep below to the common showers.

Four hours later

I had volunteered to return a tunnel transport car to a depot on the eastern edge of the base, and was returning on foot to Pavilion-B from a direction opposite the other candidates. As I neared my destination, I noticed a beta-male Pic standing along the tunnel wall, command rank insignia on his sleeve and working intently on a tablet. He flashed me a perfunctory greeting on his muzzle as I neared, not really noticing me. Was he even aware he had said hello? It struck me how much he was trusting me by being so nonchalant. I was an alien creature twice his height and we were in an isolated tunnel, and he seemed totally relaxed about it. Feeling adventurous, I decided to try a conversation.

"Excuse me. Are you the commander of the station?"

He looked up and gave me his attention. "Hello, Steven. You may call me Christopher." He thought for a moment before speaking again. "The Pic military is more relational, compared to the Earth's military hierarchies. It's approximately true that I'm the current base commander."

I was intrigued by his answer, and how it differed from my candidate training, which had included a crash course in warfare. "More relational? Is that possible? Don't militaries need chains of command to function?"

"Oh, the chains are there when needed. We train to function under a variety of protocols. It's a tradeoff both our species struggle with, adjusting the ratio between efficiency and flexibility. Compared to humans, we Pic opt for more consensus when possible. Not just for mission execution — I'm speaking of mission definition."

"Ah, thank you. This is all very interesting. I never heard this before, about your military I mean."

"We hide so much, but our reasons are valid." He flashed me a complex muzzle pattern I wasn't sure how to interpret. A sigh? Regret? Some combination of the two maybe.

"But you're telling me now…"

He nodded. "The interviewers and command-rank personnel are allowed discretion. Conversations will be free for everyone after the transfer, and I'm not anticipating anyone declining the jump. Are you?"

"No, I suppose not. Sorry if I disturbed your work."

His muzzle flashed a simple negative. "I appreciate my opportunity to practice English with a native. How do I sound?"

I decided he wanted honest feedback. "You're very understandable. There's a bit of a high pitch at the end of your sentences."

"Ah." He took a deep breath. "How's this?"

"Sounds good. Thanks for the chat."

He nodded and got back to his tablet. I resumed my walk and a few minutes later climbed four flights of stairs to Pavilion-B. The main floor area was full of people. I seemed to be about the last human to arrive. Four hundred and eighty humans milled about and there were at least an equal number of Pic present. But in spite of the crowd, the hall seemed remarkably quiet. Lifelong ties were about to be broken, and unfortunately the few small pavilion windows were showing a pure whiteout condition outside, depriving us humans of one last view of an Earth landscape. It was a sobering thought to realize our native planet would soon be a place of memories.

Six genders of Pic were mingling with us, and it was interesting to see all three gender types about equally represented, though for the mode, females were clearly more numerous. It was easy to tell the females by how they dressed and the distinctive curves in their necks and hips. Amazingly, it was the Pic females who wore skirts, just like humans. And as I looked around, I realized the group socializing with us now was mostly the adolescent group, our guides. I had missed them yesterday during the parties but they were back with us now.

Many of our young escorts were rising up on their hind legs and giving us hugs of encouragement, asking if we were sure of our decisions. Such a new experience, hugging and being hugged by creatures who were not my species… especially getting hugged by one young gamma female who had a feather-fur so blue that it was breathtaking. I discovered that beta feather-fur was as soft and silky as it looked, alpha feather-fur was coarse and stiff by comparison, and the gammas were somewhere in between. The Pics' concern for us and the happiness in their eyes and muzzle patterns that we were joining them made all the difference in the world to me. My heart was at peace with my decision.

A few minutes before 18:00 U.T., Christopher walked to a podium and asked for everyone's attention. "Greetings and welcome! Given the weather, we'll be using the tunnels to enter the transport. The path is heated, so you'll be leaving your outdoor gear in the closets below. There will be a short intake process once you board the ship, including a description of portal transfers. Afterwards, there will be a longer briefing at your campus."

Christopher paused for a moment, standing upright on hind legs to survey the crowd before dropping back down. "A final reminder, by our treaty with Earth, entering the transport voluntarily is the action that officially grants you provisional Pic citizenship. You will be fully subject to our laws once you cross that threshold, and I appreciate the leap of trust you are making, because you do not know what those laws are. Let us begin! Humans, please allow your escorts to begin sorting and guiding you to the ship. Portal transfers will occur in groups of sixty by two."

I quickly learned that Christopher meant we would leave in groups of sixty Pic with sixty humans. A long double-line formed and then marched to the levels below the pavilion, sixty humans side by side with adolescent Pic escorts. Fifteen minutes later, the process was repeated, then again around 18:30. With the reduced crowd, it was much easier for the remaining humans and Pic to mill around.

While we waited our turns, I chatted with friends and a few former interviewers. I waved goodbye to Jorani as she paired with an alpha male named Max and left with the third group. Shortly afterwards I met a young beta female who seemed particularly interested in getting to know me. She introduced herself as Julie and spoke English like a native, better than many of the human candidates. We shared a few minutes of pleasant introductions, then in spite of her super fluency, she asked if I would tell her a story using Pic sign language.

I gulped at the challenge. As candidates, we had all been exposed to a crash course in Pic hand and muzzle signs, three one-hour sessions per day for eight twenty-five-hour days. I was taught the basic emotional content of muzzle patterns, and the form and grammar of a core vocabulary of hand signs. And I had a big advantage over the other candidates. I had a twelve-year-old cousin back in Whitehorse who was deaf. I had learned ASL years ago.

But could I carry a conversation now in a completely new sign language? I didn't think so, but Julie's muzzle pattern looked so hopeful I decided to try. I chose a tale of how I got lost in the Vuntut National Park. It didn't seem funny at the time, but when I was a kid, I was lost in the woods overnight due to a comedy of errors both on my part and my parents.

Pic whistling bursts can carry a vast amount of information in a short period of time. By contrast, there's a wonderful intimacy that overlies their slower sign language, a cultural standard that's used by friends as an expression of closeness, or by others either for emphasis or for going out of the way to take the time and be polite. My following hour with Julie was delightful, her gentle hands often guiding my fingers through the forms. I learned there was a lot of subtlety to Pic hand signs, far more than I would have guessed from my previous classes. Julie introduced me to an entirely new level of communication where the hands were touching and the information flowed not just through visual positioning but also tactile sensing.

Four more groups of humans and Pic left the pavilion during my lesson, but I was so involved with Julie, I hardly noticed. She would occasionally burst out laughing, not because of my story, I think, but because I was probably signing something completely different from what I intended. To a human ear, a Pic laugh sounds like a high-pitched hiccup. Julie's cries of amusement sounded rather sweet, and by the end of my story, I thought I'd be able to recognize her in a crowd of Pic just by the sound of her whistle.

It was finally our turn to leave. We were in the last group, and Julie guided me to the very end of the departure line. Just about every Pic I could see was flashing Julie complex muzzle signs as we approached our place, and for a moment I wondered if they were telling her to hurry up, but Julie's own muzzle patterns were far from the general patterns of distress, quite the opposite in fact.

We reached our position and stood behind Hariz, an emigrant from one of the new spinoff nations of Indonesia. He was escorted by a beta female whom I didn't know. On some unknown cue, we all began to walk forward just seconds after Julie and I completed the line. Our group quickly descended to a storage level where we dropped off our coats, then two levels below that we entered a well-lit tunnel. We walked the length of it before stopping. Up ahead at the start of the line, I could see an open bulkhead door. It was our entrance to the Pic transport.

This was it! I shivered a bit and took a deep breath. Looking down on my right, I noticed Julie giving a subtle hand sign. It was an offer to hold hands, which in itself was a basic sign, but Julie had added a gentle inverted curve to her wrist, signaling she was asking as a friend who very much wanted to hold hands. There was nothing of this in my courses on Pic sign, and I wouldn't have understood the subtlety without her previous tutoring. I felt quite touched by her offer and gladly accepted. A moment later the female beta ahead of us noticed what Julie and I were doing, and she made a similar offer to Hariz, but without the inverted curve.

Hariz looked startled, glanced at Julie and me for a moment, then signed back to his Pic a basic circle, which is the root for yes, but with the middle finger extended, which is the semaphore for reverse. In other words, he was giving a polite refusal, to which his Pic replied with a polite sign for understood. I looked at the long line ahead of me. As far as I could see, I was the only human holding hands with a Pic.

A minute later, Hariz's escort glanced back at me. I gave a friendly smile and signed with my free hand, "Your partner is probably just nervous."

She gave the polite sign for understood again, then signed, "My name is Kathy," using letter-finger positions that the Pic have mapped to the English alphabet.

I signed back, "I am Steven," spelling out my name.

Kathy's muzzle flashed an emotion of gentle amusement and she signed back, "I know."

I heard a crisp high-pitched whistle and we all began to move forward. Perhaps there were faint hesitations by a few people, but the line proceeded smoothly. As I approached the threshold, Julie hung back ever so slightly, not wanting to lead me. I let go of her hand after lightly stroking her palm with my index and middle fingers, a sign of appreciation for her thoughtfulness. I then entered the transport a step behind Kathy and became the last of the four hundred and eighty candidates to receive Pic citizenship. The bulkhead began to seal as soon as Julie entered.

Our group split and entered three different rooms. I was asked to sit in a chair obviously meant for humans and be examined by a Pic doctor. The room was unusual. It appeared to be a well-equipped medical room, but there were also flowers everywhere, strange and beautiful flowers. The odors were remarkable, spicier than Earth flowers, I thought, very complex. Julie was across the room quietly whistling with other Pic, but when the doctor was finished with me, Julie came and sat Pic fashion, her two rear legs and rump forming a tripod on the floor. With both of us seated, our heads were close to equal height, and she flashed a color pattern on her muzzle that indicated friendly concern. "Everything okay?"

"Me? Oh, I'm fine."

"Breathing easily?"

"Yeah. Wow, these bouquets are really something, aren't they? The colors are a riot."

Julie nodded. "Did the doctor explain it to you? The flowers are testing you for allergic reactions."

"Yeah. He downloaded some extra health monitoring into my assistant too." I absently looked at the ubiquitous bracelet at my wrist. The doctor had also asked me if I'd like my calendar program set to Pic time, and the display on my assistant was now far outside the range of a human clock. The hour indicator was showing a value of fifty-eight. I groaned at the thought of adjusting to such a different daily cycle, but then noticed how fast the seconds were racing, at least double the speed of an Earth clock.

The doctor had said the clock was set for Far Rockaway time, the city of our first transfer. Far Rockaway? Wasn't that in New York somewhere? And why did I know that? There was something familiar about the name. And the doctor mentioned a first transfer. I guessed that implied we'd be making more than one jump. I took another look at the time index. What was a negative time zone?

Well, time to figure that stuff out later. Julie had been patiently waiting while I was lost in my thoughts. I turned to her and asked, "Anyone have a problem with the flowers?"

Julie's muzzle turned a dim pattern showing uncertainty. "The doctors didn't mention anything. That would be unexpected. The treatments last night were comprehensive, pro-viroids." Julie was referring to a series of fast-acting shots that were supposed to improve human immune system behavior.

I rubbed my arm at the memory. "I was injected with… what?"

"I had to make up an English word for it; a live virus that avoids an antibody response and makes beneficial changes. Pic introduced humans to the concept when we first landed on Earth." Julie's muzzle flashed an emotion of sorrow and she added quietly, "The program was stopped when we found evidence humans were weaponizing the technology."

"Yikes. Who was doing that?"

"The more difficult question to answer is, who wasn't. Uh… Actually, I'm limited in what I'm allowed to discuss with you on this side of the portal. Hold off a bit, okay? We'll have lots of time to…" Julie paused. "Okay?"

"Yeah, sure. Christopher told me about the restrictions."

"You spoke with Christopher? Cool."

A few more minutes passed quietly until the doctors were satisfied with us. We then rejoined our two subgroups and hiked through the ship to a large interior space. In the center was a huge spherical chamber I immediately guessed was the portal. Surrounding it in 3-D were four much smaller spheres aligned as a tetrahedron circumscribing the great sphere. Everything was connected by massive struts that seemed to continue through the walls beyond this core room.

We were given a brief description of portal transfer from a gamma male. The four smaller spheres were connected through entangled spacetime to a gas giant in the Pic's home star system, and through portal exchange of virtual photons, they were the ship's source of propulsion and energy. The massive struts around us were used to transfer virtual momentum to the ship's hull. And the central sphere provided continuous communications with the Pic home-world and would take us to a jump cluster at the city of Far Rockaway. The hub was run jointly by the military and the planetary Parks and Conservation department, and from there we would make a second transfer to our campus home.

The description of our pending travel was consistent with Earth's conjecture on portal capability and limitation. It was not a routable system. Rather, a pair of spacetime regions were permanently entangled, and each end of the dipole could provide transport only to the other. The implications for our eventual return to Earth were ominous. If the system on the Pic transport failed, the only way to reestablish contact would be to send another portal through normal space. And how long would that take?

The description of our pending trip continued. Currently we were in the Darwin Mountains at a height of eighteen-hundred meters. After we climbed in and the chamber sealed, our air pressure would be boosted about twenty percent to match conditions at our first destination. The twin transfer chamber on Pic was sixty meters above sea level, which corresponded to an average pressure about two hundred meters above sea level on Earth. Marvelously close numbers!

After pressure equalization, our sphere and its entangled counterpart would be quantum-isolated. Portal interchange of the entangled pair of spacetime continua would be instantaneous. We would know the transfer was complete by noticing a slight change in weight. Gravity at our destination would be 9.622 m/s^2, about two percent less than Earth's. I breathed another sigh of relief at the closeness of the numbers.

And that was it. Without further explanation, we crowded into the sphere, twenty people and twenty Pic standing on each of three floors in a simple cubical structure inside the sphere. The lighting inside was dim but adequate. I was on the bottom floor in a corner with Julie, the room about seven meters square, the ceiling slighter lower than a normal human dwelling but not a problem. I yawned a few times as the pressure increased, and Julie shook her head side to side as if to clear it. She then rested the side of her neck against my upper thigh, and the gesture was so much like my dog greeting me that without thinking I reached down and stroked the thick downy feather-fur under her throat. I felt her shiver slightly.

"Yikes! Julie, I'm so sorry!"

"Huh?" She looked up at me, her muzzle pattern flashing from enjoyment to a state of simple confusion. "Sorry about what?"

At that instant it felt as if the sphere had begun to descend, and I heard the entrance doors slide open above us. I was on another planet!

Chapter 2

Northern Summer 57, 3483 Common Era 41:27 (Time Zone 30, Providence)
Southern Winter 58, 3483 C.E. 11:27 (Time Zone 0, Haven)

I felt disoriented from the effort to assimilate so many points of information, and my throat felt a bit hoarse from whispering notes to my assistant. We (all the new human citizens) had been getting briefings at the campus auditorium for almost ten hours now (over four Earth hours), with just one short break to hit the restrooms. Almost everybody was looking shot. I was probably one of the very few who had managed a decent amount of sleep recently. Jorani! She was so right, worrying about the difficulty of adjusting to new units. It was almost like being a kid again, starting everything from scratch. There was so much basic stuff to learn.

There were fascinating parallels between the Pic home-world and Earth, including a fixation on sixty. It reminded me of the Ishango artifact on Earth, prehistoric humanity making rows of sixty notches on a bone. But the Pic did us one better, sixty seconds to a minute, sixty minutes to an hour, and sixty hours to a day. There were sixty time zones too, numbered -29 to +30. To get to Universal Time at the world capital, simply add the local time zone number to the hour of the local time.

There were also sixty days to a season and four seasons to a year. The planet's tropical year (my year too now) was a hair more than three hours shy of 240 days (three short Pic hours, not Earth hours). So fast! I knew it was coming, but it would be another thing entirely to live it.

Our class and the university professors had a lengthy discussion on terminology. Rather than learning names for whole new sets of units, the faculty had decided years ago to keep Earth names like kilometer and Watt and kilogram and so on, but have them refer to Pic metrics. All our textbooks would follow this convention. An hour meant Pic hour, and we would say "Earth hour" if we meant otherwise.

Every nineteen years, the Pic had a leap day on Northern Summer 59, the last day of the year. The year starts at Northern Autumn with the season day at zero. It might seem a strange time to start the year, but it's also the first day of spring in the Southern Hemisphere, and that's where the world capital is. The Pic translated the capital name as the city of Haven on the island of Genesis.

And by leap day, the Pic meant that the day didn't exist. It was leaped over. They found it amusing that their whistle for a calendar day thrown out is the same Earth concept as sticking an extra day in. It was all a matter of perspective, I guessed, on whether the calendar leaped forward in time (the Earth's perspective), or the Pic way, where time leaped forward on the calendar.

The two hundred and forty days in a year translated to two hundred and forty degrees in a circle. The Pic said its origin came from two hundred and forty notches on a stone sundial almost seventy thousand years old. This meant the Poles here are at sixty degrees latitude North and South, and the radian to degree conversion is 120/pi. This was going to take so much time getting used to! But at least their temperature scale was the same, using zero degrees and a hundred degrees for the melting and boiling points of water.

What else? The sidereal day here was twenty-five Earth hours and twelve Earth minutes, making a Pic hour equal to 25.2 Earth minutes. There was other stuff too, both wonderfully similar to Earth and profoundly different. The local solar mass is only eighty-four percent of Earth's sun, but our new planetary home got about the same incident solar power density as Earth by having a much closer orbit. That was what caused the faster year and the increase in solar tides (Pic's solar tides were as strong as Earth's lunar tides).

The planet had a very circular orbit; its eccentricity was a small fraction of Earth's. But the tilt, wow! On Earth right now and using Earth degrees, the tilt was about 23.4 degrees, heading down and about midway between a 1.7 degree wobble that has a 41,000 Earth-year cycle. Here, the tilt was now very close to its maximum value of 25.3 degrees (38.0

degrees in Earth units), the high end of a 2.1 Pic-degree wobble with a cycle time of 143,000 Pic years.

And as for the name of our new home, the logical whistle translation would be Earth, but that would be confusing, and the Pic asked us to use the word Pic for their species and not their planet. So we debated the issue until another USNA emigrant, Cindy from Missouri, suggested we consider how the Pic refer to their planet, a rising three-note chord that seems to want to continue but abruptly ends. She suggested the English translation as Whistlestop, and the name stuck.

Whistlestop is a water world, a planet of islands with one great global ocean that covers 82.3% of the planet's surface. The plate tectonics here were far different from Earth. There are no large continents. Instead, scattered across the deep global ocean are forty-three primary islands where habitation is legal, a total land area of thirty-eight million square kilometers, with the inhabited islands ranging in size from Earth's Iceland to the largest approaching the size of Australia. These were Pic square kilometers. A Pic meter is about 1.43 Earth meters, making their square kilometer slightly more than double an Earth square kilometer.

There were also 4.7 million square kilometers of thousands of smaller islands, almost all of which were dedicated nature preserves and off-limits to development without a special decision by the central government. That's where our campus was, a beautiful nature preserve, an oval-shaped island over eighteen-hundred square kilometers called Providence.

There was so much other stuff to think about, but I thought what was most on my mind was the mingling of us humans with an equal number of Pic freshman students. Our escorts from Earth were making the transition to adulthood too, volunteers just as we were. They had separate dorms but would join us in class and social activities. What a great idea, and so much to think about. Fortunately, classes didn't begin until Autumn 0. There were a few meet-and-greet gatherings with the faculty before then, but nothing like today. My only action item tomorrow would be to pick my one elective course. Basically, we'd have a bit of time to settle in.

As our long briefing finally closed, people got up and stretched, most looking at their welcome packages and campus maps, studying the routes to their assigned dorms. I exchanged a few quick greetings with people who were looking very sleepy, then headed out myself, wondering what my living quarters would be like. My welcome map showed it to be a corner room on the top third floor of a nearby building.

As I walked outside, I experienced the fresh air again, sweeter and cleaner than I had ever imagined air could be. It was a pleasure to breathe it. I decided to do a little exploring and drifted away from the crowd of humans heading for the dorms.

I walked about the quiet campus and compared it to the scenes we were just shown of Pic cities. Pic architecture was simple and elegant, with even more interior headroom than what was standard on Earth. The same was true for public entrances and exits, though there were occasional old-style exterior doorways on homes where any human taller than a young child would have to duck.

In their building designs, the Pic liked to mix multiple shades of polished gray stone and flexi-glass walls in clean geometric shapes. Rectangular was the standard for residential, other polygons for public, and cylindrical yellow was a special designation for restricted. The portal complex was the only such building on campus. There was also a standard not to have anyone far from an exit. From our lecture, we were told of occasional exceptions for major public structures, but the vast majority of buildings on the planet had at most two levels above the ground floor and one level below.

I turned a corner and at the other end of the building saw a Pic work crew tending plants. They didn't appear to notice me and I took a moment to observe their work. It seemed an extremely relaxed approach to weeding and mulching; over half the crew were just standing around having animated conversations with the rest of the crew doing the work. Did gardening really need that much supervision? I soon realized I didn't understand the group's dynamics; roles of worker and supervisor were frequently being exchanged. Puzzled by the behavior, I wandered over to say hello.

For a moment we paused and studied each other. *Old*, I thought. The crew was made up of multiple genders but older than any Pic I had ever met. And while I had become acquainted with a hundred Pic over the last two weeks, I was probably the first human they had ever seen. I didn't want to make sudden moves and startle them. So we just stared at each other for a while until I gave a sheepish hand sign of greeting, to which they replied in kind. They slowly got back to their work and conversations. I continued my walk.

In spite of all the differences, I decided the campus would be nothing more than innovative design on Earth. Even the shallow pools that Pic used to wash their feet before entering buildings would be nothing more than small reflecting ponds on Earth. Nothing caught my eye that seemed bizarre or nonfunctional. The plantings along the walkways, while perhaps more plentiful than an Earth designer would have chosen, were very pleasing to the eye. I walked to one particular row of plantings and had to smile. They were unmistakably Earth blueberry bushes. For a moment I gazed at the ripe fruit and thought about going back and asking the work crew if I could sample a few. Did they speak English? I sure didn't want to make a communication mistake with my limited hand sign ability. Maybe I should pass on the idea. Meanwhile Julie trotted up behind me. "Hey, hi! There you are! How did your orientation go?"

I turned and smiled. "Just fabulous. Julie, your world is so beautiful!"

Her muzzle flashed too briefly for me to read, but her happiness was apparent. "Thanks! I want to ask you, do you want more information now? Or maybe you want to sack out?"

I blinked. The lecture had described how our escorts would have an enduring one-on-one responsibility to mentor us in our transition to life on Whistlestop, but I didn't realize how seriously Julie would take her role. "Wow, Julie, were you waiting for me all this time?"

"No. We had our own orientation, mostly reviews of what our responsibilities are. Some of the legal stuff goes on forever. I just got out an hour ago."

"Ah. Well… actually, yeah, chatting would be nice. Thanks for taking such good care of me. Want to go for a walk?"

"Sure. You'll find the nature trails interesting, or we could tour the campus. I'll show you my dorm pod if you like, or we could hike down to the beach."

My eyebrows rose. "How about the beach?"

It took a short half hour (a short Pic half hour) to stroll down garden pathways to a steep southern cliff that led to the shore. Our Pic hosts were so thoughtful. Half the gardens were growing Earth fruits and vegetables. With an approving nod from Julie, I munched raspberries as we walked, and Julie would occasionally nibble native green berries on squat circular grass-colored shrubs that were only as tall as my ankles. Julie confirmed that it was a Pic custom to grow free food along public walkways. What a great idea! It left me wondering why the practice was unknown on Earth.

And beyond the gardens was a very impressive switchback stone stairway leading down to the beach. As we descended, I made a comment to Julie how gentle the slope was, far less than what would be typical on Earth. Julie replied that the stairs were a standard rise and run for exterior use, and I noticed they were a perfect match for her easy loping gait.

At last we reached the deserted beach. Julie studied the dunes and the cliff for a moment and said, "Hold off just a bit, okay? This ocean looks irresistible!"

And so saying she threw off her clothes and galloped into the surf, diving and riding the waves and whistling with delight while kicking her powerful hindquarters up and down, undulating her backbone like the tail of a whale. I watched her mesmerized, realizing that no human could ever hope to compete in a water sport with a Pic. Julie was as graceful as a dolphin, in an element that seemed her second home.

As I waited for Julie, I looked around the beach. It was a beautiful place, fine powdered sand, the ocean a marine blue just like Earth, the sky and surf populated with multiple species of whistling birds, and the dunes near the cliff covered with short plants crowned with tiny, bright red and purple flowers. The only piece of technology present was a moderate-sized jetty far off to the west. There was one vessel docked there. It appeared to be a fishing vessel.

I noticed Julie returning from her swim. She rode a wave in and trotted back to me, shaking the water from her feather-fur like a dog before coming close. "Oh boy, that felt good! Help me keep an eye on the cliff, will you, Steve? We don't use swimsuits, but on the beach I've got to put my clothes back on if any Pic show up."

"Uh, yeah, sure."

It was late afternoon and the sun was warm. Julie and I were soon in the soft sand. I sat down and Julie stretched out, her muzzle pattern a mixture of contentment and excitement, plus something else I didn't understand. She watched me stare at her muzzle and sighed and whistled a quiet laugh. "Among alpha and gamma males, adolescent beta females are known as cheap dates."

I blinked. "Say again?"

"They watch our muzzles. Beta females are the last gender to gain control of their chromatophores, later than the other genders. I'm just beginning to control mine. We use chromatophores to convey emotional content."

Recognition set in and I blushed. "They wait until they see you're interested, and then move in?"

"Something like that, only… Well, it's not as brutal as Earth can be, if I understand your cultures. Sure, visual image is important, at least initially. But Pic arousal is based on trust and friendship. It's true for all genders. Rape is unheard of here. I can't imagine a male being physically capable of it."

I nodded thoughtfully. "Such a gift your species has."

"Yes. And before we discovered humans, we didn't even recognize the gift." Julie paused and gave a crying whistle. "Steve, I've just insulted you, haven't I?!"

I gave her the sign of a closed fist, the root for anger, but with my middle finger extended. "No more than the truth ever does."

"Huh? Oh. Right." A brief pause, and then a softer "Thank you," plus the pure hand sign root for gratitude. "Steve? Don't think I'm gloating that Pic are morally superior to humans. We're not. You'll be learning our history over the years, the good and the bad. The bad is really awful. We've used humiliation as a weapon of war too, just as rape is used to humiliate in human wars. Pic humiliate in different ways. That doesn't make us better. Just different."

I got up and sat back down very close to Julie's head. We stared into each other's eyes for a moment. It felt strange and wondrous to see compassion in such non-human eyes. My hand came up and stroked the side of her neck. "I love your openness. We humans never talk to each other like this."

Julie sighed in contentment as I stroked her neck. She glanced cross-W-eyed at her snout. "See the pinkish blue with the sliding brown freckles? I don't think that was described to you. That's me being happy and affectionate with a new friend. But there's nothing sexual with this pattern. That would be grossly inappropriate."

I nodded at her unspoken meaning. We could enjoy physical contact with each other, but we were also responsible for not letting it manifest as sexual desire. "Julie?"

"Hmm?"

"I'm curious about the incoming Pic class. I couldn't help but notice, there're a lot more females than males. Why is that?"

"Ah! Our reproductive sciences... that hasn't been explained to you, has it? We'll be having a joint meeting after breakfast tomorrow. My guess is the faculty plans to tell you then." Julie paused. "Personally, I'm surprised Earth hasn't figured this out yet. Or maybe some governments have captured traces of our DNA, and they just don't want us to know what they know."

"Uh, what?"

Julie saw my confusion. "Don't worry. I'm staying on topic. Reluctance to yield our bio information might seem paranoid, but Earth has such a horrible history of creating bio-weapons, especially during your last century. Insane behavior, but your species seems driven to it."

"Yeah, I know." I thought for a moment of modern Earth warfare and realized what Christopher said was true. "Your fears are valid."

"But you candidates will have access to the knowledge, so I don't see why I can't spill the beans now. Is that the right Earth phrase?"

"Yep!"

"Okay! So, Steven, how many sex chromosomes for humans?"

"That's easy; two. X-X for female and X-Y for male."

"That's right; and the human male is basically a modified form of a human female. That's what the Y chromosome does. For hex-sexual reproduction, it's the reverse; four sex chromosomes with one key chromosome that turns you female. Without it, you're a male."

"Sounds complicated. Any idea why our two worlds are so different?"

"There are conjectures, sure. Both worlds started life about the same time, but the jump to multi-cellular life happened more quickly here, at least two billion years ago."

I blinked over how monumental this information was. "So Earth species are more primitive?"

"That sounds too judgmental. Bisexual reproduction is common here too. Only mammals and some predatory bird species are hex-sexual. There are advantages to it. Want a detailed explanation how it works?"

"Sure!" I was fascinated. Julie went on to explain the following table.

	alpha	beta	gamma
Male	Y-Z	X-Z	X-Y
Female	W-X	W-Y	W-Z

"Four sex chromosomes W, X, Y, Z; with the W turning you female and two distinct conception processes: bi-catalytic fusion producing a female and transformational fusion creating a male. Four distinct sex chromosomes result in six possible pairs; each pair producing a different gender. Assume an alpha female is procreating with a beta male; W-X with X-Z. The W is always at the end of a temporary four-chromosome super-chain at the instant of conception, either W-X-X-Z or W-X-Z-X. Two X chromosomes together catalyze the creation of a W-Z cell, the conception of a gamma female; or the W-X-Z substring transforms into a Y chromosome for a Y-X cell, a gamma male. That's why alpha males and females are infertile with each other. There's no common chromosome pair for catalytic fusion, and transformational fusion would theoretically create a Y-Y or Z-Z cell, but that's not a viable combination. Steven, for humans, what's the ratio of boy to girl births?"

"Uh, 1.06, I think."

'That's the number I learned too. For Pic, transformation fusion is a slower and more complex process. It occurs less often. Across all three gender types, the ratio of transformational conception to catalytic conception is about 0.44."

It took a moment for the implication to hit me. "Wow!"

"Yes, about forty-four boy births for every one hundred girl births. Surprised at how different our world is?" Julie blinked her large eyes at me.

I was shocked. "I never really thought about it. One to one just seems…"

"Natural? Yes, it is for Earth. But even there, heredity can have skip-generational issues. Granted, nothing as what happens with hex-sexual reproduction."

I shrugged and got up and stretched; beginning to feel very tired, but my mind was still racing. I turned to Julie. "Earlier today, before the portals…"

"You wanted to ask me something?"

"Yeah, so many questions…" I wondered where to begin. "I saw some Pic doing gardening here, and they were having such active conversations about it. Is pulling weeds really that big a decision?"

"Ah…" Julie hesitated a moment, rubbing her hand across my knee. "No, of course not. This is related to the free food along public walkways. You were seeing us practice our religion. I should clarify," Julie said as she saw me blink, "that using the English word religion is a rough approximation. The literal translation of the activity is: The gifting and the purpose. This could be an extended conversation. Perhaps we could talk about this later?"

"Sure, later's fine. Julie, how about your life, your family, what's it like? Wait. I think I see some movement on the cliff."

Julie sprang up gracefully and quickly got dressed. "Thanks for keeping watch. Steven, you must be exhausted. How about we walk to your dorm? You can wash up and sack out."

"Is the ocean safe for me to swim in?"

"Yes. You'll find it less briny and far cleaner than Earth's oceans. Maybe tomorrow we can go for a swim. But for now…" Julie took a few steps towards campus and beckoned me to follow. We began retracing our way up the gentle walkway.

I turned to my beta escort, resisting the urge to touch the silky feather-fur on the side of her neck. "And how about the island? Is it safe, too?"

Julie paused for a moment before answering. "Here on campus and the nearby nature trails, totally. The interior, though, is a wilderness. Providence is a major nature preserve, with one one-hundred-and-sixty-kilometer Class-B road that hugs the circumference. Think of it as an ellipse with major and minor radii of thirty and twenty kilometers."

"Yes, I know. We were shown maps during our orientation. We're on the southern end of an island that runs mostly north-south." As we began hiking up the walkway, I converted to Earth units and did a simple comparison in my mind. I reminded myself that a Pic kilometer was about 1.43 Earth kilometers, closer to an Earth mile than an Earth kilometer. Our island was considerable, about double the size of Maui in the Hawaiian Islands.

Julie continued. "The interior is mountainous as you saw, a central plateau with great radial ravines leading to the shore. If you pass certification classes, you'll be allowed to hike and camp anywhere on the island. That'll be safe too, once you understand the ecology. It is a wilderness, though. You have to respect its power."

After passing a group of Pic heading down, we crested the cliff face and then turned for a moment to admire a golden sun setting into the blue-green ocean. The sun was almost touching the horizon, and as I gazed at the beach below us, the scene was so lovely and pristine that I wondered if I could be fooled into thinking this was magically some uncharted island on Earth. The sky color and clouds seemed just the same, though the sun was larger and more golden than the butter-yellow sun of Earth, resulting in an unusual pinkish hue on the horizon. The gravity was also a touch too light, and the shore birds were whistling in multiple simultaneous frequencies, clearly nothing Earth had ever seen. How could a bird with a beak whistle? Something to ask Julie about sometime. And the beats of the birds' double sets of wings were subtly different too, strange slicing motions that seemed foreign to my expectations.

And yet, the ecology, while alien, was one of profound wholeness and goodness. I whispered to Julie, "Such a privilege to think of this as home."

Julie sighed, caught as I was in the peace of the moment. "There's an ancient Pic saying: Nature has to be shared to be appreciated."

"Yeah. Is the whole island always this beautiful and serene?"

Julie whistled a laugh and hugged me, one arm low on my thigh and her neck pressing against my hip. "Always this serene? Just wait for a summer storm! And as for beauty, take the certification courses. We can go on hikes and you can judge for yourself." My hand came and lightly held her neck. We stood there for a long moment, watching the last of the day's orange-gold light and drinking in the world with all of our senses. My escort gave a deep, contented sigh and gave my rump a friendly pat. We resumed our walk.

We took the long way back through the gardens, Julie showing me the layout of the southern part of the campus. She also showed me she had not forgotten my earlier question. "My father is a gamma. You're sure to meet him soon. He's a professor here at the university. You'll have him for freshman physics. I also have two mothers, a beta and an alpha, and I have an alpha sister and an alpha brother..."

I blinked. "Yes! Both born from your beta mother, and you were born from your alpha mother."

"Of course. The three gender types joining in marriage is our most common family unit, a male and two females, and my dad and moms have two daughters and a son. That makes us an arch-typical family. We have two distinct whistles to describe the maternal relationships." Julie gave a short burst of sound. "That means birth mother." And then another whistling burst, quite different from the first. "And that means... It means..."

"Hmm?"

"Actually, I don't know if humans have a word to describe the concept. I'm tempted to say teacher mother; that's what our linguists put in the translation dictionary, but that doesn't capture the essence of the bond."

"Ah... And your brother and sister, are either of them here?"

Julie laughed. "No! My brother is halfway through college already, and my sister is four years my junior. You're right though. With two mothers, they could have been pregnant at the same time. In practice, that's rarely done."

I nodded and yawned. "Yeah, I can see that. So your dad's a professor, huh? How about your moms?"

"My alpha mom is in the military. My beta mom is a councilor in the world government. She chairs the committee of the Parks and Conservation Department. She was a primary decision-maker in changing the status of Providence."

"You mean to site the campus here?"

"Uh huh."

"Ah. I'd like to meet your family someday."

Julie gave another whistling laugh. "You've already met my birth mother."

I stopped short in my walk. "I have?"

Julie nodded. "She was one of the interviewers in Antarctica. You know her as Ellie."

"Oh wow, really? Ellie is your mom? Your birth mom?"

"Uh huh. She'll also be the instructor here for wilderness training."

"Hey, that's great…" We continued walking. I wanted to say something nice about my interview time with Julie's mom, but I was so sleepy, I couldn't think of anything that made sense. I yawned instead. "All your parents are very involved then, with bringing humans to Whistlestop."

"Whistlestop?"

"It's the English name we gave your planet."

"Whistlestop… I like it."

"So all three of your parents were involved with bringing us here?"

"Oh, yes! We're…"

I waited a long moment for Julie to continue. It took me that long to notice her muzzle pattern was a mixture of sadness and embarrassment. Was there something she was still not allowed to talk about? In kindness, I tried to change topics. "So, how about your grandparents? All still alive?"

Julie's muzzle pattern changed to relief and happiness. "Yes, twelve wonderful people. I couldn't ask for a nicer family."

Twelve grandparents? "Uh… Well, I guess it's great they're all still with you."

Julie looked at me curiously. "Steven, how much do you know about Pic longevity?"

My ears picked up. "Well, from the literature you've shared, Earth thinks a Pic's lifespan is similar to a human but maybe a bit longer."

"That's about right. The oldest Pic on record died a few centuries ago. He was one hundred and ninety-five years old, about ten percent older than the oldest human on record, I think."

"Hmm…" It took my tired mind a moment to realize Julie was using Pic years.

"If our lifespans were too different, we probably wouldn't be doing the fusion trial. Our perspectives on life would be too different, don't you think?"

I thought for a moment and yawned. "Yeah, maybe. A factor of two or more would be tough."

Julie also yawned. "A big day for me too," she muttered. Another yawn. "Perhaps I should tell you, most of my great-grandparents are also alive. That's typical for a person my age. We're very proud of our health services. Over eighty percent of children born reach eighty percent of the longevity record without debilitation. Earth is nothing like that."

I looked at Julie. "No, it sure isn't. Your medical science is way beyond ours."

Julie nodded. "It's common for people to play with their great-great-grandchildren, one or two extra generations compared to Earth. Pic normally have children between thirty to fifty years of age. "

"Hmm… That's about the same for us, twenty to thirty-five in Earth years." I could feel my mind wandering. "It must be tough on the guys, though, not having children of their own type."

"Well, it is possible for marriages to have multiple male partners, usually two males and three females. It's not as common as it used to be. My father's parents are a five-set. Otherwise, husbands have to be patient and wait for the arrival of their children's marriage partners. And if not that, at least the grandkids will match."

After a moment, Julie added, "There are many forms of marriage. Couples often remain monogamous. And many marriages become quads, the husband taking a third wife, a…" Julie gave a whistling burst. "… a companion wife, a female of his own type. With the low ratio of men to women, husbands are often in short supply."

"What about having more than one husband or wife of the same type?"

Julie shook her head. "That's not our tradition. It might happen once in a while. There's nothing illegal about it. It's just that, well, jealousy can be an issue."

I blinked. "And jealousy isn't an issue if the men or women are different types?"

"Not much. Personally, I wouldn't see an alpha or a gamma wife in my marriage as a competitor. They're just not my gender." Julie looked at me curiously and shrugged as she recognized my bewilderment. "Maybe you have to be Pic to understand the perspective."

"Yeah, maybe." I yawned. "Honestly, I don't get it."

"Well, think of it this way. If I married an alpha, my husband taking a gamma wife would be my route to motherhood of children of my own type, something I want very much. And I don't think you understand what a companion wife is. She would be my companion too, and within our marriage, her birthright could transfer to me. And I should add that legally, I have the right to accept or reject any addition to my marriage. It's my free choice, just as much as my husband's."

"Legally, yeah, but how about in practice?"

Julie's snout showed a pattern I recognized as a blush. "Well, in practice a Pic wife will try to please her husband, but it works both ways. A husband will propose to someone who has already developed a close friendship with his other wife or wives. There's a lot of discussion involved. To do otherwise would be crazy."

"Hmm…" I smiled sleepily. "And what do you women do before committing? I mean, where everyone is unattached. Do you fight over the men?"

"Well… We compete for them. But it works both ways. The boys chase us too, in spite of their fewer numbers, and the girls love being chased. It's a complex dating scene, very exciting. You'll see." Julie stared at me for a moment. "Steven, you look so tired."

I yawned again. Julie was right. I was totally out of gas, desperate for sleep. As we walked, a delightfully cool evening breeze began to come off the ocean. The smell was wonderful, faintly salty and so clean and alive. I loved its fragrance. "Julie?"

"Yes?"

I asked in a sleepy voice, "How is it you got to be my escort?"

"Ah… I'll tell you someday, I promise. Not now."

"Okay."

The sun had set by the time we reached my dorm. In evening twilight we said goodnight and I went inside. The area where I entered was adjacent to the campus portal complex. I studied my map and found my room on the other end of the building. Walking down a quiet hall, I remembered something pleasant from the orientation. Primary and secondary school children from cities across the planet had donated funds to buy each of us a gift. I wondered what mine would be.

A minute later I discovered that my dorm room was both large and luxurious. It had its own private bathroom and a small balcony overlooking the southern gardens with a view towards the ocean. And my desk was magnificent, an enormous work area of gleaming, highly polished hardwood, deep swirls of rich orange, purple and burgundy running through the grain. The desk was obviously a one-of-a-kind work of art. I opened a drawer and found it empty except for a small note: "Greetings and welcome from the primary school students of Fair Meadows."

I looked around the room and sighed. Would my time here seem like one long vacation? I took a quick shower and climbed into a huge and comfortable bed. Through screened windows, I could hear the distant sounds of both shore and inland birds whistling in the night. So much to think about. A religion based on pulling weeds? Definitely something to ask Julie about tomorrow.

Would I get to sleep tonight? I glanced at my assistant. The time now was 46:26, an hour after sunset, and sunrise tomorrow would be at 14:41, so I had over twenty-eight of the short Pic hours for sleep. I guess that made sense. The equinox was only a couple of days away, when there'd be thirty hours each of day and night. I played with the numbers on my assistant for a while. At the solstices, the campus would get about fifteen hours of light or darkness out of the sixty-hour day. My capital city of Whitehorse in the Commonwealth of Yukon had something like that, perhaps even a bit more extreme. But the summer solstice here would have the noonday sun almost directly overhead, and daily incident power averaged over forty-five hours of sunlight would be phenomenal. Whitehorse never had anything like that. I wondered how hot the island would get.

I turned off the lights and my head hit the pillow. I was planning to review the day in my thoughts, but my brain had other ideas. I fell asleep very quickly.

Chapter 3

I was twenty minutes into my two-hour lunch period, and after nine days on Whistlestop, I was finally acclimated to how much time that was (and wasn't). Carrying my lunch out of the blue-coded section of the serving area, I waved hello and walked past a large table of fellow students, a few adventurous Pic but mostly humans from the West African Union. For some reason, most humans and Pic were still finding it difficult to sit side by side for a meal. Hopefully that would pass. I saw an empty table for two and sat down with my sandwich and drink and waited for Jorani.

What a strange life! A week on Whistlestop was ten days, with six weeks to a season, and a typical week here had seven school days followed by a three-day weekend. For all schools including colleges, the school year was twenty weeks per year, the first five weeks of each season, with the last week for vacation and independent study activities. For my one elective, I'd enrolled in the two-semester wilderness certification training with Julie's birth mom, whom the class addressed as Lieutenant Ellie. If I passed the first course, I'd get a junior permit that will allow me to go camping with Julie near the winter solstice. We had a plan.

Days zero through five of the week had a fixed schedule for courses. The school day started at 20:00 and ran till 40:00, six three-hour periods plus a middle two-hour lunch break. Today though, the last day of classes before the three-day weekend, was what the Pic call the "dessert day" for learning, guest speakers from across the planet joining the permanent faculty for special presentations. I'd come to appreciate how the Pic method of teaching focused heavily on class involvement with relatively little homework. The philosophy gave students more time for unstructured and independent learning. For example, Julie, Max, Jorani, and I had planned an all-day nature hike along the beach three days from now. I was really looking forward to it.

It was a very full life, challenging to everybody, humans and Pic. And especially challenging for the humans, I thought, because of all the extra nonsense we'd been loading on ourselves. It certainly didn't take long to start. I didn't think the sun was up on our first morning here before a group of people were running around organizing a student government. At first it was nothing I particularly wanted to be involved with, but it would have been insane to boycott what was happening and not have a voice in decisions later on.

And that wasn't all. After a stunning morning lecture on reproductive responsibilities on Autumn 0, the new human student government decided to keep tabs on dating couples. Jorani and I signed up as dating each other just to get out the detailed reporting unattached people were being asked to do.

Keeping logs of dating couples might seem insane, but perhaps there was justification for it. A lecture on Autumn 0 opened our eyes to the potential sacrifice our escorts had made for us. Every adult citizen of Whistlestop, both males and females and eventually us humans, had a birthright to sponsor the creation of one child, and individuals could apply for more. Based on the desired size and growth rate for the total population, extra birthrights were handed out in a weighted lottery.

Reproduction without a permit involved heavy social penalties. If the male and female both had their original birthrights but no permit, the single pregnancy would count against both birthrights. Without original birthrights, a double negative count must be borne either willingly by family or friends, or by a penalty lottery that cancelled the birthrights of two random citizens. Those citizens could then lay financial claim on the persons who had stolen their birthrights, but the real punishment comes from the social stigma. The crime was public knowledge, and stealing birthrights was as bad as being labeled a child molester on Earth.

Our escorts! They had pledged their individual birthrights against the possibility of humans reproducing outside the system. Without permits, if Jorani got pregnant by me, the pregnancy would cancel both our birthrights. If we did it again and didn't have two other humans give up birthrights for us, both my escort Julie and Jorani's escort Max would lose their birthrights. Further pregnancies would randomly double target our remaining Pic classmates.

Such trust our escorts had placed in us, and compared to Earth, this was such a different way of controlling world population. It is the individual's moral and social responsibility not to steal another's birthright. Earth's population now was about nine billion, down from peak numbers in the 2060s. Wars were a factor, but the primary causes were pandemics and hunger from the continuing collapse of Earth's overstressed ecologies.

Whistlestop's world population was tiny by comparison — barely one percent of Earth's, less than ninety-seven million and it had been slowly drifting down for centuries. It was in the middle of a neutral range set by the world government. Below one hundred and twenty million, extra birthrights for first-time petitioners were automatically granted, but above that the lottery started to bite. And the population would have to fall below eighty million before previous winners of the lottery could reenter. Modern Pic had a strong aversion to a large number of children from a single pair. In ancient history, the practice led to clan warfare.

Their family structures were so profoundly different from Earth's. People here had even more siblings and cousins than is typical on Earth, but they did it without population growth, using multiple marriage partners instead. So there was lots of individual freedom in choosing family size, but the global Pic population and growth rate were tightly controlled. We were told that the world population has been within the neutral regime for more than three thousand years, almost since the beginning of their current calendar system that marked the formation of their world government.

We humans were just beginning to grasp Pic law and what our positions truly were. Legally, we were children and wards of the world government. Thirty years was the threshold for adulthood and claiming birthrights. I was born on November 17, 2081. That's Northern Summer 0, 3457 on the Pic calendar, so I have to wait until Northern Summer 0 of 3487 to have the legal right to leave our campus island.

It was a major point of speculation back on Earth, how much freedom we would have to explore the Pic home-world during our undergraduate years. Now we knew there would be three years of confinement to Providence. Personally, I'm comfortable with the schedule. None of us were ready to start wandering around Pic cities, and besides, Pic years were short, and three was a lot better than six.

I saw Jorani leave the buffet area and waved hello. We were very close in age. She was a month older than I am, born October 22. On her way over, Jorani greeted a few people on the student council then lightly kissed my cheek before sitting with me. "What a day! Sorry I'm late."

I made a Pic hand gesture dismissing any need to apologize. "Everything okay?"

"Hmm? Oh yeah, just insanely busy, that's all." Jorani took a bite of her lunch. "Hey, this is good!"

I started eating my own lunch and mumbled an agreement. "So, what did you pick for your afternoon?"

"A double lecture on quantum routers. The abstract indicated some major differences from Earth designs. The signup was filling up fast. I'm lucky I got in." Another bite. "How about you?"

"A double lecture from one of the artist unions — micro-stone mosaics."

Jorani gave me a playful grin. "All this new technology, and you're taking an art class?"

"It's what Julie picked. She mentioned the artist is world renowned." I cued my PA. "Pity he hasn't picked a human name. I won't know how to address him. And as for my choice, there were lots of Pic but no other humans on the signup. It seemed almost disrespectful not to have at least one human there. The guy's giving the lecture in English!" That was the standard for all campus instruction.

Jorani blinked. "You're absolutely right. Well done…" Jorani finished her meal and glanced at the time. We still had a few minutes. "I was talking to Max before breakfast. We were chatting about the lack of celebration for the New Year. Autumn 0 came and went with no parties, no fireworks, nothing at all. Max just laughed and said from the Pic perspective, celebrating something as inevitable and boring as a clock tick seems absolutely…" Jorani giggled. "Well, you get the idea." My registered dating partner looked around to see if she could be overheard, then added quietly. "Max said something else too. He talked about the special physics lecture we're having."

I nodded. After our electives, there was a mandatory-for-humans physics lecture at 37:00 that would finish our first week of classes.

Jorani continued in an even lower voice. "Max said the physics lecture is going to be on portals."

My eyebrows shot up and I half shouted, "You're kidding!"

Jorani frowned and hissed, "Not so loud, Steve! Professor Feynman is Julie's dad, isn't he? I know Max and Julie spend a lot of time talking with each other. I'm assuming she is Max's source of information. Didn't Julie mention any of this to you?"

"No," I whispered back. "But Julie's not an alpha."

Jorani looked puzzled. "What's that got to do with anything?" Before I could reply, a couple of friends came by and we wound up walking out with them, off to our various choices. Given what Jorani said, I wondered if I would pay attention to my art class, but to my delight, it was a fascinating presentation, covering both artistry and the history of how stone mineralogy changed mosaic methodology. The instructor also mentioned that his union had accepted numerous commissions involving the construction of our campus, and he released us early, urging us to view some of the artwork before our next class.

The teaching area of our university had three large lecture halls, each one quite beautiful. One would seat primarily humans, the second hall was for Pic (who didn't use chairs), and the third would easily hold both groups plus the faculty. The upcoming physics lecture was in the first hall, and I arrived there more than an hour ahead of schedule and started to study the interior walls. I soon began to feel ashamed of myself. The artworks were breathtaking, masterful, and I had been in this hall several times before and had ignored them. One image in particular captivated me. Even close up, the image looked like a painting or photograph, a masterpiece from a national museum. I held my PA a few centimeters from an artwork and magnified the display. It was only then I could see the tiny slivers of stone chips creating the image.

Eventually humans began drifting in, filling the hall for the physics lecture. I sat next to Jorani near the front. Professor Feynman took the podium and began the lesson with a history of Pic science, laying out the grand progression of Pic knowledge from primitive stone tools to the beginning of mathematics to relativity and generalized spacetime. It was a progression both remarkably similar and remarkably different to Earth's, spanning a much longer time scale, and having periods when technology was lost for tens of thousands of years. It was near the end of the lecture that Feynman dropped his bombshell.

"And now we come to what is undoubtedly the crowning achievement of..." He gave a complex whistle and then continued, "... a name we translate for you as the Third New Kingdom." He pointed to an area on a large chart showing the timeline of Pic history. "It was near the end of this era that the theory of entangled spacetime was discovered and portal engineering developed." The room became absolutely silent.

"Let me digress a moment. There is public knowledge of this history on our world, and it would be impossible to run a fair trial of fusing our two societies and insist you not stumble onto common knowledge. So, I'm very happy to announce that starting this weekend, world network access will be opened for the campus. From what I understand, there is mail for each of you from thousands of school children who would be thrilled with getting a reply and a question or two answered. Please feel free to respond or ignore this mail as you wish.

"As far as we can determine from ancient nano-crystal records, both Type-I and Type-II portal pairs were manufactured early in the last century of the Third New Kingdom, some thirty-six thousand years ago. Type-I portal pairs allow the full exchange of matter-energy, while Type-II portals are limited to the momentum exchange of virtual photons. All known Type-I portals were bundled with four Type-II portals. The Type-I portals also support the transmission of continuous modulated virtual photons; information necessary to synchronize the interchange of spacetime. The pair twins of the Type-II portals are embedded at the bottom of the gravity well of a gas giant several light-hours from here. The Type-II portals appear permanently anchored there, through a mechanism not understood."

Professor Feynman stared at the silent audience for a moment before continuing. "About thirty-five hundred years ago, just a few decades before the formation of the current world government, a total of 1512 Type-I portal spheres were discovered stored in a deep polar valley on our local moon, along with limited documentation on how to operate them. Once their momentum-exchange abilities were understood, the portals were transported to Whistlestop and put to use. Testing of the Type-1 portals revealed the collection to be comprised of two hundred and sixteen joined pairs and one thousand eighty half-pairs. The two hundred and sixteen joined pairs form the backbone of our world's inter-island transport system, and they are also our prime source for energy. As you know from physics, a free source of external momentum can easily be converted to a free source of energy.

"There is convincing nano-crystal evidence that portals gave the Third New Kingdom virtually unlimited transportation and energy abilities. Perhaps the most impressive use of the technology was the elemental conversion and storage done during this period. The planet Enigma, our rough equivalent to your Mars, was used as a master warehouse, holding gigatons of virtually every stable isotope in existence. Our access to these vaults now eliminates any conceivable need for mining."

The professor sighed. "The reason new portals have not been constructed is very simple. We don't know how, though the matter has been researched for millennia. The few scraps of knowledge we have from the Third New Kingdom on portal physics are baffling, and there is no known record of the engineering techniques used in their construction. In fact, the technology is so foreign that there is conjecture that portals are not a Pic invention at all, but came from an interaction with an alien species, just as Earth learned of portals from us.

"Returning to the present, the world capital Haven is the central hub of the civilian portal system. In addition to the public system, there is a restricted subnet run by the military and the Parks and Conservation Department. All of our interplanetary links to our moon, to Enigma, and to our interstellar probes are part of this subnet. One thousand eighty probes in groups of three apparently left Whistlestop approximately thirty-six thousand years ago, in great radial or spiral tracks from this planet of origin. Their normal cruising speed is about half the speed of light relative to the local background of stars.

"Solar system mapping is an automated process. Probes typically spend one to three years in planetary orbital surveillances before resuming interstellar flight. One hundred and seventy years ago, on Southern Autumn 45, 3313 Current Era, July 4, 1982 on Earth's calendar, one of these probes entered your star's heliosphere and shortly afterwards detected modulated radio frequencies from the inner solar system. The mission plan was altered to investigate and after a decade of discreet Earth observation, the probe was moved to a powered high orbit around your solar system. It took the Pic government a lifetime of debate before deciding to make contact."

The professor pointed to his historical chart and gave a long, sad whistle. "The fall of the Third New Kingdom was catastrophic. We believe it happened within a few days and perhaps within a few hours. We believe that portals were used not just for transportation but as momentum weapons in ways we do not understand, and we know for a fact that the time of barbarism afterwards was in excess of thirty thousand years. We almost became extinct. Survivors after the war numbered a few thousand in a single mountain stronghold, where great efforts were made to destroy all knowledge of the Third New Kingdom. For tens of thousands of years, engaging in archeology was a crime punishable by death. It was the most severe technology fall in our history, and as you can imagine, there is still some... debate concerning the wisdom of relying on portals for our transportation needs, our energy needs, and of course, debate on using portals to mingle with an alien species which both astonishes and in some ways horrifies us. I refer you to the world network to view these debates, and since it's 40:00, it's time for me to stop."

Professor Feynman closed his notes. "For those of you taking physics with me, I encourage you to understand fully what we've covered on precession and nutation. We will be expanding these concepts to nuclear magnetic resonance next week. And now, kindly consider yourselves dismissed. Enjoy the weekend!"

Northern Autumn 9, 3484 C.E. 22:21

It was six hours after our sunrise departure from campus, and Max, Julie, Jorani and I were making excellent time hiking along the beach. We were halfway to our destination, the famed Flowering Dunes of Providence, and Jorani and I were already mesmerized by the beauty and spicy aromas around us. There were dazzling flowers everywhere, from flowering shrubs to flowering high willows with trunks and dense canopy that reminded me vaguely of beech trees.

Julie and Jorani were walking ahead of Max and me, far enough away for private conversations. It was a pleasure to get to know Jorani's escort. He had spent the last six years at the capital Haven going to the same high school as Julie, and before that he had lived nine years at Tranquility, the city that Julie's beta mom represented in the world government.

Tranquility was one of fifteen cities on Long Island, Whistlestop's fourth largest island. The way Max described it, Long Island was roughly the shape of Madagascar on Earth but ten times the size, a very considerable piece of territory. My walking companion was giving me a very interesting look at what it was like to grow up in Pic society, and also telling me how fond he was of Julie. I gathered she and Max had been dating for a number of years.

"A nice coincidence," I remarked, "that both you and Julie and Jorani and I are going together."

"Not exactly a coincidence," Max replied. "Julie picked you first, then suggested I choose the woman you went on a hike with, back in Antarctica, I mean."

"Oh, wow. So the escort pairings weren't decided until the very end?"

"Of course. The interview selection process had to complete first."

"Oh, yeah, right." It was embarrassing to miss something so obvious. "But Julie seems to know me so well. What if two escorts wanted the same human? How would that work?"

Max paused for a moment, his muzzle showing he was uncertain what to say. "It's a little complicated. Julie is your escort. She should be the one to explain it to you."

"Ah. Okay."

After that, we just walked for a while in silence, enjoying the smells and the scenery. I found myself drawn to look at the tracks Max's bare feet were leaving in the wet sand. I shuddered involuntarily. The gesture did not go unnoticed.

"Problem?"

I felt a bit sheepish but decided to answer honestly. "It's your footprints. They're similar to bear tracks on Earth. My mind sees you as a person, but you're leaving animal tracks. It's a little unsettling."

Max looked at me thoughtfully, his muzzle holding a pattern of polite amusement. "This is really funny. I've been fighting not to show a similar reaction. There aren't many large bipedal mammals on Whistlestop, and the ones that are tend to be venomous, quite dangerous actually. I see you as a person and a friend, but you're twice my height and your footprints are alarming!" And so saying, Max walked sideways and bumped into me hard, almost knocking me off balance. Alpha-male Pic were solid muscle.

I took the gesture for what it was, friendly horsing around. I returned the gesture with a stiff tug on the brown feather-fur on his back, and Max snorted and trotted ahead to Julie and Jorani, leaving me a very impressive set of tracks to admire. A few minutes later Jorani dropped back to walk with me and I told her about my conversation with Max.

Jorani grinned at me. "You were worrying about your feet? This is weird. Julie and I were just talking about our hands." She stared at her palm. "I still shiver sometime when I see a Pic hand. It looks exactly like a human hand, but attached to something unearthly. Julie confided she sometimes has a similar reaction with human hands. She still avoids looking at them when she's trying to eat with humans."

"Really? I hadn't noticed. We both enjoy holding hands with each other." I gestured to our two escorts and smiled. "And she certainly seems happy now." Up ahead we could see Julie and Max preening each other as they walked.

Over the next several hours of hiking, our two Pic friends appeared to become infatuated with each other, openly caressing each other between bursts of stylized dancing, hopping across each other's backs in a braided version of leap-frog, alternating flashes of black and brown, pink and gold. By the time we reached the Flowering Dunes, both Max and Julie were panting heavily. Julie led us up to a dune of spectacular color and tried to start a lecture, but she wasn't sounding coherent. Max, meanwhile, was a few meters away stamping his front feet. He finally let out one incredible howl of an impatient whistle and ran back to the beach where he shed his clothes and dived into the surf. Julie was panting heavily as she watched Max and she turned to follow him.

I threw my arms around my escort's neck and restrained her. "Julie! Are you okay?"

"Never felt better!" she growled as her hands pulled her hiking pant-skirt off her hips and down her rear legs. Jorani came to stand near us, and we all heard another blast of Max's impatient whistle coming from beyond the breakers. Julie shivered in my arms and her hips were rocking with an arching motion that seemed unmistakably sexual. She made an urgent tug to pull away. "My dear friend, let me go!"

Julie's muzzle was a dazzling display of neon yellow with rippling black zebra marks. I did something almost unthinkable, because I had been taught how sensitive and personal the chromatophore area on a Pic's snout is. But I grabbed Julie's muzzle now with my free hand and asked, "Julie, this is your pattern for sexual arousal, isn't it?"

"Oh yeah!" Julie was trembling. My hand on her snout was equivalent to me grabbing Jorani's breast. "Steven, let me go!"

"Julie, I don't want you to get hurt! You're like us, years from claiming your birthright!"

Julie blinked and tore her gaze from the surf, staring into my eyes for the first time. "My dear friend! This is not the copulation that gets me pregnant! Let me go!" She wiggled impatiently in my arms, showing me her strength but not physically using her power to break free. She licked my hand instead. "Please, Steven?"

"Let her go, Steve," Jorani echoed quietly.

In respect, I let Julie go, but my heart was full of distress. The sight of Jorani and me momentarily pulled Julie from her arousal. "Steven, Jorani, promise me, you will stay on the dunes or on the beach, okay? The forest is not safe for you. You won't recognize the dangers!"

"We promise," said Jorani. "You have our word."

Julie gave a crying whistle of thanks and then galloped towards the ocean at full speed, flying across the sand and singing out to Max as she ran. She disappeared very quickly beneath the waves.

Jorani gave a long sigh followed by a thin smile. "How about we gather their things and wait for them on the beach?"

A few minutes later, Jorani and I were sitting with our gear near the edge of the dry sand, a short distance from the surf. Jorani took off her hiking boots and socks and began to play with the sand with her bare feet. The day was warm, and after a few minutes, she stripped down to just her shorts and sports halter and then lay down to soak up some sun. I also stripped down to shorts and sat close by, smiling at my partner. "You clearly know something about Max and Julie that I don't."

"Yes, and that astonishes me. I thought the male human mind is obsessed with getting it on with females, yet you never researched how the Pic have sex?"

"And how could I do that?"

"What do you mean, how? They opened up their world web to us last night."

I stared at Julie with wide eyes. "Well, I was kind of tired last night. I responded to a few school children and that was about it. You researched how the Pic have sex?"

"Well, not just that. But they are our classmates, you know. Sex is as important to them as it is to us."

"Uh, yeah... So... Tell me?"

Jorani grinned. "Max was helping me. If you forget the head and arms, Pic bodies are a bit of a cross between the torso of a lanky dog and the neck of a pony."

"Well, vaguely. Their hip joints are very flexible, more like a bear's."

"From what I've read, Pic sex is incredibly pleasurable for both partners. It's more enjoyable than..." Jorani stopped suddenly and blushed. "Well, I don't want to get too explicit. Read it yourself!" Jorani gave me a playful look of incredulity and asked, "You spent your time reading children's e-mail?"

"Not just children, but mostly, yeah. Replying too."

"What did you think of the translation software that puts their web into English?"

"A credibly good job, here and there a bit flaky."

"That was my impression too. Very strange."

"Hmm? How so?"

Jorani shrugged her shoulders. "Their Internet! Max showed me the network topology. It's been around since the time of Aristotle on Earth, yet their web seems like something from the early 2000s! What have these creatures been doing all this time?"

"Well, their encryption is okay, from what I understand. And their quantum computing technology is superior to…"

"Steve, I'm not talking encryption or hardware. I'm talking network orchestration, the policies and the protocols."

I couldn't help but smile. "Wow, someone had a really busy time last night!"

"I'm serious, Steven. They have nothing like a modern connoisseur in their security layer. I don't think they even have a security layer! I think they're going directly from data link to net address to transport."

I groaned. "The ancient firewall design?"

"Yeah, maybe, something like that. The Black Hats on Earth would run wild here!"

I paused for a moment before replying. "There's been cyber warfare on Earth for more than a century. I don't think the Pic… They're just not interested in fighting that war. And now they just welcomed four hundred and eighty potential Black Hats to their world. Shows you how much they're trusting us."

Jorani blinked. "I didn't think of that… I hope the other candidates don't do anything stupid."

"I admit, the Pic run a very open society compared to Earth. But security never publicizes everything they do. Try to keep an open mind."

Jorani paused for a moment and nodded. "Yeah, always a good idea… Maybe they'd like some help with a few things, certainly with the semantics. I have a few ideas." Jorani lay back and relaxed in the sand, her arms folded behind her head as a pillow. I watched the gentle rise and fall of her breasts beneath her halter bra. I had never seen so much of Jorani before. I knew she was pretty but never realized she was drop-dead gorgeous.

Jorani meanwhile seemed unaware of my staring. She was looking out and admiring the ocean before us. "Such a beautiful planet, Steve. Maybe so beautiful and peaceful, it doesn't matter that their Internet is not secure. Kudos for planning this trip."

"Thanks, but the real credit belongs to Julie."

"Ah…" Jorani looked at me for a moment, her eyes stealing glimpses my bare chest. "So, what did you say to the kids?"

I lay down by Jorani's side, close but not quite touching. "The e-mails? They were… interesting. I guess the majority of the letters were friendly, but not all of them. For several, I had to write back and say we're not monsters and I hope our future behavior will demonstrate this."

Jorani turned on her side to stare at me, propping up her head with an arm. "Pic kids think we're monsters?"

I nodded. "In some ways, we are monsters. A beta girl from Fair Meadows who said she was twelve asked when I fought, would I refrain from raping my enemy if she were too young or pregnant."

Jorani cringed. "The war news! Kids here are watching war news from Earth?"

"Evidently." Jorani's free arm crossed my stomach and she held my rib cage with her hand. The warmth and softness of her bare sandy arm resting on my stomach was both arousing and deeply relaxing. I took a slow, deep breath and sighed.

Jorani leaned close and kissed my cheek. "You were busy getting out a very important message. I'm sorry I mocked you."

"Hmm?" I mumbled. Lying with Jorani in the sand was so nice. My arm came up and I hugged her close to me. She had a beautiful, athletic body, and I was holding her side in the bare area above her shorts and below her sports halter. Physical desire for her filled my mind. All other thoughts were evaporating.

Jorani sighed. "Earlier, I mocked you for not exploring their databases."

I shook my head and mumbled, "You were just being playful." My hand caressed her ribcage.

Another kiss on my cheek, and this one I returned. Jorani's hair and her body smelled so clean and alive. A moment later we were hugging each other, lying side by side and pressing our bodies together. A few more kisses and I was losing track of everything except the softness of Jorani's body. I rotated and pushed myself on top of her. More kisses, and then Jorani's hands were against my chest, the palms of her hands pressing upward against me. "Whoa, settle down, tiger!"

"Hmm?"

She gave me a little bump with a forward hip thrust, and I realized what she meant. I was fully aroused and had been humping against her. She saw me blushing and laughed. "I kind of like it! But it's a little fast. Steve?"

I rolled off her and worked to get my breathing under control. "Yeah?"

"We signed up as dating each other. Want to do it for real?"

I smiled and nodded eagerly.

"Good!" She leaned forward and gave me another kiss, this one on the lips. So soft! It felt as if I were kissing an angel, so soft and light. The world seemed full of goodness, and we wound up with our arms around each other again. Nothing in the universe seemed to matter outside this wonderful moment of holding Jorani and being held in return.

A piercing whistle came to us from beyond the breakers. I recognized the voice as Max, and it sounded like a sliding progression of ultra-high trumpet blasts. And underneath the sound of Max was Julie, weaving into Max's whistle in sweet complex harmony. "Wow, listen to Max," I said. "It sounds as if he's boasting."

Jorani opened her eyes and after a moment nodded. "Julie too. You can hear joy in Julie's whistle too."

"Yeah. It's nice to think she's so happy. I guess she must be serious about Max."

"Well, of course. From what I understand of Pic courtship…" Jorani was silent for a long moment and then gave me a playful rise of her eyebrows. "I believe this is what they call a courtship copulation. Couples do this as they pledge to each other. It's touching that they're sharing their intimacy with us. Do you know they've been going together for years?"

"Yeah. Max told me." My worries returned. "I hope they're being careful."

"Steve, the Pic are more advanced medically than we are. I'm sure they have effective means of birth control."

I sighed in relief, feeling a bit foolish. "Right, of course."

"Well…" Jorani shook her head and gave the deepest blush I've ever seen. "Actually, from what she said about…"

"Hmm?"

"What were her words, Steve? This is not the copulation that gets me pregnant?"

"Yeah, something like that."

Jorani blushed again. "From what I read... It's their custom... I think Julie is taking Max in her rump."

"What?"

"Oh, don't judge them, Steve! They're not human!"

"I know."

Another trumpet blast from beyond the breakers. Jorani shivered. "Max sounds absolutely ecstatic."

I gazed out to sea. Our Pic escorts were not visible but we could still hear them whistling merrily. "Okay," I said. "I'll try not to judge. And you're right. I shouldn't be applying human standards."

"You really shouldn't, Steve. You and I both know what that kind of sex is like for humans..."

My eyes went wide and I gave Jorani a very playful smile and tapped her butt.

"Stop that!" she cried with a laugh. "You know I don't mean personally! But in Pic courtship, it's an easy coupling and it's Julie's way of expressing her acceptance. Max is asking for her engagement, something like that. From what I read about Pic tradition, they won't mate again until a formal public commitment is made."

"Hmm... You know, mating is such an interesting topic..." I had my face close to Jorani as we lay, my nose sniffing an ear under her black hair. I felt awash in desire. I caressed her earlobe with my nose and slightly stroked her bare midriff with the back of my hand. Jorani lay on her back and became very still, accepting my caresses. The sounds and smells around me seemed to fade away. After a moment, the tips of my fingers began gliding across the sensitive skin of her navel, and I leaned close to lick her ear. I gazed down at her body. *Such a beautiful skin color*, I thought, *such a rich golden brown*. Her bare stomach felt like a velvet smooth covering over hard muscle and I bent to kiss her neck, meanwhile pushing in with my middle finger just above her abdomen, penetrating the navel. Jorani took a sharp breath as my lips caressed her and she wiggled in my arms. "Ticklish?" I asked.

"Not exactly," she whispered back. "Aroused. And nervous."

"Oh," I mumbled. "Sorry." I sat up and returned my hand to my side.

Jorani shook her head to dismiss my apology as she turned to me. "Steve, you're like me, aren't you? You got involved in the Pic competitions in 2097, right?"

"Sure. That's probably true for everyone here." It had taken two Earth years for all the nations to finalize their quotas and decide who their candidates would be. The summer and fall of 2099 were particularly brutal as the contenders were whittled down to less than a thousand. And then the Pic made their final selections to reduce class size to four hundred and eighty.

Jorani nodded. "I was too young to have much of a dating relationship before the competitions, and afterwards, there was no time." She frowned and burst out, "The elimination rounds! My final month in Phnom Penh..." Jorani looked troubled, as if she wanted to say more but couldn't find the words. I became still and wondered if Jorani would finally tell me about her training or her family life in Cambodia. She had dropped a few hints earlier that she had led a rough life but had never filled in the details.

But the words just wouldn't come. Jorani finally seemed to give up and took a few deep breaths to calm herself. "How about you? Did you leave a girl behind?"

I sighed and lay on my back. It took me a moment to switch gears and collect my thoughts. "Her name was Cossette. We were in the same class at Whitehorse until last summer when I moved to finalist training in Colorado. We were as close as..." I was silent for a while wondering how to describe what happened. "Cossette was furious at me for continuing the competition. She said I was abandoning her, which was true."

Jorani looked at me and then out to sea. "Ah, sorry. That must have hurt. I didn't mean to pry." She idly rubbed some sand between her fingers. "I guess what I want to say is... I have no experience with... and I'm feeling all the emotions and..." She paused and added softly, turning but not quite meeting my eyes, "I need a little space, that's all."

I nodded. "Sure. I'm happy just to have you."

A relieved smile. "Thank you." She lay back down and cuddled against me. I wrapped an arm around her and gave a contented sigh. And then I remembered something else that Jorani had said. I kissed her lightly and asked, "So what else did you find out last night?"

"Hmmm? Oh, yeah. Something really interesting. Max suggested I read about Enigma."

"...funny name for a planet." I thought about what I had learned of the local solar system. For their other planets, the Pic had chosen rough analogies to their own mythologies. Enigma, though, had been renamed during the last century of the Third New Kingdom.

"Yeah, but it fits. It's one strange planet. Its atmosphere is a crazy mixture of deuterium and helium-3, with rich additions of neon, krypton, and xenon, and with a residual one percent carbon dioxide."

"That sounds like a joke, completely unnatural, except maybe for the CO2."

"Exactly. That's probably the only natural part, outgas from rocks. The Pic have nano-crystal records the planet was transformed during the last century of the Third New Kingdom. What grandeur, using an entire planet as a giant warehouse for the elements."

I still felt confused. "But you can't... The sheer volume of it, and that isotope mix is absurd. Professor Feynman compared the planet to Mars. That's not massive enough to hold an atmosphere."

"No, not forever, though Enigma does have more gravity than Mars. The denser gases are concentrated at the surface. The top layer is almost pure Helium 3 and deuterium. That escapes first. But the solar wind here is not as fierce as Earth's solar system, and Enigma has a magnetic field. The Pic estimate Enigma's exponential loss rate for the top layer to be about fifty million years. In a few billion years, maybe the planet will be more like Mars. But for now, surface air pressure is higher than Whistlestop's."

"Makes sense, I guess. The heavier gases build the pressure in layers."

Jorani sat up and looked out to sea. "The references in the nano-records are even more bizarre than the portal network... some super-secret technology that allowed the transmutation of matter. I read there are at least six billion tons of iridium bars on Enigma, half Iridium-191 and half Iridium-193. There are similar breakouts for the other elements too, ten huge underground facilities the size of Pic cities holding the ten stable isotopes of tin. Can you imagine?"

Before I could make a comment, Jorani cried out, "Oh, look! Max and Julie are returning!"

Our Pic escorts were a bit hard to read when they rejoined us. After brief hand gestures thanking us for our patience, they donned their clothes and began their lectures on dune ecology as if nothing had happened. Jorani and I spent the next few hours learning the biology and connections of the different species, sometimes walking up to the very edge of the interior forest but never quite entering. The interior looked very wild, bursting with life. I noticed that Julie was especially attentive of the forest whenever we were near.

As the time approached 33:00, Julie pointed out to Max that we had a long hike ahead of us and we wouldn't get back to campus until well after sunset. So our escorts cut the tour short and we started our return journey. The four of us walked together as we ate our lunch, but afterwards Jorani gave Julie and me a hand sign and then pulled ahead with Max for a private conversation. Eager to be alone with Julie, I didn't mind a bit.

"Earlier, Julie, apologies for grabbing your snout like that."

"Huh?" Julie gave a laughing whistle. "Oh, yeah! I was so pumped up, I had forgotten. No foul. Just forget about it. Your concern for me was very sweet."

"I take it you and Max are a couple now?"

Julie nodded. "We're going to register ourselves as betrothed."

"Ah… And what does that mean?"

"Well, it's not quite marriage. You have to be an adult for that. But betrothal is not far from it. Breaking a betrothal is the same legal process as divorce."

"Oh. I've never thought of that. Divorce with multiple people…"

"Yeah. It's not common, nothing like Earth. But yeah, it can be messy."

"Well, anyway… Congratulations, Julie. Will you have a long engagement?" I spent the next few minutes describing what an engagement was, and was surprised to learn Pic didn't follow the practice. Julie expected to have a simple ceremony with Max and their families and friends next weekend. I digested that for a moment and asked, "And sometime in the future, a gamma female will join your betrothal?"

Julie shook her head. "Many word translations were picked for convenience. They don't have the same meaning as on Earth. Here on Whistlestop, betrothals are for couples before they reach adulthood. For older singles, sometimes a triplet will form, three pairs of relationships all at once, but it's unusual for young people to do that." Julie looked up at me. "We've talked about this before. Some couples remain monogamous for life, and it's also not uncommon for a marriage to grow beyond three. The legal maximum is six."

"Six, huh? One for each gender?"

Julie gave the Pic equivalent of a shrug. "Probably any combination you can think of exists. Homosexuality is much rarer here compared to Earth, but there's nothing illegal about it. But the limit of six has more to do with how we socialize. Beyond six, a group can't have an unstructured conversation. People will break into sub-groups. It's a Pic tradition that marriages shouldn't be like that."

"That's really interesting. I think humans have about the same limit..." An unusually strong wave washed our feet as we walked. "So these same freedoms will be given to humans when we reach thirty?"

Julie gave a chirping laugh. "I suppose so. Do you want a husband or two?"

I grinned. "Definitely not."

"How about five wives?"

This question took slightly longer to answer. "Uh, no, I suppose not."

"I didn't think so."

"I admit, the idea is a bit intriguing."

Julie stared at me before deciding I wasn't being serious. She shrugged. "For what will really happen, who knows? Everything is fluid."

"We humans know almost nothing about the endgame. What's the vision for when our trial is over?"

Julie took a long moment to decide what she wanted to say. "I've had some conversations with my beta mom about this. Best case, the human population will be assigned a maximum growth rate limit and a long-term cap, perhaps as many as half a million citizens, plus a much smaller number that can come from Earth on visitor permits. My mom mentioned there was even discussion of giving humans some limited form of autonomy on Providence."

"Hey, that's great!"

"Limited, Steven, limited. We are not going to hand over our planet to you." Julie added quietly. "And this is the best case."

I nodded. "Assuming we humans can adapt to Pic's form of population control, you mean."

"Among other things."

"Can escorts use the lottery if humans cancel their birthrights?"

Julie shook her head. "No. The penalty has to be real for it to be effective. A cancelled birthright disqualifies a person from the lottery. If you and Jorani have two kids without permits, my marriage with Max will be childless."

"Unless you add someone with a birthright to your marriage."

"Unless that, yes, but the lack of our own birthrights would make us an unattractive couple to marry. This is no joke, Steven."

I frowned and felt horrible over my power to ruin Julie's life. "Part of the trial, huh?"

Julie saw my distress and decided to reply with playful sarcasm. "I could be wrong, but stealing birthrights might not be the best way for humans to gain the world's approval."

We walked several hundred meters before I spoke again. "So, I've been reading kids' emails."

Julie nodded. "Yes. I want to thank you for copying me on your replies. As you saw, there's a lot of resistance to the trial."

"I can see why. You people have such a beautiful and cared-for planet, while we humans have trashed Earth."

Julie stared at me. "Did you study the network debates on this?"

"Uh, not yet."

"The kids I'm not sure about. Mostly I think they're just excited about having an intelligent alien species on the planet. The adults though…"

"We're that bad, huh?"

Julie sighed. "So many issues — wars, poverty, drug abuse, exploitation, insane bioweapons, destroyed ecosystems… The language doesn't help, either…"

"You mean English? What's wrong with English?"

"Not just English. To the Pic ear, human speech is all low register. Humans sound as if they're growling all the time. Pic who are against the trial sometime refer to humans as growlers." Julie noticed my frown. "Yes, yes, I know! Not very nice, and completely irrational! The fault is ours! But the Pic mind is like the human mind. We are both more and less than rational. It took me a year of practicing English before I felt I was no longer growling at people. But not many people will make the effort to learn." Julie paused and added softly, "Most adults are against the trial."

I blinked. "Then how…"

"By a cute council maneuver that declared Earth an ecological disaster area. Once that was done, it opened up automatic rights to do disaster relief, and the opposition couldn't muster a sixty percent vote to stop it. No one surprises like a gamma! They pushed the vote through. The majority of the alpha and beta councilors were against the idea of social fusion." Julie gave me a long, thoughtful look and offered her hand. I gladly accepted.

And she began to sign to me using the intimate form of communication through tactile touch. She was lightning fast, a burst of hand forms against my palms and fingers, and she had to repeat herself twice before I got it.

I said out loud, "You're offering to give me private lessons on hand signs?"

"Oh, you are good, Steven. I was signing at expert speed." She reached up and gave me a brief hug, low on my hips. "And how did you know the sign for private? I didn't teach you that."

"Uh, I just guessed from context, index finger pad double strength against my index finger pad is the sign for you, and then index finger rotating and hiding behind middle finger. I guessed that meant private you."

"Brilliant and correct. Steven, it's time I told you how I got to be your escort."

I looked down at Julie and smiled. "I'm all ears."

"Huh? Oh, I get it. Anyway, I got to be your escort because I earned the right of first choice. Steven, you were ranked top choice by both the alpha and beta interviewers in Antarctica."

I blinked and half shouted, "Really?"

"For one person to get two top picks was unexpected. The three types look for different qualities, and across the full candidate population, there's considerable diversity among their selections. For someone to be picked number one by two different types is remarkable."

"Julie, are you trying to make me blush?"

"And the first shall be last."

"What?"

"Don't you remember? We were at the very back of the line, the last pair to enter the transport. It's a Pic tradition that the first go last. It's a position of honor."

"Oh…" The memory came back to me, so many Pic escorts flashing Julie muzzle signs as she and I walked to the end of the line. They were congratulating her, me too I guess. "Was the whole line ranked?"

Julie laughed. "Of course not! What possible reason could there be to humiliate the people at the head of the line? The last position was a place of honor. Everything else was random."

"Yeah, makes sense…" I looked at Julie curiously. "You had access to the all the scoring?"

"Uh, I don't think I'm supposed to comment about that."

"Huh? You mean the other escorts know the scores of only their humans?"

"I don't mean to imply that either."

"So what do you mean to imply? Why do you know my scores?"

"All the escorts know your scores."

"What?" I thought silently. But before I asked Julie to explain, my curiosity pulled me in another direction. "So, how did I do with the gammas?"

"Uh, you did fine, an acceptable rating." Julie looked up at me and stared. "Sorry. That wasn't the question I was expecting."

I felt a bit disoriented. Where was this conversation heading? "I'm relieved. I thought I did poorly with my gamma interviews."

Julie just laughed. "Well, sure, gammas! They'll tie your mind in knots if you let them!"

I couldn't help but laugh too. "Spoken like a true non-gamma!"

"Well, I am my father's daughter!" Julie's snout was showing a pattern of extreme playfulness and challenge.

And I tried to meet her challenge, still avoiding the prime question before us. "So what was the exclusion process like?"

"From each of the three interview teams, every candidate received a score between plus two and minus two: two points for top choice, one point for acceptable, zero for no confidence, minus-one for rejection, and minus-two for rejection with prejudice. A candidate needed a positive net score to come to Whistlestop. Each team was allowed one top choice and as many of the other scores as they wished. Your score was plus five, obviously the highest."

I smiled. "Obviously... A modified version of pass/fail, huh? That's not what I would have guessed. How did they break ties?"

"There were further conditions that had to be met," Julie said evasively.

"Ah. Sounds tough. Were many excluded in the pass/fail round?"

For a moment, Julie's muzzle flashed sadness tinged with embarrassment. "Over half, many more than anticipated."

"What?" I took a deep breath. "What was the problem?"

"In a word, nationalism. A majority of the candidates seemed focused on bringing their nationalism and religious beliefs to Whistlestop."

"Well, yeah, sure. They wouldn't have made it to the finals otherwise."

"But that's not the purpose of the trial, Steve. We're trying to augment our culture, not replace it."

"So what happened?"

"The interview committees dropped below target maximum. But that would have been a very poor way to start the trial." Julie gave an idle hand gesture that I didn't know how to interpret. "It was rough on the interviewers, and the escorts too. We're all volunteers who wanted to make the fusion trial a success. We were also given the mandate to pick a fair and objective representation of all of Earth's cultures. It was… difficult to align the two goals." Julie paused and added quietly, "In the end, the committees agreed to rescind a number of their rejections."

I stared at Julie. "This is really fascinating. And what do you mean, rough on the escorts, too? Are you saying our Pic classmates were part of the selection process?"

"Uh…" Julie unexpectedly flashed a confused color pattern. "I have legal responsibilities that limit what I'm allowed to tell you. Let me research how I can answer that."

We walked past several dunes before I felt like talking again. I looked at Julie and saw her snout had switched back to playful challenge mode. I felt my resistance crumble. "Okay! I give up! Why do all the escorts know my scores?"

Julie's muzzle flashed a sign of victory and she answered my question indirectly. "Because of what your scores portend. I got a call from my beta mom last night. Early yesterday, the council had a private meeting. They approved you to be the liaison between the Pic government and humans. If you accept, they'll make their decision public." Julie paused to adjust her backpack. "A government official is coming here tomorrow to discuss this with you. Don't worry. I have permission to tell you. And it's not really a big secret among the escorts. The gammas are the main drivers of this trial, and they're thrilled both the alphas and betas will have their number one choice for the job… assuming you'll accept, of course."

My mind was filled with questions. Where to begin? "Shouldn't the student government be part of this decision?"

Julie's muzzle flashed something I vaguely associated with horror. "That would be a disaster! Steve, the world government is asking you to be a liaison, not an ambassador. Your primary job would be to represent the Pic government to humans. The relationship is tenuous already. We really, really don't want to be in a situation where the human student government is telling the world council to work with someone else."

"Holy shit!" I hissed. "This is going to go down with the student government like a ton of bricks!"

"Well, maybe… How about you tell them you're accepting because of your sign language abilities? You're more skillful than the other humans, you really are. Hostile councilors will not learn English!"

I thought for a while. "Yeah, that might help. I could also promise to convey student concerns."

"Sure you could! Uh, does that mean you'll accept?" The hope in Julie's muzzle pattern was unmistakable.

"Hmm… What would I have to do, exactly?"

"In quiet times, not much except make occasional trips to meet with councilors and build relationships. With the portals, there's minimal travel time. On the plus side, you'll get to see the world three years sooner than your classmates. Our cities focus on gardens and integration with diverse local ecologies. I think you'll find our planet beautiful." Julie tried to inject a bit of playfulness into her answer. "I imagine you'll have to get used to being gawked at, especially by kids."

But my mind was on other things. "What about the not-so-quiet times?"

Julie sighed. "Yeah, I know. That could be anything." She offered me her hand and this time it was just for holding. We walked a long while in silence. The day was still delightfully warm and bright, but the wind and surf were picking up. Far out at sea, dark clouds were forming on the horizon.

Chapter 4

Early next morning, Northern Autumn 10, 3484 C.E. 13:29

It was three hours before sunrise, and usually I was a sound sleeper, but there had just been a staccato series of thunder claps that was impossible to ignore. Fully awake and having missed last night's dinner, I decided to get dressed and raid the self-service area of the cafeteria. As I was leaving my dorm room, I met my next-door neighbor, one of the emigrants from Germany.

"Emeric! Want to join me for breakfast?"

"Uh, sure. Just a minute." He tapped his PA. "Hey, Rebby, change of plans. Steven and I are heading down to breakfast. You ready for the next step? ... Great. See you there."

"Rebby? That sounded like Rebekah. The alpha female?"

"Ja. She's my mentor. Do you know her?"

"Sort of. She's in my physics class, one of the top students, very sharp. We've never chatted."

"Well, here's your chance!" Emeric said with a beaming smile.

The self-service wing of the cafeteria was divided into three parts, a large blue-coded area in the front with food certified for both humans and Pic, a red-coded area in the back left for Pic-only food, and a yellow-coded area in the back right (yellow was the traditional Pic color for danger) for human-only food. The cafeteria trays were similarly coded: blue for only blue-coded food, red when selecting anything red coded, and yellow for anything yellow coded. No one was supposed to put red and yellow coded foods on the same tray.

Both humans and Pic could easily live on the ample selections from the blue-coded area, but the Pic wanted to instill in us humans lifelong habits of eating awareness. For this morning, I opened a blue cooler and was happy to find a native meal my human classmates jokingly call carrot

76

cake with shrimp — pastry-wrapped shredded orange vegetables with chunks of peppery seafood. I thought it was delicious, and with a local vegetable drink and some Earth fruit, it made a very satisfying meal.

Emeric sat down opposite me in the deserted dining area, his blue tray holding all Earth food except for a small cup of native nuts. Meanwhile Rebekah trotted into the cafeteria and flashed us a quick muzzle hello and a hand sign not to wait for her before disappearing into the self-service area. "Quite a storm last night," I commented as the two of us began eating.

Emeric grinned. "*Ja, ja, aber…* are we talking about the weather or the student meeting?"

"Yeah." I grinned back. "Fireworks in both."

"You're okay with the outcome?" Emeric asked as he stared thoughtfully at a purple nut before popping it in his mouth.

"Sure. I have to report to the student council. But that's what the job is anyway."

Emeric made a satisfied smile at the taste. "Any idea when you might leave the island?"

"Nothing definite. For a while, the government councilors will be coming here. The first one's coming this evening, one of our advocates. And in two weeks, I'll meet Longfellow, the leader of the trial opposition."

"Ah, good luck with that…"

Rebekah joined us with her own blue tray, sitting on the floor Pic fashion by Emeric's side while deftly plucking a strawberry off his plate without asking and munching on it. Emeric returned the favor by helping himself to a couple of the purple nuts on her tray. "These are great. Taste like buttered popcorn and a whole lot more."

Rebekah sampled one herself. "These are the best quality, the wild version from the lakes region, the northern part of Genesis. Very nutritious." She looked at me and added, "It's a dangerous ecology. The nuts are harvested with drones. Would you like to try one, Steven?" Emeric and Rebekah then gave each other an affectionate hug.

I smiled. "You guys are an inspiration. You really are."

Rebekah flashed a gratitude emotion on her muzzle. "I want to thank you for this opportunity. This is my first attempt eating with multiple humans and no Pic. Being together in class and recreation is fine. Eating together is surprisingly difficult."

"Ah." I sliced a thick wedge off my plum and offered it. "Try this... How was it?"

"Feeling good," she replied, correctly understanding my question. "Taste is good too."

"I know many humans are still queasy about eating meals together," I said as I accepted a nut.

Rebekah flashed a shrug pattern. "It's a bigger issue with us Pic. A much bigger issue. But we're all working on it."

"Ah. So you practice with Emeric before breakfast?"

"You mean today? No. We were heading to the greenhouse, our gardening group."

My ears picked up. "The gifting and the purpose?"

Rebekah flashed a bright smile. "Exactly! I didn't realize other humans had picked up on this. Our guidance was to avoid spiritual issues with humans for a while, or at least not initiate them. The concern was conflicts with Earth religions would make our human classmates uncomfortable. Emeric and I wandered into a religious conversation by accident."

"I know almost nothing," I admitted. "Julie offered to tell me but I never got back to her about it."

"If you're interested..." Seeing me nod, Rebekah looked at Emeric. "You want to start?"

"Sure..." Emeric took a moment to gather his thoughts. "What I really objected to with the religious revival movement back in Germany was its rigidity. People insisted that their beliefs were as valid as scientific perspectives, that both ways of thinking should be taught in schools."

I nodded. "The USNA suffered through the same thing a century ago, an Earth century, I mean, back when it was the USA."

"But it's not a matter of choosing a perspective," Emeric continued. "It's a matter of choosing a direction. Let me teach you two German words. The first word is *scheinheilig*, the German adjective for hypocritical. *Scheinen* is the verb to appear, and *heilig* is holy, and *scheinheilig* at its root is the appearance of holiness but without the

78

reality of it. The second word is *Wissenschaft* which means science. *Wissen* means to know, and *schaffen* means create. Our word for science literally means knowledge creation."

I grinned. "That is genuinely neat."

Emeric frowned. "What the fundamentalists are doing is *Scheinwissenschaft*, the appearance of science without the reality of it. Rather than using data to create knowledge, they have these divinely revealed, closed-minded beliefs that they're trying to push back into the data. They're running the scientific process in reverse!" Emeric looked at his mentor. "No data will ever be viewed without bias, because what data could possibly refute the revelations of God? But data are like people. If you torture and cook them long enough, you can get them to tell you anything you want. What the Pic are doing, though… It's the first religion that ever made total sense to me. Rebby, you want to take it from here?"

"Sure… Steven, I'm still a novice at reading human emotions. This isn't offending you, is it?"

"Heck no. Go on."

"Okay. What we Pic do, it's so different from what humans do, I don't know if you would call it a religion. On Earth, religions use divinely revealed truth to frame the physical world and a person's existence. We Pic do the opposite. We use observations to frame our spirituality. There's never a conflict with science because we don't recognize an immutable revealed truth. If our understanding of our observations change, it can change our spirituality too… Would you like an example?"

I was captivated by the thought. "Sure."

"Before the current era, males on Whistlestop were considered inferior to females and suitable for slavery. We females had the dominant numbers. It was judged that we should dominate in other ways too." Rebekah grunted while flashing a disgust pattern. "It's hard to imagine how such ridiculous logic was ever accepted. But it took the rebirth of modern scientific attitudes to reveal our moral error, and that changed our spirituality. Because of the intrinsic brutality of the institution, slavery should never be accepted. The point is spirituality should always be a work in progress. Never close your mind to critiquing your principles."

She finished her plum slice before continuing. "So I look at the universe with an open mind and what do I see? I see a created universe. The evidence is overwhelming. There are no steady-state eternal models for the universe, nothing that can explain what we observe. The next question is: What kind of universe was created? Again, the observational evidence is overwhelming. It's a universe that has been gifted with life; layer after layer of interlocking optimizations that are needed to support the existence of life. There're optimizations in quantum mechanics. Its framework provides the physical basis for consciousness and free-will. There's optimized-for-life fine structure in the nuclear excess-mass curve, optimized fusion reaction rates in stellar furnaces, optimizations in cosmological genesis and evolution, the grand pattern of self-organization and thermodynamic entropy thriving in each other's counter flow. Optimized-for-life everything! Sure, if you imagine ten raised to the ten to the one-thousandth power of universes, perhaps this is just the one universe against quasi-infinite odds with life in it, but how does that argument survive the principle of simplicity? Cut out what you don't need; what you can do with few assumptions, you do in vain with more. What you can do with one universe, you do in vain with requiring an infinite number of them."

I tried to hold the number mentioned in my mind. "I'll have to work on what $10^{(10^{1000})}$ means."

Rebekah smiled. "And the gifting implies the purpose, because gifts are meant to be appreciated and enjoyed. Our purpose is to enjoy our lives and to help others enjoy theirs. Again, look at the observations. Have you ever seen anyone act as if life had no free will, no purpose, no desire for enjoyment?"

I thought for a moment. "It's possible, I suppose; some profound form of depression or autism. Why interact with a reality if it has no meaning?"

"Ah, that's a good point. But those are forms of mental illness, not the perspectives of a healthy mind."

"All right, I'll concede the first part, about wanting to enjoy life… But the second part? Not that I object to it, but is it that obvious our purpose is to help others?"

"Sure. We're in a universe where we must live with the consequences of our decisions. We're also in a universe where we live with the consequences of other people's decisions. Can an island of happiness exist surrounded by an ocean of misery? Wouldn't the jealous ocean rebel in fury and drag the island into its depths? It's a human saying, isn't it, that misery loves company?"

"I suppose. But I'm thinking of Earth history. There're many examples of people taking over governments, seizing power and acting sadistically."

Rebekah flashed a dissonant array of colors, a sign of confusion. "One moment. I'm not familiar with that word." She queried her assistant. "Interesting. Sadism. We return to mental illness. The Pic equivalent word for sadism means inflicting pain or distress with immoral pleasure. It has a strong, automatic connotation of mental disease, a damaged mind. Is it the same in English?"

I thought for a moment and frowned. "I have to say no. People will call you nasty and maybe curse you for hurting them, but there's no automatic leap to think sadistic behavior is mental illness. I like the thought though. Maybe that's part of our trial, to shift to the Pic way of thinking."

Rebekah flashed a distinct sign of gratitude, specific to thanking me for accepting her position. "Yes, perhaps. It's the core of Pic spirituality, that the universe was gifted with life by a creator, and in love, the universe was created where the life has purpose, where our love has purpose and our sadism does not. Everything beyond that… well, is conjecture. That's what we do when we're gardening, contending all our different ideas about what is eternal and what is not. On top of all the unfairness in life, what are our personal responsibilities to our creator? We should help each other, yet life at the biosphere level is by the creator's design in deadly competition with itself. How to we reconcile, how do we interlock these two truths? Earth religions seek unity on this. We Pic seek contention."

I had to grin and barely restrained myself from laughing. "You're right; this sure doesn't sound like Earth! A religion based on seeking opposing views?"

Rebekah countered, "And what's wrong with that? Our creed is simple: Always approach the creator with an open mind. Think! We learn by contending our different ideas. That's how humans and Pic innovate, how we advance. And our religion is not raw conflict... We use gardening to unite in common purpose. We get to know and trust each other. The key thoughts are that trust has value, that contention has value, and that trust and contention together unlock each other's value." Rebekah finished her drink and stood up with her tray. "I need to be going. Thank you for your help with my breakfast, Steven. And it was a pleasure talking with you."

"Same here. Fabulous lesson. Thank you." Rebekah nodded back and trotted out. As she left the room, I said to Emeric, "I think I just fell in love with your mentor."

Emeric stretched. "*Ja*, Rebekah. It is impossible to know her and not love her. She can be a bit brisk at times, but the amount of trust and loyalty I'm offered... she acts like an older sister to me." He paused and added in a quiet voice, "Speaking of love, mind if I change topic? I saw you and Jorani return from your field trip yesterday."

"Hmm?"

"I want to give you a friendly heads-up. You might have some competition for her."

I managed a playful grin. "Hey, Emeric. You moving in on my girl?"

"*Nicht ich, Dummkopf*! I have my sights set on Marisa! Do you know her?"

"The emigrant from Brazil? Sure. She's in my wilderness training course. Good choice, Emeric! She's a wonderful person." I tried to give Emeric a casual look. "So, who's my competition?"

"Uh, I'd rather not say. I could be wrong."

I studied Emeric's face. He didn't look uncertain. "What did you see?"

"Just someone buzzing around Jorani."

"Oh... Was she buzzing back?"

Emeric thought for a moment. "Not that I noticed."

"Well, that's good." We both had classes starting at 20:00. Our second week of school was about to begin. I headed off to the library to meet Julie for my first morning hand-signing lesson.

Chapter 5

Two weeks later:
Northern Autumn 28, 3484 C.E. 57:57 (Time Zone 30)
Earth time: January 24, 2100, 11:47 PM U.T.

The weather was unusually warm for this time of year, and I was relaxing with my tablet on a lounge chair on my bedroom balcony, enjoying the night air and the fact that tomorrow was another vacation day. Jorani's dorm room has a fine view of the northern part of the campus, but mine faces the southern park that leads to the ocean. There was more than enough light to appreciate the view. Whistlestop's moon was full and high in the southern sky and supported by bright clusters of starlight and Hera, the solar system's gas giant. It had the mass of Jupiter and Saturn combined and with about Saturn's orbital radius. Whistlestop was considerably closer than Earth to one of the two major spiral arms of the galaxy. The deep night sky here was spectacular. The only thing missing now was the Blue Diamond, an incredibly bright star that could currently be seen only in the predawn twilight. I made an idle effort to trace some of the ancient Pic constellations Professor Higgins had mentioned. A tight string of stars high in the southeast was the Arm of the Beta Grandmother. There were some interesting differences in how humans and Pic named their constellations; the biggest shift was that ancient Pic didn't see animals in their star patterns.

I was very relaxed, having spent most of today and yesterday trying out various sporting activities with my Pic classmates. What fun! And I had learned a tremendous amount of material. It didn't seem like work at all. Was the first term really more than half over?

At the start, the thought of three-day weekends sounded nice but I wondered if it would be a grind to go through seven school days in a row. But it isn't a grind at all. The Pic run interactive classes, and it is very engaging to experience how human and Pic classmates together explore and debate material. And our course schedules are only fixed for six days a week. The seventh day provides a wide assortment of guest lecturers.

I stretched and took a deep satisfying breath of fragrant ocean air as I sat in my chair. Perhaps I should have turned in, but I wasn't sleepy yet. Just about all of us humans here were still adjusting to the longer daily cycle. And the daily news package from Earth would be available in a half hour. I decided to wait for it, setting a tablet alert then turning off my review lesson on the history of physics. Professor Feynman was teaming up with history Professor Higgins and giving us a whirlwind tour of Pic advancement, taking us from the invention of sundials to the discovery of portals. My mind drifted back to the latest lesson, the one on Whistlestop's astounding transportation network.

Slightly over thirty-five hundred years ago, Pic discovered hidden in a lunar valley a combination of complete and partial pairs of a total of 1512 Type-I portals. The current civilian jump network consisted of two hundred and six pairs linking all cities to the world capital's hub. The Pic had an additional ten pairs for local use, plus more than a thousand half-pairs whose other ends were spread across the galaxy in a vast sphere, originally under the control of ancient computers at the lunar valley. Such an amazing leap of exploration the Pic made so long ago, to send so many of their priceless assets into the heavens. The most distant probes are now more than two thousand light-years distant.

Was it really a Pic decision? The archeological evidence from the New Third Kingdom was based almost exclusively on encoded nano-crystals, and it was so confusing. Where did the invention of portals come from? It seemed to have sprung from nowhere, no preceding scientific insights that would have led to it. And yet, there was no mention in the ancient records of contact with an alien species. It was one deep puzzle.

Of the ten extra local pairs, currently seven were in use providing access to the elemental riches of Enigma, one pair linked Whistlestop with its moon, one pair was held in reserve, and finally one pair was assigned to provide a portal link from Providence to the polar-latitude city which the Pic have given the English name of Far Rockaway. This far northern city was located on one of Whistlestop's thirteen single-city islands, and it contained the hub of the military and Parks and

Conservation department. The name Far Rockaway was picked by Julie's dad, and was a very loose translation of the ancient Pic whistle for Distant Island of Rocky Foothills. I thought Julie's dad did it as a joke. He spent his early childhood on the island, just as the original Professor Feynman on Earth grew up in Far Rockaway, New York.

And as for the one thousand and eighty half-pairs still at Whistlestop, Pic life would be very different without them. The portals had limited bandwidth, perhaps twenty-thousand people transfers per day per city considering two jumps were needed if Haven was not their origin or destination. In practice, the average daily passenger number was about eight thousand per city, with a small amount of high-priority cargo filling the difference. The vast majority of inter-city commerce was done with nine hundred and sixty modified half-pairs, used not as portals but as cargo vessels similar to the transport on Earth. A Pic city typically had two hundred and forty cargo landing sites, both for commerce and for emergency evacuations if needed. It would take weeks to evacuate a city through the portal connection to Haven.

I put my portal thoughts aside and took a deep breath of the sea air, thinking about the games I had played this weekend. Tennis and wallyball! What wonderful sports to bring our two species together. With our different physiologies, there were some sports where Pic eat humans for lunch, such as any water sport or their wild, steeplechase version of soccer. Imagine playing soccer on an oversized pitch against creatures who galloped like small ponies and the landscape was filled with moguls, hedgerows, sand pits and even water hazards! Definitely not my sport to play, but with virtual reality, oh man, was it ever fun to watch!

And yet, there are some sports where the Pic couldn't compete with us. Golf is a good example. The Pic had set up a trial three-hole course past the greenhouses at the far eastern edge of the campus, and we'd found the Pic body (even when upright on rear legs) just couldn't torque much body momentum into a golf swing. What a decent human golfer could cover in two strokes, a Pic would require four or five. They were good putters though, and the betas on campus had been experimenting with the game. They found it intriguing.

But tennis was perfect for our competition, opening up a fascinating contest between our strengths and weaknesses. Pic were faster on the court. You almost never wanted to try a drop shot on them. But as in golf, they couldn't crank up the power of a human swing. The alphas in particular had fallen in love with the game, and our current status was that their average player beat our average player, but our better players beat their best players.

Julie and I played C-league tennis, which didn't focus much on winning but rather on having fun. Tomorrow we were playing mixed opposite escorts, and by the luck of the draw, Max and I would be playing against team Julie-Jorani. A few hours before sunset today, Julie, in an extremely playful mood, predicted a victory for herself and Jorani, boasting in front of her betrothed Max and a crowd of his friends and all the while giving a very suggestive arch with her hips. It was the one and only time I'd seen a blush on Max's muzzle. Max would never throw a game, but the way I play, I thought he might be in for a very enjoyable time tomorrow night.

And then there was wallyball. Imagine a 3-D box like a handball court, but closer in size to a volleyball court. There was a high net in the middle that went down to a springy floor and either four-person teams or six-person teams played against each other. You were not allowed to touch the net and you got a generous four touches on the wallyball before it had to go over the net. A point was scored every time the ball hits the floor, and there were almost no other rules.

You lost a point if you served the ball into the net or floor, but you physically couldn't serve the ball out-of-bounds. There were no out-of-bounds. Multiple bank shots off the walls and ceiling were allowed. You could jump on a teammate's back if you wanted, in order to get a better swing at the ball. It was a common Pic maneuver.

It wasn't a Pic suggestion to call it wallyball. They called it gender-ball, and it was a popular game across the planet. Their rules stated that a six-person team should include all six genders, and by unwritten tradition, there were always four genders on the four-person teams. That was true for all their team sports. The Pic had a strong focus on gender integration in team sports, very different than Earth, and also a tendency to forget about competing and switch to zany playfulness. If they ever got interested in American football, I'd expect them to uncork a triple reverse at least once a game.

And here was something really fascinating: With our mixed four-person wallyball teams, we had found that two humans and two Pic were superior to any other combination. Our two species complemented each other's abilities to dig and spike the ball. We had plans to have our college games viewable on the world web starting next season. What a wonderful symbolic message on the benefits of our two species working together.

The name World Web, by the way, was a concession the Pic made for us humans. There are insects on Whistlestop that spin webs, but the Pic never associated insect webs with their Internet. The two-chord, six-note whistle for their World Web has the literal translation of Digital Rivers.

My tablet chirped, and I spent the next few minutes browsing the news headlines from Earth, frowning when I read about the succession referendum in the city of Besiane. Several of my classmates from the Balkans predicted it would be a mess and they were so right. The voting had devolved into a major riot, and by nightfall Serbian army units were engaging with roving bands of Albanian paramilitary. Hell of a way to run a vote, the start of another war maybe, just what Earth needed. I was just deciding to turn off the tablet and call it a night when I sensed a flicker of movement. Someone was walking around in my dark bedroom.

My burst of apprehension faded as I recognized the silhouette of Jorani. We had become close enough to exchange free access to each other's dorm room, but I was still surprised she had entered without chiming. Jorani slid open my balcony door and without a word beckoned me inside. I came in and told my wrist PA to turn on the lights. Jorani looked upset. I had never seen her this tense before. "Are you okay?"

Jorani just groaned in reply and sat on my desk chair. I decided to sit on the bed. "Want some tea? I picked up some lemongrass from the care packages this morning."

"My favorite," she replied softly, avoiding my eyes. "Yeah, that would be great."

I prepared the tea quietly, allowing Jorani to unwind. She straightened her hair and looked semi relaxed by the time we took our first sips. "This is good, thanks." We locked eyes and Jorani gave a long sigh and then grimaced. "Phirun," she whispered. She was referring to the other emigrant from Cambodia.

I nearly choked on my tea. "What? What happened? Are you okay?"

"Yeah… No… Oh hell, Steve, what a mess…"

I noticed for the first time it wasn't just her hair. Her clothes looked disheveled. "Jorani, were you molested?"

"No. But it seemed…" She paused for a long moment before continuing. "I envy you. You have such a large group from the USNA."

I nodded. We had thirty-nine candidates, and twenty were selected.

"What was it like, Steve, with your group during training? Were you close to each other? Were you friends?"

"I guess so… Actually, I guess it was a mixed bag. Colorado was two thousand competitors crammed into a final pressure cooker. I guess I was friends with some; the others I just tried to respect. The competition was fierce!"

Jorani stared into her tea. "The finals for us were horrible, a thousand people competing for two slots. So much effort and so many promises to make, else I would have been eliminated. Phirun and I weren't selected to be Cambodia's representatives until December, less than a week before Antarctica. That final month…" Jorani bowed her head and seemed lost in thought. I waited quietly for her to continue.

Getting to know Jorani these past few weeks had been such a joy. She was smart, courageous, gentle, one of the most wonderful persons I had ever met. And even with our hectic schedules, we found the time to get to know each other. I felt extremely fortunate to be dating her, and she was so distressed now, it was an effort not to spring up and hug her. But somehow I felt it just wasn't the moment for it.

Jorani finished her tea and put her cup on my desk before she spoke again. "There was an undercurrent, a vision that Phirun and I would be representing Cambodian culture and values if we were both accepted. I swear, my government thinks of me as a naga."

"A naga?"

Jorani shrugged. "A dragon. It's our creation story, how people came to Cambodia. A female dragon falls in love with a wandering prince and transforms herself to human form so she can marry him."

89

I smiled and said, "Well, sure. That sounds reasonable." And then it hit me. "Oh shit."

"It didn't get bad with Phirun... until tonight."

"How long has he been bothering you?"

"I guess ever since you and I signed up as dating each other."

"And you never told me?"

She looked at me hard, her eyes bright with tears. "Are you upset with me?"

I felt completely bewildered. "With you? About what?"

"I used you as an escape. And I didn't even tell you." She wiped her eyes on her shirt sleeve before continuing. "It wasn't bad the first week. I told him we were just friends and had signed up for convenience. That was true at first, and Phirun seemed to accept it. But he's convinced I should be there for him, when it's time..."

"Time for what? This is totally ridiculous!"

A soft whisper, "I used you, Steven."

"Bullshit! Jorani, it's an honor to be your boyfriend!" I shook my head in disbelief. "I'm thrilled that you want me."

Jorani replied with a soft wail. I couldn't contain myself any longer. I got off the bed and knelt on the floor next to her chair, hugging around her waist. She was stiff for a moment, and then hugged me fiercely back.

"Jorani, what happened tonight?"

She ran her hands up and down my back before replying. "Phirun came to my room. He insisted I honor my agreements. He thought... he wanted to have... he grabbed me..."

"Jorani, this is starting to sound like assault. We should take this to the student government, maybe the Pic courts."

"No! A few seconds of groping, nothing more. I said something that stopped him."

"What did you say?"

"I said..." Tears were running down Jorani's cheeks. "I said that I loved you. Funny, isn't it? I told Phirun before I told you. I told Phirun even before I told myself."

It was my turn to cry. Words wouldn't come, but it didn't matter. They weren't needed. I stroked the bottom of Jorani's back as I held her.

"I'm not asking for anything, Steve. We both know we're not ready."

I sighed deeply, breathing in the smell of Jorani's body. Jorani guided my head until I was pressing lightly against her chest, one ear cupping a breast, Jorani's hand caressing my other ear, cheek, and throat. So soft, so warm. I started to drift in the shelter of her arms, then she pushed me gently away. My eyes opened.

"I should go home," she whispered.

"You're sure?"

"Uh huh. A hot shower and bed, that's what I need."

"I'll walk you back."

Jorani stared at me. "You can't protect me forever."

"I know. But I can walk you home tonight."

A smile. "Okay."

I was half expecting Phirun to jump out from behind a bush or something as we walked out of my dorm building, but the late-night campus was deserted. Only distant night-birds were breaking the silence. Jorani offered me her hand, and she gave me a squeeze and picked a westerly route that would be the long way back to her dorm. "I didn't think I'd ever be called on it," she muttered.

"What exactly did you promise?"

"Honestly, I'm not sure. So many commitments, and the words kept changing. I guess you could interpret them to mean I promised to have children that would propagate... my national heritage. Phirun expected me to submit tonight. Not to have kids of course, not yet. But he wanted to claim me."

I squeezed Jorani's hand. "You're not a toy. You're not a sex slave."

Jorani grunted. "A sex toy! You don't know how close..." A deep sigh and a change of thought. "It was so strange, Steve. I didn't even meet him until November. What was I to do? Resign after two terrible years of competing, just when the prize was before me? No! So I rolled the dice." We came to a nature trail that runs along the western edge of the campus. Jorani guided us onto the trail. This would be a long walk, indeed. I put my arm around Jorani's waist to keep her warm.

She snuggled against me. "I thought the odds at twenty-five percent that Phirun and I would both be here. Silly me! The real odds were so much higher." She lifted her head off my shoulder and looked at me in the moonlight. "Any idea why?"

I understood her question. Besides Cambodia, there were over a hundred countries that had two candidate slots, and almost all of them had chosen one man and one woman to be their pair, from tiny Cyprus to mighty Australia. Why such disparity? What else would you expect with the U.N. General Assembly running the show? They pushed through a motion that every country with at least a million people would get a minimum of two candidate slots. And then the Pic magnified the bias by accepting eighty percent of the two-candidate pairs. The fusion trial was a lopsided representation of Earth, favoring the representatives of small nations.

I thought for a moment how to answer Jorani's question. I hadn't been invited off our island campus yet, but during the last couple of weeks a number of government officials had come to see me. "I have a few ideas. The councilors that I meet keep dropping bits of information, and Julie has very close relationships with her moms. Ellie in particular was deeply involved with the selection process. She co-chaired the alpha interview committee, back in Antarctica... Julie sometimes tells me things."

"Anything you can share?"

I looked at the starlight for a moment as we walked. "Well, I was never asked to keep silent about anything, not directly, but I think that's mostly because the Pic don't realize how many odd pieces of information I have. Jorani, you have to keep quiet about this, okay?"

"You have my word. I'll tell absolutely no one, not even Max."

"Oh, if I'm right, Max knows everything I'm about to tell you. Just don't let him know you know." I went on to explain my conjectures. One of my primary guesses was that the Pic followed our lead on the importance of man-woman pairs and originally accepted or rejected candidates by country pairs. A lack of a positive score for one candidate would exclude the pair. But that led to too many rejections. Jorani listened to the very end of my explanation, and then gasped. "Forty? You think forty rejected candidates were allowed to come here?"

"Yep. I knew it was a substantial number from Julie, and then yesterday I was with Longfellow. Julie was there too, as a backup when

Longfellow had trouble with English. Longfellow made a comment about you, Jorani."

"Me? Something bad?" Councilor Longfellow was the leader of the faction opposing the fusion trial.

"No, just the opposite, quite a nice compliment actually, then he gave a quick hand sign to Julie, reminding her that the doubling to the forty could not be mentioned."

"Uh… What?"

"It was really amusing. Longfellow didn't realize how intensively Julie has been teaching me Pic sign language, how much I've picked up in two weeks, or maybe he thought his short message would be too cryptic for me to understand. Longfellow signed Julie at expert speed, while I had been doing some basic signing with him much more slowly. But I can read sign much faster than I can express it. Julie was superb. She just replied to Longfellow with a quick sign of affirmation. She knew she didn't have to tell me anything. She knew that I already knew."

Jorani took a deep breath. "So you're saying the Pic were forty candidates under quota, and they made it up by accepting twenty candidates that they didn't want in order to get twenty candidates that they did want?"

"That's exactly what I'm saying. You and Phirun are the only pair I'm sure about. I know I'm pulling bits and pieces from a number of conversations, but it all fits. Longfellow's compliment about you and then immediately his hand sign to Julie, what other interpretation is there?" I sighed. "I try not to think of who the other nineteen might be, though sometimes… it's hard not to guess."

Jorani shivered in the cool air. "This is impossible, Steve! How can an alien species judge us better than we judge ourselves?"

"Yeah… Do you know Kathy?"

"Hariz's escort? Sure. What a sweet personality, even by beta-female standards."

"She's in my statistics class. We've become friends. She stopped by my dorm room a few nights ago, asking if I could advise her."

"About statistics?"

"No, about Hariz. Kathy's having trouble relating to him."

Jorani was silent for a moment and then blew a full load of air through her cheeks. "Talk about culture shock. I guess I'm not surprised. I know them both. Hariz has a devout, conservative background. Kathy reminds me of Julie. They're both free spirits with playful outlooks on life."

"Remember our hosts at the parties in Antarctica, at the end of the interviews? It was the base personnel. The lack of interviewers I understood. But I couldn't figure out why the escorts weren't with us. After talking with Kathy, I finally know why. Escort selection was the second phase of the process. The escorts chose which humans they would be paired with."

Jorani seemed startled. "The escorts ranked everybody?"

"Not exactly. They picked one-at-a-time from the pool of candidates that passed phase-one."

"That would mean the escorts were also ranked."

I nodded. "This I know this for sure. Julie was the number one escort. She got first choice. Then the number two escort picked from the remaining pool, then number three and so on."

"This is amazing. The Pic let adolescents run the last phase of the selection process?!"

"Yep. You could have a positive interview score, but if you weren't selected by any of the escorts, you stayed on Earth. That was the original plan. The Pic were expecting the majority of candidates would pass the interview process."

"Kathy told you all this?"

"Well, not in so many words, but yeah. She gave me the final pieces of the puzzle I needed to figure out everything. As you said, Kathy is a free-spirit. All the escorts have a legal responsibility not to give specific information of a human's rank in the selection process. Kathy has a liberal interpretation of what that means."

"But we all know you're number one!"

I smiled sheepishly as I reached over and held her hand. "What can I say? As liaison, I'm an exception to the rule. But I have no idea who the gamma's top pick was. By the rules of the trial, no other human should know either."

The nature trail we were on eventually reached its northern limit. Up ahead we could see a dimly lit monorail station, straddling a high fence that separated the campus from the great wilderness part of the island. On a whim, Jorani walked to the entrance of the station, and as I caught up with her, the door's status indicator blinked green, signaling it would permit entry. "We're allowed in?" she asked.

"The door's picking up my ID," I replied. "Ellie's starting to take us on field trips. Class members have higher access status."

"You're allowed to operate the monorail system?"

"Not for outgoing." I was referring to a one hundred and sixty kilometer track, sixteen stations about equally spaced. "Class members have the authority to order a return to campus, just for emergencies."

"Ah. Mind if I look inside?"

"Uh, sure. Not much to see…" I touched a control and the door slid open. The small room had panoramic views of wilderness bathed in moonlight, windows everywhere. Below the windows were storage areas for first aid and camping supplies. To the right was another door exiting to wild forest on the other side of the fence, and on the left a set of stairs led to the monorail.

Jorani climbed the stairs and I followed. She spent a moment running her hand along a sleek car. "I thought about taking the wilderness training series next year, but the faculty is saying there are not enough students to run the program again. I'll have to wait until at least three more students apply."

"I know. Our current class is a dozen students, three humans besides me. The rest are Pic. I'm surprised more humans weren't interested."

"Oh, I'm not. Two hundred years ago, maybe even one hundred years ago, you might have a point, but things are so different now. Think what Earth culture is today. Think of how the finalists were chosen."

"We're all focused on technology?"

Jorani looked at me. "Totally, otherwise we'd never have made it to Antarctica. Insight into Pic technology will be worth billions, maybe trillions, assuming any of us make it back to Earth." She paused and added playfully, "You, however, are a throwback, spending your life in the Yukon wilds. How did you ever become a finalist?"

I laughed. "Well, I did come in from the woods once in a while, you know, when I wanted to learn to read or something." A pause. "The USNA had thirty-nine candidate slots, Cambodia had two. We could afford to target variety. I was judged exceptional in my ability to make interesting conjectures out of diverse bits of data. My government thought that might be a useful skill for our group. They tried to pick the best team, not the best individuals."

"Ah. What a luxury." She then smiled playfully. "I thought it might have been your whistling ability. You're really excellent at carrying a tune."

"Huh? I can't whistle with Pic multiple frequencies. No human can."

"I was joking…" Jorani turned and spent a moment admiring the canopy softly lit by the station lights, and then we headed down. I happened to walk by the wilderness exit door. The door flashed from white locked to warning red and yellow, then displayed an icon to contact campus security. I quickly declined the offer.

"Steve, tell me more about your family," Jorani asked as we left the station, and we started describing our past lives, holding hands at first and then each other's waists. The nature trail paralleled the fence for a while and started to bend south, slowly returning us to campus. After I finished a story about my cousins, I coaxed Jorani into describing her childhood in detail. She had told me previously of being somewhat shy as a young girl but little else, almost no details. It was my private conjecture that her shyness might have hidden her childhood brilliance from the world. I considered Jorani to be one of the smartest persons I had ever met.

What she described now was shocking — a broken family bereft of love except for her anchor Rachany, a dear older sister. But when Jorani was thirteen, Rachany enlisted as a U.N. peacekeeper and was killed soon afterwards in one of Earth's pointless wars. Jorani started to tremble in my arms, and the words of betrayal came pouring out. Her last years before becoming a fusion-trial candidate were horrible. She joined the competitions because she overheard her father discussing selling her into prostitution. I was speechless, trying and failing to imagine the betrayal and fear.

Our campus was coming into view, and I didn't want our walk to end on something so painful. So I steered the conversation back to our time in Antarctic, the rigors of the interviews and how everyone looked so relieved afterwards at the reception. Jorani seemed very grateful for the change of topic. She eventually commented, "And while we were partying, our escorts were having a very hectic time."

I nodded. "Oh, yeah. Their student government is much better organized than ours. Kathy said they were negotiating madly with the interview committees about the rejections. The adults eventually caved in. That's why we have a full class of four hundred and eighty."

Up ahead we could see the lights of Jorani's dormitory. She blurted out, "The Pic! Sometimes they fill me with awe! They're so non-human! I can't imagine a human society letting adolescents play such a central role in interstellar contact."

I nodded. "The Pic generations, they trust each other more, respect each other more. Look at their communal showering practice."

A giggle. "Yeah. Has Julie's pod invited you yet?"

"They have. How about you? Has Max's pod invited you?"

"Yep!"

"Thinking of accepting?"

Jorani laughed as she squeezed my waist. "You're joking, right?" It was great to see the return of her usual cheerfulness. And then she became serious. We were about to lose the security of our private conversation. "I can see why we have to keep quiet about this. Thank you for trusting me."

The main entrance opened as it sensed our ID tags. I walked Jorani up to her dorm room. The long walk had done us enormous good. We were both at peace. I kissed her goodnight. She kissed back, and the kiss turning into a hug and then a lingering embrace. Neither of us wanted to let go and end the magic. We had bonded. We could both feel it, the intimacy that comes with complete trust.

And Jorani got playful. She licked my ear several times. I sighed with the pleasure of it and patted the upper curve of her butt. "I love you too," I whispered.

"I know." She pulled back a bit, her hands taking mine, her eyes staring into mine. "Your hands, they're cold."

"Oh, I'll be all right. I'll take the quick way home."

"It's late," she whispered. "Want to sleep here?"

I took a deep breath and whispered back. "You're sure?"

"Uh huh. Nothing too sexy, just to be with you."

I couldn't speak. I just nodded and followed Jorani into her room. She tucked a clean sheet over her lounge chair and got out a spare pillow and blanket for me. And then, in spite of looking very tired, she excused herself and went to her bathroom for a hot shower. Given her encounter with Phirun, I wasn't surprised she felt the need.

I stripped down to underwear and sacked out in the chair. It was like mine, the lowest level fully horizontal, quite comfortable for sleeping. I spent a few quiet minutes admiring Jorani's desk lamp, a myriad of milky pastel curves of blown glass giving the illusion of impossible Escher geometry. It was a lamp that would have caused even Louis Comfort Tiffany to stop and stare.

Jorani came out of the bathroom drying her hair and wearing a loose sleep garment. She looked so pretty in the soft clothing. Then she turned out the light. I could still dimly see her though, from some of the campus nightlight coming through the windows. Jorani could have lowered the shades and made the room pitch black, but she left the windows as they were. We exchanged quick calls of goodnight and she crawled into bed.

And for the first time on Whistlestop, I had trouble getting to sleep. An hour passed, then two. It was a unique and somewhat unpleasant feeling, tired but not sleepy. Was I aroused? Not exactly, though the feeling seemed related somehow. Anxious maybe? I turned on my side and looked at Jorani, who was lying on her side a few meters away, facing away from me. My eyes rested on the curve of her hip, the shape clearly defined under a thin blanket, so pretty. Sold into prostitution?! I wanted so much to… *"You can't protect me forever."* Jorani's warning echoed in my mind. I gave a deep sigh as I continued to watch her. She was right of course, but damn it, I could still try! And she was also leading by example, letting go of her anxiety and falling asleep. I thought of a relaxation technique from my Colorado training: hands on belly, a light focus on breathing, and a peaceful mantra. *Jorani loves me, she's so pretty… Jorani loves me, she's so pretty…* The quiet of the moment and her beauty finally rested my mind. I began to drift off…

…until someone shined a bright light in my eyes. No, not someone. I was alone. Jorani's windows face southeast, and an orange sun was emerging on the horizon. I looked at the time, 19:23, and gave a sigh of relief there were no classes today. Jorani had left a note suggesting we meet for lunch. I picked up my things and headed out.

Chapter 6

One week later, Northern Autumn 38, 3484 C.E. 14:41 (Time Zone 30)

It was six hours before local sunrise and about sixty hours since I had last slept when Julie and I walked out of the spherical portal. Getting back to campus now was a simple walk down a corridor and passing through a control gate. With a nod to the operations personnel, we left the portal room.

My journey today with Julie was amazing, my first excursion off campus. We went to Far Rockaway then to the world capital Haven then to the city of Sundance. Sundance was located in a mountainous region on the largest island of Whistlestop. The city was in the same time zone as Providence but near the equator. It was an area of spectacular beauty, the highest and driest of all Pic cities, semi-arid but still nothing compared to Earth's deserts. And it was where Julie and I just had a very stressful meeting with our lead opposition member of the world's executive council.

As we humans learned in Professor Higgins' history class this week, Sundance held a special meaning to Pic. It was the key high-altitude city in the recovery after the collapse of the Third New Kingdom. In addition to conventional warfare, there was evidence that monstrous ocean waves were created, hundreds of meters high. Coastal cities across the globe were obliterated. The focusing mechanism used to accomplish such horror was a mystery, though the momentum-exchange capability of portals was a prime suspect.

Julie and I were now at the exit. As the interlock began to cycle, Julie surprised me by rising on her hind legs and hugging me in an extremely intimate manner, an arm wrapping around me and coming under my arm to hold my breast, while her other hand came to my throat. Her fingers on my neck, she signed to me, "I stand with you to the close."

It was the type of commitment usually reserved for close family members comforting each other during funerals. It was also my privilege to see Max and Julie exchange that vow during their betrothal ceremony.

My eyes wet with emotion, I returned the pledge, pressing a hand against one of Julie's breasts while my other hand came to her throat where I repeated her signs. And then with fingers still on her throat, I added something of my own. "Love lasts forever; forever and for real." We both knew the interlock area was still part of the military zone and that we were being monitored, and we both didn't care.

And then the exterior gate opened and we walked out of the complex and onto our campus home. Waiting just outside the gate were all six members of the human executive council. I wasn't surprised. Also milling about were hundreds of other students, probably the entire human population and almost as many Pic. The air was cold and damp, seasonal for the time of year and day, hovering just above freezing. I gave a hand sign of greeting to the student president and called out in a tired voice, "Hi, Karim."

He gave me a nod of recognition and asked if I would give an immediate briefing. I agreed and also suggested representatives of the Pic student union be allowed to join us. Karim was amenable and a few minutes later, we were taking off our coats and sitting down in a large huddle-room inside my dorm building. There was a lounge area nearby where many of the other students were congregating. I managed to catch sight of Jorani and wave hello before Karim closed the door. Julie silently signed me a suggestion. Out loud, I asked Karim to activate the room's audio so the others could listen.

I didn't waste any time diving into the details of what everyone was dreading. With Julie by my side, I began my report. "We met with our opposition councilor-in-charge within an hour of reaching Sundance. Longfellow confirmed everything we received in yesterday's data burst. On Tuesday, February 2, 2100, at 12:25 U.T., Northern Autumn 37, 6:43 local time for us, there were two nuclear explosions along the coastline of the eastern Mediterranean. Earth is reporting that both explosions were plutonium based. The first explosion occurred in the Tel Aviv area, centered in the harbor west of Old Jaffa. The yield was very small, estimated to be sixty tons TNT equivalent, and damage was limited to the harbor area. There's evidence that the bomb was much larger but failed to achieve its intended fission burn.

"The second explosion occurred seconds later at the port city of Haifa, and this one was massive, in excess of thirty-five kilotons. The primary blast spilled over into Jordan." Everything I was saying so far was confirming information we received the previous day at 34:18, the time we got our latest Earth-daily data burst.

I looked around the room and grimaced before moving on. "There are new developments. Minutes before the twin blasts, a fishing trawler traveling at high speed was sunk by an autonomous hunter-seeker mine outside the harbor area of Eilot, Israel's southernmost city. Sensors at the site are detecting a heavy concentration of plutonium in the Red Sea. Salvage work for the trawler is occurring at this moment, and if it identifies the origin of the bombs..." I was silent for a moment, struggling to compose my thoughts.

Karim asked, "How often are the Pic getting updates from Earth?"

"I didn't ask; more than once an hour, I think. The information Longfellow kept sharing with us was very fresh." My tired mind paused and then I added unnecessarily, "I mean more than once a Pic hour."

"What was Longfellow's attitude?" asked Taamraparnee, another member of the student council.

"Yeah, hi, Parni. At least here, I've got some good news. Julie and I found our oppositional councilor polite and personally as compassionate as I've even seen an alpha Pic. He assured us that despite his general opposition to social fusion, he would not use this development for political advantage, and would also urge others in his faction not to do so. We are not in danger of having our trial end because of what is happening on Earth, at least not directly."

"But Pic's presence and involvement with Earth is hanging by a thread. The Pic transport is currently restricted to the Darwin Mountains and it's manned by a skeleton crew. All other personnel have been evacuated to Whistlestop. If attacked or if nuclear war breaks out, the transport will lift and attempt to monitor Earth from a safe distance. If that's not possible, most of the remaining crew will attempt to evacuate, and volunteer command officers will stay behind and ensure the destruction of the portal. I really don't have anything more to report. Our next data burst is scheduled for…" I glanced at my wrist assistant, "…31:10 today. What I'd like to do is grab some sleep and be up for its arrival."

"So the Pic know how to destroy entangled spacetime," someone commented.

"Not being insane," I replied with a yawn, "I didn't press for details."

But Karim wouldn't let the issue rest. "It's public knowledge that you can't send entangled spacetime through entangled spacetime. Maybe that's how you destroy it, by attempting to do that."

The same thought had occurred to me once, but I was surprised Karim verbalized the idea, especially with the intercom system on. Perhaps he was just as tired as I was, tired enough to welcome distracting thoughts and speak without thinking.

Another voice in the room called out, "What do you mean, our trial is not *directly* at risk?"

I shrugged. "It's obvious, isn't it? The Pic realize we people can't influence Earth's descent into nuclear war. But if our Jewish and Muslim members bring Earth's war to Whistlestop, that's another matter entirely. If we react badly, especially with physical violence…" I gave another big yawn. "I don't have to elaborate. Guys, I really need to get some sleep. I don't have anything else to report, other than to repeat that the Pic response so far has been kind and supportive, even from the opposition against us." I gave a third yawn and blinked my eyes. It wasn't just being up for the last sixty hours. I felt emotionally drained. Karim seemed to realize this and suggested I head for bed. I didn't wait for the motion to be seconded.

I met Max and Jorani in the lounge area outside the huddle room. For a moment, Max looked as if he wanted to say something, but then Jorani offered to walk with me to my room, so Julie and Max simply gave me polite hand-signs for goodnight and departed. A few minutes later my dorm door chirped and opened when it recognized our ID chips. Jorani followed me into my room and closed the door.

Oh, boy, home! It was such a relief to be back, and I was too tired to be embarrassed about the room being messy. Jorani made an offer to change my bed sheets while I took a quick shower and I gratefully accepted. Ten minutes later I found the room looking tidy and a nice, clean bed turned down and waiting for me. My desire to lie down was so strong, I just mumbled some thanks to Jorani while I shed my towel and crawled under the sheets.

It was the first time Jorani ever saw me naked. I turned to say goodnight to her and found her standing next to my bed looking intently at me. "Want me to stay?"

I nodded. Jorani turned the room lights to almost off and began to undress. A waning crescent moon was shining enough light in the room to see Jorani clearly as she shed her clothes. I caught a glimpse of a very cute, thin butt and then she turned and slid under the bed covers. "Get comfortable," she said softly. "I'll pet you."

I rolled on my stomach. Jorani massaged my back for a while, working the tenseness from my muscles. And as time drifted, her hands became light and caressing, long, light strokes down my butt and the backs of my thighs. I felt a tap on my legs and spread myself. A moment later Jorani's searching hand slid down and cupped me into her palm. I let out the deepest sigh imaginable.

"Just rest, my love," Jorani whispered. "You don't have to do anything."

My universe transformed into pure pleasure. Nothing else mattered except the slow strokes of Jorani's thumb. I tried to mumble something, tell Jorani that I loved her, but my body was so relaxed and my mind floating so peacefully that I never managed to speak. My fears disappeared as if by magic and I descended into a dream filled with goodness and a deeply sexual love.

A half day later.
Northern Autumn 38, 3484 C.E. 39:00 (Time Zone 30)

A mixed group of humans and Pic were having a late lunch in the campus cafeteria and a jam session about events on Earth. Jorani and I were sitting at one end of the table, and the southwest windows nearby were giving us a fine prospect of the setting sun. I did a calculation in my head: eight long Earth minutes of daylight left.

"Another cracker, Steven?" asked Flossie, gesturing to a nearby blue tray. Flossie was a gamma female classmate, and gammas in general had a lock on being the brainiest students on campus. Flossie though, she was a cut above everybody, certainly the most brilliant student on campus and probably at the very top worldwide. She also had a feather-fur so blue that the first time I saw her in Antarctica, I wondered if she dyed it. Julie has since explained to me that from the Pic perspective, coloring feather-fur would be so bizarre that it would be a flag for mental illness.

Flossie had thoughtfully prepared a tray for us humans, offering us a traditional Pic snack using ingredients certified safe for humans and Pic. Calling them crackers was an injustice. Think of a light and crispy pizza crust with subtle cheese-like flavors and sharply spiced dried vegetables that are not subtle at all. I loved these things and had quietly and hopefully asked Julie an hour ago if she knew how to make them. Julie just rolled her W-eyes at me in reply.

Signing Flossie a hand gesture for gratitude, I picked up another large cracker and took a bite. We had been discussing Earth for a couple of hours now. In the last one hundred and fifty-five Earth years, the nuclear-war genie had escaped its bottle twice. Could it be re-bottled again? Well, our native planet hadn't blown itself up yet, though our daily news burst was describing an incredibly tense situation. Iran and the other Arab nuclear powers were disavowing any involvement in the attack, but still twisting the knife by accusing Israel of reaping what seven generations of Zionist arrogance had sown. Meanwhile, the underwater salvage work near Eilot continued. To find out more, we would have to wait for the next midnight data-burst (Universal Time) on Earth, which would be tomorrow late morning for us here, Autumn 39, 28:19. Hopefully we would get no news till then. Anything sooner would probably be the Pic government telling us Earth had blown itself up.

Earlier today, after getting the latest data-burst, we students had a joint Pic-human meeting and voted to proceed with our normal schedules. So tomorrow, our scheduled tennis and wallyball matches were still on, and our normal class week would resume the day after. There was just one more long school week before thirteen days of end-of-Autumn holidays.

Out of the corner of my eye, I noticed a woman passing by. It was Marisa from Brazil, Emeric's girlfriend and the person who had Flossie as her escort. Flossie and Emeric's mentor Rebekah both noticed Marisa and made hand gestures to an open chair at our jam session. After several minutes of listening, Marisa looked at me and asked, "So, Steve, what was it like getting off The Island?"

"It was kind of nice," I admitted. "All I saw at Far Rockaway were corridors and a couple of transfer rooms, just like our first day here. But Haven, the majesty of the portal hub, you have to see it to believe it." I went on to describe the vast transfer cavern at the world capital. The facilities for staging goods and personnel for transfers were stunning. I'd read on the web that at full throttle, the system could make exchanges with every city on the network at a rate of two to three cargo transfers per hour per city. My impression passing through was of a dream version of the 3-D train station, so grand and automated as to seem unreal. My mind didn't want to accept the scale that my eyes were seeing.

"And what did you think of Sundance and Treasure Island?" asked Flossie.

Before I could answer, Emeric piped up. "Is Treasure Island really an accurate translation of the Pic whistle? It's the world's largest island, almost the size of Australia! Calling it Treasure Island makes it sound like some small atoll with a chest of gold buried in the beach."

Flossie stared at Emeric. "It's an accurate translation. The island is named for its geological formations. They take your breath away." She paused for a moment and added, "Maybe you have a point. How could a chest of elemental metal be called a treasure? Are we talking about the same concept?"

"Well," I said, coming to Emeric's defense, "in a primitive society, metal might be valuable enough to be called a treasure."

Flossie turned back to me. "Agreed. But both our societies have moved beyond that stage, haven't we?" She then gave me a hand sign asking me to answer her original question.

I knew Flossie had spent nine years of her life at Sundance. "I agree with you. Sundance is incredibly beautiful. Images on the net don't do it justice. It reminds me a bit of a mountainous version of San Francisco on Earth. Everything is so three-dimensional!"

Flossie gave a chirping laugh. "If you think Sundance is 3-D, look up Wuthering Heights, same island but a thousand kilometers distant, directly on the equator near the western shore." Flossie paused and then said with a playful grin. "It's also the only city on Whistlestop that wasn't built by my species."

"What?" croaked Jorani as she choked on a cracker.

Flossie replied cryptically. "I suspected you humans hadn't stumbled onto this yet. Cross reference the city with Old Kingdom anthropology." She paused for a moment and added to the humans at the table, "I have a lot of fond memories of growing up at Sundance. If any of you ever get the chance to hike around there, sign up for the excursion to Hidden Valley. It's eight days of walking and worth every step."

An alpha female named Circes piped up. "Yes, I concur. I did that tour last year when the high meadows were in flower. Beautiful!" She also took a moment to survey the human crowd. "At the end of the second day, you enter the valley through a half-kilometer cave system. It's spectacular the way they have the rock formations lit."

Flossie nodded. "The valley is steeped in history. DNA data suggest it was the sole community to survive the Third New Kingdom war and technology crash." She turned to me. "There are hostels along the way. It's usually a young crowd during vacation weeks, couples and triples and quads with children, very friendly."

Flossie paused and stared at us humans. "Wow. I've really changed. Just a few weeks ago, I was feeling queasy about eating side by side with humans, and now I can't imagine what my problem was. But the other citizens? Truthfully, I don't know. The hostels are primitive, complete family-style living with all the adults responsible for not getting too sexy in front of the kids. I really don't know how other Pic would react to sharing their children and meals and sleeping quarters and restrooms with humans."

From my own experience with shared restrooms, I found the smell of Pic feces very easy to take. The faint odor was like fresh cut hay. And with six genders worldwide and a campus with eight, the Pic never bothered to segregate the public restrooms. The social standard was to politely ignore everyone. I smiled now at Flossie and replied, "I think most of us were nervous at first about living with each other. Kudos to all of us for making the transition. We don't see each other as Pic or human any more. We see each other as people."

"But that's because we know you," commented Circes. "You should hear my parents talk. My dad says there's a rumor at Falls Island that the human dorms at Providence are being quietly searched. People are afraid humans might have smuggled weapons to our campus. Such nonsense! Steve, did you see any of this insanity at Sundance?"

Was it really that crazy a rumor? Every human was allowed to bring one cubic meter of baggage from Earth. There were no weight restrictions, and several exceptions were made on size. One person brought a cello, and there were several Steinways on campus.

But weapons were absolutely prohibited. Did anybody (or any group) try to beat the system? I occasionally wondered about the issue. My mind returned to the present and I realized Circes was patiently waiting for an answer. "Uh, not really. But to get to our meeting with Longfellow, Julie and I had a military escort and avoided public areas. We didn't have time to mingle." I sighed. "I think you escorts will be the key to our acceptance. Walk with us as friends. It'll show people it's okay to trust us."

Rebekah nodded back to me. "Well, that's the grand design, the idea behind the escort system and the joint class."

Marisa spoke up. "I love the Pic system of teaching! So little homework and testing, yet I'm learning a tremendous amount of material. My class time is filled with lively discussion and short exercises to test concepts. This is so different than what schooling is like on Earth!"

Without much thinking, Marisa's escort Flossie gave a complex hand signal in reply, conveying standard gratitude for a compliment, but with subtle extensions of her long Pic fingers indicating gentle amusement over Marisa not getting something quite right. As Flossie began to wait for a question that wasn't coming, I realized I was probably the only human at the table to get Flossie's full message.

I decided to head off the awkward silence that was about to happen when Marisa didn't ask her escort Flossie what she found so amusing. "The way I understand it," I said, "we're in a high-achievers program. The standard Pic school system has more homework and more testing, including the colleges. Isn't that right, Flossie?"

Flossie gave me a thoughtful blink with her W-eyes before she replied. "Yes, but it's not exactly achievement. In the general Pic population, most people will probably ignore or even mock things they don't understand. Is it the same on Earth, Marisa?"

"Yeah. I hate to admit it, but yeah, I think so."

Flossie continued. "But some people will be fascinated by what they don't understand. That's what our primary teachers look for, children who are fascinated by what they don't understand. Our school system identifies these children and places them in programs that channel their fascination into a love of learning. We try to do that for all students of course, but it's only with some children that the process goes... #!#!, as we whistle on Whistlestop, supersonic. We don't have much certification testing here on campus because we don't need it. We study for the joy of learning, and to help us be explorers when we do our summer theses. Nobody studies for the test. We study to fulfill our love."

An alpha male classmate named Isaac was with us. He was the Pic equivalent of an Eagle Scout, and he was Lieutenant Ellie's teaching assistant for wilderness survival. Isaac looked up from the cracker he was eating and signed to Flossie from across the table, "Very well put." Flossie seemed startled by the compliment.

Marisa laughed as she gave her escort Flossie an affectionate hug. "I love you guys! Nobody on Earth talks like this!"

A few minutes later, we broke up. I headed back to my dorm room to prepare for Julie's dad's final week of lectures, fulfilling my love, I thought with a smile. Flossie was trailing behind me as we crossed the commons, and she caught up with me shortly after I entered my dorm building. Walking down a deserted corridor, I looked at Flossie loping at my side and gave her the hand signal for "what's up?" She offered me her hand in reply.

"I want to thank you for rescuing me. I almost embarrassed my mentee. It was completely unreasonable for me to expect Marisa to know what I was signing." Flossie was tactile signing at expert speed, almost faster than what it would take to speak the words.

"Huh?" I signed back in standard form. "Flossie, it was nothing, really. Marisa wasn't offended. And I thought your point was great, illuminating in fact."

"Wow," Flossie signed. "You're slow but your form is excellent. Julie is teaching you well."

I smiled and signed, "Yes, two two-hour sessions every day, usually one before class and then again in the evening. We haven't missed a day yet. Well, yesterday was crazy. But we practiced during our trip."

Flossie gently squeezed my hand with her long fingers, a sign of affection, and then resumed signing. "I'd like you to know, I came in first in the competition to be your escort, but was disqualified later because of something in my background."

"Ah..." I signed. "That's interesting to know. Are you and Julie friends?"

"Well, we respect each other. We're both very competitive. Julie was better in some scores. I was better in others." Flossie paused and added, "I guess I agree with the decision. Julie's family has much better connections to support the human liaison, and her language skills are legendary." Her hands then dropped into an unusual sub-form, extremely playful and usually reserved for male-female sexual banter. "I, however, am a *much* better chef!"

I laughed out loud and signed back in the same sub-form, "That explains it! I asked Julie if she could prepare your snack dish, and she surprised me with a very playful gesture."

"Good!" Flossie answered, switching to standard form. "Julie is teaching you the intimate form as well."

I nodded and also switched back to standard. "Yes. I can feel why it's called the intimate form. All the patterns drop into light caresses." We came to my dorm room. I looked down at Flossie and signed into her palm an affectionate goodbye, staying in standard form.

"Before you go," signed Flossie, "I want to offer, if you ever need a favor, just ask."

"You don't have to do that," I signed back.

Flossie ignored my protest. "Even if it's a big favor, just ask, okay?"

It was very sweet offer for her to make. I know how serious Pic are about pledging their word like this. I stroked Flossie's palm with my thumb, my other fingers pressing into the base of her fingers and gently holding her fingers away from my thumb. It's the way to express acceptance of open-ended commitment in intimate form. In a vague way,

I was expressing my right to dominate her with a future desire. Flossie sighed and nodded and then she was gone. A short time later I was at my desk trying to review my physics lessons. But my mind kept wandering back to Flossie.

Chapter 7

Time: Fifteen days later, Northern Autumn 53, 3484 C.E. 32:46 (Time Zone 30)

"We'll be taking the left fork," I announced to the group. The Pic were stoic about my decision, but I heard a few groans from Marisa and the other two human classmates.

It was my turn to be pathfinder, and I had just returned from surveying the two possibilities before us. We only had four short hours of sunlight left, and the left fork would have us hiking across numerous rocks, not an easy feat with the loads we were packing. The right fork appeared a much easier route and would definitely get us to our destination in time to make camp before sunset. The left fork was debatable.

"Did you recognize any dangers?" asked Isaac. He was the leader of our expedition and was asking questions and keeping notes on all our decisions.

I nodded. "There's fire-grass ahead on the right fork. It doesn't look too bad from here, and I know it's not the season for it, but there's no reason to take the risk."

Isaac gave me a curt nod and jotted for a moment in his log. "Anything else?"

"Nothing worth mentioning."

Isaac's muzzle briefly flashed a faint pattern of uncertainty.

I paused for a moment, wondering if the dim flashes were involuntary. What was his point? "Are you worried about the pike-owl nest?" I was referring to a nest high up in a tree about a hundred meters distant along the left fork. The rare Providence pike-owl was the only dangerous flying animal we had to face. Normally shy, the birds were very territorial near their nests, and their talons were powerful enough to penetrate a Pic or human skull. Once riled from their nests, they were ornery enough to do just that.

"You recognized the nest," replied Isaac. "Very good. And you've judged the fire-grass the greater danger."

I shook my head and gestured with my arm. "That nest is abandoned. It's not an issue."

Isaac blinked, took out his binoculars and studied the location. "The nest appears to be in decent condition. How did you decide it's abandoned?"

"Look into the foliage above the nest. There's a patch of poison creep-weed in full pollen. A pike-owl would be crazy to live up there. The pollen would burn its feathers off."

Flossie had her own binoculars out and was staring at the tree. "He's right, Isaac."

Isaac took another look and bowed his neck to me. "Excellent, Steven. I stand corrected."

It was one of the things I really admire about Pic, the alphas in particular... their instant willingness to admit mistakes. I gave Isaac a hand sign thanking him for the compliment and called out to the group in a cheerful voice, "Let's roll!"

I was enjoying this trip immensely. We were in the middle of the thirteen-day end-of-season holiday, and had been spending the last three days hiking across the rugged mountainous interior of Providence. It was impossible not to love the ecosystem. Even now near the winter solstice, there was still so much life to see, including much plant life still active in the freezing weather, so different than Earth. And the mountain views stretching to the great ocean were magnificent.

Julie didn't make this trip. She didn't need any certification credits. After years of training with her alpha mom, Julie was a registered Ranger-Three, qualified to be anywhere on the planet. And she was looking forward to showing me just how beautiful Providence was. But being a Level-II or Level-III Ranger gave you automatic reserve status in the Pic military, and at the end of classes, Julie was ordered on a week-long training mission at Polaris, one of the hottest islands on the planet this time of year.

I looked around at the deepening shadows as we hit an easy stretch between some rough rocks. This would be the last night for our expedition to be at altitude. At about six hundred meters and at this time of year, it was enough to keep the temperature below freezing sixty hours a day. We were hiking northwest now towards the ocean, just starting to come off the high interior plateau. Occasionally through the trees I could see far below the great shoreline road that circumnavigates the island.

I never bothered to understand the definition of a Class-B road until recently. It was not just a two-lane road with overhead monorail. It was also a fantastic piece of engineering. Question: What can you do with solar panels rugged and flexible enough to drive a dump truck over? Answer: Solar panel the roads! And that was just what the Pic do. Providence didn't normally have a portal, and our campus didn't need it as an energy source. The monorails and the conservation facilities that were expanded to become our campus were powered by the solar-paneled road, with a hydrogen disassociation plant making such ample fuel reserves that fishing vessels often refueled when they dropped off food for us. And this philosophy of backups to portal magic was implemented across the planet. Would humans have remained so vigilant after three thousand five hundred years of rock-solid portal performance? I doubted it. Somehow the Pic had managed to remain skeptical about something they'd used for millennia but don't understand, and I admired them for it.

The fork I had chosen turned out to be easier than it first appeared. We arrived at our intended destination with ample daylight left. Almost everybody started making camp, but Flossie and I got busy collecting the gear we would need for a special survival test we had volunteered for. Isaac, meanwhile, was off to the side, whistling on his comm link and staring at the western horizon with his binoculars. I left Flossie and walked over to him.

"We're in for a storm tonight," Isaac said, "It's an issue; sustained winds over twenty kilometers per hour."

Old habits died hard. I did a conversion in my head. A kph here was 3.4 times an Earth kph. I grunted and took a moment to study the clouds myself.

"Steven, I'm close to deciding we cancel the survival test."

I shook my head. "What for? Our gear is superb. You people with the exposed tents are going to have more trouble with the wind than Flossie and I will."

"You think so?"

I looked at Isaac and smiled. "If you need to be rescued, just call."

Isaac stared at me for a moment and then gave a humph snort and laughed.

I tried to reassure him. "I've done winter camping all my life, in colder weather than this. Flossie and I will find a good spot to bed down." I decided to get an unspoken question out in the open. "Are you okay with the test itself?"

Isaac looked me in the eyes. "Oh, I trust you. I trust Flossie too."

"Fine. Then she and I better be going. We need to find shelter while it's still light."

Isaac nodded. "All right. Go to it!"

Flossie and I found an excellent niche in a rocky slope about two hundred meters from our group's camp. Deep and over a meter in height, the niche was large enough to hold our gear, had a smooth and almost level floor, and our small tarp would cover the entrance almost completely. We even had enough time to gather wood for a cooking fire and a thick bed of pine-like needles as twilight marked the end of the day. After arranging the bedding, we sat on rocks and ate our heated dinner packs, a protein and vegetable assortment for Flossie and a great fish meal for me. It was a species the Pic didn't eat themselves but caught for us. The taste was between salmon and peppery crabmeat, and I loved it. Flossie and I chatted during dinner as we watched oncoming clouds obliterate the evening stars.

And the world transformed. Our small campsite became surrounded by a universe of blackness. The wind started to howl and the air was filled with stinging ice crystals. Flossie and I quickly killed the fire and retired to our sleeping bag.

I must admit, at first I was a bit embarrassed. I hadn't bathed since the start of the trip, and I had no idea what Flossie would think of my smell. But Flossie took off her clothes, standard practice for Pic sleep and also to provide extra insulation from the ground, and I followed suit. We positioned both our faces near the one small opening in the sleeping bag, a short tunnel to the outside air. Side by side, I scooted back into Flossie and was in for a sensual surprise.

The back of a gamma's feather fur is a bit coarse, but on the chest and underbelly, it's all downy softness. Cuddling back into Flossie was as warm as cuddling into a heated down pillow. She stretched her neck to position her snout near the air opening, warming my head with the feather-fur on her throat. A moment later Flossie lightly draped an arm and two legs on me, tapping a message in sign on my stomach, "Warm enough?"

I had to laugh and I tapped back a message on her hand. "I had no idea the survival test would be like this. Yes, thank you, delightfully warm. And you?"

"I haven't been this comfortable the whole trip," Flossie signed back, then switched to verbal. "Calling this a survival test seems a joke."

Neither of us was sleepy, and we had over forty hours until daybreak. So we resumed our earlier conversation of what I was learning in my first semester of Pic history. The Pic had an incredibly rich heritage, over sixty thousand years of recorded history, and another eighty thousand years before that of stone tools to paintings and ornamental carvings. Their very earliest written record was a stone fragment, believed to be part of a pictorial love poem written by a female to a male.

Pic history was absolutely fascinating. These creatures were like us in so many ways, and in other ways, so incredibly different. The Pic had suffered through numerous technology collapses, violent rejections of science and brutal elimination of their intellectuals. The only things that came close on Earth were perhaps the Middle Ages and the loss of Roman engineering, or maybe the horrible Chinese cultural revolution. But nowhere in human history was there evidence of technology collapses on the scale of Pic's. For example, the Second New Kingdom some forty thousand years ago was more advanced in metallurgy than the Pic are now. And the Third New Kingdom, in addition to its portals, had the remarkable ability to manufacture quantum-perfect, defect-free nano-crystals for data storage.

But in the long, dark times between industrial societies, the Pic female genders had a habit of enslaving the males. Over the last sixty thousand years, it was generally accepted that the males were enslaved at least two-thirds of the time. I guess there are some Greek legends of Amazons doing something like this on Earth, but the Pic did it for real, and they did it wholesale. I brought up a point to Flossie. Was pre-industrial Earth really that different? Perhaps women back then weren't universally enslaved, but it was a rare culture where they had true equality of rights.

During our last week in history class, we had a fascinating discussion that integrated Pic history with modern medical knowledge. In humans, our male brains are wired to pursue opportunities for copulation. And with male Pic, their desire for sex is on par with ours. For Pic females, the desire for sex is recognized to be significantly stronger than a male's. And without the veneer of civilization, this sex drive along with the greater female numbers resulted in the subjugation of the males, time and again.

It was a very sobering history, yet for almost four thousand years now, the Pic had maintained a stable society based on gender equality. How had they managed this? What changed? I put the question to Flossie.

In reply, she sang me a fragment of an Earth tune that I couldn't quite place. "Till by turning, turning, we come round right."

"What?"

"There's a religion on Earth that encapsulates much of modern Pic philosophy. Unfortunately for Earth, it has almost no practitioners."

My mind thought of Jorani. "Buddhism?"

Flossie laughed. "No! There are many Buddhists on Earth, and I admit, that religion has interesting ideas. But I was speaking of the Society of Friends."

"Oh, the Quakers…" Recognition hit me. "Now I remember! 'Tis a gift to be simple, tis a gift to be free'."

"Yep, that's the one." Flossie began to sing, vocalizing the English words in "under", and accompanying herself in "over" with flutelike whistle chords. " 'When true simplicity is gained, to bow and to bend, we shan't be ashamed. To turn, turn, will be our delight. Till by turning, turning, we come round right'." She let out a deep sigh. "I don't want to sound condescending, but comparing my course on Earth religions with

Earth's news reports, I don't think many people on Earth understand the Quaker concept of simplicity."

"I think I do."

Flossie pressed her point. "Do you also understand the Quaker principle of relationships?"

"Uh… Well, maybe not. Tell me?"

"I'll be happy to. Their principle is this: A relationship is right if helps all parties of the relationship to flourish. A relationship is wrong if it causes one or more parties of the relationship to be degraded. Till by turning, turning, we come round right. That's the great Pic hope. This is by far the longest we've ever held a civil society. Perhaps we finally turned our society to come round right, in the Quaker sense of the word."

I felt stunned. "It seems so obvious, and I've never thought of this before."

Flossie hugged me. "You are such an unusual person, Steve. Humans in general are so strange, so reluctant to admit failings or ignorance. It's almost as if your species is ashamed of not being perfect, ashamed that your religions are not perfect." She paused. "Tell me, Steve, what is the purpose of an economy?"

"Huh?" The question caught me off guard and I pondered for a moment. I was scheduled to take an introductory course in Pic economics in the coming semester, but knew almost nothing about the subject now. "Well, to promote the wellbeing of the society, I guess. Do you want something more specific?"

"No. Actually, I want you to think more broadly. Your definition is exactly Earth's problem. The entire focus is on promotion, growth, improvement, increasing productivity so that consumption can also increase. But Earth's ecosystems are failing under the stress. Your species has a wrong relationship with your planet. Consumption is flourishing at the cost of degrading your biosphere."

After a moment, I whispered, "And this is the core of our trial, isn't it?"

"A big part of it, yeah. Can humans and Pic build a right relationship, one which helps both to flourish? We really don't know." Flossie gave a deep sigh. "There's a saying from the Old Kingdoms: Alphas are for action, betas are for probity, and gammas are for innovation. What we're doing with the trial is adding a fourth dimension, a human dimension, without really understanding what the addition will do. Many citizens are upset that we're exploring something so dangerous."

"Because of Earth's wars and overpopulation?"

"That's not the worst of it," Flossie replied quietly.

"What could be worse? Our pollution?"

"In a sense." Flossie stirred uncomfortably. "I'm thinking of your species' abuse of drugs. The behavior is disgusting. People here are terrified that humans will one day pollute us with the practice."

"Huh? Are you saying Whistlestop never had a drug problem?"

"No. I mean yes, I'm saying that Whistlestop never had a drug problem, nothing like Earth's."

I gasped. "My God, I never knew. No problem at all?"

"Well... Perhaps I shouldn't brag. Medical science here is considerably more advanced than on Earth. We've known how to cure addictions to pain killers since ancient times."

"You're being too critical of humans, Flossie. Once you're addicted, you have to think of it as a disease, not a moral failing. The addicted brain is damaged."

"Agreed. But Earth's drug abuse isn't just with pain killers. Think of how other addictions start. I've read your news reports, wrote a paper for one of my classes. You humans often walk into your drug addictions willfully, with your eyes open, using drugs to avoid stressful situations, not just physical pain. But life is all about meeting our challenges, not avoiding them. Humans, though, some of them exchange their challenges for such cheap pleasure."

Flossie gave me an affectionate hug then hammered her point home. "The pleasure of a good meal nourishes the body. The joy of knowledge discovery nourishes our insight and self-esteem. The joy of sex nourishes our close relationships and the promise of a new generation. But the only things an addiction nourishes are delusions and a feedback loop of craving, and where's the value in that, Steven? Where's the value?" There was a long moment of silence, and then an added whisper. "I hope I haven't offended you."

I sighed. "You haven't."

"I shouldn't boast. Much of Pic history is incomplete. I shouldn't have said we never had a drug problem. Nobody really knows... And you're correct, once present, it is a disease. The addicted brain is damaged. Addicts deserve compassion and medical support for healing, not condemnation. But think of the initial choice, Steven. The uncertainty of the future stresses all of us. To respond to that challenge with recreational drugs, there is no other way to frame that choice but as a profound error. It should never be condoned... It's our religion. Life is a gift, and gifts are meant to be enjoyed. But using drugs for recreation? That dishonors the gift." Flossie shook her head vigorously, a Pic gesture for changing topics. "The other worries you mentioned aren't so bad, wars and overpopulation. Overpopulation is insane, but at least it's understandable. If we tried to run our world with as much poverty as Earth has, we'd probably suffer from overpopulation too."

"You talk as if poverty were a choice."

"It is a choice!" Flossie insisted. "At least where overpopulation is concerned. You let selfish individuals accumulate such vast amounts of wealth and power. You let public power fall into private hands. When you set up a society where all the wealth and power are tied up like that, people can't count on their neighbors and government to care for them. Survival instincts kick in and they have lots of kids."

I groaned. "You sound like a communist. That form of government doesn't work. It's the most effective poverty enhancement program imaginable."

"Steven, I'm not talking about one-party dictatorships pretending to be socialists. Whistlestop has tried basing societies on pure capital markets. Study the history of the New Kingdoms. That form of government doesn't work either."

"So what's better?"

"How about a government with a passion for protecting both individual liberties and social responsibilities?"

I chuckled. "Protecting responsibilities? You Pic are so strange. No human would phrase it that way."

"Why do humans insist on separating liberties from responsibilities?" Flossie countered. "Can't you see that the right to speak freely is also the responsibility to speak truthfully?" She then laughed. "It's you humans who are strange! You take what should be an excellent social glue and turn it into odious burdens on rich people. Where are your brains?!"

"Uh… What?"

"I'm thinking of another paper I wrote, on medical care in the USNA. You make it the responsibility of the rich to pay for the healthcare of the poor."

"What's wrong with that?"

"Silly! It should be the responsibility of everybody to pay for everyone's healthcare! Acts of caring are what bind us together. They create social glue, feelings of generosity and gratitude. With the USNA system, the rich resent the burden and the poor feel entitled. There's no glue. At best, the system is ripe for abuse, and at worst, it can lead to class warfare. Study the end of the First New Kingdom."

Flossie took a deep breath and gave a summary judgment. "With your system, there's no solidarity woven into the capital structure, and an economy can't succeed if the society underneath it fails. Just look at the data, Earth's birthrates by country. You know what I'm talking about."

I thought for a moment. "Yeah, I guess I do. Countries on Earth with the better educational and social programs have lower birth rates."

"Well, of course they do. And as for wars…" Flossie paused to hug me, giving me time to collect my thoughts.

I'd noticed something remarkable when conversing with gammas. Humans had difficulty with the gammas' amazing ability to move back and forth effortlessly through various levels of a conversation. Even the alphas and betas joked about it, calling it the gammas' ability to tie your mind in knots. But in a deep sense, it was just the opposite. A few days ago at the start of our hiking expedition, Flossie told me an ancient Pic truism: No one sees like a gamma; no one surprises like a gamma; no one makes the rules like a gamma. At the time, I wondered if it meant that traditionally gammas were the dominant genders, as on Earth where people who make the rules are called rulers. But since then, I'd realized the Pic truism was speaking from a system engineering perspective, that gammas were the best process designers.

Human conversations and alpha and beta conversations are often random walks. That was normal for us, the way our brains follow wandering threads of thought. A gamma conversation was much more holistic, the gamma brain keeping track of original conversation threads even while exploring child threads. Jorani once made an analogy to me that human conversation was meandering text while gamma conversation is hypertext. And here was Flossie now, being super considerate and waiting for me to catch up to her phenomenal multi-threaded mind. I caressed her hand to show her I was ready.

"Wars will test everyone's morality. By definition, they're wrong relationships, because the purpose of war is to degrade your enemy. But what do you do when a foreign group develops a vocation for domination? You can resist with war, a short-term wrong relationship, or submit to your enslavement, a wrong relationship that has no end. Whistlestop would fight back if Earth tried to enslave it."

I made a humph noise. "Not much chance of that, is there?"

"Who knows? As Lieutenant Ellie keeps reminding us, the future can be full of surprises."

"So why take the risk? What can we humans offer you? Why do you even try?"

"You're studied Pic history, Steve. Can't you see the answer?"

I pondered Flossie's question for a while before answering. "Not really. I mean, I see some value in sharing our cultures, our literatures, our... aspirations. And the human cerebellum is more integrated with fine motor control, compared to a Pic. It allows us to do things with our hands that a Pic cannot."

"That's true. The abilities of trained human musicians are breathtaking. I wouldn't be surprised if many of our human classmates eventually find employment in the performing arts."

"But Flossie, that can't be the answer!"

"No, it isn't. Pic have a deeper need for human interaction. You were very correct to mention aspirations, Steve." Flossie gave a deep sigh. "Take a look at Pic science over the last three thousand years. Maybe you haven't had much time to study this yet, but you'll see some development, sure, incremental improvements, but very little that's revolutionary. Since the discovery of the portals, there have been only a handful of real advances."

"Well, you have an excuse for that. We humans have a saying: Necessity is the mother of invention. Why make an effort to invent something inferior to the magic you already possess?"

Flossie grunted. "The issue is deeper than that. Pure mathematicians would probably disagree with me, and maybe the medical community too, but not the physicists and engineers. We've lost our desire to be explorers. We had steam engines four thousand years ago. Where will Earth be four thousand years after steam engines?"

"Assuming we don't blow ourselves up."

"Yes, assuming that."

"The Pic want humans to be their explorers?"

"No. The trial is for true social fusion."

The light finally dawned for me. "Ah. I get it."

"It's the grand argument of the gamma councilors. Earth is too unstable. Whistlestop is too stable. Let's try to build a right relationship that allows both to flourish."

Flossie gave my hip an affectionate pat and continued. "You want an example? The budget to monitor the space probes gets reviewed every three years. They represent a thousand gateways to the galaxy. Humans would never ignore such opportunities. Here on Whistlestop, it's a struggle just to find the budget to monitor the telemetry and maintain the gateways for occasional field trips. The probes would be recalled if they weren't so far away. Fortunately, the closest is about twelve hundred light-years from here. It would take at least seventeen hundred years to get it back, too long to be on anyone's time horizon."

My curiosity was piqued. "Where does the number seventeen hundred come from? Why not twelve hundred?"

"Ah, the flight controllers need a safety buffer on the time dilation effect. The probes are barely controllable at seventy percent of light-speed."

"Oh, really?" I felt a warning message in the back of my mind, but I was so interested in what Flossie was saying that I ignored it.

"Yes, and the effect is asymptotic. At 86.6% of light-speed relative to the portals at Far Rockaway, the time dilation reaches a factor of two. Physicists believe that breaks the entanglement of spacetime…"

Flossie gave a sudden, piercing whistle and her entire body jerked as if shocked. I recognized the awful whistle as a vulgar expletive and I cried out, "Flossie! What?"

My survival companion let out a whistling wail. "Steven! I'm so sorry! I don't think that's public knowledge!"

"Huh?"

"I'll try to explain! Five years ago… before the announcement of the trial… I won a science prize!" Flossie gave a few gasps for breath, trying to calm herself. "I got to be a scientist and work with military specialists analyzing deep space data. That's where I met Julie's dad. I was having lunch with the theoretical staff, and we got into a discussion on reality interchange physics. Professor Feynman mentioned the dilation limit, and I probed for details. I don't think any of this is in the public domain!"

Flossie shook again then moved her head and surprised me by starting to lick the back of my neck. It was an intimate Pic custom used by gamma females for expressing a grievous need for forgiveness. A quiet minute passed as I wondered how to respond.

"Ah, that feels so nice," I mumbled in an intentionally sleepy voice. "What were we talking about, anyway?"

Flossie paused from her licking. "Huh?"

"Pic and humans having a right relationship, right? Something like that, anyway. I'm so sleepy, I can't remember."

"Oh, yeah… I can't remember either. It must not have been important." Flossie let out a large yawn and returned to cuddling with me. "I'm sleepy too. Want to sack out?"

I gave a relaxing sigh. "Sounds like a plan."

Just a short meter away, a winter storm was howling in fury and snapping our tarp fabric, but inside our shelter, all was warmth and acceptance. Flossie quickly fell asleep, a slow, very distinctive breathing pattern. Yet, Flossie continued to cuddle with me, her arm and legs tucking me into her soft underbelly. And her hand, she was pressing it lightly into my stomach, holding the pattern for love. Such trust, to accept in sleep a creature from an alien planet. Was my species worthy of this?

I finally dozed off, and had strange yet delightful dreams. I dreamt I was being caressed by a universe of warm, downy pillows.

Chapter 8

Five days later.
Northern Autumn 58, 3484 C.E. 33:34 (Time Zone 30)

I took a moment to look at my wrist assistant, and saw I still had four hours to sunset, though the sun was only about four degrees above the horizon. So I turned and walked to the surf's end and began heading home, the churning ocean hitting my side with bits of spray.

Our midnight U.T. news package had arrived on time again today, 31:11 local time. Everybody seemed to take the continued lack of hostilities as very good news. But I kept thinking that nothing had been resolved. It had only been about three short Earth weeks since Israel had been attacked with nuclear bombs… three strange and short Earth weeks, weeks with only seven days in them. Israel was saying absolutely nothing about what their analysis of the Eilot trawler was revealing. Everyone in the news room here on campus was happily thinking that this was one more day without nuclear war, as if the nuclear genie would return to its lamp through boredom. But nothing had been resolved.

In two days, it'd be the winter solstice and the first day of our new school term. Course schedules were released at noon today. I got all my first picks except one. Julie's alpha mom had rejected me from her second semester of wilderness training. It would have been a very easy course for me. I thought I knew all the material, but I needed the course for my certification. Ah, well, the course had a schedule conflict with Pic Economics 101. As the human liaison, I had to admit that economics made more sense for me.

I pulled my collar tight against the stiff wind coming off the ocean. It was about 2 C and a brisk day with the gusts, but nothing like what Whitehorse could be in December. The ocean surrounding Providence was just too great a thermal reservoir for the island shoreline to go into the deep freeze. And it worked just the opposite in summer. Julie said I would find the summers delightful.

I jogged easily along the beach, and after five kilometers, got back to campus. I climbed the stone walkway and turned for a moment to admire the long shadows across the dunes. Then I headed back to my dorm for a shower. This evening after dinner, we humans were going to see a movie that had arrived in Earth's data package. From what I understood of the reviews, it was basically a chick flick, but with enough sex and violence to keep the guys happy too. Should be interesting.

As I neared my dorm, Isaac trotted up and began walking by my side. "Good day, Steven," he signed politely.

"Hi, Isaac," I replied verbally. "Coming to the movie tonight?"

"Uh… Maybe…" He seemed startled by my question. "Steven, a word with you?"

We were already talking, so I assumed he meant in private. "Sure. I'm heading to my room. That be okay?"

Isaac answered politely with a basic circular hand motion. We walked the rest of the way in silence, and I picked up my pace a bit, sensing Isaac's eagerness. After we entered my room, I closed the door behind us. "So, what's up?"

"First, it's my pleasure and duty to give you this." Isaac reached into his shoulder pouch and pulled out his PA and whistled a series of commands. A few seconds later my own PA beeped, informing me of a high-priority update. I gave a command to view my status registry.

The Pic written language is a complex hybrid of a glyph-rich symbolic set combined with pictograms and semaphores. Becoming fluent in it would require years of study. But I knew enough to understand what I was looking at. I turned at Isaac astonished. "I'm a Level-One Ranger?"

He nodded. "Lieutenant Ellie has more authority than you might have realized."

I stared at the image again. "I thought… Wow, this is really something. The ecology restrictions, am I reading this right? Does this cover all of Providence?"

Isaac nodded. "Yes. You are cleared for solo travel anywhere on the island, and you can act as a qualified guide for people with a junior license. Test it as you wish. The monorail should respond to all your commands." Isaac smiled at me. "Congratulations, Steven. You've joined a very select club. You're living on a planet of city dwellers. Not many people achieve Ranger qualification."

I still couldn't get over it. "This is absolutely fabulous. Thanks, Isaac!"

Isaac shook his head. "Thanks are inappropriate. I did nothing but log the truth as best I saw it. Ellie confided she has great hopes about you. A few hours ago, she called you a... a..." Isaac paused and gave a complex, sliding harmonic whistle.

I grinned. "Which means?"

Isaac thought for a moment. "It's difficult to translate. You haven't taken the intro course on Pic mythologies, have you?"

I shook my head and sighed. "I'd like to, maybe next year."

Isaac gave the complex whistle again. "A prehistoric legend... a wily, ancient creature of the forest. But there's no negative connotation in this. From Ellie, it's the ultimate compliment." Isaac paused before continuing. "Level-One requires wilderness testing. Level-Two requires an extended solo field survey. Advancement to Level-Three is almost automatic if you put in the study time. It's a set of written tests. Of course, in your case, you'll have to wait three years before field testing in another ecosystem." Isaac looked thoughtful for a moment and then added, "Being a Level-Two Ranger also creates a binding auxiliary relationship with the military. It would endure into your adulthood. You might want to consider that before advancing."

"Yeah, I know a little of that from Julie." I made an intuitive leap. "Ellie said something else too."

Isaac stared at me. "I've always suspected humans can read minds."

I gave him a playful grin. "I knew of course you were going to say that. Mind reading is our most endearing quality."

"Indeed?" He smiled for a moment and then the smile morphed to a sad muzzle pattern. "Ellie made another comment, please don't misinterpret this, but she made a comment that if humans abandoned the trial and went to live in the forest, Ellie thought you'd be the only human she'd have trouble hunting. Please don't misinterpret this. Ellie is very supportive of the trial."

I nodded. "And as a military officer, she would obey orders. Of course I understand. No offence taken."

Isaac nodded and stood for a moment in silence, looking rather awkward.

I gave him a friendly smile. "So, what else you do want to talk about?"

Isaac stared at me. "Mind reading again?"

"Once you start," I confided, "it's a hard habit to break."

"Yes, I would assume so. Well…" Isaac shuffled his feet and looked even more awkward than before. I had never seen him like this. "Actually, Steven, I was wondering if I might impose on you for a favor…"

Two hours later.

I was walking down a corridor in a Pic dorm complex, making friendly eye contact with casual friends as I passed. Pic dorms had a very different setup from the human residences. The recreational areas were fully hex-sex integrated, but the sleeping and study rooms were grouped into unisex units called pods. Each pod contained five private rooms for sleeping and personal storage, a large, comfortable study area with five huge wrap-around desks, and a cavernous common shower and toilet area. Students within a pod tended to be very supportive and protective of each other. The pod would become a second family.

After a few turns, I went down a long corridor unit I reached the unit I was looking for, FC22, the last pod on the wing. I announced myself on the intercom. A female gamma answered, and a moment later Flossie was on the line. I asked her if we could chat for a while.

"Ah, one moment, Steven," she replied, and then I heard several seconds of rapid whistling. "Steven, my pod is about to shower. Would you care to join us?"

Well, Isaac's visit had delayed my plans for a shower, and the invitation, while unexpected, carried an unspoken offer of trust and friendship. All five pod members would have signed off on the proposal. After reflecting a moment, I took a deep breath and accepted.

Pic showering was preferably a communal activity, so completely different than human practice. It was universal that generations within a family will readily shower with each other at all stages of life, from infants to full adulthood. In sharp contrast, Earth cultures would go ballistic over the thought of mothers and fathers washing and being washed by their adolescent children.

But outside of family, group washing was unisexual except under well-defined conditions. For example, since Max was betrothed to Julie, he was welcome to shower in Julie's pod, and Julie was welcome in Max's pod. But if they were fully married, it would be inappropriate. Don't ask me to explain the logic. It was all based on traditions that are thousands of years old.

And with the arrival of humans, the traditions have expanded. Our Pic classmates voted to allow humans to experience communal showering by invitation. The social standard was that bodies would do what bodies do, but making any sexual overture through language or gesture would be considered extremely anti-social. Julie once confided to me with a grin that both times when Max showered with her pod, his penis was hanging to the floor by the time her pod was finished with him. Julie and her four pod companions ignored it, or at least pretended to, and since Max behaved politely, he was welcome to come again.

The pod door opened and a gamma female named Ann welcomed me. She offered to add my clothes to a fast-cycle laundry they were doing, and I nodded and stripped. A moment later Ann shed her bathrobe and we headed for the tiled shower room.

The other four members of the pod were already there waiting for us, and as Ann and I entered, Flossie activated the shower. It only took a moment for the room to be filled with hot mist and sprays. I worked one of several wall dispensers and soaped myself down, and before I rinsed I got my first whiff of gamma female musk, far stronger than I had ever smelled it before.

And as the communal showering continued, I realized what a delightful practice it was. There was friendly chattering, lots of mutual washing, a gamma even backed up into my leg and asked me to wash her, a common request since it was difficult for Pic to reach between their own deep shoulder joints. I worked a generous amount of soap from a dispenser and squatted to wash her.

Such a strange feeling! I'd washed my dog back on Earth countless times and never thought anything of it. And here was a creature much farther removed from me genetically than any dog. But this creature was also a person, not human but still a young woman, someone with hopes and fears and aspirations just like me, someone who could be in my class and support or contend my positions. And as I felt her ribs and backbone under the suds, I wondered if I would do a repeat of Max with Julie's pod.

The gamma wasn't Flossie. The feather-fur under my soapy hands was a creamy white, only lightly tinged with blue. I thought it might be Ann, but with all the steam, I...

She chirped a brief thanks, and I recognized the whistle. It was Ann.

Ann remained still after I finished washing her back and sides, and I took the hint and began washing the rest of her, arms, hands, forelegs, hind legs and flanks, neck, head, even her snout, chest, underbelly and rear, thoroughly cleaning the area around her musk glands... I finished off with soaping each of her four feet, working the suds between the tough pads before rinsing her clear.

I finally stood up and gave Ann a friendly tap on her flank to let her know I was finished. She disappeared into the mists, and shortly afterwards I heard a lot of short whistling. Flossie asked me if I were done. When I said yes, the sprays stopped and hot, dry air was blown into the room. We all enjoyed our blow drying, everyone except me shaking and fluffing their feather-fur.

Afterwards, we walked to the pod's large study room, where Flossie handed me a huge towel to wear until my clothes were ready. I looked around and admired the study. It was on the third floor and had a great view of the island's interior. I followed Flossie to her room. I had been in many Pic dorms before, but this was my first visit to a bedroom. "Wow, big bed," I commented.

Flossie looked at me thoughtfully. "We Pic are so different than humans, especially in our sleep patterns. It was a big debate issue in the past, about running the fusion trial, I mean."

I gave Flossie a hand sign to continue.

"For humans, child sleep is separated by gender, and your adult sleep partner is usually your sexual partner. For Pic, sleep partners are for bonding and trust building. Children and adults have private bedrooms to sleep alone if desired. Having that backup is necessary, but not the common choice. For my pod, we usually pair in twos and threes. It's very informal, we move around a lot. As the day is winding down, one person will start inviting." Flossie chirped a laugh. "Usually the person with the cleanest room that day! I haven't seen a refusal since I came here."

"Yeah, I can imagine a refusal might be awkward."

"It's easier than you think. I would just hold a muzzle pattern, like this, to show I needed some alone time."

I stared and shook my head. "I don't see much of a difference."

"Oh." Flossie paused and seemed to concentrate. A pale green with faint zigzag brown lines appeared at the base of her muzzle.

"Okay, that I can see."

The colors disappeared. "That was extreme. It would be impolite to open a conversation with anyone holding such a pattern." Still without clothes on, she took a large comb and started to work on some tangles in the feather fur on her left flank.

I wandered over to a chest of drawers and saw two pictures on top. The one of the left was of two older Pic, an alpha female and a beta male. "Are these your parents?" I asked.

"Uh huh. They'll be here next weekend for a visit. I can introduce you if you'd like." Flossie switched hands to work on her right flank.

"Sure, sounds good…" I muttered as I studied the second frame. I wasn't completely comfortable with Pic mathematical symbolism yet, but it was still impossible not to recognize Maxwell's equations. "You've framed the equations for electromagnetism?" I asked with a grin.

"Beautiful, aren't they?" Flossie replied. "It's the language our creator made for electrons and photons to talk to each other." She turned and gave me her attention and completely misinterpreted my smile. "Oh, I know. Photons talk to other particles too. Magnetic resonance imaging, photons convincing hydrogen protons to spin polarize, and what humans call the Mossbauer Effect, a single gamma ray having a conversation with an entire lattice array of atoms. But photons and electrons, that's the real chatterbox of the universe." Flossie handed me her comb. "Can you help me between my shoulder blades?" As I worked a knot out of the soft fur, she asked what I thought of Pic showering.

"It's great. I love the social nature of it."

"Yes, for me too. It's my favorite time of day. Think the idea will catch on with humans?" I was finished with the knot. Flossie walked to her dresser and laid a white undershirt and panties on her bed, and then a blouse, but no shoes, of course. Pic feet were tough. I hadn't seen Pic footgear since Antarctica.

I shook my head at Flossie's question. "There's not a chance in hell we humans will ever adopt the practice. And I never realized till now what a pity that is."

Flossie turned her head to me. "Really? This was your first time?"

"Yeah."

"Wow, I'm surprised. Ann wasn't, though."

"Oh, nuts. Did I do a bad job washing her?"

"She whistled that you did an excellent job washing her. But Ann was expecting you to kneel and be washed. As our guest, all five of us were expecting to wash you. Steve, this is what communal showering is all about. Communal, get it?" As we were speaking, Flossie was still undressed but laying out more clothes on her bed.

"Oh, boy. I hope I didn't offend anyone."

"No. Ann whistled she thought you didn't understand the custom. You're very welcome to wash with us again, if you wish." Flossie paused. "I'm surprised Julie's pod never invited you."

"Uh, they have, several times actually. I've been a little shy about accepting."

Flossie had already slipped on her undergarments by this time. She was halfway through pulling a dark gray skirt up her hindquarters. "Hmm? Shy about what?"

"Well…" I struggled to find the right words. "The problem is… Well, showering with five women; even though they're not human…"

Flossie looked at me thoughtfully for a moment as she finished with her skirt and buttoned a cream-colored blouse, then she jumped up on her bed and got into a comfortable lounging position, tucking all four legs beneath her. "We wouldn't be compatible as sexual partners," she said softly, "even if we wanted to be. A Pic vagina would crush something as thick as a human penis, and a Pic penis is strong enough to drill a human cervix and enter the uterus. Both your genders would find sex with us excruciating."

"Yeah, I know." I paused for a moment. "Did the councilors who voted for the trial ever consider…"

"I don't know, Steve. Do you think it's part of the trial, exploring the fusion of two sexualities? I don't know. Maybe you can ask Julie's beta mom."

"Hmm? You think so? We haven't met yet. I don't even think she knows English."

"So what? Just send her an e-mail. You humans have done a great job improving the reverse language map."

"Just like that? It's such a touchy question to start off with."

"So start off with another question."

"Uh… Yeah, well, there's an idea. Any suggestions?"

Flossie thought for a moment. "Steve, do you know the breakout of the pods here on campus?"

"You mean the gender counts? Sure. Thirty male pods, ten of each type, and sixty-six female pods, twenty-two of each type, for a total of four hundred and eighty Pic students."

"Right, and the ratios match the general population. You must also have observed that every single human male has a female Pic escort."

"Sure. We humans have a lot of theories about that; my guess was to help us with the procreation restrictions, that it would weigh on a guy's conscience more to steal the birthright of a woman."

"I doubt that's the answer. Why don't you ask Julie's beta mom?"

I nodded slowly. "Right… Flossie, do you know what questions the councilors want the trial to answer?"

Flossie jumped off her bed and stood on her hind legs to hug me before replying. "In a broad sense, sure, maybe not the particulars. I know what my questions would be. Can we show loyalty to each other? Can we be affectionate with each other? Can our love and fears bind us together? I sure hope so! But wanting to copulate with you? I treasure you as a friend, but I'm just not feeling any sexual urges. You don't either, do you? You don't find Julie sexually attractive, do you?"

I gave a deep sigh and hugged Flossie back, my hands burying themselves in the clean feather-fur of Flossie's bare midriff between her blouse and skirt. "It would be so easy and so polite and so socially correct to say no, but truthfully, where's the boundary between sensuality and sexuality? The answer seems undetermined somehow, so incredibly undetermined. I look at this moment and I'm enjoying holding you and your feather-fur is so soft. Humans only have two genders, you know. I think of you and Julie as women!"

Flossie looked and stared at me with her large W-shaped eyes, nodding slowly, her muzzle caressing my cheek. "Then it's part of the trial, at least for you. In time, your answer will have to form." And then she laughed and patted my rump before breaking our hug. "Enough of this seriousness! What brings you to my pod, Steve?" Flossie jumped back on her bed and sat down, picking a small comb to work on her feet.

I sighed in relief. "Ah, yes. I'm seeing the new Earth movie with a bunch of friends tonight, and afterwards we'll be munching on snacks and playing board games. Want to join us?"

My friend's demeanor changed from open intimacy to instant wariness. "Friends? Who?"

"Oh, just some people you know. Julie and Max, and Marisa and Emeric."

"Ah, yes, Marisa did mention something about this."

"And an Italian couple, Daria and Gilberto."

"I know them too. Anybody else?"

"Jorani will be there, of course… And uh, Isaac…"

"Isaac?"

"Flossie, what?"

"Did Julie set this up?"

"Huh? No, not at all. I admit, I did mention it to her. She thought it was a great idea. Flossie?" I took a chance and came over and sat on the bed, signing a desire to hold hands and adding a slight inverted curve to my wrist.

Flossie did more than accept. She lay down and stretched out on her bed, resting the side of her head in my lap, looking away from me and out the window, her neck resting on my thigh. I tentatively reached out and began stroking very lightly the edge line between her feather-fur neck and her smooth dolphin head. After a moment, Flossie began to emit low-pitched, rhythmic chirps. It was the Pic equivalent of crying. I didn't say a word, just kept stroking her, occasionally letting my fingers dip into the soft clean fluffiness of her neck.

Flossie slowly settled herself. It was a long while before she spoke. "You don't know how I envy you humans and your monogamous relationships."

"Hmm? Pic relationships can be monogamous."

"But it's not the rule! Every human woman can have a man of her own."

"Uh, I don't think life is ever that fair."

Flossie added with a half sob, "And you humans are so tolerant of diversity!"

I blinked. "We are?"

"Are you blind? Of course you are! The women in particular! They dye their hair, add color around their eyes, their nails; they can even pick unnatural colors and no one minds. Everyone just enjoys the diversity!"

"I never really thought about it that way. It's true, I guess."

"Sure it's true! Pic culture is very traditional by comparison. I really stick out."

I let the flat of my hand stroke down the soft richness of Flossie's neck and shoulder. "The blue, huh?"

"You've noticed?"

"Flossie, I'm not trying to be sarcastic."

Flossie ignored my protest. "It's unheard of, a genetic mutation."

"Oh wow, really?" I was genuinely curious. "Do you know if it's recessive or dominant?"

Flossie sighed. "Unknown. I'll have to wait for grandkids, assuming I'll find someone to exercise my birthright with."

"Either way, I'm guessing they'll be beautiful."

"Other Pic might not think so. I was… teased in high school…"

"Oh, shit," I whispered. "Badly?"

"It was unmerciful," Flossie whispered back without elaborating.

"The teachers wouldn't stop it?"

Flossie sighed. "The kids were careful, choosing their time. And I was so embarrassed, I guess I… I never said much to the adults. All the anxiety turned inward. I started to suffer from body dissatisfaction, started to have trouble with my eating patterns…"

I groaned and hugged her. "Flossie, my dear friend. There is so much I admire about you, and I'm not just talking about your intellect. You're full of grace, in the old meaning of the word, in body and mind… You're not unhappy about yourself now, are you?"

"Oh, no! This campus is so different, a dream, an oasis of kindness. I have a true home. My pod loves me!"

"Great! So why not join us tonight?"

"Julie must have warned you," continued Flossie, ignoring my question. "This campus here, it's the best of what we are. The rest of the world is much less tolerant of change."

"It's the same for us," I admitted. "Our class is the best Earth has to offer." I took a deep breath and ventured, "I think Isaac would enjoy your company," attempting to pull the conversation back on track.

Flossie gave a vulgar whistle. "Steven! Isaac must be the handsomest guy on campus! He'll see this as a… what do you humans call it? Something about losing your vision."

"Uh… Oh. A blind date?"

"Yes, that's it. You have Jorani. Julie and Max are betrothed. Daria has Gilberto. Marisa has Emeric. Isaac is going to be forced into seeing me as a dating partner. It will be his duty to keep me entertained. Steven, I would die of embarrassment!"

"What makes you think he won't enjoy being your partner?"

"Have you forgotten the ratio of Pic women to men? A guy like Isaac will have a hundred women chasing him."

"Maybe he wants just one."

"What?"

"Have you ever seen him chasing back?"

Flossie shivered and asked again, "What?"

"Flossie, I'm not being hard to understand! Have you ever seen Isaac dating anyone?"

There was a long silence. "I just see Isaac in survival class. I don't socialize much. I prefer to bury myself in my books."

The obvious occurred to me. "So this is what you did before college, huh?"

Flossie sighed and nodded. "My great escape."

My hand still on her neck, I struggled for a moment how to proceed. "You know, females aren't the only genders that can be shy. Guys can be shy too." I started playfully to ruffle the leg that Flossie had just combed.

Flossie raised her head and stared at me. "Steven, what are you doing?"

"As they say in American football, I'm calling an audible." I sighed and committed myself. "It was Isaac's request that he join our party and that I invite you."

Flossie replied in the faintest whisper. "Truth?"

"I would never toy with you about something like this. Isaac thinks you're the most beautiful creature who ever walked the planet."

"Steven!"

"His words, not mine, I swear it! And I think he would be mortified if he found out I told you. Flossie, he's just as shy around girls as you are around guys."

Flossie got up and paced about the room in silence, walking in circles several times before finally opening a drawer and pulling out a new blouse and skirt. The new skirt was wine red with a wide gold sash, far richer than the one she was wearing. It also had a geometric pattern woven into the fabric, both bold and intricate and an exact color match to Flossie's feather-fur. The new blouse was snow white with shorter sleeves for the arms and forelegs and ending in open lace. "What do you think?" asked Flossie timidly.

I smiled and made a prediction. "I think you're going to knock Isaac off his four feet. He's not going to have the faintest memory of what the movie was about."

Flossie blinked. "You have my word, Steven. I will never tell Isaac you called an audible, though someday you should explain to me what that means." She shivered. "When should we meet?"

"Movie starts at 48:00. How about we meet in the foyer at 47:00?"

"Okay…" Flossie blinked. "47:00? I need to get ready! Steven! Scoot!"

I got up and walked to the door, thinking my clothes should be dry by now.

"Wait!" Flossie called out. "Should I bring anything?"

"Just yourself. Any particular games you like?"

"Do you know what Isaac likes?"

"I saw him playing backgammon once."

"Oh, I love backgammon! Maybe set up Pic Scatter Stones too, just to be safe."

I had to smile. Flossie perhaps had the most brilliant analytical mind on campus, yet she had chosen another game where good rolling would beat good strategy. "You got it. See you soon." I left Flossie's room with a song in my heart. This was my very first time playing matchmaker, and it felt great.

Chapter 9

Time: Thirteen days later, Northern Winter 11, 3484 C.E. 51:11 (Time Zone 30)

It was the second week of the freshman winter term, and Jorani and I were studying in her bedroom. She was at her desk reviewing functions of a complex variable, material on a multi-year course in mathematical physics that we were both taking with Professor Feynman. I was comfortably sprawled out in her lounge chair studying Pic civics. I took a moment to relax and admire Jorani. She was so pretty. Jorani sensed me watching her and looked over and grinned. Then we both got back to our coursework.

The Pic have such a different way of building a government, using targeted drawings rather than elections to fill seats. I don't think any Earth culture has ever tried anything like it. The closest thing I can think of is being selected for jury duty in the USNA, or maybe the ancient Athenian or Biblical traditions of electing people by casting lots. Perhaps the place to start understanding Pic government is to understand their island system.

There are forty-three inhabited islands holding a total of two hundred and seven cities. Cities are designed to accommodate populations ranging from 380,000 to 900,000 with two exceptions, tiny Wuthering Heights with 40,000 and the capital, which is designed for 1,400,000. This adds up to total room for one hundred and twenty-five million, not coincidently the target maximum for world population. The Pic will replace old housing stock as needed but have no intention of expanding it. People and families would have to start doubling-up in the event the population ever did exceed one hundred and twenty-five million, a strong incentive to reduce procreation as the maximum neutral limit is approached.

City population profiles are remarkably uniform, typically at seventy-five to eighty-five percent of capacity with only a handful above that. Regardless of size, each city has a council representative in the two-hundred-and-sixteen-member legislative government, with the nine most junior members serving at-large. The whistle for the world government body is the same whistle for "council", and the members are called councilors.

Councilors serve nine-year terms, usually with one new councilor being appointed every ~~year~~ week (more if unplanned vacancies occur). Appointment is through a combination of qualification, self-nomination, and random drawing, with the incoming councilor matching the gender and labor guild of the departing one. It is a system that keeps all six guilds and genders equally represented, even though there are a lot more females than males on Whistlestop.

The world council acts as a supreme legislature, combining executive and legislative functions and having ultimate authority over the judiciary. The council has the last word in defining what a law means. Strictly speaking, a forty percent minority vote can cancel any law, and a sixty percent majority is needed to create or change a law, but there is a strong tradition for avoiding minority opposition. The simple majority rules unless strong principles are involved, such as with the fusion trial.

It is a zero-party system. And without political parties, committee membership is done by talent and interest. Except for the city appointment during a councilor's second season, there is very little seniority involved, a true citizen's government. There are several million citizens who have put in the extensive special study needed to qualify for council membership. The qualifications are broad, with testing in ethics, civics, economics, and the sciences. You don't have to believe everything that is accepted by science, but you do have to demonstrate the logic of why such beliefs exist. I remember expressing a concern to Jorani about this, excluding people who didn't qualify on the testing. She replied that as far as she knew of all countries on Earth, you had to pass a bar exam to practice law, so why not an exam to write the law?

The system has the fascinating quality of no politicking. By law, councilors are simply to act their conscience, and without political pressure, they tend to think globally when considering issues, even after accepting the responsibility for advocating specific city issues.

A large part of what makes this work is the mobility of Pic society. Citizens don't own houses or land, but rather have cheap government leases on housing where they choose to live. After nine years, it is possible to apply for one-year extensions to stay in the same place, but that becomes exponentially more expensive. After three years, a new cheap lease can be obtained in any city except the current one, with all moving costs borne by the government.

End result? Pic spend their lives sampling the full range of climates and ecologies, equatorial to mid-latitude to polar, shoreline to forest to grassland to river valley to mountain, usually moving every six to nine years, often in groups of extended families. The practice keeps the city populations from forming territorial exclusivity. Oh, there is still competition, but with none of the raw aggressiveness and lack of compassion that is so common among the nations of Earth.

As I sat on Jorani's bed, an idle fantasy occurred to me. Could Earth ever be persuaded to try something like this? Swap homes with another nation? I blinked. There was nothing in human history anything like this, yet the Pic had been doing it continually for over three millennia. The thought hammered home just how alien the Pic were, and what a leap of faith they were making to run the fusion trial.

I tried to get back to my civics study, but my mind just didn't want to engage with it, and I wound up admiring the scenery outside Jorani's windows. Situated at the northern limit of the campus, her room faced the core of the university, and through light snow falling across the commons, I could see the lights of multiple buildings. The sky itself was quite dark, of course. But even now this early in winter, there was a hint of things to come. Today we had a full extra hour of daylight compared to the solstice, sixteen hours compared to fifteen. The school days, though, from 20:00 to 40:00, were still beginning and ending in pitch darkness. For me, it was very much like winters at Whitehorse, but without the bitter cold. Winters here at Providence were idyllically pleasant in comparison. My wrist PA gave a soft beep, and I spent a few moments working with it.

"The daily update?" Jorani called out from her desk without looking up.

"Yeah. It's just past midnight Universal Time. Thursday, March 11th has arrived in Greater England."

"That's nice. Earth doing okay?"

"Checking now." A minute or two went by. "I guess so."

"Great. Any in particular?"

"Oh, I don't know, haven't read much yet. Maybe I'm afraid to look."

Jorani sighed. "Yeah. What a mess, and not just the Israeli issue. There's a new wave of blasphemy executions in Pakistan, and that war in the Balkans sounds horrible. Did you read yesterday's report?"

"Uh, no, not about the Balkans."

"Doctors from Save the Planet claim both sides are using bio-weapons. The idiots!"

I muttered an agreement while I scanned some other news. "Wouldn't be the first time... Ah. Here's something interesting. The BBC is saying the Pic transport might visit India soon."

"Really? Hey, that's great, their first trip since the bombs. Maybe things really are getting back to normal."

"Yeah, maybe. I'm still..." I paused for a moment as I scanned my mail folder. "Oh my gosh, look at this. Julie's beta mom responded to my email."

Jorani swiveled in her chair and gave me her full attention. "Did she answer your questions?"

"Even better. She says we should meet. She's suggesting this weekend at Haven."

Jorani's eyes arched playfully. "Thinking of accepting?"

I grinned back. As the human liaison, refusing any councilor was unthinkable, let alone our prime advocate.

Five days later.
Time: Northern Winter 16, 3484 C.E. 21:32 (Time Zone 30)

I was midway through my first period class, Pic Economics 101, and we were in a computer lab running simulations of the world's economy.

Tomorrow at this time I would be halfway across the planet, but for now I was engaged in a deeply engrossing task. Nearby was a familiar double-beep distress signal. Another classmate had let his simulation slide into self-sustaining growth. This was so incredibly different than Earth. Back on Terra Firma, economic ministers would be praised for such results. Here on Whistlestop, self-sustaining growth was viewed as economic cancer.

This class had hammered home to me how alien the Pic were when it came to economies. My textbook seemed to have been written by a combination of mathematicians and poets. In Chapter One, I learned that the purpose of an economy is to give life to our dreams, and to do this by nurturing relationships. I was sure no society on Earth has ever operated on this economic principle. No human society ever came close.

The Pic civic framework is a fascinating mix of socialism and capitalism. The government acts as a universal banker with absolute control of the capital market. It holds everyone's worth, both individual and corporate. The labor market, on the other hand, is held by the citizens. And once every three years at the end of southern winter, there's a convention at Haven where the two markets meet. The convention sets economic policy for the next three years, wages, funding for infrastructure and special public projects (such as the fusion trial!), innovation grants, business start-up capital, absolutely everything. And every three years, the workers congregate and negotiate for slices of the economic pie. But they don't negotiate with the government. During this time, the government workers are just other unions looking out for their own salaries. The workers negotiate with each other, so it's not labor versus management. It's labor versus labor, with volunteers from the capital judiciary acting as mediators. Strikes are almost unheard of. People at large would feel guilty if any group walked away from the convention with a bad deal, and the top-level guilds would be intensely embarrassed about pushing for unreasonable compensation against the objections of the other guilds.

The labor groups are loose hybrids of Earth's modern unions and medieval guilds. At the top level are six guilds roughly equal in size that set budget, policy, and standards; underneath them are hundreds of unions that manage their personnel and implement the policies and standards. The six guilds consist of education, healthcare, industrials (which included construction and non-portal transportation and utilities), consumer staples (to which all children including me belonged under the botanical unions), consumer discretionary (which included the artist and entertainment unions), and finally the government. Adult citizens choose one primary guild and as many secondary affiliations as they want, and if qualified, they have the freedom to migrate to a different primary at any time. It is your primary guild membership that ensures your base salary for living expenses.

The education and health guilds are the two primary cost centers of the economy, since almost all educational and health services are free. The industrial and consumer guilds are the primary profit centers, and the government guild is a hybrid. Calling it a government is a very loose translation of the Earth concept. Various governmental unions run portal operations, financial services, the integrated police and military services, and the deep-ocean fishing vessels.

All business and real-estate assets belong to the government. Individual incomes are tax free, as are business-to-business and personal transfers, but there is an astonishing one hundred percent sales tax on everything businesses sell to consumers. Wholesale prices of goods and non-exempt services are determined by material and labor costs, then the price is doubled for retail sale. Inheritance is taxed in a similar manner, the government getting half of everything. And the money from all this funds the annual salaries for every citizen on the planet, from newborns to retirees and even us humans. The unit rate to which everyone is entitled is enough to cover basic living expenses, and if you want, it's possible to drift through life without working since the botanical unions kept no record of your gardening. People would think you were strange, though, for not wanting the satisfaction of contributing.

What is remarkable and downright astonishing about this system are the throttles that prevent individuals from amassing fortunes. Salary rates are set by the guilds, with the median working adult earning about twice base rate and with a maximum cap of five times base rate that in practice is impossible to reach. Across the world, there are only about two thousand people paid over four times base rate. People just don't care much about amassing great fortunes, and the society is geared towards not being able to do much with great fortunes even if you had one.

In practice, almost every capable adult works, at least to a token degree. Many elders return to the universal job that children participate in, rejoining one or more of the numerous botanical unions under consumer staples and tending the edible plants and flowers that were grown along public walkways. And the Pic have a tremendous advantage in the age profile of their society, compared to the nations of Earth. Rather than pyramids (too many kids) or inverted pyramids (few workers and a crushing load of retirees), the Pic age profile have the shape of a pencil, rising uniformly for the first hundred and fifty years, the normal age for retirement, then tapering to a point in the next forty.

Yikes. My simulation was presenting me with a problem. Reclamation workers were insisting on more benefits. I couldn't ignore the issue. That would have direct environmental impact.

Reclamation work is managed by one of the conservation unions under the industrials guild, and it is a huge industry. The basis for this is a profound truth: You can't have a truly sustainable society if you are using landfills, because as the name implies, landfills fill up. So for three thousand years, the Pic government ran on a policy of recycling far more than they produced, exceeding the one hundred percent mark by factors of ten by searching for the garbage of lost eras. It was only a few hundred years ago that the law of diminishing returns finally kicked in. A hundred thousand years of accumulated waste had been made to disappear. There was nothing left that made economic and ecological sense to go after.

Our campus is no exception to this rule, nor is the Pic outpost in Antarctica. Every bit of waste is either processed for reuse, converted to nutrients for some organism in the biosphere, or sent through Whistlestop's marvelous intra-stellar trash chute. One of the deep space portals at Far Rockaway has been modified to be a trash-collection transport and it dwarfs the transport on Earth. As needed, the transport will position itself several million kilometers from Whistlestop, kill all its angular momentum relative to the sun and release its cargo. About forty-two days later the trash (or what was left of it) reaches the solar surface.

Releases are not done often. The cities of Whistlestop are in friendly competition with each other to see who can be the lowest per capita trash producer. I guess now I know why everything on Whistlestop seems so pristine. And I can't fault Earth for not following the practice. It is possible only through the Pic's infinitely abundant and infinitely clean energy source and trash disposal system. The original debates were remarkable. The founding citizens of the current government were terrified of depending on a system whose physics were so impossible to understand, but in the end, the lure of the benefits proved irresistible.

And to their credit, the Pic never allowed complacency to overcome their terror, not completely. For seasons with a leap day, they attempt to run Whistlestop without portals. Every nineteen years for fifty-nine days, cities make do with solar power, inter-island goods are transferred by the military's transports and fishing trawlers, and inter-island communications are channeled through satellites. It isn't a perfect test of course. The Pic will make exceptions for medical emergencies, and there is a special exemption for their contact work with Earth.

Back in class with my simulation, there were some minor technology advances in the previous year's game cycle that might cover the demands for wage increases. But was that the Pic way of running an economy? I popped up a help menu and studied my options, becoming completely absorbed in my toy-model universe.

The following day.
Time: Northern Winter 17, 3484 C.E. 21:17 (Providence, Time Zone 30)
Time: Southern Summer 17, 3484 C.E. 51:17 (Haven, Time Zone 0)

I was on the island continent of Genesis, in a corner conference room at the capital city Haven, on the top floor of the world government complex. I'd been waiting over an hour to meet Julie's beta mom. Some sort of unexpected legislative work had delayed our meeting. I didn't mind. The delay provided a good opportunity to survey the city through numerous windows.

At least, I thought I was on the top floor. On a side wall near the entrance, there was a flight of ascending stairs. Curiosity finally got the better of me and I decided to check it out. Near the top, the stairs curved to an exterior door, and through that to an open-air corner turret. The stonework in its canopy was beautiful, master craftsmanship. The brisk dry wind was warm but a pleasant change from the air-conditioned room below, and the panoramic view was superb.

Directly below me was a vast public square with a curved obelisk forming the center of a giant sundial. I knew why the few antique analog clocks on Whistlestop ran in a counter-clockwise direction. Sundial shadows moved counter-clockwise here in the Southern Hemisphere, just as they did in the Southern Hemisphere on Earth. And on Whistlestop, it was in this Hemisphere where ancient Pic first used the sun to measure time.

Outside now the sundial was in shadows. The city was catching the very last moment of hot sunlight, so I knew my campus at Providence was just about to meet the dawn. A line from my campus drawn through the center-of-mass of the planet would eventually emerge within the city limits of Haven. Our sunrises and sunsets were forever locked in perfect opposite synchronization. Julie once told me she found the coincidence amusing. The divided world government had placed the social fusion experiment as far from the capital as it possibly could.

Haven was no exception to Whistlestop's general rule not to build more than two stories above ground, so my view from the turret above the sixth floor of the octagonal capitol was magnificent. The city lay in the fork of a great river wider than the Mississippi, and beyond the city to the north I could see great stretches of rivers and cultivated grasslands. Haven was breathtaking both in its scope and its cleanliness.

I was in the most densely populated region on the planet. Thirty of the forty-three populated islands on Whistlestop had more than one city, and for these islands, it was common for cities to be located close to each other in groups of two or three. But nothing compared to the city cluster around the capital. Haven was located in the interior region of the world's second-largest island, and there were six other cities surrounding it in a great hexagon a hundred kilometers to a side. Haven and its six satellite cities had a current population of over five million.

And as I looked across Haven now, I saw a city alive with pedestrian activity, acting as the bread-basket of the world, the seat of world government and the top university and research centers, and also as the

148

central repository of historical treasures. Julie told me it would take a season to appreciate all the museums here. She should know. Haven had been her city of residence for seven years now, ever since her mother became a councilor.

And the cleanliness here, that was what I thought I'd remember most. I was walking the streets in the downtown area, and the air, while hot, was almost as nice as Providence. It was the time of peak heat for the capital, and outside right now the temperature was 35 C, near a record high. Julie assured me that Providence with its surrounding cold ocean reservoir was unlikely ever to match this.

The journey here was an adventure in itself. With the government's permission, I came to Haven accompanied by a dozen Pic classmates, no military escorts, and we all walked in plain sight from the portal hub to the government complex. Boy, did we turn heads. And the Pic children, they were so cute! They pranced as they walk, especially the young ones.

I understood at that moment the tremendous advantage the Pic have over humans in city design. Able to trot speedily and comfortably for kilometers without much exertion, the Pic didn't need much of an urban transportation system, just a sparse underground rail system which got you within a few hundred meters of your destination. Surface vehicles were usually remote-controlled and used for moving cargo and physically handicapped Pic.

Julie's beta mom was in the eighth year of her nine-year council term. She was both a lawyer and psychiatrist by profession, specializing in how Pic society responded to changes in law, and as such she was a superb ally to have on our side. She was one of the original sponsors of the bill that created the social fusion trial. And on Southern Summer 0, 3486, her replacement could be just as supportive of us or our worst adversary. There was no way to know which, but the odds favored us getting an adversary.

A polite knock on the door pulled me from my thoughts. As I turned, a single beta female wearing a councilor's sash entered the turret. From pictures Julie had shown me, I recognized the councilor as Julie's beta mom. I signed an appropriate greeting and started to apologize for leaving the room below.

She signed back that she should be the one apologizing for the delay, and then, "I thought I should learn English before picking an English name, but I never put aside the necessary study time. However, you deserve a human name for me, so I've chosen…" then she said verbally, "Maayan." She stood by my side for a moment and we shared the view. "I had forgotten how beautiful it is up here," she signed, then she gestured that we go below.

Four hours later…

My wrists were getting stiff from their workout, but otherwise I had only a dim sense of how much time had gone by. My experience of conversations with betas was that they were wonderfully open, thoughtful, and gentle, and my meeting with Councilor Maayan was no exception. We were into a conversation that should have been deeply embarrassing, but somehow wasn't.

"Have you noticed that we don't keep pets?" Maayan signed to me.

The question made me pause. "No, I guess not." I signed back. "I'm thinking of what I read in literature class and on the web…"

"Web?" Maayan interrupted with a smile and a gentle hand sign.

I realized I had given the hand sign for an insect web. "Sorry, Digital Rivers. Pets were never described. And I can't think of my Pic classmates ever talking about their pets. But I never realized it was an absolute."

"It is."

I gulped. "That's a real difference between us. Do you find us weird?"

"Personally, I find your ability to love pets fascinating and admirable. Look at the priceless relationships you humans have with your dogs and horses. With the right care and love, those animals will work their hearts out for you."

I sighed. "That's true. I used to go hiking in deep forest with my dog. There was a time, an encounter with a…" I paused to display an image of a grizzly bear on my wrist PA. Maayan nodded.

I continued signing with my hands. "I think my dog was ready to sacrifice her life for me. She provided a diversion for me to get away. I think she would have given her life without hesitation."

Maayan gave me a thoughtful look and signed, "I've read the interview notes of my wife on you. I remember one of the stories."

I nodded and tried to pull the conversation back to our primary topic. "And this is related to human-Pic sexuality?"

"Of course. Humans find it easier to bond inter-species, just as Pic apparently find it easier to bond intra-species."

I stared at Maayan and signed, "That first part seems right, given Pic don't keep pets, but how do you measure relative intra-species bonding?"

"By diving into the fabrics of our societies, how they are woven. Consider all the social factors that motivate individuals."

I made a simple hand gesture asking Maayan to continue.

"There are basic motives of course, individual desires for food, safety, and ability to procreate. Species without these motives would go extinct. And then there's the social level. We model species by their positions on a four-dimensional passion index, a desire to conquer and hold territory, a desire for knowledge discovery, a desire for acceptance by a group, and finally a desire to express."

"Express?" I asked with another simple sign.

"Of course. Poetry, creative writing, performing arts, sexual activity, championing political positions, these are all activities of expressive passion."

"Ah, politics, like the fusion trial."

Maayan gave me the Pic version of a beaming smile. "Exactly! It's an emotional struggle for us. You humans are testing our morality, forcing us to turn our familiar ways of thinking to something unfamiliar. Some find this exhilarating. Others find the new ideas dangerous. I'm embarrassed to admit my gender type sees mostly the danger."

Maayan paused and added, "Perhaps because it's the beta type has the strongest parental instinct, the instinct to protect progeny. It's common within Pic marriages for the betas to assume what on Earth would be the primary motherhood role." She paused again and laughed. "No one nurtures like a beta; no one seeks beauty like a beta; no one follows the rules like a beta!"

I had heard this truism before, but never in sign. Maayan used a hand sign unfamiliar to me, similar to "nurtures" but different. I signed a request for a pause and dived into references on my wrist assistant.

Interesting. I could see why the Pic used nurture as a verbal approximation. The true word was without a direct English equivalent. Its definition was: to represent the interests of the future to the present. The verb was also flagged with the same marker that "teacher mother" had, indicating that Pic linguists considered the translation ripe for revision.

Meanwhile, Maayan had walked over to a console and was now displaying a large chart on the wall opposite the windows. "We believe there are two significant social differences between humans and Pic. Humans have a greater passion for conquest, while Pic have a greater passion for acceptance. In the other two areas, knowledge discovery and expression, our base passions are almost identical."

I studied the scaling on the chart for a moment and then signed, "Even the two differences don't seem very large, compared to the underlying range."

"No, of course not. Large differences would make the fusion trial impossible. We wouldn't be able to empathize with each other's desires."

"Wow…" I signed. "Our greater desire to conquer, do you think it's because humans evolved from hunters?"

Maayan smiled. "Many herbivores are territorial." She gave command gestures to the console again and soon had a large portion of the wall filled with videos of animals from both Earth and Whistlestop. "I've sorted these animals by their passion for holding territory. See the pattern? It's not diet. All creatures will work to secure their food supply, regardless of diet. Even plants will do this. Consider the battle to be the top plant of the canopy." Maayan finished creating her display. "See how the desire for conquest lies along the mobility axis? Migratory animals are less concerned with holding territory."

"Sure, makes sense." A light dawned. "I see! Prehistoric Pic were migratory herds. Now Pic migrate to different cities and humans don't because we're more territorial. And are you saying the human desire for territory inhibits our intra-species bonding? Our neighbors threaten our territory?"

"Very good, Steven, though perhaps compete would be a better word than inhibit. Allow me to make an analogy. Think of something that isn't sexy, not the least bit."

"Uh…" I spun a holding pattern with my fingers for a moment. Maayan was gently guiding our conversation to my original email questions on human-Pic sexuality. "School assignments?"

Maayan smiled. "I was thinking of something physical, not an activity."

"You mean like a bridge or something?"

"Perfect. How about a suspension bridge with lots of cables? You wouldn't want to copulate with a bridge, correct?"

I blushed and grinned. "I rather doubt it."

"What if the bridge were magically conscious? What if the bridge showed loyalty and concern for you, asked you to be its friend? Would you want to copulate in return?"

My fingers stretched aimlessly for a second, then I asked, "Copulate how?"

"It doesn't really matter, does it? Imagine holes in the steel or concrete somewhere. Would you find the holes arousing?"

I shook my head no and signed, "I dimly see where you're heading. A human would be judged mentally ill for getting sexually aroused by a bridge. Is that the way the Pic see us?"

"Some, I admit. But Steven, the fault is ours, not yours. Humans have such incredible versatility in forming inter-species bonds. My expectation is that one day Pic will break through and share this ability with you."

"Assuming the trial is allowed to go forward."

"Yes, assuming that. And in return, I hope we can teach humans to let go of their insane excesses and religious rigidity. There is so much our two species can teach each other!"

Four hours later.
Time: Northern Winter 17, 3484 C.E. 29:49 (Time Zone 30)
Time: Southern Summer 17, 3484 C.E. 59:49 (Time Zone 0)

For a capital city, Haven was remarkably quiet at night, but then again, remembering Whitehorse in early summer, most of the locals were probably taking advantage of the brief darkness to get some sleep. Meanwhile, my classmates and I were hiking back to the global portal hub. The streets were well lit but empty, and as we neared our destination, we were passing through the large warehouse district that surrounds the portal hub. Earlier on our way back, we made a brief detour to see a water fountain that was four thousand years old. There were flowers everywhere, and the stone carvings worn but beautiful.

It was nice to be sight-seeing with a dozen friends, two from each gender, and a great commercial of Pic and human enjoying each other's company. And the short duration of our Haven trip made it easy to jump over jetlag effects. We had departed our campus after an early breakfast and would be back in time for a late lunch. It did feel strange though, walking in dark Haven now a few minutes before midnight. Instantaneous travel didn't cause jetlag. It felt more like jet sonic boom.

Thinking about the rest of the day, I paid no notice of the many cargo transports that were parked along our route. But as my group walked alongside one particular transport, there was the click of an electronic lock disengaging, followed by an explosive impact that flung the cargo doors wide open. In the open archway was a creature straight from anyone's worst nightmare.

I wasn't scheduled to take Pic zoology until next semester, but from my course with Lieutenant Ellie I had a good idea of what I was looking at, a hexapod duckbilled tiger, alpha male by his markings, and easily twice my weight. I was staring in shock at the deadliest land creature on the planet. The creature gazed down at our group and opened its mouth to issue a roaring whistle, almost above my hearing range and painful in intensity. Then the creature and I locked eyes with each other. True to his nature, the eyes were full of murderous intent.

My mind went into hyper-drive. I could sense everything around me in slow motion with crystal clarity. My classmates were beginning to whistle in horror and arch their backs, the first move for a Pic to gallop. Flossie's whistle was ear-splitting, a shriek of pure terror.

An old adage of forest hikers popped into my mind: You don't have to be faster than the bear; you just have to be faster than the other guy. My group was beginning to scatter, leaving me to remain with the tiger as the slowest member by far. I had sometimes wondered in the years since my childhood, if I could ever act as bravely and selflessly as my dog had once done. Almost the exact situation was now before me.

My odds for survival were zero. I knew what this creature was capable of. Its terrible, giant duckbill was filled with hundreds of serrated teeth. That was its primary killing weapon. It also had lightning-quick reflexes and powerful forelegs for slashing and much smaller arms with extended finger nails that it used as pincers. But if I could just keep the tiger occupied for a few moments, at least my classmates would have time to run away. My death would not be in vain.

So I intentionally locked eyes with the creature again and relaxed my body and thought out a message for my eyes to convey. *"Hey, big guy, think you're a predator? Guess what? I'm a predator too. I'm not much interested in fighting right now, but if you insist, don't go crying to your mama after you lose."*

Incredibly, beyond my wildest imagination, the tiger paused and seemed to consider my eye message and lack of flight. Then he turned and leaped for Ann, the nearest of the departing Pic.

Blinding speed! With one powerful swipe, the creature tore open Ann's flank, flipping and spinning her to the ground. The creature pivoted to make his kill and begin his feast. *Decision time!* I could live! Ann was sounding a piercing whistle of pain and had the creature's full attention. All I had to do was walk away and leave Ann to her fate. It was a surprisingly easy decision to make. I yelled at the creature and charged.

As far as I knew, all humans in the fusion trial had at least some training in martial arts. It was certainly true for USNA members. Unofficially, my government's position was, "Show the Pic they have to pay a price when they take on a human. Even if things are hopeless, don't go out meekly." That attitude was drilled into all of us.

I had picked Shaolin style for my training, and the tiger before me reminded me of the moves based on animal behavior, where human legs became the ferocious Shaolin tiger legs and dragon tails of the sky. Guessing my opponent would not expect a leap, I flew over the tiger's low swipe at my hips and did the one move I was really good at… dragon whips its tail.

My target was an area my Earth combat instructors had taught me to attack. After studying information on Pic physiology, they concluded the ear opening at the side of the head is the thinnest part of a Pic skull. I made a guess it would be the same for the hexapod tiger.

Success! Perhaps the best whip kick of my life, full spinning momentum delivered directly on target. My body began to vibrate from the tiger's ultrasonic scream, but the monster was far from defeated. A lightning quick backhand with his forepaw knocked me through the air. *Such power!* I rolled from the ground just in time to meet its charge.

No time to think! No time to move! So fast! The tiger grabbed my sides with both forepaws, immobilizing me and raking his claws against my ribs, seeking to secure a lethal purchase. Meanwhile the great head was turning sideways and the duckbill opening wide. I was literally about to have my head chewed off.

I might have time for just one arm blow. My right hand whipped my PA off my left wrist and I rotated my arm in a high overhead arc, twisting my hips and shoulders against the raking claws, trying to build as much power as I could. I swung down and hammer-punched the edge of my PA against the tiger's bleeding ear with absolutely everything I had. The universe exploded in pain and blackness.

A foggy time later...

I was drifting and confused, floating in darkness. Why was I having trouble breathing? The sensation was a little like drifting in deep water and trying to reach the surface, but never quite making it. There were soft whistles in the distance. I fought for a while with some fuzzy thoughts of a struggle, then in a burst the memories of the duckbilled tiger returned. Well, I was still alive, but where was I? It took a long moment of concentration just to realize I was lying on my back. Hell. The tiger was a setup. Did the Pic who set the trap kidnap me? I struggled to become more awake.

More whistles, closer this time. With infinite relief, I recognized the voice of Lieutenant Ellie. "Steven, try not to move. Just rest."

I mumbled back into the darkness. "Ann okay?"

Ellie whistled something I didn't understand, then asked, "Better shape than you. You've just come out of major surgery. You're in a recovery area now. I..." There was a pause. "Steven, why did you attack?"

I tried to answer. "Ann would have died. I couldn't leave her."

More whistles. I sensed the presence of numerous Pic nearby. "Steven, the doctors are ordering me to leave. Try to rest."

I took a painful breath and tried to say goodbye, but the waters closed and mercifully the world faded from existence.

Time: Northern Winter 18, 3484 C.E. 39:00 (Time Zone 30)
Time: Southern Summer 19, 3484 C.E. 9:00 (Time Zone 0)

Feeling stiff but remarkably free of pain, I opened my eyes. I was in what was obviously a hospital room. Warm summer sun was streaming into the room from a bank of windows on my left. I recognized the city. I was still in Haven, and a glance at the clock told me it was just a few minutes past sunrise, more than a day after my encounter with the tiger.

I looked around the room. I was plugged into an impressive amount of exotic monitoring equipment, plus an IV drip that would have looked right at home in any Earth hospital. I guessed there were a few basics that just didn't change, even across the universe. And Julie was with me, lying asleep on a low cot near the side of my bed, wearing what looked like a Pic version of a hospital gown. She looked exhausted.

A moment later several doctors entered the room. Julie woke and acted as interpreter, which was very useful since I didn't know the hand signs for many medical terms. The news was fabulous, high hopes for a complete recovery. In time, even the scars would be made to disappear. Before departing, the doctors did something remarkable. They all bowed to me, splaying their arms and forelegs. Then they left. I took a look at Julie and saw her muzzle holding a pattern of deep shame. I asked if she were okay.

She looked down shyly, not meeting my eyes. "You're not angry with me? With us?"

I blinked. "For what?"

Julie was tongue-tied for a moment. "It was only last season when I made my pledge to you. 'I stand with you to the close.' I had no idea how empty my words were."

"Hey, kiddo, don't think that way. That monster was a nightmare."

Julie shrugged, still not meeting my eyes. "It's from the lake region, the northern area of Genesis."

"I know. Your alpha mom covered the animal in a seminar."

Julie finally looked at me. "And now you're taking Pic anthropology with Professor Arnold. You know this is the birth island of our species."

I nodded. "Sure, the lake region, the prehistoric Pic remains, millions of years old. You and the tigers go way back." I had found my anthropology course fascinating. With almost double Earth's tilt and wobble, the Pic home world underwent substantial periodic changes in climate. And the lake region of Genesis was perhaps the most challenging, predator-filled land ecology on the planet. The Pic theorized that the highly stressful environment honed their intelligence through the ages.

Julie continued. "Ancient humans formed hunter-gatherer communities. Ancient Pic formed migrating herds. It's not our nature to confront physical danger." She came closer and we were soon holding hands. "When our probe first contacted Earth, we stated we were peaceful creatures. Ever notice that we never said we were courageous?" Julie paused for a moment then cried out, "Steven! We were supposed to be your escorts!"

I let go of her hand and touched her face. Julie rested her head on my bed and looked at me with pleading eyes. I knew what she wanted, and I was soon stroking her neck, from the smooth skin on the back of her dolphin-shaped head to the soft feather-fur down her neck and shoulders. Julie let out a deep sigh, closed her eyes and let out a low, purring rumble. We were performing the latter part of an ancient Pic ritual for granting and accepting forgiveness.

Forgiveness for major issues was a formal activity in Pic culture. There were thirty-six different rites for two people to use, depending on the gender of both the forgiver and forgivee. For example, the rituals for a gamma female asking forgiveness from any male gender involved licking the back of the male's neck. In Julie's case, the full ritual with me would be complex, but I was currently unable to participate in the positions. So Julie had moved to the final part of the ceremony. I didn't mind a bit. I really didn't think there was anything to forgive her for, and besides, I always enjoyed physical contact with Julie.

Her eyes still closed, Julie spoke in a quiet voice. "The rest of our group... Isaac suggested you might want your forgiveness for me to represent forgiveness for the whole group. We would plead individually, of course. Rebekah wondered if you might find that embarrassing."

"Oh, she has the right idea there. Seriously, Julie, I see no transgression."

Julie sighed. "Except for Ann. It was her life you saved, even as she was abandoning you. She would very much like to plead personally." Julie's purr descended in frequency, her muzzle pattern indicating a state of deep relaxation.

"She doesn't have to do that," I said softly.

Julie mumbled back, "I think I agree with Ann." And then her eyes popped open. "Your forgiveness is putting me to sleep."

I smiled and briefly stroked her muzzle directly on the chromatophore area. The caress completed the forgiveness ceremony. "You look really tired. Why don't you go back to sleep?"

Julie glanced longingly at her cot but shook her head. "Circes is going to relieve me soon. I'll stay awake till then. And it's not just our group. Every single Pic student on campus has offered to come and assist you. Flossie is arranging the schedule."

"Flossie, yeah…" A faint memory came back to me. "How's she doing?"

"Flossie? She wasn't hurt." Julie flashed a muzzle pattern of confusion about what to say. "I admit, she was hysterical after the attack. I didn't think you would know that."

"I didn't, just a feeling… I'm glad she's okay."

"Yeah. Anyway, every Pic in our class wants the honor of assisting you. One of us will be with you at all times until you're ready to return to Providence."

I gave a hand sign of appreciation. "Any idea when that will be?"

"Probably not for a few weeks. The doctors want you walking comfortably before they release you. Don't worry, the rehab facilities here are superb. And if you want, we can set up a video link for you to participate in classes."

"Sure, sounds good."

Julie nodded. "Steven, are you up for discussing what happened? The past day has been incredible. It's changed the world."

I nodded eagerly. Julie began her briefing. "The attack was captured on several video monitors. Your rescue of Ann has been playing around the world without stop, that and your responses to my birth mom in the recovery room. You offered your life to save Ann, someone you barely knew. The world is going absolutely crazy!"

I grinned. "Want to know a secret? It feels absolutely great to save someone's life." I thought for a moment about what Julie had said. "So the warehouse area is monitored?"

"Not everywhere, but near the transport hub where we were walking, yeah, extensively."

"I suppose there're no images of someone dropping off the truck."

"Transports are usually autonomous, but they can be manually operated, and that's what happened here. But there are no images of the drop-off."

"No?"

"No. That's part of the world's craziness. Almost two hours of video logs are missing. We know the truck wasn't there at 56:00, and that the truck was there at 58:00. But for the time in between, there's a hole in the security logs."

I stared into Julie's large eyes and whispered, "Wow."

"Yeah, really. The authorizations necessary to wipe both the video and the access logs are incredible. My beta mom says it suggests collusion within the military at high levels. And even with that, it should have been impossible, yet the files simply aren't there. It's as if they never existed, as if we had a two-hour leap-time and those moments never existed."

"Wait a minute. If there are no records, why are people so sure the truck was manually operated?"

"Why else wipe the video logs?"

"Well, perhaps to mislead people into thinking the transport wasn't autonomous."

Julie's snout displayed a burst of bewilderment. "What a strange idea. I'll have to tell my moms about it."

I laughed. "An ancient Chinese general once commented that all successful military campaigns are based on deception. How did you Pic ever fight your battles without it?" I took a deep breath. "What about the transport itself? Who owns it?"

"Property of the City of Haven. Its last log entry shows it entering a transport barn more than a week ago."

"Somebody stole a transport and nobody noticed?"

Julie shook her head. "We're a peaceful society, Steven, or at least we thought we were. Why should we verify inventory? Can you see why the world is going crazy? Imagine you're living in a democracy all your life, and then one day discovering it's a fake and a hidden dictator is pulling all the strings. That's what's happening on Pic right now." Julie paused and smiled. "It's a crisis filled with opportunity for the fusion trial. Longfellow is sponsoring a bill to recognize you with the council's Citizen Award. This is historic."

I had never heard of such an award, but Julie's muzzle and body language were saying it was a very big deal, and from the leader of the fusion-trial opposition, no less. I gave Julie the Pic hand sign for happy astonishment.

"Yeah. What a change, huh? Needless to say, this attack will kill the idea of you having a student escort away from campus. There're military right outside the door, and they'll go wherever you do, even to therapy inside the hospital. Don't expect to have any privacy except in this room. And don't expect more trips abroad, once you're back at Providence. Our government wants to understand what it's up against first."

I groaned. "Great. So the military is back to guarding me, and this is the same military that was involved in attacking us?"

Julie sighed. "They operate the surveillance systems. A purely outside hack seems inconceivable." A shy smile. "On the bright side, the world loves you almost as much as I do."

Julie and I looked into each other's eyes for a moment, then I returned her smile and asked, "Are all Pic assassins this moronic?"

"Hmm?" Julie's muzzle flashed a pattern of confusion. "What do you mean?"

"I'm just thinking, the capture, the transport, the setup of a duckbilled tiger, the effort and risks must have been monumental."

"Oh, no doubt."

"How did they ever have enough time to set this up?"

"My alpha mom thinks your invitation to Haven was intercepted."

"Huh?" I was a bit surprised. Whistlestop used the same communications security as the best networks on Earth. "You can't clone an entangled signal."

"I know. The intercept must have to be done at a portal relay center."

"Wouldn't that leave a trace?"

"People are searching. Nothing so far."

I returned to my original point. "But why bother with a tiger? Why not a simple bullet in the back of my head?"

"You think their goal was to kill you?"

Julie's question startled me. "No?"

Julie shook her head dismissively. "Think of the bullet scenario. Your classmates would be running for help and crying and trying to keep you alive. Steven, the goal of our assassins was to discredit our claims of friendship and loyalty with each other. Your death was just a means to that end."

I thought about Julie's point for a moment. "Ah."

"Think of the most likely scenario. Your escorts flee, nobody protects you, and the tiger eats you. All our talk of loyalty and faithfulness would be a lie, and the average citizen would now feel embarrassed to be around a human. We as a species had failed you. The assassins would suffer short-term condemnation for their act, but would reap profound long-term benefit."

Julie continued. "Scenario two: For some reason, the tiger chooses a Pic as its prey. Everybody else escapes. There's video all over the world of all of us but especially you abandoning a classmate to a horrible death. Duckbilled tigers are renowned for eating live prey. Death would have come to Ann as a mercy sometime during the tiger's meal."

I shivered. "I remember that from the seminar."

Julie beamed at me. "Our hero, you've changed everything! In all of history, there's not one record of another species offering its life to protect a Pic. You humans have your dogs, but for us, this is an entirely new experience. The military documented your concern for Ann as you came out of surgery. It was the only thing you talked about. Don't you see? You've validated everything we've done!"

162

Chapter 10

Three weeks later.
Time: Northern Winter 46, 3484 C.E. 14:00 (Time Zone 30)

It was about three hours before dawn and six hours before the last day of classes for the winter semester. Tomorrow would be the first day of a thirteen-day vacation period, and I didn't have a clue how I wanted to spend the time. Well, I guessed something would come up. Having some down time with Jorani would be nice. We had a plan for tonight. And as for the rest of the holidays, maybe I'd just spend time in social gardening and curl up with a good book or two. There was a lot of spring planting to do. The greenhouses were bursting with life.

I returned to Providence two days ago, and this was the second time I'd woken in the middle of the night and couldn't get back to sleep. So I got up around 9:30 and checked Earth's news report. Everything was still okay. It was April 16, 2100 in Greater England now.

I went out walking on the beach, and was now returning to campus with less than a kilometer to go. It felt good to be alone, and I welcomed the solitude. Everyone at Haven's primary hospital had been very kind, even my guards, and no effort was spared in my recovery. Pic medical science was more advanced than Earth's, and Pic had spent considerable resources adapting their skills to human physiology. But I'd never had a chance to be by myself, not until now.

I tried some easy jogging for a few hundred meters, then paused and stretched and admired the cold stars while I caught my breath. One star was impossible to miss, my oldest memories of it lost in early childhood. From Whitehorse, Yukon, it was the lower right star in the rectangle of Orion, and its name was Rigel. But here on Whistlestop, its whistle name translated to The Blue Diamond. Its celestial position was near the local sun when we first got here, but now it was half a year later and The Blue Diamond owned the night sky.

It was an impressive star even from Earth, but Whistlestop was twenty times closer and hence the star appeared four-hundred-times brighter. Its variable nature was clearly apparent, varying every few weeks from 4.4 to 5.6 times the maximum brightness of Venus as seen from Earth. The Pic, with their excellent eyesight, had no trouble reading by it. In fact, it was an ancient tradition for Pic lovers to read poetry to each other by Blue Diamond light.

And for humans, it was a great pointer to our native land. Earth, Rigel, and Whistlestop lay along almost a straight line. Earth's sun lay less than one degree from Rigel in the Whistlestop sky, towards the southern horizon from Providence.

My eyes fell from the stars and my mind returned to the surroundings as I resumed my journey home. There was a little snow on the beach but not much, and the sand was pleasantly soft, perfect for walking or lazy jogging. I had to laugh at myself occasionally during my outing. My eyes would dart across the dunes to the forest, searching for a new deadly monster springing from an open cage. But Julie was right. Our adversaries would gain nothing by simply killing me, not while I was alone. Logically, I was safe. But as Julie had once taught me, Pic and human minds are both more and less than logical. I was without a military guard for the first time in weeks, and I was feeling vaguely naked.

Results from a worldwide seasonal poll were published a week ago. The previous poll had been done a few days after the nuclear explosions on Earth. For the question of whether people wanted the fusion trial to succeed, the previous range was the lowest ever recorded, by gender thirty-two to sixty-three percent, with beta females being our most severe critics and gamma females our best advocates.

The changes in the latest poll were phenomenal, a range of forty-nine percent approval from beta males to an astonishing eighty-seven percent gamma female approval of the trial and hope for its success. The three female genders were now more supportive of us than each of the three mode counterparts, and with the greater female numbers, our overall approval rating was over seventy percent in the general population.

Did my single act on Northern Winter 17 cause this? I tried to be a modest guy, but I also tried to avoid false modesty. I thought I'd done it. But the problem of being a hero was that I was going to get killed if I kept this up. I had killed a duckbilled tiger barehanded, something the Pic would have considered impossible for a human. Some apparently still do. The day after my encounter, a rumor began to circulate on Digital Rivers that the video was a fake, done in order to boost approval for the fusion trial. The government was very interested in tracking down the source of the rumor, but it wound up chasing smoke, pointers referencing non-existent quantum routers.

I reached the cliff and began climbing the long gentle stairway to campus. Halfway up, I paused to catch my breath again and take one more look at the nighttime ocean and the beautiful winter dunes of Providence. God, it felt good to be home again. I felt a profound sense of belonging.

Wow, where did that thought come from? But it carried the ring of truth. Earth was now a place of memories. Providence had become a true home, and four-legged creatures with extra arms and dolphin heads had become more than friends. They had become my people, and some had become as close as family. I looked at the star-filled sky again, rich and expansive but alien. I listened for and heard the distant hoots and whistles of the shore and forest night birds, beautiful creatures and miraculously not alien. Would I ever understand this? I stretched my hips and resumed my climb.

Forty hours later.
Time: Northern Winter 46, 3484 C.E. 54:17 (Time Zone 30)

"Turn over," Jorani commanded in a seductive voice. I was lying on my back on her dorm bed wearing just my shorts. This was the first time for us to be alone together since my return from Haven. With a sheepish grin, I rolled onto my stomach, my arms up and relaxed surrounding the pillow under my head.

Jorani's gentle hands continued tracing the scars along the muscles from my ribs to my backbone. "They don't bother you?" she asked for the second time.

"No, not really."

"Remarkable. From the video, the tiger seemed to tear you apart. You must have seen its death spasm."

"From the recordings, yeah." I gave a big yawn. "I don't remember much directly."

"You sound pretty tired."

"Yeah…" I yawned again. "The last two nights, I didn't sleep much."

"Ah… Jetlag?"

"I don't know. Something like that. My mind just doesn't want to let go of thinking. I wind up walking on the beach."

"You seem sleepy now, though."

"Yeah. What you're doing is really nice… relaxing…"

"That's good…" Jorani kissed the back of my neck, then her fingers left my back and started probing the scars on my thighs. "You're sure this is okay?"

"Delightful." I sighed in contentment. "Maybe just a little itchy. It makes me want to scratch."

"Oh hell, I'm sorry."

"Oh, don't stop. It feels really nice."

"Hmmm… okay." The gentle fingers returned for a moment, then Jorani paused to remove her shirt and bra. I turned my head and watched her, transfixed by the sight of her breasts. She briefly hopped off the bed to take off her shorts and panties. Then her gentle tracing fingers returned. After a moment, I felt a tug and I lifted my hips as Jorani slid the last of my clothing down and off my legs. I shivered in the warm room. This was the first time Jorani and I had gotten fully naked with each other. Oh, there had been lots of intimate moments before, but we had never let things go to full sexual arousal and release, not yet anyway. I gazed at Jorani's relaxed nakedness and wondered if she were ready. I wondered if I were. The danger of rushing and burning out relationships was a concern for all of us.

166

It had happened to a few couples already, with awkward consequences. We were a small group imprisoned on an isolated island. A person could break up with someone, but people wouldn't get away from ex-lovers for the next five years. And no one wanted a reputation for not being able to hold a relationship. We were living on a beautiful, idyllic campus, but in some ways, the social pressures were anything but.

Jorani's fingers meanwhile were caressing my butt, pushing my legs apart and lightly probing the backside of my scrotum with her fingertips. This was so different than my few sexual encounters with Cossette, my girlfriend back in Whitehorse. Those were super-charged episodes of passion with the added spice of fear of detection by our parents. Being with Jorani now was so different. The sexual desire was just as strong, but the spices now were peace and gentleness. I was excited and relaxed at the same time, and the combination felt both mysterious and wonderful.

Jorani kissed the backs of my thighs before her hands dropped and began caressing my calf muscles. "You're in good shape. I thought after all that time in the hospital..."

I gave a quiet laugh. "Pic therapy is intense, but it sure does produce results."

"Yeah..." murmured Jorani as she started to massage my feet. "Any decision yet when you receive the Citizen Award?"

"No final date," I mumbled. "Maybe sometime next week." I wanted to say more, talk about the additional negotiations between Maayan and Longfellow. But I didn't want to disappoint Jorani if the deal fell through. So I just sighed in contentment.

Jorani gave a playfully wet and lingering kiss on my instep, the sensation both ticklish and wildly erotic. Her two hands were firmly holding my foot as her tongue and lips caressed me. I shivered when she briefly suckled a toe.

She got up and turned off the lights. The outside campus lights were our only illumination. I felt a clean sheet then a comforter settle over me, then a delightfully soft body was pressing into my side and a warm hand cupping my butt cheek. "Stay with me?" Jorani asked in a whisper. I turned to hold and kiss her.

The urge to caress and mount her was becoming irresistible. I stroked her arms and breasts and belly. Soon my fingers were in the silky softness of her pubic fur. Jorani began to shiver.

"Cold?" I whispered.

"No." She squirmed in my arms. "A bit hot, actually."

"Ah. I could open a window…"

Jorani giggled. "Not that hot." A fast moving snowstorm had arrived in the afternoon and the wind was blowing outside. "Here, just a second…" Jorani told her P.A. on the night table to lower the room temperature. In the dim light, I admired the beautiful curves of her upturned breasts. Jorani's nipples looked large and hard, and I reached up and pinched one. I was right. Her nipple was rigid. Jorani went absolutely still for a moment then bent forward slightly, offering her breasts to me. I brushed her aroused point back and forth with the back of my hand, then started kissing the underside of her breasts.

I was just about to suckle her when she gasped and pulled away and put her head against mine. "Steven," she whispered hoarsely near my ear. "Are we ready for this?"

I was tongue-tied. Jorani's question pulled me from my arousal. What was she talking about? Sex? Commitment? Was Jorani considering this a marriage proposal? We wouldn't be the first human couple here to unite in a betrothal. But was I that sure of myself? Was Jorani?

I reached and held her for a while, cupping her warm breasts and kissing the side of her head, cheek to ear and back again. I wanted so much to be gentle with her, to do the right thing, yet she was so overwhelmingly desirable. Waves of passion were washing over me. I started to tremble, then I rolled and half laid my body on top of her, my hand descending to hold her ribs, her flat belly, caressing down across her hip bone to her thighs. Jorani opened her legs wide as I began my return stroke, and I accepted the invitation and rubbed the flat of my hand along her inner thigh. So soft! I pushed my hand hard against her vulva. The outer lips parted and my fingertip curled into a wet vagina.

Jorani groaned and twisted away from me. My mind was moving so slowly. I was just beginning to worry that I had offended her when a light, wet embrace descended on my groin. My erection seemed surrounded by hot, vibrating feathers.

Jorani broke her suckle and released me from her mouth. "What should I do?" she cried softly.

My only reply was an incoherent grunt.

"What do you like? Tell me!"

I gasped. Jorani had told me before she had no experience with dating, but I never appreciated how completely frank she had been. "Do anything!" I answered idiotically as I thrust my hips into empty air. "What you were doing was nice!"

Jorani's mouth returned, driving me to ecstasy, both from the physical pleasure of it and the sweet innocence she was offering me. I cried out her name as I came, and Jorani held firm and caught all my spurts. I was floating mindlessly by the time she finally released me with a pop, turning to lie with me side by side, her body sweaty. I loved the smell of her. She cooed and kissed me. "Wow…"

I gave a deep sigh. "Yeah, wow…" I struggled to stay awake and do something for her in return, but the urge to just hold her and continue floating was so strong.

"What a taste," Jorani mumbled, draping an arm over my hips, "a lot sharper than I imagined."

"Jorani… Dearest…." I raised a heavy arm to hold her.

"It's okay," she murmured. "We can talk in the morning."

"Hmm?" There was so much I wanted to tell her, but my mind switched off before I could say another word.

Time: The next morning, Northern Winter 47, 3484 C.E. 14:55 (Time Zone 30)

I awoke feeling totally relaxed and rested, probably for the first time since coming back to Providence. It to me a moment to remember I was in Jorani's bedroom, and another moment to realize the delightful warmth pressing into my groin was Jorani's butt. My arm was draped over her, and I could feel the steady rise and fall of her breathing.

I sighed and looked at my PA on the night table. It was two hours before dawn, which meant that predawn twilight should be just around the corner, though the room was still dark. I studied the windows. Last night's snow storm had turned to rain. Winter at Providence was fast coming to a close.

My beautiful and precious Jorani. I curled around her and sniffed her hair, her ear. She stirred a bit but did not wake. I did want her, so very much. So what was I worried about, that I'd change my mind? No. So why not… I closed my eyes to shut out distracting thoughts, and soon drifted into a light sleep.

Then I popped my eyes open. It was two hours later, just after dawn, and there was a lot of gray light at the windows illuminating the rain. Jorani was awake and watching me, her head propped up on a forearm. "Well, I know one good thing," she said with a playful smile.

"Yeah? What's that?"

"After two nights of careful observation, I'm convinced you don't snore." She bent forward and kissed the side of my nose.

I smiled back inanely. "Well then, it's settled."

"What's settled?"

"Our future life together."

"Ah…" Jorani grinned at me and then got serious. "Welcome home. You finding the adjustment okay?"

I thought for a moment. "I guess so. I was surprised there was an adjustment to make. But you're right. It feels different being around humans again."

"Being around me too?"

"Oh, that definitely feels different, yeah." I reached under the covers and caressed her body. The caress descended to her hips, and my fingers played with her pubic fur. "This definitely feels delightfully different."

Jorani smiled and gripped my penis firmly, giving it a few tugs to get it interested in life, then forming a locking ring with her forefinger and thumb at the base. "I think you're different too. It's so nice that we can appreciate our differences."

I give a forward hip thrust into her gripping hand and grinned. "Yep. Appreciating differences can be a beautiful thing."

Jorani nodded. "It can be creative too. We have to be careful." She released me, paused for a moment and then added, "It's been a little rough around here without you."

"Hmm? Do you mean in general, or something in particular?"

Jorani shrugged. "Haven't you talked with people yet?"

"Sure," I answered before understanding Jorani's question. I had gotten so used to thinking of Pic as people, it took me a moment to realize what she was asking. "Oh, I don't know. Maybe not. Lots of hellos and welcome backs, but no real conversations. The last couple of days, I guess I've been keeping to myself. Jorani, what's up?"

"You are. You've changed everything. For the first day or so, everybody just cheered. Score one for Earth! But then reality set in. Steven, you set the bar too high. Our escorts are asking us if we would die for them. People don't know how to respond. Of course we like the jump in the polls. But it's based on a lie!" She looked as me exasperated. "How did you ever decide to attack? You had no chance!"

"I admit, I was totally outgunned in speed, power, weaponry. The jaws were a nightmare. But my chances weren't absolute zero. I survived, didn't I?"

"Steven!"

"I just make the most of my one advantage."

"Uh, what advantage?"

"I knew my enemy, and my enemy did not know me."

Jorani groaned. "Oh, do be serious! It's a miracle you're alive. Admit it — you were throwing your life away as a gesture. Why did you attack? What's the true answer?"

I leaned back on a pillow and stared at the ceiling for a while. Jorani was demonstrating her unsettling ability to see into my heart more clearly than I could myself. Is that why I love her so fiercely? An additional unwelcome thought popped into my mind. Would I ever fear her ability to do this? I blinked and tried to answer her question. "I know. I've been asking myself why I attacked and I don't know the true answer. Well, maybe I do. But what I mostly remember is how easy a decision it was. How I made it…"

Jorani was sharp, catching my every word. "What's your maybe answer?"

I gave a deep sigh. "A couple of weeks before going to Haven, I showered with Flossie's pod."

"I remember you telling me, the night we went to the movies with Flossie and Isaac. So?"

171

"I washed Ann. I washed her thoroughly." Jorani gave me a bewildered look. I continued. "Have you ever tried communal showering?"

"Uh, Max's pod did invite me, and I'm sure they would be polite. But stripping naked and getting washed by five alpha-male Pic? I'm not ready for that!" Jorani looked at me askance. "What are you saying? You attacked the tiger because you're hot for Ann?"

"No! Not exactly, anyway. Being with you, it's a lot different…"

"Well, I would hope so!" Jorani's body went rigid and a deep frown appeared on her face. "Steven, I don't want to be jealous of a Pic! I don't want to compete for you! Do you understand me?! Do you want me and only me?"

I groaned. "This isn't coming out very well, is it?"

"What?" Jorani took a second to catch her breath, and she said in a strained voice, "Do you need time to think about this?"

I shrugged helplessly. "It might help." Jorani looked as if she were about to cry. "Wait! It might not. I don't want to leave the conversation hanging like this."

Jorani half-shouted, "So talk to me! All this talk of Pic-human sexuality, I assumed it was just sweet you being thoughtful. But do you really want to mount a Pic?"

"Uh… Let me answer that in a bit, okay? I need to tell you some stuff first."

Jorani struggled for a moment, I think deciding whether to tell me to get the hell out of her dorm room. "Go ahead," she said stiffly.

"Well…" Where to begin? "A number of councilors visited me in Haven, including people who used to be part of our opposition. One beta male, a councilor named Kester, he told me why I was ranked number one by both the alphas and the betas back in Antarctica. He said it was my scores on honesty and frankness. Alphas and betas prize those traits. It's important to gammas too, but…" I continued with my explanation.

I gave Jorani a lot of credit for her patience. She let me talk without interruption, and I went on for quite a while. When I was finished, she leaned over and silently stared at me for the longest time, our eyes gazing into each other's souls. I think it was during this silence that Jorani changed her mind. I saw her eyes soften, and she began to smile at me.

And when she finally spoke, her voice was gentle. "You don't like telling social lies, do you?"

"Social lies?"

"Uh…" Jorani frowned. "Damn, my English…"

"Your English is excellent. Want to hear me try to speak Khmer?"

Jorani shook off my pathetic attempt at humor. "What's the phrase for hiding fleeting asocial thoughts? The ones we all have?"

"Huh?"

"You know, the lies we tell not to hurt other people's feelings."

"Oh. You mean white lies?"

"Yes, that's it, the color. I can't remember you ever telling one."

I sighed in relief. "I try not to. During the qualifiers, I think I was almost disqualified for the trait. But the Pic prize honesty so much, the psychologists on Earth decided to let me through." I reached up and caressed Jorani's cheek. "It would be so easy to hide desires I don't understand, never express them. But I've been living in a pure Pic world for weeks! Everybody was so open!"

"Yes, I've noticed that too, how open they are, how friendly… and how honest."

I nodded. "I have a theory about that. During my hospital stay, several groups of school children came to wish me well. They're so cute, Jorani, and their muzzles are alive with emotions! My theory is that Pic are honest because as children, it's physically impossible for them not to be. If a Pic child tries to tell a lie, his or her muzzle turns flaming yellow from embarrassment, and they feel physically ill. So they grow up with honesty as the center post of their morality. They have no other choice. And then the habit carries into adulthood."

Jorani sighed wistfully. "Sometimes I envy the Pic with their chromatophores. But it's one strange adaptation. It defies evolution."

"You think so?"

"Of course. Think about procreation pressures on Earth. The successful males who sire the next generation are either the toughest or smart enough to be the sneakiest. But you can't be sneaky with your emotions on display. I'm amazed evolutionary pressures didn't eliminate the adolescent Pic lack of control. How in the world did it ever dominate when it first started?"

"I never thought of that… but they have control when they're adults, when they're procreating."

"Yeah, that's a point, I guess. But did you know that Pic are the only hex-sexual species on Whistlestop with chromatophores? The only species! Don't you see how weird that is?"

"That does sound strange. But maybe some evolutionary pressure…"

"No, it's deeper than that. Pic pigments are based on cell types that are otherwise found only in marine invertebrates. How the heck did that get into the Pic genome without intermediate steps?"

I frowned at the problem. "Maybe the intermediate steps became extinct during the portal war."

Jorani shook her head. "No. The issue was recognized during the First New Kingdom."

"So what was their answer?"

"Independent evolution wandering back to an old solution. It sounds absurd, but what other explanation is there?" Jorani sighed and got back to our earlier discussion. "Flaming yellow is embarrassment. Reminds me of Julie's snout, our time at the flowering dunes."

I chuckled. "But without the rippling black stripes!" And then I thought for a moment about Jorani's insight. "You're right. Embarrassment and arousal, the two emotions seem connected somehow, their agitations vaguely similar."

Jorani nodded. "They share a common desire to release tension." She lay down by my side, smiling and putting a hand on my chest. "Remember our old tennis game with our escorts? I remember Julie hugging me after we beat you and Max. Such softness! It's very sensual compared to the hugs I get from Max." A light caress across my chest. "Do you trust me? I promise I won't get angry again, no matter what."

"You don't have to promise that."

Julie tilted her head. "So tell me, you're around a cute female Pic who's being very friendly. What do you feel?" Her tone was one of pure curiosity, no condemnation at all.

"Well, I'm not aroused, not physically." I paused for a moment to collect some thoughts. "Remember my girlfriend Cossette before the trial? Maybe it's sort of what it was like being alone with her younger sister. I was polite and I knew nothing was going to happen, even when she was being playful and flirting. It's just that, in another mental universe, if my imagination could create a whole new universe where things were very different, things might happen. I never got physically aroused over Laure. I never let myself go there. As Julie would say, that would have been vastly inappropriate. But that's the value of imagination, isn't it? It lets you explore fantasies without being responsible for their consequences."

Jorani sat up fully in bed, the covers falling to her hips and revealing her breasts. The return of Jorani's easy semi-nakedness with me was wonderful. I took it as a very hopeful sign. She was grinning at me and watching my eyes closely. "So, Steven, oh admirer of cleavage, can you tell me, will you cleave only to me?"

"Certainly, cleave only to your cleavage."

She nodded thoughtfully, her eyes twinkling. "Seriously now. No other Earth woman, no other Pic?"

"No other woman, human or Pic. I promise. Only you."

She stroked my cheek. "You're sure? I don't want push you into something you feel is a trap. And I won't push you away again if you're uncertain about this."

"I'm sure, Jorani. I want you. I want only you."

Jorani shivered and said in a burst, "Now and forever?" She seemed to give a small hiccup afterwards.

"Now and forever." For a moment the room became absolutely silent. *What the hell am I waiting for?* I asked myself. I seemed to speak before deciding. "Jorani, will you cleave only to me?"

Jorani sucked in a long, slow breath and let it out even more slowly. "I want to," she whispered. "I want it so much." Another slow breath. "Can we keep this private for a while?"

"Sure… if you want."

"What I want… Damn, this feels strange! I want to tell everybody, and I want no one to know; I want both at the same time. How is that possible? Am I making any sense?" Jorani lay down beside me, our eyes locking, our noses almost touching.

I reached and caressed her cheek. "I hope so. I feel the same way. Julie once told me that Pic and humans were alike because we're both more and less than rational. Maybe our feelings are wrapped in the poetry of that truth."

We sat up and hugged. The hugs turned to kisses, the kissing turned into arousal, and things were just getting really interesting again when Jorani pulled my hands off her breasts and smiled. "We can work on cleaving to cleavage later. I want to shower and head down to breakfast." She gave me a very playful smile. "You should shower too."

I took a deep breath and nodded. "Yeah, okay. Want to go first?"

"Oh, I wasn't thinking of taking turns! Given this is how you bond, I think I need a private lesson in communal showering!" And so saying, she took my hand and led a very willing me to her bathroom.

Three hours later

The food was fabulous. The Pic were getting so good at making synthetic food for us that, without looking at the menu board, I couldn't tell if my eggs, bagel, and lamb sausage were from a care package from Earth or from their actual point of origin, Polaris, Whistlestop's southernmost city and one that specialized in bio-molecular manufacturing. Jorani and I came out of the cafeteria selection area and Jorani suggested we take a large empty table. It was a good intuition. Within a few minutes, a large group of people had joined us, including most of the top members of the student government.

President Karim was sitting across from me. "The day before you returned, the Pic held a special meeting with us. They started talking about career possibilities. You know about this, right?"

I swallowed a bite of egg and nodded. "Sure. There was a conflict with my rehab schedule, otherwise I would have joined you through the link." I sipped my orange juice and added, "But I got my own briefing in the evening."

"So you know the proposal?"

"Uh huh. After our graduation, the world university system is considering opening up two associate faculty positions in Earth studies in every city, even the capital, four hundred and fourteen positions." I took another sip of juice. "I thought it was a very generous offer."

Karim nodded slightly. "That was my first thought too. But it would break us apart, scattering us like that."

I looked at Karim. "The idea was to convert an area adjacent to the world hub into a new campus for us and give us priority for using the portal system. It makes a lot of sense. We can work wherever we want, and our children will be able to socialize with each other. The Pic understand all this, how important it is." I paused for a moment and added, "We have years before we have to decide."

Karim shrugged. "True, but I'm concerned now about what the Pic are suggesting."

I allowed a bit of exasperation to creep into my voice. "Karim, look, thirty-six years from now, you might have a point, but not in six. We need the exposure! We need every citizen on the planet to feel that humans are part of their society, and not on some far-off island. If we don't start thinking of ourselves as immigrants, the Pic never will. Whistlestop has to be our home. Our first loyalty has to transfer to here."

Karim raised his eyebrows. "Has that already happened with you?"

It was my turn to shrug. "Honestly? I think it's a work in progress."

Karim's face was expressionless. He gave me a small hand sign signifying the end of the conversation. I started to lose my appetite for the rest of my excellent breakfast. Jorani, my superb diplomat, came to our rescue, trying to end the topic by vaguely supporting both of us. "It would be a little difficult, don't you think, being a community at Haven but working all over the world like that? Our jobs would be in so many different time zones, all our sleep schedules... But I don't think the Pic were trying to force anything. My impression was they were just asking if this was something we would like."

Parni, the VP of the student council, was at the end of the table and piped up, "Is it because of what you did that we got the faculty offer?"

I felt myself blushing, but tried to answer truthfully. "I guess so. From what I understand of the trial, Pic would begin discussing career options with us after our third year here or when there was sixty percent council approval of the trial, whichever came first. The general population poll is at seventy percent. Our council approval isn't quite that high, but well above sixty percent, so we're having these discussions now."

Parni thought for a moment. "We learned in civics that with a sixty percent majority, the council can do anything."

"Yep."

"So if our approval is there, any chance the trial might end early?"

I blinked. "That's not something I'm expecting. The sixty percent approval is to run the trial, not to end it. The only councilors in favor of ending the trial now are our opponents. And if we ever sink to sixty percent disapproval, that's exactly what'll happen."

Jorani added, "That actually happened with the general population once. Fortunately, not with the council." We finished eating and a few minutes later excused ourselves. Last night's storm had ended and the day was turning quite pleasant. The sun was melting the last bits of slush and our campus had a rich, damp, earthy smell that reminded me of a wet spring morning at Whitehorse. My sweetheart and I went for a walk around campus. "So," said Jorani, "besides the award, what are your plans for the holidays?"

"Uh, nothing in particular, outside of gardening. We have a really interesting discussion going."

"Oh yeah? Who's in your group now?"

"Emeric and Marissa, and our three mentors of course. You should join us sometime."

Jorani smiled. "Maybe. My group is interesting too, Karim and Parni and our three mentors. At first, all K and P wanted to talk about was politics. That was kind of boring. But then Max suggested we talk about the three-way synergy among belief, trust, and doubt."

"Doubt?"

"Sure. Without doubt, belief becomes extremist and trust becomes blind. Who would want trust with no vision? Who would want such a thing? … Anyway, what are you guys talking about?"

"We're building a pyramid model for morality, with belief on the bottom, and with beliefs supporting values, values supporting attitudes, and finally attitudes supporting actions. Rebekah is such an optimist. She started with a conjecture that all moral failing is rooted in errors of belief."

Jorani looked thoughtful. "That would imply the solution to cruelty would be rigorous and unbiased observation. If only life were that simple…"

"Exactly. Our next step added a feedback loop from attitude back into belief. It's so dangerous to let your attitudes color your beliefs. But we're all guilty of it; a core part of human nature probably…"

Jorani idly hand-signed a symbol for speculation. "I wonder if the Pic are more resilient. They seem to keep a healthy separation between their beliefs and self-serving behavior."

I nodded. "Yeah, that's the danger. Once you become self-serving, any people and facts that don't serve you, you just dismiss them as enemies and fakery, no matter what the reality is."

"Arrogance, holding yourself to be source of all truth. The great weakness of course is that you start believing your own lies… Yeah, this sounds interesting. Where do you meet?"

"West corner of Greenhouse One, look for the tomatoes."

"Okay. I'll talk with Max about switching." Jorani stretched and took a deep breath of the morning air. "What a beautiful day! Let's do something outdoors. How about a picnic lunch later on the beach?"

"Sounds great. And maybe some tennis after?"

"Sure." She gently patted my ribcage. "You up for that?"

"I'd like to try. Don't expect me to go diving after balls…"

Jorani laughed. "Have you *ever* dived after a tennis ball?"

Well, Jorani had me there, but before I had to respond, I was saved by a beep on my PA. I glanced at the message, sent a reply, and said to Jorani, "Ellie wants to meet with me this afternoon."

"The award ceremony?"

"I don't think so. From the message, it's probably to answer some questions I asked her. Ellie and Maayan were the people who briefed me on career opportunities."

"Ah. Did you get a different briefing than ours?"

I paused for a moment. "Yeah. Ellie said there's always a need for rangers in the Parks and Conservation Department. And Maayan suggested there'd be a big political benefit if I joined the Pic military."

"Oh my gosh!" Jorani blinked and then grinned. "Won't the student government be thrilled to hear about that?"

"Right." I laughed. "Can you imagine Karim's face? Parni's too. Maybe I'll tell them I'm heading back to Earth early to command the Pic transport!" We both laughed. "Anyway, this is all years away. A lot will change by then."

"Yes, I would hope so." Jorani offered me her hand, and we walked for a while in silence. I thought of bringing up our conversation from earlier in the morning. Did we commit to each other? *"I want to,"* Jorani had said. Did that mean yes? And then she asked me to keep this private. Keep what private? Did she consider us betrothed? Should I ask?

I looked at Jorani and gave her hand a gentle squeeze. She squeezed back and gave me a warm smile, standing on tiptoe for a moment to kiss my cheek, her eyes full of promise and happiness. That was more than enough for now, I decided. *Let the matter rest. We both need time to adjust.*

One week later.
Time: Northern Winter 57, 3484 C.E. 44:10 (Time Zone: -28)

"Wow," whispered Jorani. "Wow, wow, wow…"

I nodded in agreement as we both sat down in adjacent lounge chairs. "I've kayaked the Grand Canyon in the USNA. This matches the best spots."

Jorani smiled. "So beautiful… I was reading about the history of Wuthering Heights last night. The residential side is in the Southern Hemisphere; the equator runs right along the river. You lease there by the season, up to a full year. It very popular with the artist unions."

"Julie gave me a lecture on the Storytellers. She said the literal whistle for them would be lunatics, but that would suggest a completely inappropriate association. In native Pic, a lunatic is someone who tells stories by moonlight. So that's why the Pic give the English translation as Storytellers. The building facades here play mathematical games with lunar shadows." I stared at some of the nearby stone architecture. "It would be nice to come back someday and really have time to explore this place."

Jorani glanced to the depths below and took a deep breath, savoring the air. "I can also see why it's called Wuthering Heights. Listen to the wind blowing through the trees. What a soothing sound."

"I think the name is just the Pic being playful again." I closed my eyes and listened. "But it is nice, very relaxing. The trees are nice too; the fruits look like figs, don't you think?"

Jorani drank in the scenery for a while and then sighed. "Maybe. Their smell reminds me of home in Cambodia, the jackfruit trees. I'm so glad I'm getting to see this. I hope the others won't be jealous…"

"They might not have to be. Maayan is trying to get a bill passed that would allow other humans to leave Providence."

Jorani turned and looked at me. "So soon? How would that work? Could anybody just leave?"

"No, not on their own. They would have to have some official purpose for leaving. Some organization would have to sponsor the trip."

"Ah. Like us now?"

"Yeah."

"More humans as bait?"

I shifted in my chair. "More than that. I think attitudes are changing…"

Jorani and I were sitting in lounge chairs and holding hands on a breezy hostel balcony. We were about fifty kilometers from the west coast of Treasure Island, in the city of Wuthering Heights, watching the setting sun illuminate the vast expanse before us. What an incredible place, and not just the canyon. The city made San Francisco look like a flat pancake. Built into the northern and southern walls of a tremendous gorge, the city had a larger footprint when viewed from the river than when viewed from above. There was a single switchback road on each of the two shear canyon walls, effectively creating a vertical city. Small areas on Earth might look like this, but nothing the size of a city holding tens of thousands of people.

And no Pic would build like this either, though they did maintain the city in beautiful condition. The city was the creation of a second intelligent species on Whistlestop, one that became extinct at the close of the Old Kingdom era fifty thousand years ago. This was much grander than the different hominids that once lived on Earth. Like the Pic, the species that had built Wuthering Heights was hexapod. But the builders of Wuthering Heights were on a very different branch of evolution. They were bipedal, with two arms, two legs, and two large leathery wings. Somehow, that made them much more alien to me, compared to Pic. I couldn't justify my bias. It was just there.

Could Storytellers fly? The Pic weren't sure, though the single pair of wings were huge and there were ancient accounts that Storytellers had gliding ability. And they definitely didn't look like angels. They were nocturnal, carnivorous, reddish brown in color, with huge eyes on a lizard-like head complete with venomous fangs. It was a common joke among us humans what a Storyteller reception would have been like if they had visited the Earth a thousand years ago. The medieval church would have completely misinterpreted what they were looking at.

Wuthering Heights was another example of how different species come up with different ideas. On Earth, this place would have been looted or at best preserved as a museum. The Pic had turned it into a living city, admittedly one with unique permits. The northern side where we were now had hostel accommodations that leased by the week. The system gave everybody on the planet the opportunity to experience living here.

"Can I see your hockey puck again?" asked Jorani.

"Sure." I handed it over, complete with blue neck ribbon.

Jorani hefted the disk in her hand. "I can't get over how heavy this feels."

I grinned. "My neck's a little stiff from wearing it this morning."

"I can imagine. How heavy is this thing, anyway?"

"Circes told me two and a half kilos. That's why they made the ribbon so wide."

"Uh huh. Pic or Earth kilos?"

I asked for a conversion on my wrist assistant. "Pic, of course. That's... 2.16 Earth kilos." I raised my eyebrows slightly. "You're still thinking in Earth units?"

"It just feels so heavy, that's all, more like two and a half Earth kilos." Jorani passed the gleaming medal back to me.

"Yeah. Well, back on Earth, it would feel even heavier," I replied, thinking of Earth's slightly greater gravity. "By volume, it's forty-five percent iridium and forty-five percent gold. Maybe it feels so heavy because it's so dense."

"Yeah, maybe." My partner sighed. "Some habits are hard to break. I'm okay with most things, about seven Earth Newtons to a Pic Newton, ten Earth Watts to a Pic Watt, stuff like that. Those are easy, I think, because they're calculations. But mass, that's stuff you feel. Feelings are harder to change, don't you think?"

Jorani and I had arrived here earlier today for my award ceremony. The Pic, they were so thoughtful. They turned the Citizen Award into a medal ceremony even though the practice was unknown to them. Jorani was right to call it a hockey puck. It had the full diameter and thickness of one. But mine had a core of solid gold and iridium, covered by a steel shell polished to mirror brightness. The blades of Earth's finest samurai swords would be an apt comparison, and across the face, the stylish Pic pictogram for commitment. The symbol emerged through open areas in the mirror-like steel, pure gold and the silvery yellow tint of iridium. The medal was an exquisite work of art, admittedly a very dense one.

Tomorrow Julie and I would be touring archeological sites around the city, incredible stuff from the Old Kingdoms, paintings and sculptures from a species that went extinct more than fifty thousand years ago. Tomorrow would be a day of wonder, then the magic would end. We returned to Providence the day before spring term begins.

There was more to this outing than meets the eye. Jorani and Max and Julie and I were asked in a secure meeting if we would mind being bait to tease a response out of our adversaries. We still had protection, an elite military unit that was remarkably discreet. Max's and Julie's opinions were that absolutely nothing was going to happen, and we should just relax and enjoy the show. And even if nothing did happen, Ellie made a vague reference to me that useful data might still be collected. A team of researchers was quietly doing net traffic analysis on the news coverage of our stay here.

Jorani and I were sharing a hostel suite with two bedrooms. We'd decided to follow Pic custom and refrain from sexual activity until we announce our betrothal. I was eager for Jorani, yet I thought waiting was a wonderfully correct idea. We'd spent loads of time this past week sharing not our bodies but our souls, what it was like growing up, our dreams, our secret fears. I'd never trusted anyone as much as I trusted Jorani now. And the sweet anticipation of having sex with her almost made the waiting bearable. Almost.

I sank down into my lounge chair and enjoyed the soothing breeze and holding Jorani's hand. She signed "I love you" to me. *Ah. Life is good.*

A week later.
Time: Southern Autumn 7, 3484 C.E. 51:20 at Canopy (Time Zone 28)

Ever worry about something that turned into an absolute delight? That was what happened to me two days after Jorani and I got back to Providence. I received a request to spend the upcoming weekend at Canopy with Keon, a beta-male opposition councilor, a person who had some of the most logical and persuasive writings on Digital Rivers about why not to run the fusion trial. I started to prepare myself mentally, going over protection protocols with the Pic military while imagining what questions Keon would ask, what my responses would be. My understanding was Keon spoke passably good English. Would he want to converse in that? What if he misinterpreted what I said? Jorani was playful in chiding me for worrying, saying just give honest answers and that's all that mattered.

I started doing some research on Canopy, the city Keon represented. It was the tenth largest city on Whistlestop with a capacity for 870,000 residents, and that wasn't counting extensive college and graduate student housing. Canopy was the home city of the health services guild, and it rivaled Haven for its teaching hospitals. The city is over one hundred square kilometers of center-city with an even larger ring of student housing and suburban residences. An east-to-west river cut the city in half, and beyond was a vast redwood-type forest in all directions. It brought back memories of my childhood, though Canopy's trees were much taller and the climate much wetter, frequent fog in the mornings burned off by afternoon sun.

It was one of the most peculiar aspects of life on Whistlestop, how portals both enabled near instantaneous access to any city on the planet, yet also throttled the flow of people between the cities. A single portal could handle at most twenty-thousand citizen exchanges per day, or forty-thousand evacuations per day if they didn't have to unload exchanges from the portal of the evacuating city. I read that the population of Canopy's resident and college student population is over eight hundred thousand. It would take two full weeks to evacuate the city in an emergency.

One of the design rules for city locations was that it must have a class-A road connection to at least one other city, but that rule was waived for single-city islands, such as Canopy or Far Rockaway. Instead, each such city must have a class-A road to a seaport within twenty kilometers, but that rule was also waived for Canopy. The city was situated nearly sixty kilometers from the coast due to its unique setting for water and wild food availability. There was also a siting rule that every city on the planet be independently capable of meeting its own food, water, and minimum power needs without use of a portal. That rule was never violated.

The weekend finally came. Three hops through the portals and I arrived at Canopy just before dawn and was greeted by Keon, two of his staff, and unexpectedly his entire family. He had a quartet marriage with all three female genders, plus five children ages seven to twenty-one. Their oldest, Brian, spoke English fluently, telling me it was an elective he had chosen since entering primary school, and he was proud to be present and help with any translation difficulties. Brian was also beta-male, which puzzled me a bit.

It was a short hike through the damp to a breakfast restaurant along the riverfront. I was amused to see a large college-age crowd attempt and fail not to stare at a human presence. Meanwhile through sign, his kids peppered me with questions just about everything, and I returned the favor, getting details about their childhood educations. I had to admit, the Whistlestop system was impressive.

A student would enroll in the season (not the year) they turned three years old, and spend six years each in play school, primary school, secondary school, and high school. Their youngest, who didn't speak English but picked the name Amy just for me, was in her fifth year of play school. Brian was in the last season of his first year of high school. The profiles matched almost exactly with the USNA school system, once

I adjusted for the shorter Whistlestop years. I thought the Pic method of keeping classes within a sixty-day window of age was a real plus.

After breakfast, I expected Keon and his staff would pull me aside for more serious questioning, but after a short burst of rapid whistling, the kids left with the staff. The four parents then took me on a day tour of the open and airy central region of Canopy, teaching me how the city worked. The design was fabulous, long rows of greenhouses on both sides of the river, and a circular street design surrounding the portal hub connected with radial spokes and with numerous tunnels and bridges spanning the river. Every street intersection was labeled with a pair of numbers. The first number was the number of circular streets from the portal hub, and the second was the compass azimuth from the portal. We spent the entire morning touring Canopy's medical complex. All three of Keon's wives worked there. Perhaps Keon would too, except he was a councilor. He had worked as a physical therapist before that.

It was late afternoon and sunny by the time we retired to Keon's home in the most outer residential ring that surrounds the city. What I saw there took my breath away. Most Canopy homes had an Earth-type setting, but the last ring of residences rose high into the canopy of the forest. The circular multi-family structures were connected by tunnels and surface paths, and the homes inside were modern and spacious, but otherwise, it was as if they were living in middle of the canopy. The common-room views were mesmerizing with all the wildlife. Modular bedrooms were in the interior cores of the buildings and were linked as needed.

And then, another surprise! Keon asked me to look after his kids while he and his wives went out for the evening. Was this a test? Of course it was a test, but one I gladly accepted. Keon was offering me the opportunity to see what domestic Pic family life was like.

The older kids did most of the work preparing the evening meal, spending extra time to involve me; the two oldest girls taught me how the appliances worked while Brian talked about ecological history and the various wildlife outside the windows. "This type of forest is unique to the island. There was a big climatic shift about five thousand years ago, other islands shifted with it but Canopy kept these trees. We get more moisture from the ocean that most... See that pack of reddish animals with the bushy tails? Think of them as carnivorous squirrels. In the early days of the city, they were more than a nuisance. But they're smart animals, passing memory from one generation to the next, and we have the superior weapons, military drones protecting the harvester drones. It's peaceful coexistence now." Brian paused and looked at me. "You're too big to be of interest, but a human child before primary school might be in danger…"

I nodded. "Brian, I'm impressed how fluent you are in English. You've been studying it for nine years now? That was well before Earth was told about the fusion trial."

"Well, the Pic decision for the trial happened years before that. I was beginning my third year of primary school. But the elective to learn English is… maybe it started a century ago. All of your literature and different ways of thinking… you have to understand the language to appreciate it."

"Well, thanks for making the effort. It's a pleasure talking with you…" A flock of bright parrot-like birds flew in and started to chatter just outside the windows, a beautiful panorama with the last of the orange sunlight filtering through the leaves. Double sets of wings, of course. All vertebrate life on Whistlestop had hexapod origins. I also recognized that this particular species was bi-sexual. Both the males and females had beautiful plumage, bright green and yellow for the females and green and orange for the males. "I bet these canopy homes are highly sought after."

Brian flashed a laugh. "Thousands of years ago maybe. Now it's just the opposite. The current resident population of Canopy is about 684,000, I think, not counting the college students. Most of the vacancies are here in the outer ring. Everything else is packed."

I blinked. "This building is thousands of years old?"

Brian's muzzle flashed a pattern of uncertainty. "I'm not sure. I know Canopy was the last city to finish primary construction, and the outer ring wasn't finished until 1700 C.E. or so. A lot of debate about building residences with twenty floors. I could check the age with city records if you like."

"No, that's okay. It's just that everything looks so new."

Brian gave a Pic shrug gesture. "Interiors get redone. I was talking about the… the bones of the building. I think that's the right English phrase. A big difference with construction here, compared to Earth. We build with diagnostics and full maintenance access to everything, including the foundation. It's slow going and a lot more effort, but once you do that, you can make changes as needed and keep the building forever. Someone from the industrials guild could give you better details…" Brian paused as he and I saw a predator bird catch our attention. It looked like the love child of an owl and a hawk, and I watched it silently pivot through covering branches and catch one of the parrot birds in its talons. Brian commented, "Yeah, so beautiful. My dad and I love the nature too. It took a while for my moms to get used to it, the hunting of the carnivores."

After dinner and sunset, the kids pulled out the gameboard for Scatter Stones. Amy settled down by my right side as we sat on the floor, choosing me to play before her. I had never realized how complex the game could be with multiple players, with the kids pushing the board into positions not to attack one another, but to challenge each player with various problems. I finally learned how to cooperate and give Amy puzzles she could solve. The kids were all in bed by the time the parents returned, and I was offered Amy's vacant room for the night.

And now I was sacking out, beginning to drift, thinking about Canopy. How could it not be my first choice for where to live after graduation? Jorani would surely like it too… The faint sound of the bedroom door opening pulled me from those happy, sleepy thoughts. In scooted Amy, followed by Brian, both without clothes, which was the Pic standard for sleeping. Amy jumped up on the bed and curled up by my leg after giving my foot a gentle caress, a warm bundle of white fluffiness. She wouldn't get her blue tinge until puberty. I looked at her older brother. "Brian, what's up?"

"Hi. Our parents asked Amy and me to sleep together tonight."

"Yeah, I know. In your room, maybe?"

"Uh, they didn't say that. I assumed it was our choice. We often sleep with guests."

"Any of these guests human?"

"Well, no, I suppose not. Amy really wanted to sleep with you. I had no objection. Do you want us to leave?"

I looked at Amy. She was peaceful and already drifting, or at least pretending to. Her muzzle was still indicating an alert state. "Well, you kids are great. But can you check with your parents and make sure this is okay?"

Brian acknowledged with a hand sign and left the room. It was almost an hour before he returned. By that time, Amy was sound asleep for real. Brian curled up by my leg opposite of Amy, his muzzle indicating he was open for a conversation. So was I. "How did it go?"

"It was… complex. You were right. What we did was unexpected. Dad was hesitant. All three of my moms were supportive. They kept pointing out your Citizen's Award. Dad finally agreed."

I smiled. "This is my first time sleeping with Pic kids. Thanks for choosing me… Your dad?"

"Huh? Oh. Yeah, not my birth dad. The gamma is my birth mom. She divorced years ago."

"Ah. I'm sorry."

"Thanks. It's okay. Sometimes things just don't stick." Brian's muzzle pattern faded to neutral and he started to sound sleepy. "Big change in our schedule today… We kids weren't expecting to see you again after breakfast…" and then he became still. I stayed awake for a while. Sleeping with children was such a new sensation. *Bonding and trust building.* I remembered Flossie's words. I looked down at Amy and felt so incredibly protective of her — Brian too, I guess. I really had to admire Keon and his wives. They were doing a superb job raising their children… Sleeping with them… So different than Earth… How did we lose our way so badly? I finally drifted off to sleep with my warm feet leading the way.

Chapter 11

The end of the season.
Time: Northern Spring 58, 3484 C.E. 52:20 at Providence (Time Zone 30)

I was at my favorite battle station for studying, a second desk Jorani had requested for her dorm room shortly after spring term started. The summer season would both officially start the day after tomorrow, and the near-solstice sun was filling our days with light. It was still shining outside, though about to set for a brief night.

And in a real sense, our summer term had already started. It was a college requirement for Pic students to do a thesis each summer, a special project to augment their regular classes. That was what the spring break period was used for, to prepare thesis proposals for the faculty. Jorani planned to do her thesis on Pic language arts. I hoped to work on a project complementing my upcoming second course on Pic archaeology with Professor Arnold. I'd be presenting my idea to a faculty review committee tomorrow, on a puzzling topic I'd become fascinated with.

"Listen to this, Steve," Jorani called out from her desk as she removed her headphones. "I never realized how logical Pic whistling is." She activated her desk speakers. "Here's the whistle for kilogram — three simultaneous modulated notes. Let me break them down." Jorani played the wobbly notes in series. "The first means standard, the second mass, and the third note by itself means one, but used together with the other notes means unit. To whistle the word second, just replace the middle note with the modulation root for time. Neat! And get this: The whistle for Northern Summer is the same as Southern Winter; and likewise for the other seasons. What we humans do with eight phrases, the Pic do with four words."

I nodded. "What a different way of thinking. Think you'll ever be able to understand conversational whistling?"

Jorani shrugged at the challenge. "Boy, it's so much information so fast, I don't know. But we're going to give it a try." Max and Jorani had their joint thesis proposal approved earlier today. Jorani looked at me slyly. "You up for talking about your proposal yet?"

"Julie's been asking about it too," I said evasively.

"Julie's not your one and only," Jorani reminded me. "This is first time you've withheld something from me. You have my curiosity running wild."

I sighed and looked up from my notes. "I'm going to tackle an archaeology project."

Jorani grinned. "With Higgins and Arnold on your committee, I've already guessed that!"

"I want to explore a problematica."

Jorani frowned for a second then queried her PA. A moment later she read to me, "Problematica, noun, a term used for fossils in paleontology or artifacts in anthropology that contradict current beliefs in the field." She looked at me thoughtfully.

"Are you familiar with the Bayside archive?"

Jorani paused. "No, not at all. Bayside? Do you mean the coastal city on Long Island?"

"That's the one. It was mowed flat by a tsunami at the end of the Third New Kingdom, estimated wave height in excess of three hundred meters."

Jorani glanced out a window and shivered. "It's unimaginable… what a terror it must have been to see that coming."

"A small artifact was found on Long Island, found twice, in fact. It was found the first time about 3800 years ago, during the start of the planetary cleanup efforts. The object was found again four hundred years later, in the year 79 Current Era. This time people realized what it was, an encoded nano-crystal."

Jorani gave me a funny look. "So it's either Second or Third New Kingdom technology."

"Actually, nobody believes either possibility. But the crystal was fabricated to Third New Kingdom specs, sort of."

"Sort of? What do you mean, sort of?"

"It has the data schema of NK-3."

Jorani blinked. "Oh, hell, Steve. Wouldn't it be safer to pick some other thesis?"

"Yeah, I know. But that's where the problem is, or should I say problematica? I've become fascinated with this issue. The crystal appears to be an official harbor log. It shows Bayside as a thriving commercial seaport, freighter schedules, manifests, dock reservations... It's very detailed."

Jorani visibly relaxed. "Ah, okay, something from the early part of the era then?"

"No, exactly the opposite, and that's exactly the problem. The crystal has about three seasons of data on it, ending abruptly five hours later than any other record from the era."

Jorani's eyes went wide. "A direct record from the war? I thought there was no such thing."

"And that might be true. The crystal is discounted by historians. People don't believe the time index. They don't believe anything about the crystal."

"Why not?"

"Because it doesn't fit with all the other information about the final years of NK-3. Supposedly the world was running a global portal network before the war, far bigger than the one we have today, had been for almost a century. There would be no need for commercial shipping."

"Uh..." Jorani looked unhappy as she searched for an explanation. "The Pic use fishing vessels now. They're a major part of world food production."

"The Bayside harbor logs weren't just for fishing vessels. I'll show you the manifests."

"Still, current-day Pic sometimes ship cargo. Every nineteen years, don't they spend a season living without portals?"

"Yeah, but that's because they don't want to be completely dependent on something they don't understand. But portals were invented by NK-3, so why would they also run a completely inferior technology? Plus there's nothing in their last century of nano-crystals that suggest that they did, nothing except for this one crystal."

Jorani was silent for several minutes, turning and staring out the window. The sun set before she spoke again. "We've covered the Third New Kingdom with Higgins, four hundred years of turbulence, the shortest Kingdom in history. There are thousands of crystals from that era that survived the war. The ones from the last century verify the existence of the portal network. And forgive me for pointing out the obvious, but that network is real. It's how we got here."

"Yep, hence the Bayside crystal is a problematica."

"There must be some theory to explain it."

"Sure. It's universally accepted that the crystal is a fake, some ancient Pic's version of an extremely weird joke. Being a nano-crystal, there's no way to tell its physical age." I thought for a moment and chuckled. "It's not as if you can distinguish a modern electron from an antique electron."

"Make a fake nano-crystal and just hope somebody finds it? That would be one determined jokester." Jorani smiled. "But I can see why you're fascinated with this. Give me some details."

"Okay. Imagine life on Whistlestop 3800 years ago. The planet is a collection of island nations. Male slavery has recently been abolished, but females are still running the show. Technology is in its infancy. The premier power source is the steam engine. A male work crew is reclaiming a ruin with giant steam shovels about ten kilometers inland on Long Island. An alpha sees something sparkling in the dirt and takes it home."

"He doesn't know what it is," Jorani whispered.

"At that time, how could he? Nobody would know what it was. Fast forward to the year 79 C.E. The guy's descendent, a beta female, dies of old age, and her alpha daughter dutifully takes the crystal to be inspected to see if there's any of the new inheritance tax due. That's when the crystal is recognized for what it is, an encoded nano-crystal."

"It took that long? I thought… Was it stored in a shielded location?"

"No. This particular crystal's resonance tag was damaged, damage that was consistent with a pressure wave shock."

Jorani frowned. "I wish I knew more about this technology. Are you saying you can kill the RF tag with a shock wave and the crystal is still readable?"

"I was surprised by that too. I'll see if Professor Feynman has an answer, otherwise I'm proposing to research that point in my thesis."

"Well, in any case, it doesn't prove the crystal got hit by a tsunami. Someone could have smashed it with a hammer." Another frown. "But if it was found before the current era knew about nano-crystals, how could it be a fake?"

"The assumption is that a fake nano-crystal was substituted for the original find."

"Ah. And the alpha daughter couldn't tell the difference?"

I shook my head. "The crystal had been in storage for centuries, totally forgotten."

"Nuts. Well, if it is a fake, it was one lucky faker to be able to piggyback on a genuine find. I wonder if the original crystal was…" Jorani's eyes lit up. "What about defects?"

I gave Jorani a hand sign complimenting her for her astuteness. "Oh, you are good! There are lots of defects in the Bayside crystal. It's worse than current-day crystals and nothing like the super-clean lattices of other late NK-3 crystals."

"Defects caused by a shock wave?"

"No way. The original physicists who researched the crystal stated flatly that the logs wrap around the defects, just as they do today. The defects were there before the logs were written."

Jorani thought silently for a moment and then said, "Let's review the history. NK-3 began using nano-crystals during the second century of its existence. Within fifty years, the technology began replacing all other media for long-term data storage, similar to what's happening on Earth now."

"Right."

"By the beginning of the Kingdom's third century, RF tags were added to the crystals so they could be queried remotely about their location and contents, and at the start of the fourth century, the Kingdom switched to their remarkable quantum-perfect crystals, about the same time as the emergence of the portal network."

"Yep, good summary."

"And the Bayside crystal has the problem of containing end-of-NK-3 data but using the earlier crystal technology, the one with defects, a technology that could have been duplicated in the year 79 C.E.?"

"Uh huh."

"Well, that clinches things, doesn't it? The crystal is a fake."

"Gee, you think so?" I gave a hard frown. "Jorani, I'm really unhappy with that explanation. Do you know the resources involved in reverse-engineering the Third New Kingdom's data schema? I've been researching this. Making crystals is easy, but modifying nano recording equipment to write in NK-3 format is not."

"How hard is it?"

"Well, for one thing, you would need a different type of X-ray laser. We're talking a lot of work here, a job for a government or a corporation, not somebody playing a joke."

Jorani considered my point and finally shrugged. "Okay, I give up. It doesn't make sense. And nobody cares?"

I gave a Pic hand gesture echoing Jorani's shrug and said, "Whistlestop is just like Earth. People see what they want to see and disregard the rest."

Jorani looked at me warily. "So what do you see? What's your thesis about, exactly?"

"What if the Bayside crystal is accurate, and all the other crystals are not?"

"What? All of them? Impossible!"

I grinned. "You have a lot of company with that opinion, as far as I know. Every Pic on the planet."

"Steve, you're not making sense." Jorani took a deep breath. "Were any postwar shipwrecks found, you know, big commercial freighters?"

"That's another thing I want to research, though I don't expect to find much. At the beginning of the reclamation, people weren't paying attention to what they were recycling. Records are scarce. And people were just coming out of a thirty-thousand year period when doing archaeology would get you executed. Any old hulk would probably be dismissed as a fishing vessel or from an earlier era."

Jorani shook her head vigorously. "Steve, you're still not making sense. We've both learned the history of the Third New Kingdom. Some of it is a bit confusing, sure, but it's also a massive body of interlocking evidence. There's no way all the other records could be in error."

"I'm not suggesting they are in error, not exactly."

Jorani looked perplexed. "So what are you suggesting, exactly?"

The next morning:
Time: Northern Spring 59, 3484 C.E. 21:52 (Time Zone 30)

I repeated my answer to Jorani's question a half day later to the three faculty members of my thesis committee. There was my history instructor alpha-female Professor Higgins, my instructor for anthropology beta-male paleontologist Professor Arnold, and Julie's dad, gamma physicist Professor Feynman. It was a Pic tradition for a student to invite all three gender types to be on his or her first thesis review committee, and these were three Pic of whom I held an extremely high opinion. I was delighted that they had all accepted my invitation to be my summer thesis advisors.

Professor Higgins was so shocked by my answer that she cried out, "Are you mad?" before signing me a brief apology for rudeness. She then turned to Professor Arnold and got into a furious snout conversation, patterns flashing at dazzling speed. I turned to Professor Feynman. His eyes were boring into me, but he was also nodding.

"I understand now why you asked for a physicist to review a history thesis. Very thoughtful, Steven. But do you understand the risks?"

"Somewhat, I guess."

"There are two people on campus with knowledge that's forbidden to you. You're looking at one of them."

"Flossie," I replied without thinking.

Another nod. "So you know. Flossie is an outstanding physicist with the potential to become the premier theoretician of our time, yet she chose to postpone her life's vocation and study Earth cultures instead. There was considerable debate before either of us was allowed to come here."

"The trial won't last forever. That was the grand agreement, no second-class citizens."

"Yes, and in thirty-six years, you'll be safe or back on Earth. But in the interim, Steven, have you considered the risks?" He paused. "Have you discussed this with anyone?"

"Jorani, last night."

"And what was her opinion?"

"It was a lively debate, but in the end, she promised to support me."

"Ah, the courage of the humans, it is quite remarkable." I'd learned a lot about reading Pic emotions. Professor Feynman was looking at me, and his W-eyes were full of kindness. "The risks are real. I could lead you in good faith to knowledge that could get you blacklisted. I'm not a god. I can't see the future."

"But you're willing to help me?"

Before he could answer, Professor Higgins broke into our conversation. "Fakes? All of them?"

"Just the defect-free ones from the final century. It's an idea I'd like to explore," I answered simply.

"But there were no cargo ships! There were no shipwrecks, nothing that would fit the Bayside description!"

I countered, "The power that transformed Enigma could also make a bunch of shipwrecks disappear, don't you think?"

Higgins' snout flashed a mixed pattern of rebuke and pity. "But that would imply the transformation technology survived the war. Steven, people will think you are paranoid for suggesting such a massive conspiracy."

Professor Arnold also spoke. "Let me make an analogy. Suppose a student wanted to question the reality of our senses. Suppose the conjecture of the thesis was that our brains are floating in jars in some hostile alien lab, and the aliens were feeding fake data to our sensory neurons to simulate what we perceive as reality."

"That's a horribly scary thought, Professor." I admitted.

"Yes. And how could you ever disprove such a thing? But it would be paranoia to fear it. We trust that our senses are showing us reality. All other belief would be mental illness."

"It's not paranoia if the fear is real," I insisted. "You people prize honesty so highly, deception is so repugnant to you, that I think you might be missing something here."

Professor Arnold replied, "But do you also see the other side of the argument, that humans are so in love with conspiracies that they discard simple explanations?"

"Oh, I know," I admitted. "Earth tabloids. We go insane with our suspicions and fantasies."

Professor Arnold nodded. "The Bayside crystal does not meet the manufacturing standards of the era it claims to be from."

"Exactly! Don't you find it odd that someone would go to such great effort to make a fake when it would be so easily rejected?" I noticed Professor Feynman's eyes blink when I said this.

"Steven," spoke Professor Higgins, "there are valid reasons why that piece of rubbish from Bayside is discounted. Think of what your scenario implies. Hostile interstellar beings invade our world, drive us almost to extinction, and then what? They go through elaborate godlike measures to hide their crimes, plant thousands of nano-crystals to describe a fake history, and then take off, leaving us all their toys? It's absurd!"

"Well, yeah, if you put it that way..." I was beginning to feel a little sheepish. "Uh, what if their motive is completely alien to us, not understandable?"

Higgins made a humph noise. "We are all bound by the same constraints of reality. Any species so bizarre does not belong in our universe. It would go extinct!" She then turned to Professor Feynman, the senior faculty member present. "I propose we tell this student to choose a new topic."

Julie's dad gave the Pic snout equivalent of a deep sigh. "No. I'd like for us to support his research on Bayside."

"What?" Professor Higgins made a chirp that sounded like a hiccup. "Explain, please?"

"It's the point of the trial, humans and Pic working together to augment our strengths and diminish our weaknesses. Steven's alien conspiracy theory might be wrong. But he's raising some intriguing objections to current belief. Our discounting the Bayside archive might be wrong. Can a new and better understanding emerge if we contend our different ideas? Of course it can."

"Well..."

"Great leaps of effectiveness can occur when one discovers a new perspective."

"That's true of course, but…" The conversation went on for almost a half hour, but in the end, Julie's dad proved persuasive. All three advisors voted to support me, and the word of a Pic was money in the bank, or at least it would be if the Pic ever got around to printing legal tender.

Professor Arnold made a thoughtful suggestion at the end of our meeting. He urged me to edit my proposal. In written form, it would only mention a general historical study of Bayside and some nano-crystal physics research, none of my wild speculations. I readily agreed.

Four weeks later:
Time: Northern Summer 40, 3484 C.E. 57:55 (Time Zone 30)

It was late evening at the start of the last week of summer classes, and I was in Specialty Lab Six. With me was Professor Feynman assisting me with my thesis, and Flossie who was doing her thesis on human problem-solving techniques. Basically, her thesis was to study how I did mine. It did make me feel vaguely uncomfortable that all my trials and errors were being meticulously recorded, but in my love for Flossie, I had accepted her request. The feeling was similar to writing a paper with someone looking over my shoulder and watching me create and edit every word.

Julie had been with us until an hour ago, when she had stretched her neck and given a big yawn, hugged me goodnight and headed off to sleep. Flossie's best friend Ann, though, was still in the lab with us, purely out of curiosity.

I had built a tabletop collision experiment, using the lab's small ballistics chamber to replicate a shock wave that would damage the RF locator on a nano-crystal without obliterating its encoded information. Professor Feynman had procured dozens of blank crystals for us to use, more than I thought we would need. But his intuition was correct. The box was empty now, our last crystal mounted in the chamber, and we had not come close to accomplishing what we were attempting to do. I was beginning to think it was impossible.

Our current test was a series of high-speed, light-mass, shallow-angle collisions, not the regime where we had hoped for success, but the last place to try. After receiving confirmation from the diagnostics and safety interlocks, I began the firings, thin metallic threads vacuum-fired with increasing impulse by a magnetic rail gun.

Professor Feynman stopped firing after a dozen impacts. The RF tag was still functioning, but the crystal was registering as unreadable. I sighed and did a poor imitation of Julie's earlier yawn. It was very late. But as least we had our results, though not the ones we were expecting. I felt very tired.

Professor Feynman, on the other hand, was quite animated. "This is a considerable puzzle. How was the Bayside crystal formed?" He then looked at Flossie and noticed she was even more animated than he was. He whistled something to her in native Pic.

With a start I realized I understood the initial part of his chirp. At the risk of embarrassing my favorite professor, I called out, "Cute adolescent gamma girl?"

Professor Feynman turned to me astonished. "You understood!"

I nodded. "Jorani and Max have been practicing for weeks, and I guess I've picked up some stuff through osmosis."

Julie's dad nodded and gave me a complimentary hand sign. With a start, I realized the finger positions were complimenting my morals, not my ability to understand Pic whistling. Julie's dad was complimenting me for my honesty, rather than preserving my ability to understand future conversations secretly.

And in regard to calling Flossie something vaguely inappropriate in an equivalent Earth setting, it was just something I found charming about Pic culture. Males and females within the same type would often banter with each other when no other type was present. For example, if an alpha or a beta were here, even if it were just his own daughter Julie, Professor Feynman would never have referred to Flossie so playfully. Ann was with us, but she was also a gamma.

"May I ask?" asked Julie's dad. He didn't have to verbalize the question.

"You saw my limit," I replied. "A quick three or four word burst if I know the notes. Jorani can get a full sentence if it isn't too long."

"Remarkable, and a major piece of news."

Flossie spoke with a muzzle grin, "The rest of his comment was that my snout was going to explode if I tried to stay silent much longer!"

Professor Feynman turned to Flossie and chirped something totally incomprehensible to me.

Flossie gave him a hand sign dismissing any need to apologize, then she added something that touched my heart. She added a back-and-forth rocking wrist pattern that has no exact Earth translation, the Pic bidirectional possessive meaning both "He is I" and "I am he."

The Pic-English dictionary translates the term as "soul mate", though its full meaning is deeper and more difficult to describe. On Earth, soul mates share interests and perspectives and secrets. On Whistlestop, to refer to another with a bidirectional possessive means that you consider the other person part of your conscience and morality. Flossie was saying that the concept of shame could not exist between us unless we were ashamed of ourselves. It was not a sexual bond at all, though in its own way just as deep. I was finally beginning to understand the lesson that Maayan had tried to teach me.

After her hand gesture, Flossie replied in English to Professor Feynman's earlier comment about her snout. "My role here is to observe problem-solving techniques, not to stomp on what I'm trying to observe."

It took me a second to realize what Flossie was talking about. "But you think you know how the Bayside crystal was formed?"

Flossie heard the hope in my voice. She nodded and flashed Professor Feynman a rapid series of chromatophore patterns. A moment later they were at the lab's electronic whiteboard, drawing equations and lattice configurations and whistling madly at each other. Ann and I stood aside and watched quietly. It was a sight to behold.

After a while, Ann tried to fill me in on what was going on. "Flossie is going over a lot of math on vacuoles and interstitials. I think... I think I'm getting this right. She's arguing that certain arrangements of lattice defects could strengthen the data area of a crystal. She's arguing that we need to examine the actual Bayside crystal."

"What's Professor Feynman whistling?" I whispered.

"He's insisting that it would be extremely unlikely that such a strengthening configuration would occur by chance, and… uh, that it's beyond even current technology to do it on purpose. I think that's what he said." Ann pressed her head against my hip and looked at me with her W-shaped eyes. "Most of this conversation is beyond me."

I grinned and scratched her neck affectionately. "You have a lot of company there, probably everyone else on the planet."

I looked at the clock again. It was approaching midnight, and at 20:00 tomorrow morning, Jorani and I would be in our two-semester course on Old Kingdom history with Professor Higgins, someone who insisted her students be bright and alert. But I couldn't just wander off now and leave Flossie and Professor Feynman here working on my thesis. It just seemed a rude thing to do.

Fortunately, they came to some kind of agreement. Professor Feynman announced he would try to get access to the Bayside crystal, which was currently in a museum on Long Island. We broke a few minutes later, Professor Feynman heading to faculty housing where he lived with Lieutenant Ellie, Flossie and Ann back to their dorm pod, and I hiking alone across a silent campus to my dorm. There was a stiff sea breeze coming off the ocean. It was almost cool enough for a jacket.

Along the way I could see the open field on the western edge of campus where a complex for married student housing would one day be built. It wasn't needed yet. Almost every student here would turn thirty in the year 3486, both humans and Pic, and that was the minimum legal age for marriage and officially living together. Where someone actually slept though, nobody cared, and right now Jorani was waiting for me in my dorm. I picked up my pace as I headed home.

Something wonderful had happened two days ago. The two student bodies, human and Pic, voted overwhelmingly to ask for integrated married housing. We'll have our small private family areas, but all the dining and recreational and childcare facilities would be shared. Our kids would grow up playing with each other, and that would be truly beautiful.

How long will it last? Perhaps for many years. Over the past semester, Karim persuaded the Pic that it would be more effective to bring Pic students to a human-culture university, rather than spread us humans out as teachers across the planet. After our graduation, perhaps a thousand or more new Pic undergrads each season would come to Providence for five weeks for Earth cultural immersion taught by us. That was the current plan, anyway. And I have to admit, Karim was right on this and I was wrong. We would learn to see each other as equals when we live side by side in groups, and not by having isolated pairs of humans living in cities with a half million Pic.

The option wouldn't appeal to everyone, of course, and it wouldn't last forever. The Pic were quite insistent that we adapt to their cultural norm of switching cities every nine years or less. But at the start of our adult careers here, it'd be an attractive opportunity to many, especially for couples who wanted to start their families early. Would it be the right choice for Jorani and me? I didn't know. We both had a lot of wanderlust. And the Pic military was very interested in eventually enlisting some humans. I'd had discussions with several officers already.

The Pic military... I remembered a conversation I'd had with Max a few days before he and Julie were betrothed. With one global government, the Pic debated whether to translate their law enforcement name as military or police. The group functioned as police, but also assumed many other responsibilities, including operating the world's deep sea fishing vessels. They had enlistment similar to Earth's armies but their operational authority was distributed to include organizations such as health services and ecology management. It was an interesting hybrid mix, and perhaps the word police would be more accurate. But the Pic were reluctant to tell Earth that they didn't have a military.

I finally reached my dorm, and took one more look towards the western stars before entering the building. This had turned out to be a very long day.

Two weeks later.
Time: Northern Summer 59, 3484 C.E. 56:53 (Time Zone 30)

After a couple of days of going our separate ways, I met Julie on the beach as planned, and we put down our towels a short distance from the receding surf. "Three hours to go," she commented. "Want to go for a swim?" The ocean was calm and the night unseasonably warm, and the light of the waxing gibbous moon was providing enough light to entertain the possibility.

"Sure." I turned and called out to a group of Pic classmates who were glad to be our lifeguards. The water was nice, about 22 C, just past the high point for the year, and it was a pleasure to swim past the breakers and float on the gentle rollers, holding hands with Jorani and gazing at the small, bright moon.

Our surrounding Pic were unusually quiet, floating peacefully with us and just appreciating the night's beauty. I felt a slender hand gently grab my foot, followed by a quick chirp. It was Julie, complimenting Jorani on her idea of coming out here. Max echoed the chirp nearby.

The moon was in the southwest sky and appeared to be a small version of Earth's moon, but appearances could be deceiving. In reality, it was slightly more massive but also thirty percent farther away, making it appear considerably smaller. The numbers resulted in a fascinating parallel with Earth on tidal forces. Solar tides on Whistlestop were the strength of Earth's lunar tides, and the lunar tides were strength of Earth's solar tides. The swap resulted in some interesting differences. Since the solar tides dominated on Whistlestop, high tides occurred worldwide around 20:00 and 50:00 local time, every day of the year. The synching of tides with the daily cycle drove evolution in different directions compared with Earth, especially for creatures who fed in tidal waters.

The ancient Storytellers of Wuthering Heights ran their society on a lunar calendar. But were they superstitious or just extremely practical? Six lunar synodic periods on Whistlestop added up to almost exactly one solar year. A lunar leap day was needed only once every thirty-five years, compared to every nineteen years for a solar calendar. And as Jorani once reminded me, the Storytellers were nocturnal. It would be natural for them align with the lunar cycle. It was a pity so little was known about the two Old Kingdom eras. They were both pre-industrial, roughly equivalent to Earth's Iron and Medieval Ages. Jorani and I would learn a lot more about the Second Old Kingdom in a course this coming semester.

I raised my head, and against the black southern horizon, saw the silhouette of a small barge floating about a hundred meters further out. I

204

sighed and squeezed Jorani's hand. We began swimming to shore. Back on the beach we shared our towels to dry each other then settled down for the show. By this time the beach was crowded, all the humans and I think all our Pic classmates and faculty. Maybe some had come just to be polite, but I think most were genuinely curious. The night's festivities were about to begin.

I was a little leery when I first heard the news. Our four emigrants from Italy had proposed a joint summer project on fireworks, and somewhat to my surprise, the Pic approved the request. Julie and I and probably half the campus stopped by their lab at least once to observe the magic in the making. A small hut was constructed at the edge of campus with extra-sturdy walls and a flimsy, clear plastic bubble roof. (In the event of a disaster, the Pic wanted the explosion to travel UP, not OUT.) All the work was done by hand. It was safer not to have machinery around, especially anything where metal rubbing against metal could cause a spark.

The human crowd began counting down the final seconds as midnight approached, and then everyone cheered when the fireworks went off right on time. Hello, 3485! It was a short display but nice, Roman candles sparkling the ocean around the barge while mortars lobbed about two dozen shells high into the black sky. I didn't expect the emotional effect, a brief but sharp pang of loss. After a full year on Pic, I had my first bout of homesickness, short but intense. The humans cheered, the Pic clapped politely in Earth fashion, then the show was over. Morning classes and the first day of our second year of school were fast approaching. It was time for bed.

Jorani and I headed for her dorm room. Seeing Jorani in a swimsuit usually got me hot for her, especially watching her change out of one. But after some gentle caresses we both realized it would be a quiet night. We rinsed off with a quick shower and were soon under a sheet, my hand lightly resting on Jorani's hip, her butt tucked into my groin. The open windows were letting in the sounds of campus and beyond. For a while some idiot was blowing a horn, but thankfully not for long. Afterwards I started to drift asleep, serenaded by the soothing whistles of night birds.

"Asleep?" Jorani whispered.

I gave a contented sigh and kissed the back of her head, breathing in the faint smell of ocean still present in her hair. "Not yet. You okay?"

"I guess. I didn't expect to like the fireworks as much as I did."

"Yeah. Me too." My arm came up from her hip to rest against her ribcage, then I curled my hand and cupped a firm breast. "I love you."

Jorani made a soft, purring noise. "I know. I love you too." A silent moment, then she asked, "Does it seem like a full year?"

"Yeah, it does."

"For me too, and it's still summer back home. Earth years seem so slow now."

"Yeah, surprising how easy it is to adjust to Whistlestop."

Jorani grunted. "Surprising how easy it is to prefer it."

"Hmm? You think so?"

Jorani paused a moment before answering. "Sure. The faster seasons are easier to appreciate. And except for your tiger, such peace!" Jorani turned to face me and kissed my nose, her secret playful way of asking if I wanted to talk for a while.

I smiled and became more awake. "Any difficulties at all, making the transition?"

Jorani blinked. "Ah, life on Whistlestop, now there's a question... Not much comes to mind, just old trivial stuff."

"Oh yeah? Like what?"

"Well... like playing wallyball. Our first season here, I'd be taking the game seriously, game on! And then my teammates would do something insane — attempt to hit the ball with their rumps or something then start frolicking around the court. It would shock me out of my competitive mindset and I would feel frustrated. I felt like scolding them."

"Hmmm.... Still an issue?"

"What? No, of course not. Now I just laugh and join in. The Pic have the right idea. Games are for fun and exercise; winning doesn't mean anything. It just took me a while to learn the lesson... Have you ever noticed Pic seem happiest when they're being zany? They're joyful."

"Yeah. I can remember watching professional ice hockey games as a kid, seeing fights break out. The last time I watched two Pic teams playing steeple-chase soccer, right in the middle of the match, the two teams started dancing with each other. What an incredible difference."

Jorani gave me another nose kiss, delightfully lingering and brushing with her soft lips. "I have something really interesting to tell you. A team of linguists from Haven University came to interview me. Julie and Max were there too. What was really amazing is that the linguists were treating Julie as one of their own. I know she's majoring in language arts, but I had no idea how much she's already published."

I nodded with a yawn. "I think it's true with many of our classmates. The Pic paired us with the brightest students on the planet. Julie's specialty is the evolution of the Pic language, all the way from Old Kingdom to the present. She's the one who first got me interested in the Bayside crystal."

"Ah. She also told me some of the people I would meet today were on the team that cracked the English language puzzle, mapped our video transmissions over the last century into native Pic."

"Oh, wow, really? Did they tell you how they did it?"

"Vaguely. I think they still had some reservations about revealing logistical details. But Julie told me afterwards that the listening network needed to be lot closer than 9.25 light days away. It took years to provision a large array of small, fake asteroids in solar orbits halfway between Earth and Venus."

"I'm not surprised. They're probably still active too. Lots of solar power at that radius." I thought for a moment. "I think I can guess how they did it. Launch probes directly behind the sun from Earth. With the faster orbital period, they could have deployed a full ring of satellites in a few years and stayed hidden the whole time."

"Sounds right. It's fortunate they were never detected. Earth would have felt it was being spied upon."

"Well, we were being spied upon." I sighed. "So anyway, how did your presentation go?"

Jorani chuckled. "It seems my thesis demo with Max took a lot of people by surprise. The linguists didn't think the human brain was capable of doing what I'm doing."

I gave Jorani a hug and kissed her cheek. "I don't know how you do it either."

"Aw, come on. You can do a full sentence now."

"I'm nothing like you."

Jorani wiggled, a Pic custom when being complimented. "Ever know anybody who can speed-read?"

"Yep. You know her too. Wichapi Longfeather. She gave me a demo once in Colorado. Amazing stuff."

"Well, I'm speed-listening. You need a strange mix of concentration, patience, and relaxation. And then magically the gibberish suddenly becomes little snippets of conversation… Anyway, the linguists want to do extensive testing, figure out in more detail what I'm doing then develop a training program for the rest of us. They're petitioning for me to have traveling rights to Haven."

I yawned. "Sounds really great."

"Yeah. So, how was your day? Anything exciting happen, besides this morning I mean?"

"I was talking to Professor Feynman on the beach before you showed up. He said the Bayside conservators have agreed in principle to let us make a quantum map of the crystal."

"Hey, wonderful! And about time!"

"Don't get too excited. First they want to see test data on the X-ray laser Dr. Feynman is building. They want proof the crystal won't be permanently altered."

"But they think the crystal is a fake…"

"So what? Even as a fake, it's thousands of years old. If some jokester in Egypt built a fake pyramid four thousand years ago, don't you think people on Earth would still want to preserve it?"

Jorani laughed. "That's not a fair analogy! The fake pyramid would be as old as the real ones. How could you call it a fake?"

"Well, yeah, okay. How about a fake cave painting or something?"

Jorani laughed even harder. "Prehistoric forgeries? Unbelievable!"

I echoed her laugh. "In any event, our plan is to do the certification tests this autumn and then map the real crystal during the school break."

Jorani groaned. "That long? We have to wait a full season?"

I brushed her hair and cheek with the back of my hand. "Everything nice and easy, that's our motto. No rush, nothing to draw attention."

"Think you'll learn anything?"

"My gut says yes. Maybe something I'm not expecting."

"Yeah…" Jorani gave a sleepy yawn. "Speaking of surprises, how about the one this morning?"

"The field trips? Yeah." In a gathering after breakfast, the faculty astonished us by saying that at the end of the winter semester one season from now, we humans would have the right for field trips to other worlds, the same as any other college-age students. In their thirty-six thousand years of exploration, the automated probe system had catalogued dozens of planets where Pic (or humans!) might conceivably survive without advanced technology, though none were as close as the wonderful match of Earth and Whistlestop. Five such worlds had been discovered in the Common Era, and there were three portal gateways at each of them.

And the announcement wasn't just for us. The World Council made a public release of something they haven't done in a hundred years… the current location of one of the interstellar portals in transit. There was a second portal being routed to enter Earth's solar system. It was eighty-four light-days from Earth now, beginning a deceleration of one standard gravity and manned by military personnel tasked with converting the probe to a second Pic transport. The ship was scheduled to reach Earth a year from now, on or about Northern Autumn 0, 3486.

I did a quiet calculation earlier today. The portal's velocity was just under seventy percent of light-speed now. Remembering my time with Flossie on the high plateau, I was guessing the deceleration maneuver began yesterday.

Jorani's hand came and rested on mine. "Any idea where you want to go first?"

"Well, Enigma seems obvious."

"Everybody wants to go there, pick up a gold brick as a souvenir." Jorani chuckled. "Maybe we should go first, beat the crowds."

"Right… And I definitely want to visit a certain lunar valley."

"The old portal depot? I thought it was nothing more than an underground room next to an empty parking lot."

"I still want to check it out. And another world too, the one called Sorrows' End."

"Ah, the one with the alien telescopes. Yeah, that's intriguing. You're thinking of the satellite moon, right? Not the planet itself."

I yawned. "The planet."

Jorani was starting to sound sleepy too. "You can do that?"

I nodded and said casually, "...if you're there as part of a thesis field trip."

"But I thought the planet's gravity is too high."

"It's not that high."

"Well... See if you can still say that when you're standing there." Jorani gave a sleepy yawn then a small jolt. "What thesis? What are you up to?"

I laughed. "Not mine this time. Isaac was awarded a grant from the Haven Science Foundation to do a map of the plate tectonics on Sorrows' End for his summer thesis. This'll be the trip we collect the data."

"We? How did you get involved with this? And do I detect the influence of Flossie?"

"Uh, yeah, she asked me and Julie to tag along, make it a foursome. We jumped at the chance. The Pic have studied the satellite, but the planet itself is pristine. Want a mountain named after you?"

"One measly mountain?"

"No, of course not. I'll pick a big one."

"How about a mountain range?"

Inspiration struck. "Maybe I'll name a continent after you. How about Jorania?"

"Yeah, Jorania. That would be nice... but I still think the gravity is too high. Watch your step." She turned and nestled her warm rump against me again, giving a deep sigh before silence. Tomorrow would be a big day, the first day of our second year at Providence University. We finally got wise and went to sleep.

Chapter 12

Four weeks later.
Time: Northern Autumn 42, 3485 22:11 Time Zone 30

It was early morning in the middle of the last school week of the autumn term, and I was in my first-period class writing a short essay on the last years of the Second Old Kingdom. I had about half an hour left to do some easy polishing, and I took a moment to stretch and enjoy the bright sunlight streaming in through the windows. Daylight now was something to appreciate. We were approaching the winter solstice and the sun had started its brief journey along the horizon an hour ago. It would be dark twilight by the time the school day ended at 40:00.

Jorani was sitting at the desk on my right, and she was deeply engrossed in her writing. We had both found this two-semester course with Professor Higgins fascinating... First Old Kingdom (circa 53500 to 52300 BCE) during the summer, followed by Second Old Kingdom history (circa 50100 to 49200 BCE) now in the autumn. The two Old Kingdoms were roughly equivalent to Earth's Iron Age and Renaissance Era, but with many interesting differences.

Many of the differences were tied to geography and Pic physiology. The world's great ocean was a formidable challenge to ancient Pic. Though the First Old Kingdom duplicated much of the technology of Earth's Roman and Chinese Empires (concrete, metal working, bridges, sewers and aqueducts supporting urban centers), the Pic were working with two great disadvantages. They had no animal labor such as horses and no deep-sea ships. It was not hard to see why. Pic didn't have the shoulder strength for endurance rowing, and their quadruped design made it almost impossible for them to climb the rigging of sail boats. So even during the height of the First Old Kingdom Era, with urban centers holding populations of one hundred thousand or more, the only boats around were cargo rafts that would be pulled across rivers with ropes and pulleys. There were tales of incredibly bold attempts to venture beyond Genesis with drifting arks, but then city-state warfare led to the collapse of the First Old Kingdom. Further efforts to explore the globe would have to wait another two thousand years.

The era of the Second Old Kingdom was perhaps my favorite period in Pic history. It was truly an age of enlightenment, and much of modern Pic philosophy found its roots there. There was fabulous art, fine craftsmanship, the elimination of male slavery, the birth of democratic government, and great leaps of understanding in mathematics and the sciences. And in the two centuries between 49500 and 49300 BCE, the Pic went from lumbering rafts on rivers to efficient sailing vessels similar to Yankee Clipper ships, but with remarkably ingenious arrays of pulleys and jointed masts that eliminated the need to climb riggings. There were still no mechanical engines, but the Pic finally had the technology to explore their world.

And in the end, the exploration proved disastrous. Treasure Island was the last of the great island continents to be explored in detail, not surprisingly since it was on the opposite side of the planet from Genesis and filled with mountainous ravines and canyons. It wasn't until the year 49237 BCE when a Pic expedition made first contact with the Storytellers. Exactly what happened next was unclear, but it was universally agreed that the first encounter was a disaster.

There were many fragments of knowledge from the forty-year intersection of Pic and Storyteller cultures, starting off with the account of the first Pic expedition killing several Storytellers with crossbow bolts as they glided overhead. The tragedy didn't end there. Most of the expedition was slaughtered during its torturous, frantic journey back to the coast.

What followed was four decades of sporadic contact as both species slowly recognized the intelligence of the other. There were many contradictory fragments of what this time was like. Some accounts stated the meetings were stiff and awkward, while others told of the two species making considerable effort to get past their earlier misunderstandings.

And then catastrophe struck. Perhaps it was a Storyteller virus that mutated in a Pic body. Perhaps it was the other way around. Regardless, both the Pic and the Storytellers were hit with a lethal plague that collapsed their populations. The disease sent Whistlestop back into the dark ages for the next eleven thousand years, and the Storytellers did not survive the journey. When the Pic finally revisited Treasure Island near the beginning of the First New Kingdom, they found that the Storytellers had become extinct.

There was a short bong signaling the end of first-period class. I transmitted my essay and headed to my next class, Intro to Pic Poetry. My PA beeped as soon as I stepped out of the no-contact coordinates of the classroom.

"Hello?"

"Steve? It's Karim. Where are you?"

"Uh, Complex-three, southern end on the second floor. I'm just leaving history class. What's up?"

Karim allowed a hint of exasperation to creep into his voice. "I've been trying to reach you."

"Ah. Professor Higgins insists on silent PAs during class."

"Have you heard about the Earth update?"

I blinked. "No. What was in it?"

"That's just it. It hasn't arrived. Has anyone in the government tried to contact you?"

I looked at the time, 22:46, and began to worry. The report was late by two hours, and that was unprecedented. I told Karim I'd get back to him and tried to contact Maayan. There was no response.

Three Pic hours previously...

An alpha female known to Earth as Admiral Hillarie was in her command net, overseeing the smooth function of the transport's return to its berth in Antarctica. The ship had departed Brussels shortly after midnight, an hour ahead of schedule, and upon liftoff ship-time reverted to Universal, so the time display on the bridge currently read 23:35, Sunday, October 17, 2100. Other ship displays were also based in Earth units. Hillarie thought it was a bit paranoid for the Pic to hide their own measurement unit from the humans, but she had long become accustomed to the nuisance.

Ship velocity was over six thousand kilometers per hour and still accelerating, and they were currently passing the French southern coast. The seven-hundred-kilometer trip across the Mediterranean would take five and half minutes, by which time the ship would be near its planned cruising altitude of eighty-three kilometers. On large visual and tactical displays around the control room, Sardinia was clearly visible one hundred and fifty kilometers to the east. The island would be too small for legal habitation on Whistlestop, but it was similar in shape and size to a nature preserve where Admiral Hillarie earned her Ranger qualifications almost a Pic century ago, and she allowed herself an idle moment to admire and compare Sardinia's features. Then she returned to reviewing the planned test firing of the ship's weapons systems that would occur over the South Atlantic later in the flight, after the ship crossed the equator and the western coast of Africa.

A short distance to her left, a team of specialists were monitoring feeds from a dozen ground bases and satellites. The Pic transport was the most connected mobile site on the planet. A vast array of official and complimentary data feeds were giving information from every corner of the world, including prized satellite surveillance courtesy of the USNA military. Much of the data was being modulated in real-time to virtual photons and portal-exchanged to Whistlestop.

This had been their longest stay outside of Antarctica yet, lasting almost a month, and perhaps the most productive. The Pic had engaged with Earth's World Bank, and over the last three weeks had deposited kilotons of rare metals in Brussels' warehouses, to be used to sponsor worldwide environmental repair. There was also ongoing technical collaboration on a new pandemic that was sweeping the world. A highly contagious fungus had appeared in Eastern Europe that was attacking the human respiratory system. The collaboration had gone deeper than anyone had planned. Disease specialists from Whistlestop had remained in Brussels to continue their research, and Hillarie's third-in-command Captain Christopher had also remained behind as liaison.

Seconds after leaving the Mediterranean and crossing the North African coast, transport speed reached nine thousand kilometers per hour, approaching flight-plan cruising velocity. But prior to the expected decrease in portal thrust, several monitors recorded flickering lights on the eastern horizon. Multiple alarms began sounding, followed by a flashing yellow warning to prepare for emergency acceleration. Admiral Hillarie had less than a minute to override the computer-driven decision. She chirped a rapid series of questions to her bridge crew.

Her sensor and communications teams responded simultaneously. An enormous supersonic shock wave was building along the eastern horizon, something that would become planetary in scale, and autonomous ship processors had concluded it was the result of multiple nuclear detonations. Sensor specialists were saying the energy release was so intense that it had blown out the atmosphere over the blast sites, and the communications team quickly confirmed the analysis. Contact with LEO (low-Earth orbit) satellites appeared to have been disrupted by an electromagnetic pulse, but before the loss, a USNA surveillance feed had shown three simultaneous fireballs at Tehran, Qom, and Yazd four thousand kilometers to the east. Hillarie ordered an Iranian industrial map to appear on one of her tactical displays and saw that these were Iran's three principal cities engaged in nuclear fuel processing. Primary mission orders were now in effect. Grimacing at the insanity that was unfolding, she allowed the acceleration maneuver to proceed. After a final warning bong, the ship rotated and began a hard, full-vertical acceleration.

The experienced g-force would be three times standard Whistlestop gravity, including the pull from Earth, which at their current height was 9.55 m/s^2. The Pic would risk both neck injury and breathing difficulty with anything greater. Lying on her back and sinking into the net that supported her body, Hillarie thought wistfully of the g-suits humans used to withstand much higher accelerations. Years ago her recommendations were ignored that Pic experiment with the concept.

Hillarie studied a ship monitor and was alarmed by the height and density of the shock wave. "Is that going to hit us?" she chirped to her sensor team.

"Not with our current acceleration," chirped a crewman. "It'll pass underneath, miss us. Not by much…" He gave a whistle of astonishment. "Admiral, are you seeing this? I'm reading… the boulders in the shock wave! They're going suborbital!"

Seventy seconds into the escape maneuver, at a height of one hundred and thirty-one kilometers, the Pic transport received a high-priority demand for communication on a hardened military channel. After delaying as long as she dared, Hillarie whistled to her crew to open a video line, and was relieved to see USNA General James Collins, the on-duty liaison officer between the U.N. and the Pic.

"Admiral Hillarie, you have deviated from your flight plan. Your flight clearance to Antarctica is cancelled. Return to Brussels immediately."

"I have priority orders from my government, Jim. In the event of nuclear warfare, I must vacate the planet." Hillarie allowed her muzzle to express the sadness and frustration she was feeling.

The human facing her was grim. "You began your ascent seconds after the explosions. People will interpret your escape as an admission of guilt."

Hillarie's muzzle flared with annoyance. "We had nothing to do with this! Think it through! The conjecture is absurd!"

"Your return to Brussels will prove it is absurd."

"Returning to Brussels won't prove anything, and it will place my ship at risk. My first priority is to ensure this ship's technology does not fall into human hands." Hillarie glanced at her monitors. Two minutes and nine seconds into the escape maneuver, ship's altitude was two hundred forty-six kilometers and vertical velocity was now matching horizontal velocity at nine thousand kilometers per hour. Earth had only seconds left to decide whether to fire their super-fast interceptor missiles.

Give them something! Hillarie's mind screamed at her. *Give them something to hope with!*

"Jim, the fusion trial," she said out loud. "It's going extremely well. The students are in their second year of studies." General Collins blinked. This was first comment the Pic had made about the trial since it began.

"We are opening our interstellar network to them, the fruit of our space exploration, field trips to other worlds. The universe is filled with life! But intelligent life is rare. Besides Earth and ourselves, we have only one other example. It's barren now, a planet at the outer edge of the temperate zone for liquid water."

Hillarie stared at the human face in front of her and thought she had the General's full attention. *Good!* she thought. *Keep it going!* "The evidence is ancient, the Oligocene epoch on Earth, twenty-five to thirty million years ago. There are blast craters across the planet. But it wasn't always so. They had technology, enough to leave artifacts, advanced enough to leave magnificent broad-spectrum telescopes on their satellite moon." Hillarie paused. "We will not give Earth the chance to bring nuclear insanity to Whistlestop!"

The liaison stared at her. "Whistlestop?"

"The name our human citizens have given their new home."

Collins glanced at the monitors beside him and sighed. "We no longer have a flight window to intercept you. The U.N. command is standing down." He paused and added, "Did we have a chance?"

Admiral Hillarie thought for a moment of her ship's considerably defensive capability and tried to shrug despite the high-g acceleration. "No comment, other than to say I was more worried about the political fallout. An attack on this vessel would have ruined everything."

"What happens now?"

"My current orders are to remain in contact at a distance of one light-minute. Our conversations are going to be a bit awkward with the time delay."

The General tapped his earplug. "I'm directed to request your participation in an emergency meeting of the U.N. Security Council. It will start within the hour. Can you delay your departure?"

Hillarie thought for a moment. "I have some discretion, and will petition my superiors for more."

"What about the Pic at Brussels? And in Antarctica?"

"We are all volunteers. We accepted the risks." Admiral Hillarie sighed. There were more than three hundred Pic currently on Earth, and her orders were to abandon them.

At four hundred and fifty seconds into the acceleration maneuver, the Pic transport reached Earth escape velocity at a height 2,120 kilometers above the Earth's surface. Both to relieve the physical stress on her crew and as a token of trust to Earth, Hillarie cut the effective g-force on her crew to two standard Whistlestop gravities. A half-hour later when the U.N. meeting started, the ship was forty-eight thousand kilometers from Earth and achieving escape velocity from the solar system. Fully satisfied with the safety of her ship, Hillarie further reduced acceleration to standard Earth gravity and began the slow and tedious process of explaining the new relationship that would exist between humans and Pic. Meanwhile, it was eighteen Earth minutes past the end of a duty shift. Part of the crew began to interchange with replacements from Far Rockaway.

Four days later.
Time: Friday, 12:27 PM, October 22, 2100 Central European Time (11:27 AM U.T.)
Time: Northern Autumn 46, 3485 36:36 Time Zone 30
Location: Earth, 51 degrees 0' North, 4 degrees 21` East, 17 km north of downtown Brussels, Belgium

Heavy traffic slowed the motorcade as they approached the front gates, and Christopher leaned and pressed his dolphin-shaped head against the car window, gazing at the thin, silent crowd that had gathered to see him pass. The scene was one of overwhelming grayness with the midday light hidden by thick layers of rolling clouds. Trying to shake off a heavy feeling of gloom, the beta Pic concentrated on the destination before him, one of Belgium's premier medical research facilities. In spite of his fatigue, Christopher felt considerable excitement over the opportunity to be with his own kind again. Working with humans and their lack of trust was so frustrating!

It was hard judging the mood of the humans outside the car… blank, cold faces peering at him through misty rain. Rain and ash had been falling over much of Eurasia for days now, most of the world actually, but the forecast for Brussels called for brief clearing later in the day, and amazingly the ash, while bearing traces of plutonium and other radioactive particulates, was below dangerous levels. Earth seemed to have dodged a planet-killing bullet, though it was not clear how. The catastrophes in Iran were riddled with technical mysteries, riddles that were becoming more puzzling each passing day, riddles that were adding momentum to a pendulum swing of suspicions. What exactly had happened in Iran?

The motorcade finally entered the secure facility, and Christopher spent the better part of an hour passing through a series of access gates. It was a struggle not to see the complex as a multi-layered prison, but when he reached the Pic residential quarters, the joy of being with other Pic banished his gloom. All five Pic medical researchers were in a large living area, the two alphas Alice and Simone, beta Andrea, and gammas Paul and Molly. By chance, all six Pic genders were now present. Alice, the youngest member of the group, gave Christopher a very joyous chirp of welcome that included the phrase, "The set is now complete!"

"English only," Christopher replied as the researchers gathered around him.

"Why?" asked Paul in English.

Christopher muzzle flashed a dim pattern of resignation. "I assume we're being recorded, audio and visual. I don't want to hide anything from our hosts."

Molly, the team's director, nodded. "That was our assumption too, the surveillance. The lack of privacy is... a bit difficult."

Alice spoke up. "But the facilities are good. Excellent food, lots of space, a place to exercise, and yesterday the humans finished installing a proper communal shower for us." Seeing a query on Christopher's snout, she added, "Over the last few days, we've decided to accept each other as family." As she spoke, the sun peeked through a hole in the clouds and illuminated the trees outside. The group turned to see the first break in the weather.

Christopher had to admit it was pretty. Earth's sun had a more buttery, yellow color, compared to the orange tint of Whistlestop, but it was hard to appreciate the difference in the ice palace of the Darwin Mountains. Here though, the sky was filled with reds and yellows and streaks of purple, and there were large windows overlooking an inner courtyard of Acers and Magnolias. Christopher found the scene very pleasing to the eye. "It would be a beautiful planet without the damage," he said softly.

Several of the other Pic flashed wistful muzzle patterns of agreement.

"So," said Christopher, "I assume we have much to tell each other. Why don't you go first? Have you been treated kindly? Any progress on the medical research?"

Andrea spoke up, her muzzle pattern holding a rippling pattern of pride. "We've cracked the problem of the human plague! I mean the origin of it. Simone made a key finding."

Christopher flashed a muzzle pattern of congratulations as he turned to Simone and said, "Another goblin laid to rest, I hope?" Over the years, the Pic based on Earth had adopted the word "goblin" to refer to any problem that human rumors would blame on the Pic. The ability of the human mind to dream up conspiracy fantasies never ceased to amaze Christopher. The wild stories were often so fantastically convoluted and self-contradictory that he sometimes felt that the general human population was immune to data and rational thought.

"Killed entirely," replied Simone with a nod, "except for those who believe in zombie goblins." Christopher understood the term — a ridiculous idea thoroughly debunked that refused to stay dead. With their seemingly magic portals, there were some Earth scientists who speculated that the Pic could travel in time and mettle with Earth's history. The idea was absolutely absurd as far as Christopher knew, but the problem was, how do you prove to somebody that you haven't altered their timeline?

"Officially we're done," added Paul. "But you should know, the humans are asking for more. They're asking us to find a cure, a vaccine, and if possible they want help to create a bio-agent to attack the fungus."

Christopher frowned. "I can understand their desire. But we agreed on limiting the technology transfer. Can you help them with their research without revealing new methodologies?"

Andrea spoke for the group. "We doubt if that's possible, not with this. That's our dilemma. If we collaborate on researching a counter-agent, what we teach them could probably be weaponized. That's what started all this. Humans took bio-warfare to a new level, created a monstrosity. It's a painful moral dilemma, refusing to help."

Christopher frowned again, more heavily this time. "So, the plague fungus is a human creation?"

"The Balkans," replied Paul. "We have proof in the labs here, something functionally equivalent to the new plague. It's a combination of two different bio-agents from the Balkan war."

"They fused," said Alice. "A double-helix lock and key. The current plague is a genetic recombination, a Serbian viral toxin that deactivates an Albanian fungus death code. The resulting fungus is virile, able to flower and propagate. That's how the spores moved off the battlefield… It's not a true fungus, of course. It's a…" Alice paused, chirped loudly, then turned to a wall and cried out, "That's the Pic word for a fungal-virus hybrid! You humans were insane to create such weapons!"

Molly chirped a whistle burst, a Pic idiom, which loosely translated as, "You are correct, but you don't have to rub their snouts in it."

Christopher asked the group, "How much pressure are they using on you?"

"Just moral persuasion so far," replied Molly. "It's a horrible way to die. The pseudo spores do what they're designed to do, inflame the lungs, a super-allergic reaction. Humans drown on their own mucus."

"And how widespread is it likely to be?"

Andrea shuddered. "Without an effective response, I think humanity is facing a global catastrophe. Every bird and mammal on the planet is potentially at risk, though the fatalities so far seem limited to humans. It all depends on how heavily the humans tailored the viral components to their own species. We're still investigating that."

Christopher blinked. "Are we at risk?"

Alice spoke up. "Have you kept up with your boosters?"

"Of course."

"Then you should be okay. Our blood doesn't have the right pH for the fungus anyway."

Andrea added softly, "We'd like to help, we really would, but we have our orders."

Christopher nodded his understanding. "I was promised contact with Admiral Hillarie tomorrow. We'll explain the situation."

Alpha Simone's muzzle flashed a brief pattern of pleading impatience. "We were allowed to watch public news, but nothing makes sense. The new reports say you were at the U.N. meetings. Do you know what's going on? What about our people in Antarctica? Are they okay?"

"I would assume so. I've heard nothing to the contrary. And as for the rest, it's a bizarre situation. The deep answer to your question is no, I don't know what's going on. But I'll tell you what I know." The group took a moment to sit Pic-fashion without chairs, facing Christopher and waiting for his story.

"The first day was chaotic. Admiral Hillarie was granted a tele-presence at an emergency U.N. meeting. I was there too. I think the world almost destroyed itself that day. The Israelis were maddening, saying they were not responsible but refusing to say if they had the means to launch such an attack. They also started accusing Iran of launching the nuclear attack on them earlier this year. They said they had absolute proof, that all three earlier bombs bore isotopic signatures from the plutonium breeder facilities at Qom."

"So this was a revenge attack?" asked Molly.

"The Israelis deny it. Their ambassador insisted they have damning evidence of Iran's earlier involvement but had not yet decided how to respond. The USNA and maybe a few other countries were willing to give them the benefit of the doubt. Iran's neighbors, though, were threatening a massive military response. I believe the humans came very close to a planetary holocaust."

"How did they avoid it?" whispered Andrea.

"During the first day, the neighboring countries were too busy coping with ash and blast effects on their own territories." Christopher flashed a pattern of bewilderment on his muzzle. "After that, the physical evidence of the attack began to be available, seismic analysis and satellite reconnaissance. It was strange enough to make the humans pause, shift the blame away from Israel."

"Shift it to us, you mean?" asked Simone.

Christopher sighed. "It wasn't a missile attack. The explosions had to come from the ground. There was no sensor evidence of missiles, and the three explosions occurred within milliseconds. No one can time missile flights that accurately. And the seismic data are filled with strange echoes. This is all very preliminary, but Earth scientists are talking about underground explosions. But that also seems absurd. All three explosions occurred precisely at three nuclear facilities. If the

Israelis are responsible, they managed to insert massive nuclear devices into the lowest levels of three highly secure areas. Is that possible?"

"So what's left?" asked Paul.

"Just the facts," replied Christopher, "and the facts are strange. The explosions generated fantastic amounts of heat, expanses of white-hot magma kilometers in diameter, and by their lack of cooling, the humans think the pools run deep, hundreds of meters at least. The heat is creating its own weather patterns around the sites, annular convection rolls reaching into the stratosphere."

"Three volcanoes?" asked Simone. "Super volcanoes? Did the bombs crack the planet's crust?"

"Unknown. The seismic data suggests not, but the heat release suggests yes. It should be beyond even the largest fusion bombs to melt cubic kilometers of rock, but that's what happened." Christopher paused and added, "The lava appears to be boiling hot, gaseous rock bubbling up into the atmosphere."

Molly frowned. "Water vapor, perhaps?"

Christopher shook and stretched his neck high, a Pic gesture for no. "True gaseous rock. It's consistent with the estimates for the original blasts, temperatures above five thousand Celsius a hundred kilometers from the blast sites, hot enough to partially ionize the atmosphere."

Molly blinked. "There must be nothing left."

"Very little," agreed Christopher. "It's beyond carbonization. Most of Iran has been reduced to ultra-hot dust. And yet, the fallout is manageable, remarkably free of nuclear decay products. The explosions seemed to have been focused somehow; the heat footprints of the explosions focused downward into the rock."

"Shaped nuclear charges? That's not possible," Simone muttered.

"Not possible for us, you mean," countered Andrea. "Humans are more advanced than we are with nuclear power."

"Andrea, it's absurd!" Simone replied. "What would you use as a reflector for a gigaton explosion, neutron star material?"

"Would that work?"

"I don't know! My point is, where would you get it?"

Christopher flashed a muzzle pattern asking for calm. "It's impossible for both our technologies. But humans don't know our limits.

The result is a goblin of epic proportions. This might terminate the interaction between our two worlds."

"And where does that leave us?" chirped Andrea as she turned to him, for a moment forgetting to talk in English.

"It leaves us here. The Council won't risk returning the transport to Earth under such conditions." Christopher shifted awkwardly on his feet. "I don't want to give false hope. We must be realistic. We may be stranded here." Christopher flashed an apologetic muzzle pattern signaling he had nothing more to say. There was a long moment of silence, and then he was startled to see a flash of amusement on Alice's snout.

"Well," she said, "we always have the cone-head solution."

"The what?"

"It's a movie we watched last night, a hundred years old by the look of it. All we have to do is point our snouts up in the air, like this," Alice said, demonstrating, "and the humans will not be able to distinguish us from other humans. The movie proves it. We will blend in among the blunt skulls!"

Christopher stared with incredulity, then cracked a Pic smile. "I should watch the movie?"

"You should watch the movie."

There was nothing else to do, at least for a while, and after the hectic pace of the last few days, Christopher welcomed the opportunity to relax. The six Pic were soon gathered around the room's entertainment center watching a comedy from a lost age.

Not long after the movie started, Alice curled up against Christopher's side. He turned and smiled at her and thought of the group's dossiers. It was a young crowd, and every Pic here except Molly was unattached. Alice was the youngest, not quite forty, and Christopher thought she looked a decade younger. Her blouse had an open back, and he rested his arm on her lightly, curling his fingers in the stiff black feather-fur between her shoulder blades. Alice turned so that her muzzle could be seen only by him and flashed him a ripple of pure happiness. *Ah, the resilience of the alphas*, he thought. *I should learn from their courage.* With warm Alice pressing against him, he returned to watching what he considered to be a truly absurd but amusing movie.

Meanwhile, 1.5 light-seconds away...

Admiral Hillarie was alone in a small conference room near the bridge, reviewing ship status on a monitor and awaiting a report from her chief engineering tech. The report was long overdue, days late, and to relieve her impatience, Hillarie closed her eyes and contemplated the crossroads that Humans and Pic had reached. Which fork would they take?

Above Hillarie's head were six Earth-meters of dense cosmic-ray shielding, and 450,000 kilometers beyond that, Earth. The ship was in a powered twelve-hour polar orbit around the planet, roughly duplicating the twelve-hour polar orbits of hybrid GPS/communications-relay satellites much closer to Earth. The ship's orbit was a compromise, close enough to Earth for interactive conversation, but far enough away to make beam-weapon targeting impossible, especially with the high-frequency random variations that were programmed into flight control. The orbit gave the crew an effective gravity equal to home, and by traveling at 66 km/sec, they had more than enough velocity to fly out of the solar system in the event of a power loss.

The door chimed, and a moment later a gamma e-tech was standing before the admiral, apologizing for the delay and giving a report on the failure of the test firing of the ship's weapons system. It was news Hillarie was secretly dreading.

"What I don't understand," Hillarie chirped at the end, "is why diagnostics didn't pick this up. We were showing an operational system until the moment of firing."

"It was a fluke," replied the e-tech. "A cascade event, one in a trillion. A primary failure in laser control caused a secondary failure in X-ray driver electronics that created an erroneous voltage that precisely cancelled the fault signal." The gamma sighed. "We were incredibly lucky."

"Lucky?"

"We left Earth an hour ahead of schedule. If we had been at Brussels at the time of the explosions..." The e-tech gave a muzzle pattern of a fatalistic shrug. "You would have followed orders to evacuate. The humans would have had an extended window to shoot us down. And they would have succeeded! End of ship, end of us, end of everything, probably. I think the Council would have terminated the fusion trial."

Hillarie nodded then asked casually, "Could this have been a software problem?"

The e-tech flashed a muzzle frown and chirped, "Admiral?"

"Could software have driven the chips to fail the way they did?"

Her chief thought for a long moment. "Theoretically, I suppose. But it would be an elaborate process, statistically impossible for a programming error."

Hillarie worked to keep her face and muzzle impassive. "Well done, chief. Dismissed."

Meanwhile, 814 Earth light-years away...
Time: Northern Autumn 46, 3485 41:03 Time Zone 30

It was an hour after the last classes of the term, and most of my classmates (human and otherwise) were in the student lounges discussing the latest from Earth and their plans for the upcoming thirteen-day IAP (Independent Activities Period). But for me, leisure thoughts were far from my mind. The last sixty hours had been a whirlwind of changed plans and unexpected preparations, and I was currently in my dorm room making a final check of my gear. With the upcoming time-zone shift, this would be a seventy-hour day for me. I was facing a long evening of lab work followed by an overnight journey via military boat, the start of a ten-day combination field-survey survival test. My mind was racing a bit, reviewing my training this term and all the things I needed to remember about equatorial woodland environments. On the bright side, the following day would be delightfully empty, an easy day of camping, and the anticipation of it helped me from thinking of the bizarre disaster unfolding on Earth.

Leaving my room, I met Max. He had been standing outside waiting for me. He flashed a muzzle query. "Need any help?"

The true answer would have been to say I was fine, but Jorani had been coaching me about situations like this. "Sure, thanks." I handed over a couple of light bags which Max threw over his back.

"Where's your kayak?" asked Max as we started walking.

"Procurement picked it up this morning; it should be aboard the hydrofoil by now."

"Ah..."

Julie, Max, and I were scheduled to transfer to Far Rockaway to Haven to Bayside starting at 43:50 this evening. Julie and Max were going to spend their holidays visiting both sides of their extended families, many of whom currently lived in Bayside and Tranquility on Long Island. I had about ten hours of work this evening with Professor Feynman setting up hardware to quantum-map the Bayside crystal — nothing too exciting, just a tedious set-up then an even more boring ten-day period for the automatic scanners to do their job. Quantum mapping was a very slow process compared to just reading the crystal.

So when I was planning this trip early in the term, it occurred to me that it would be a perfect opportunity to qualify for Ranger-II, and I took the idea to Maayan. She was rather bemused and said I was welcome to try, but that my chances were close to zero of getting the necessary Council permission. Undaunted, I talked to Jorani about applying, and she came up with the brilliant idea of making a proposal that would benefit me even if it were rejected.

So I did some research on Parks and Conservation survey requests and found an open request on a rare species that no Pic wanted to tackle, something that would require a river journey. And true to form, the Pic fabricated a beautiful kayak for me to practice with as my request went through the approval process. Last week, as expected, my proposal was shot down. And yesterday, in complete shock, I was informed that the rejection had been rescinded.

With all the insanity on Earth, the plan seemed so out of place now. But I couldn't think of a clear reason to back out, and it seemed almost insulting to try.

"Steven? Are you comfortable doing survey work on bleeder birds?"

"Yep, the famous black turduckens of Long Island. I'm all set."

Max snorted sarcastically. "Famous indeed! Why do you call them that? Nobody off campus would know what you're talking about!" He paused and added, "I assume you're fully informed about their behaviors. I've lived on Long Island for years. It's mostly a benign environment.

Bleeder birds are the top predators on the island. They're one of the few dangers you'll face."

"Lieutenant Ellie drilled me well. Besides the protective gear, I'll have flash caps, gas caps, ultrasonic screamers... In an instant, I can be the last thing a turducken wants to see, smell, or hear."

"Well, just remember to keep your goggles on, and don't be bashful about using your defenses. These birds have a nasty reputation. Decoys will try to distract you while other bleeders go for your eyes."

"I think they're fascinating. There's a species of desert hawks in the USNA that hunt squirrels in packs, but no Earth raptors go after big game animals. No way."

"But you have the concept on Earth. It was covered in my course on historical Earth cultures: death by a thousand cuts. Once their prey is blinded, that's how bleeder birds kill." Max's muzzle showed a dim pattern of curiosity, and as we stepped outside my dorm building, he returned to his earlier question. "Why do you insist on calling them turduckens? The term bleeder bird is an accurate translation from Pic."

I smiled as I pulled up my collar against the cold wind. "Just being playful, I guess." I took a second to pull up two pictures on my PA. "The bird looks like a lanky turkey with a pterodactyl head."

Max appeared unconvinced as he studied my display. "Not really. Is the bleeder head shape called turducken on Earth?"

"No. Turducken on Earth means a mix of turkey, duck, and chicken."

"What? But none of those birds are carnivorous..." Max blinked his W-eyes. "Mix? You mean as in a meal?"

"Yeah, a meal. A turducken is a chicken stuffed inside a duck that's stuffed inside a turkey."

"What?" Max's muzzle held a pattern of total confusion. "Are you saying you want to eat a bleeder bird?"

"No, not at all."

"Then I don't get it."

"Nothing to get. Sometimes humans are beyond understanding."

Max gave a final snort. "Agreed!" As we were about to enter the portal complex, he added much more quietly, "Any idea how you got permission to do this?"

"Haven't a clue."

I awoke a few minutes before dawn to the unfamiliar but soothing sounds of subtropical shore birds and surf. The first day of my wilderness trial had been a delightfully easy time of rest and acclimation, camping on the beach at the mouth of Crooked Lazy River. Today though, I would start my journey into turducken territory. As I loaded my kayak, I took a last look at the great global ocean. It was hard to shake the feeling of being on an idyllic vacation, and I reminded myself why Pic thought a test like this was so demanding. They were very social creatures, and their Ranger-II qualifiers rarely extend more than ten kilometers from a Parks base. What I was doing, ten days of real enforced solitude, would be a truly difficult challenge for them.

I'd studied video of the ecology here, but the environment before me still seemed like something beyond imagination. My river highway into the interior of Long Island was lined with trees of riotous cartoon colors, reds and yellows and even pale purple. I was about two hundred kilometers northeast of Bayside, one hundred eighty kilometers southwest of Red Cliffs, and twelve hundred kilometers south of the equator. The climate was delightful — warm days with thirty-three hours of daylight and cool nights for sleeping. Away from the coastline, though, I expected the temperatures to pick up a bit.

My journey here from Bayside the previous night had been an eye-opener. I was on a hydrofoil skiff and it was my first mingling with military Pic who were obviously leery of me. Oh, the mostly alpha crew was professional and polite, but there was none of the easy familiarity that I'd gotten used to with Pic. The encounter brought home to me how many bridges humans and Pic still needed to build, and perhaps how many bridges to mend. There hadn't been any polls taken yet, but everyone is expecting the support for the fusion trial to collapse. The latest news was that Earth is blaming the Pic for what happened in Iran, and that was absolutely absurd.

My gear was packed and loaded. I did one last scan of the river delta and confirmed hugging the northern riverside seemed the best route. I shoved off easily and began my journey.

Three days later.
October 26, 2100 6:27 PM Central European Time
Northern Autumn 51, 3485 36:36 Time Zone 30
Southern Spring 52, 3485 26:36 Time Zone -20

"What do you mean, they weren't nuclear explosions?" Molly and the other medical research staff were gathered around Christopher, who had just returned after a two-day absence.

Christopher was disengaging from multiple hugs, and took a moment before answering. "That's the conclusion from the analysis of the seismic data. Three events, effectively simultaneous, everybody agrees on that. But the latest theory is these were not nuclear detonations."

"But what about the fallout?" asked Simone. "The ash is all over the world!"

Christopher gave a short laugh. "What indeed? The puzzle is, why is the fallout so benign? There's some radioactivity but nothing like the expected ratios of fusion or fission byproducts. Nobody knows why."

Alice frowned. "But the humans think we know why."

Christopher shrugged. "The true cause is unknown."

Alpha Simone's muzzle flashed unconstrained bitterness. "And we are unknown. Humans draw conclusions with so little data! Why worry about two unknowns when you can just slam them together and declare everything solved?" He paused and added, "Completely unknown? The seismic data must suggest something."

"It's like nothing humans have ever seen. The U.N. shared the data with our home world. We don't understand it either. The three events share some similarity to surface explosions, but other wave patterns are suggestive of deep-focus earthquakes. No one model fits the data."

Andrea piped up. "How deep? Couldn't surface explosions trigger an earthquake?"

"That was my thought too. But both the human and Pic seismologists are saying no, not through hundreds of kilometers of rock. Neither group could come up with a model that comes close to what the actual observations were. Days to untangle all the compressions and shears and reflections, and still nothing makes sense. Earth's inner core was ringing like a bell, everybody agrees on that, though the how is a mystery. But before I talk more on that, I want to say our government has agreed in principle to study the fungus plague."

The group cheered, and Molly spoke for all of them. "That's good news! And a little unexpected."

Christopher nodded. "I know. But don't celebrate just yet. There are conditions. Our government is insisting on assurances that new cooperative research will not be weaponized. Not just promises, they want technical assurances built into the methodology of the cooperation. Both governments are negotiating on what that means. But it's a start." The group continued their discussion as they prepared an evening meal.

Meanwhile...

It was a little early for a lunch break, but the small glen I had wandered into was beautiful and unusually peaceful. Mornings and evenings in these subtropical woods were filled with noisy chatter. It would be nice to rest and update my log in a relatively quiet place where I could collect my thoughts.

And besides, I was hungry. A fruit tree nearby would make a perfect complement to the fish I had caught and cooked earlier this morning. Off to my left was a dense thicket I needed to avoid. It contained vibrant growth of a distant and much more dangerous tropical cousin of the creep-weed of Providence. But even if I stumbled into it, I would still be okay unless I did something additionally stupid. My boots could resist the weed's acid for hours, and its tendrils were tough but no match for steel cutters and chemical countermeasures.

I was three days into my survey trek, about twenty kilometers inland (forty kilometers if I measured along Crooked Lazy River), and I was currently about a hundred meters from my kayak which was by the water's edge charging its solar cells. This area near the river should be prime turducken territory, though so far they had remained elusive. But the world around me was so beautiful, I almost didn't mind the lack of a sighting. The environment was completely wild and pristine, in keeping with Parks and Conservation rules. The Pic were laidback when it came to preserving their environment. On Earth, turduckens would be considered endangered, and specimens would be kept in zoos in an effort to preserve the species. On Whistlestop, the philosophy was to let nature run free, and to accept extinction as a necessary and normal part of evolution. There were no zoos on Whistlestop.

On the first day of my river journey, I had passed under a massive bridge that was part of the Class-A road connecting Bayside and Red Cliffs. Since then, it would have been easy to pretend I was the only technological creature on the planet. Oh, I was still tethered. One distress signal from my emergency beacon, and I could expect a rescue from one of the many portal vessels at Far Rockaway. But for now, the solitude was profound and deeply peaceful. I couldn't remember being more relaxed. Even the riotous banana-yellow tree trunks seemed like old friends.

As I was finishing my lunch, my chemical sensors gave a low-level alert, warning me of nearby digestive activity. I studied the report for a moment and concluded that the nearby creep-weed must have captured something over its digestive pad. Thinking it would make a good addition to my log, I cautiously approached the plant to see what it had caught. It took only a few minutes to find a safe way in. The creamy gray feathers and small size fooled me for a moment, but then I blinked in surprise. Stretched by tendrils over the center of the pad was a baby turducken, clearly alive. Its eyes were riveted on me.

Chapter 13

At first I did what any Pic Ranger would do, document my observations and record any additional conjectures. The bird was type beta, the gender mode impossible to tell but probably female. It was trapped, that was clear. The left foot and the opposite rear wing were hopelessly entwined with the creep-weed. The bird looked in remarkably good shape given its predicament. The acid burns on its wing looked mostly superficial, the first flight feathers ruined, but there was no stench of burning flesh. The condition of the trapped leg was more difficult to access, but the bird didn't appear dehydrated. I concluded it must have been captured earlier today, probably after dawn when turduckens became active.

So, I had successfully found a turducken. The find had nothing to do with passing my qualification test. My mission was to survey the area and record a population. My logs were extensive, and a count of zero was just as valid a number as any other. Still, it brought a certain amount of satisfaction to have found one. I decided to postpone returning to my river camp, and after a few minutes of observation, it dawned on me what a remarkable job the young bird was doing.

Creep-weed would discharge copious amounts of digestive sap when stimulated by a struggling animal. The bird before me was demonstrating a fascinating amount of discipline and intelligence to hold itself still while locked in an extremely uncomfortable position. We just stared at each other for a while. Did the bird regard me as an additional threat? How should I proceed? The Pic answer would be to return to camp, but I wasn't a Pic. I began to think of my options.

I was packing plenty of gear to attack creep-weed, and observing the bird's reactions to my efforts seemed a reasonable explanation for what I was about to do. In fact, it was part of my checklist to test my equipment, though the guidelines were to do so with a much smaller patch of weed. But after I surveyed the monster patch carefully, I shouldn't be in any real danger, at least not from the creep-weed. Would the turducken attack me if it had the chance? Only one way to find out.

The bird chirped. Did it chirp at me? Its eyes suggested I had its full attention. I whistled back, something melodic, hoping to sound friendly. But I still needed to map the creep-weed. I stepped out of the bird's view. The bird chirped again, and damn if it didn't sound disappointed.

It really was a monster patch, but the central nerve trunks had to be somewhere. After an hour of poking around, I thought I had everything mapped. I took out my small air pistol and loaded an appropriate cartridge, a potent neurotoxin. Several quick hits with the almost silent weapon—and that was phase one—now I just had to wait a few minutes for the toxin to reach full effect. I tested the plant with the edge of my cutters. No reaction at all. Satisfied of my safety, I stepped onto the central digestive pad and cut the bird free. The wing and foot were still badly entangled though. I gingerly carried the bird to the glen.

The next hour was enjoyable. I carefully snipped the weed, and the bird was very cooperative once it realized what I was doing. We whistled to each other as I worked, strange melodies from the bird, from me easy whistling tunes from the Clear Age Revival of the early 2040s. I even went further back in time and tried singing to it. "Out here, baby, we ain't got nothin', but you still mean, the world to me, turducken..." The bird just stared at me on that one, intense eye contact, then it squawked three words of the song back to me, like a parrot. There was nothing in my references about this mimicking ability. I thought it would be an important addition to my log.

I put some burn ointment on its leg and wing, and after I gave it some fish and fruit which it devoured greedily, it allowed me to make a detailed examination of its body under the feathers. It was male, a cute little fellow, actually. In a moment of insight, I realized why I had championed a different name for the species. Thinking of the critter as a bleeder bird would forever make it a monster. The name turducken might have been comic, but it also bestowed a certain amount of dignity.

I tested the bird's ability to walk, putting another piece of fish a short distance away. The bird hopped over and gobbled it. He looked wobbly, not a good sign, so I carried him back to camp and eventually decided to let him ride on the bow of my kayak as I made my afternoon tour of the area.

And I was in for a wondrous surprise. We whistled to each other as I paddled, mostly folk tunes from me, strange but pleasant tunes from the bird. But then I started whistling Mozart's "Eine Kleine Nachtmusik." The bird stared at me, amazed at first, then joined me in the tune. I was enthralled. We spent hours slowly paddling up and down the river, the bird adding complex harmony to the melody.

I guessed it shouldn't have been a complete shock. The bird's skull held a very large brain, easily double what any Earth bird of comparable weight would have, and turduckens were known to hunt in highly cooperative clans. Still, this was remarkable. We were interacting with each other so closely. Could I keep this fellow as a pet? I was just deciding that would be a really bad idea when my avian companion gave a piercing melodic finale to his crazy rendition of Mozart and flew away. An Earth bird could not fly with one wing, but I learned that a Pic bird can with three out of four. I whistled goodbye.

A few days later.
Southern Spring 56, 3485 14:00 Time Zone -20

It was time to return to the coast, and I began the journey shortly after dawn. By hitching a ride in the central channel, I expected to make the coast easily by the end of the day. Tomorrow would be a final day of lazy solitude at the beach, then at dawn on Southern Spring 58, a military patrol boat would return me to Bayside. My qualification test was coming to a close.

The rescued fledgling was my only confirmed turducken sighting, but yesterday I had found a fresh six-legged piggish carcass that had all the signatures of a turducken kill. I thought I had done a commendable job on the survey, and it got me to thinking. Would I want this type of work as a career? Maybe part time, I concluded. Being a Ranger was rewarding work, but I probably needed a bigger anchor for my life.

The weather was fine, dry and cool, and the center of the river was peaceful with muted sounds of wildlife along the banks. And then above the distant chatter came a haunting melody, soft at first but rapidly gaining in strength. I turned in awe, and then in utter shock. Gaining on me rapidly from upriver was a full clan of at least thirty turduckens, and in unison they were whistling Mozart.

They soon overtook me and began circling my boat, two rings of turduckens, a high outer ring of at least twenty, and a tight inner ring of ten birds flying low with opposite rotation. The inner ring was only about ten meters from me, and my sensors were screaming at me to activate my defenses. But the music was enchanting, and the flying display of opposing rings dazzling. I manually overrode the firing sequence. And then memory of the recent carcass and Max's warning about devious bleeder birds came back to me. Was I being suckered?

Possible! An Earth creature came to mind, a cuttlefish mesmerizing its shrimp prey with dazzling chromatophore displays seconds before a deadly pounce. The inner ring of birds could hit me from all directions in an instant. I pulled my hood up over my neck and make sure my goggles were on as tightly as possible. What should I do? Were these birds serenading me or setting me up? A large bird from the inner ring broke formation and came straight at me. I had my finger on the trigger to open up with everything I had when the creature plopped down on the bow of my kayak. We made and held eye contact while my mind was racing whether another bird was about to impale itself into the back of my neck. The bird on my bow with its intense gaze was a perfect distraction! I was taking an insane risk, but damn it, this was first contact! How smart were these creatures? A Pic would have fired, just as the Pic fired on Storytellers eons ago during their first contact. *But I'm not a Pic!*

I looked closely at the visitor on my bow point. It had an iridescent gamma-female crest, and she had something in her mouth, some sort of large nut, and she stretched her neck in a clear signal for me to take it. Could an animal's deception run this deep? Could the clan visualize the future, plan an attack this deep? I decided to take the risk. One hand holding the defense trigger, I leaned forward with my other arm and the bird hopped close, dropped the nut into my open hand, and then squawked, "Chain of love". I gasped in surprise.

Her eyes! Could I possibly be imagining this? For a brief moment, they seemed filled with gratitude. The bird then flapped four wings in a powerful backwards take-off and flew away, the two circling rings dissolving and following her. The leader perhaps? Was my rescued fledgling in this clan? I'd have to check the visual recordings.

For another few minutes, I could still hear them merrily whistling their bizarre version of Mozart, and I watched until they disappeared upriver. Afterwards I just sat in the boat, letting the channel current carry me. I took several deep breaths and idly admired the scenery. My mind was lost in thought. Maybe I would rethink my decision on being a park ranger. A few experiences like this should be enough to fulfill anyone's life. I looked at the nut in my hand. It was nothing that I recognized would be safe to eat, but that didn't matter. I would cherish the gift forever.

What had just happened? Days earlier, the baby turducken had read my emotions while I was singing to it, and had relayed the affectionate phrase to the clan. What other explanation was there? This was monumental, perhaps on par with the Pic's first contact with the Storytellers. How intelligent were these birds? What possibilities did the future hold?

On a whim, I queried historical measurements on my PA. The light from Earth's sun currently reaching Whistlestop was from the beginning of Earth year 1287. Kublai Khan's armies were on the move, and Mozart wouldn't write "Eine Kleine Nachtmusik" for another five hundred Earth years. Except for the portals, Mozart's musical creations would still be outside Whistlestop's event horizon. But that wasn't the real magic of what I had just witnessed. Turduckens had fallen in love with a Mozart melody. And how would the composer have felt about his music being adopted by a clan of super intelligent alien birds at a star system beyond Rigel? I'd guess he would have been thrilled.

Two days later.
Southern Spring 58, 3485 24:30 Time Zone -21

This was turning out to be one confusing day, though it started normally enough. My ten-day survival test officially ended at 18:00 local time this morning, late enough for me to sleep till dawn, have a leisurely breakfast, break camp, take a final scenic stroll along the surf's edge, then paddle out to a rendezvous point about two hundred meters offshore and wait for the hydrofoil skiff for a ride back to Bayside, where I was expecting to take down the nano-crystal mapping experiment with Professor Feynman.

Surprise number one of the day: The Pic showed up on time with a top-line military hydrofoil, and as soon as I was aboard, they informed me I was scheduled to be at a Council meeting in Haven at 7:30 capital-time. They also said that they were under orders to tell me nothing else. The captain went to full throttle as soon as my kayak was secured. We headed north to Red Cliffs at thirty kilometers per hour, the ship flying across the waters. I did a calculation on my PA. The Earth equivalent was fifty-five knots.

Surprise number two of the day: These Pic were friendly! They were treating me as one of their own. I knew my advancing to Ranger-II would include a junior officer relationship with the military, but the camaraderie I was being offered was totally unexpected. Two alpha-males volunteered to communal shower with me below decks, which I found quite touching because that was exactly what a Pic would be yearning for after extended isolation. Afterwards I had a fine snack at the captain's table, and she gave me a brief tour of the bridge before letting me have some down-time to collect my thoughts. The crew was even saluting me as I walked about the ship, a quick inward snap of the wrist with head-bow.

We were currently about an hour from port and close enough to shore for me to appreciate why the city of Red Cliffs had its name, but my mind was racing with other thoughts. I was dying for an update of the situation with Earth, yet the only information I had was of an upcoming meeting with world leaders at a time equivalent to a three AM meeting on Earth. What was going on?

Southern Spring 58, 3485 7:24 Time Zone 0

I was alone in a capitol assembly hall. There was a single chair in it, which I interpreted to mean I'd be the only human at the meeting. Along one wall was a long bank of windows facing northeast, showing me a broad expanse of Haven in bright predawn twilight. Sunrise was minutes away.

Large ornate doors opened and a stream of Councilors began entering the chamber. I walked over to the chair and sat down as a courtesy, since some Pic found the height of a standing human disconcerting. As the room filled, I had to work to hide a growing feeling of apprehension. Every single Councilor entering the chamber was a member of the faction opposing the fusion trial. The room quickly filled with about sixty Pic, then a single non-Councilor entered. It was Professor Feynman. I resisted the urge to give him a hand-sign of greeting.

Finally Longfellow entered and closed the doors. He whistled something to the assembly that was completely unintelligible to me, then he turned to me and said, "We request and require information from you. I will act as moderator and translate your answers for the Councilors who don't speak English."

I nodded and replied, "With your permission, I'll also sign my answers."

A quick nod, and then, "Question: In a situation where the interests of Pic and humans diverge, which side would you support?"

My stomach churned. What the hell happened in the last ten days? Did Earth attack the Pic transport? "Councilor, may I ask?" I replied verbally and in sign. "Where are these questions going?"

"Patience, Steven! You have worked to achieve a position within our military. We need to understand your loyalties." Longfellow paused and added kindly, "We have not forgotten who among us has earned the Citizen's Award. Can you answer the question?"

The first part of Longfellow's comment confused me. Legally I was still a child and my junior officer status was somewhat honorary until I reached adulthood. Well, time to puzzle that one out later. I tried to answer as honestly as I could, "Well, maybe not. If humans and Pic were at odds with each other, I think my support would depend on who had the better moral position. Whistlestop is my home and Pic are my people, and humans are my people and Earth is the home of what I am. It would be painful… It would be impossible to make an easy choice between the two. And I think the details of the situation would have to be before me. I can't answer in general. I honestly don't know."

I finished with a polite closing hand sign, and there was no need for Longfellow to repeat my answer. The room echoed with robust debate. Numerous Pic were whistling "Objection!" That much I could interpret, and I took it to be a very encouraging sign.

Which on Earth would be a ridiculous judgment, but in large groups, Pic debate very differently than humans. It's standard practice here to first list the points of the position you oppose, thereby demonstrating your empathy and understanding of both sides of the argument. Pic found it persuasive when someone shows deeper insight yet still rejected their point of view. Logically, I had to admit this makes perfect sense, but no one on Earth debated like this. I still wasn't used to it.

The room quieted down, and Longfellow spoke to me. "Did you understand?"

"The Councilors judged my answer acceptable?"

"Correct. Next, please inform us of your knowledge of the Pic known to you as Flossie, in particular her work on portal physics."

That was definitely not a request I was expecting, and I needed a moment to collect my thoughts. I took a deep breath and looked out the windows, admiring the first moments of a beautiful sunrise over the vast garden-city of Haven.

"I know she won a science prize about six years ago."

"Do you know why?"

"Not from Flossie. She mentioned it only once in passing, made it sound like a school contest, a science fair. But I was curious. I searched the Digital Rivers, discovered it was a prestigious scientific award, the world's annual physics competition. Flossie was a kid going up against professionals and she won! Her paper was classified. I assume it concerns the physics of reality interchange. She never spoke of it to me." I paused and added, "I want to say something else. Flossie is unique. She has a truly beautiful mind, in ways that have nothing to do with physics." I made a rocking back-and-forth motion with my wrist as I signed, "She is I. I am she."

The assembly erupted in a chorus of piercing whistles, so much so that Professor Feynman broke protocol and whistled something loud enough for everyone to hear, signing also for me. "Two seasons ago, Flossie freely affirmed this bond she shares with Steven."

Longfellow quickly called the meeting back to order and launched a series of questions at me concerning my knowledge of the structure of the Pic military, in particular the units responsible for the portal network. My answers were lengthy. Basically I said there were three groups. The largest was based in Haven and was responsible for operating the planetary network connecting the cities. Another group was based at Far Rockaway and ran the interplanetary and interstellar networks, and finally there was a theoretical staff that keeps a low profile and is scattered across the globe. Everything I told Longfellow was public knowledge.

The questions shifted to Pic civics and details about the government guild, its unions and council structure. I began to relax a bit, controlling my impatience to know what this was all about. The Pic ran a well-functioning, logical society, easy to describe and approve of, and I started to elaborate on what could have been straightforward answers, relying on the excellent lessons I had with Professor Higgins. To fill an unplanned vacancy, the new councilor was selected from the general public pool if the remaining term was more than three years, and from the pool of former councilors if the term was more than three weeks. Otherwise the position was left vacant.

About an hour into the civics questioning, Longfellow abruptly signaled me to stop talking. The Councilors whistled intensely to each other for a brief time, then Longfellow beckoned me to follow him out of the examination hall through a side door. Professor Feynman joined us. He didn't say anything verbally, but one look at his colorful muzzle told me I had little to worry about.

We walked down an empty hallway, turned a corner and walked some more. For a while I could see the bright sun rising over the sleeping city. Eventually we reached the other side of the building and walked into a spacious office with a chair waiting for me. I smiled as I recognized Maayan sitting (on the floor, of course) behind a large, low desk. She and Longfellow chirped something briefly, acknowledging each other's presence. Then Maayan did a very affectionate muzzle-to-muzzle caress with Professor Feynman. I blinked in surprise before I remembered the two were married. This was my first time seeing them together.

"Any holdouts?" Maayan signed to Longfellow as I sat down.

"None," he replied. "We'll be active supporters."

"Excellent." Maayan turned to me and signed, "This must seem so strange, given your isolation over the last ten days. But the others wanted to question you before you learned of recent events." Maayan then proceeded to brief me on the current situation with Earth. The situation was even worse than I had feared. Earth and Whistlestop were heading towards a complete breakdown of trust. Earth was demanding proof that our campus existed and that we were still alive. Whistlestop was replying that the fusion trial agreement specifically prohibited Earth from making such a demand. Meanwhile public debate on Digital Rivers was building towards cancelling the fusion trial.

"Steven," Maayan signed. We stared into each other's eyes for a moment. Such compassion, both in her eyes and muzzle, so deep it confused me. "There's more. Additional knowledge that's not public."

"Can you tell me?"

"Not as a child. You would need special military clearance. That's not given to honorary officers."

I shrugged. "So how can I help?"

Longfellow signed, "By not being a child and not being an honorary officer."

"Huh?"

Longfellow grinned. "Do you remember your civics questions this morning, the one concerning reaching adulthood?"

"Sure, age thirty or... or petitioning a court for early adulthood."

Maayan signed, "And the Council is the ultimate court, and we are unanimous on this. We would welcome your petition." I gave a simple hand gesture asking her to continue. "We also would welcome your adult enlistment into our military. Your trial citizenship would then be inappropriate. The trial would be over for you."

I took a deep breath. "How would this work? What about the others?"

Longfellow answered, "Depends on how the future unfolds. For now, only your status would change."

I nodded slowly, then had a thought. "What about birthrights?"

"Your personally sponsored progeny would be a full citizen, but not a child sponsored by a mate. And I do apologize for what an awkward situation this might put you in, but the Council is not quite ready to concede a permanent human presence on Whistlestop."

I nodded as understanding set in. A single line of descent would eventually run out of people to procreate with. Still, opening a path to early trial completion was a huge concession. It would put the trial on the brink of success. So why were warning bells sounding in my head? "I don't want to sound ungrateful, and I'm not saying no, but I'm worried how my classmates will take this. Not just my classmates. I'm worried about my personal integrity. As a member of your military, my first allegiance must be to you, correct?"

Longfellow nodded. "You would be pledging to obey orders, yes."

"What about unlawful orders?"

Longfellow seemed startled by my question. "Steven, we're public servants. If you ever found us deceiving the public or intentionally acting against its interest, it would be your lawful responsibility to denounce us. That will never change." He paused for a moment. "We would like to give you time to consider and consult, but events are unfolding. To be blunt, we're asking for an answer now, and hoping for yes."

I sat there for several minutes thinking, then signed, "If I did accept, I'd have to tell Jorani about this, tell everybody actually. Would that be okay?"

Longfellow's snout flashed for a moment with internal struggle. "There are reasons to keep this quiet."

I groaned. "I can't keep this secret. The other humans have to know where my allegiance lies; otherwise I'm a spy within my own community."

Maayan signed, "Longfellow, his point is valid."

Longfellow stretched his head diagonally, a Pic gesture for conceding an issue.

I continued. "Would I be leaving Providence?"

Maayan shrugged. "Not necessarily. But we can't go into details unless you accept."

I spent some time considering the muzzle patterns of the three Pic around me. That was what finally convinced me. I smiled and signed, "I guess all the candidates of the fusion trial were picked for our ability to leap before we look. Okay, I'll do it."

A day later…
Time: Northern Autumn 58, 3485 48:20 Time Zone 30

"I can't believe what I'm hearing," Jorani said softly. I had returned to Providence a couple of hours previously and Jorani and I were in my dorm room. I was sitting at my desk and Jorani was lying prone on my bed, her forearms propping up her head. I had just given her a brief summary of what my day had been like. Almost two days, actually. Moving from Time Zone -20 to 0 to +30 had created a one-hundred-and-ten-hour day for me.

I replied to Jorani with a big yawn, "Do you think I made the right decision?"

"I don't know. Maybe." Jorani pondered for a moment. "Yeah, I guess so. The Pic asked for your help and you gave it. Assuming their intentions are good, that has to be the right decision. But damn it, Steve, this is going to be difficult! How can you be my anchor if we can't discuss things?"

"I'm working on that. I stressed to Longfellow and Maayan how much I needed your insight and advice."

"What did they say?"

"Maayan was sympathetic. Longfellow said he'd consider the issue." I stretched and gave a really tired yawn and stared out the window. It was pitch dark outside, but I could still see it was starting to snow. "Longfellow offered a consolation prize for you."

"Hmm?"

"How would you like to replace me as liaison?"

"What?" Jorani frowned for a moment then sighed. "It's a communications job. I guess I can see their logic."

"Yours if you want it. Just let the council make the announcement." I yawned heavily.

Jorani got off the bed, came over and kissed my cheek. "Sweetie, you look exhausted. Why don't we shower and sack out?"

I nodded sleepily and we headed for the bathroom. Jorani left early after washing my back, and when I came out, I saw she had turned down my bed and was warming it up for me. I crawled in next to her and snuggled.

"What are you thinking?" she whispered.

"How nice it is we don't have class tomorrow. I think I'm going to sleep till dawn," which during the winter solstice at Providence was an impressive amount of sleep.

"Well, not quite that long. Remember the briefing you promised?" I could sense Jorani's tenseness. She wanted to talk. I sighed and worked to become more awake, petting sweet Jorani under the covers. *If that won't wake me up, nothing will.*

And this night, nothing did. My mind turned off like a switch.

A half day later…
Time: Northern Autumn 59, 3485 22:40 Time Zone 30

As planned, Jorani and I met Karim and Parni in the cafeteria, the president and VP of our student government. Jorani packed a picnic brunch for the four of us while I fended off a few questions and suggested we find a quiet place to talk. So much had changed in so short a time. Just a few days ago, I was so eager to make my report on turducken behavior, and now it seemed like a distant memory. Baskets in hand, we skipped the tunnels and hiked through an impressive amount of virgin snow to an empty classroom. From the southeastern horizon, the rising sun was bathing the campus with light and long shadows.

While I gave a brief summary to my two startled leaders, Jorani set up a meal full of tasty fruits and grains native to both Earth and Whistlestop, though nothing directly from Earth. During the past semester, the Pic transport had been docked for much of the time at Brussels and Earth had sent us a fabulous amount of food. We had all enjoyed sampling cuisines from around the world. Those days were over, but I really didn't mind. Before me now were Pic-grain pancakes, lamb links indistinguishable from the real thing, locally grown Earth peaches and a creamy vegetable drink that both humans and Pic enjoyed very much. Jorani was munching a fruit that looked like a tiny eggplant and tasted like a combination of banana and pumpkin pie.

My report ended shortly after we finished eating. Parni was the first to reply. "I guess the core issue is how much do we trust the Pic. Have you seen the latest reports from Earth? Fatalities estimates are approaching two hundred million. There were fifty percent fatalities five hundred Earth kilometers from the blast zones. A little closer and no one survived, total devastation, vast deserts of ultra-hot ash."

I nodded. "The Pic briefed me. I understand the situation."

Karim spoke up. "Did they also brief you on the fungus epidemic? The shock wave scattered it across Europe. There are outbreaks in Germany and France now, Great Britain, even South America, far sooner than people were expecting."

I grimaced. "No. The Pic didn't mention that. They're focused on understanding the explosions. The fungus is horrible, but they understand what it is and they're working on countermeasures. The explosions..." I shrugged. "They asked for my help. There's a special unit of military intelligence that's been assigned the problem. I'm attached to that group, and beyond that, I'm under orders not to discuss what hasn't been released to the public."

"But you're back here on campus?" asked Parni.

"The Pic are fanatical about not interrupting education. My current assignment is to be a student here during the week and train at Far Rockaway during the weekends. It's going to be hectic."

Parni nodded thoughtfully. "Are any of our Pic escorts involved with this?"

"I can't comment. Sorry."

"People have been gossiping about Flossie."

I shrugged and looked out the window. "I hear the forecast is for more snow tonight."

"Hmm... How did your experiment go?"

"The scan finished early. Much of the crystal is unreadable. Professor Feynman didn't wait for me. He did the analysis with Flossie. You can read about this soon. The three of us will be submitting a paper to a historical journal."

"And the results were?"

"There was a fluke arch of defects that protected the readable part of the crystal."

"Aha. So you were right all along."

"Well, Flossie was right all along. It would take millions of attempts to recreate such a crystal. Flossie's estimate is in the tens of millions, even with today's technology. The Pic understand the implications. They're not stupid."

Parni looked me in the eye. "Steve, Earth has concluded human technology is not capable of causing what happened in Iran."

"I know."

"So what about the Pic?"

"The Pic are investigating. And I'm a member of the investigating team who'll be pulled in when the Pic want a human perspective, or perhaps to confirm to Earth that we're still alive."

"The Pic might do that, let us talk to Earth?"

"Everything is fluid."

"What does that mean, exactly? Can you be more specific?"

"No, not really. And I do regret that." Memories of yesterday's briefings with the Pic military passed through my mind, the monstrous conjecture that Iran was destroyed as part of a fantastic and nearly successful plot to have Earth destroy the Pic transport. Who or what were we up against? Ghosts? The investigation into the duckbill tiger attack was almost a year old now and had led nowhere. And during the week while I was searching for turduckens on Long Island, the Pic confirmed by direct on-board spacewalk observations the location of every probe in their interstellar inventory. Each probe checked out okay.

In the classroom now, Parni's face held a big frown. "You seem to have such absolute trust in the Pic."

I sighed. "Have you ever caught a Pic being deceitful? Marisa and Flossie tried an experiment once. Flossie tried to lie."

"Yeah?"

"After a few lies, Flossie said she felt dizzy but pressed on. Marisa ended the experiment when Flossie vomited."

"Oh."

"I'm not saying all Pic are incapable of deceit. Flossie is unique, and somebody planned the tiger attack. But Longfellow told me if I ever found the Council lying, it's my responsibility to denounce them to the world."

"Longfellow said that?"

"Yep, in sign, his exact words, more or less."

"I thought Longfellow spoke English."

"He does. Remember Maayan was with us. We were conversing in sign for her."

Karim spoke up. "Steve, we haven't always agreed on things, but on this issue, I admit I am in awe. You've opened a path to early success of the fusion trial. Fantastic news."

"Thanks, Karim. I appreciate that."

Karim gave me a genuine smile and scratched his jaw. "Maybe thank the Pic. I think some of their attitudes are rubbing off on me."

Parni stared at Karim, looking as if she had just swallowed a bug, and then turned back to me, sounding more than a bit annoyed. "Is there any prediction you CAN tell us?"

"Uh… About what?"

"About anything. What about the second probe? How close is it to Earth?"

I squirmed. "I can't go into details. The public news is that it'll reach the inner-planet region of the solar system by the end of the year. I believe that's accurate." I knew a bit more information that wasn't public. The military had rescheduled their construction, reducing transit time by more than two weeks by accelerating now and adding hard deceleration later. And the interstellar probes always traveled in loose sets of three. A third probe was also completing its century-long journey to Earth. I paused and added, "The second probe had nothing to do with Iran, if that's what you're asking."

Karim asked, "Any chance of more humans getting permanent citizenship?"

"Maybe. Longfellow said events are unfolding. Earth couldn't have caused the destruction of Iran. The Pic know they didn't do it. So what's left? What are we dealing with? What the hell happened in Iran?" The four of us just stared at each other.

Chapter 14

One season later.
Time: Southern Summer 55, 3485 13:37 Haven Standard Time

"Happy New Year, Steven," Isaac commented. We had just arrived at our chosen campsite, a small flat space of land a half kilometer from the portal, sheltered by large boulders. Further down the rolling hill in the bright moonlight a great grayish ocean stretched to the horizon and beyond. The brisk and ever-present wind was filled with odors from both land and sea.

The four of us carefully unslung our packs and began preparations for a predawn breakfast. Isaac, Flossie, Julie, and I had been on Sorrows' End for five standard days now, and given the planet's dizzying rate of rotation (less than thirty-six hours), we were awaiting our ninth of ten sunrises. One standard day from now, we were scheduled to be back on campus.

I puzzled over Isaac's comment for a moment, then queried my PA. It was midnight, January 1, 2101 in Greater England now. "Uh, yeah, thanks. It's so easy to lose track of time in this place." I carefully sat down as Flossie and Julie finished unpacking our breakfast. Gravity on Sorrows' End was 121% of Earth standard. Jorani was so right. It was a lot more difficult to adjust than I'd imagined. Especially when I aligned my backbone to a non-vertical position, I was very conscious of the planet pulling me down. My three Pic companions seemed similarly affected, though I never heard them comment on it. It was a Pic's nature to complain only when advocating a change in plans. At least the atmosphere was okay — higher pressure but with less of a percentage concentration of oxygen. The combination allowed breathing without much difficulty, though sleeping was still stressful.

"Such a strange experience," commented Isaac, staring up at the fading stars. "Was it like this for you, Steven, leaving Earth and seeing such an unfamiliar night sky?"

"Yeah, I guess. This star system though is a lot stranger than Whistlestop. One planet and almost nothing else. I find it disturbing. Not sure why..."

Flossie flashed a muzzle sign of agreement. "It is unique, the only known example of such a system. And the few dwarf planets here have wildly elliptical orbits. Except for this planet and moon, the system would be typical of one having a close encounter with another star, one that disrupted all the planetary orbits. And yet, here is Sorrows' End with its circular orbit."

"A challenge question for you, Steve," Julie announced as she handed me a vegetable drink. "Do you think the humans at our campus could survive on Sorrows' End, establish a colony here?"

My first thought was to cringe at the idea, but I tried to give Julie an intelligent answer. "Do we have access to the portal network?"

"No. Assume a worst case scenario, four hundred and eighty humans abandoned here with an extended amount of camping supplies, enough to cover several years of needs."

"Yuck. We would die out. The soil is too rich in perchlorates to grow anything edible."

"The oceans here have creatures that are edible by humans."

"Well, shellfish..."

"Several kinds of shellfish, plus edible seaweed. And suppose you had genetically tailored seeds that could tolerate the salts and produce human-edible vegetables, nuts, and grains."

"Well, okay..." I took a long, slow sip on my drink and looked around at the hill. It was full of a moss-like cover and dwarf shrubs, but nothing that looked like a real tree. It reminded me of a pale version of the Arctic tundra in summer. Julie's question was frightening. In orbital radius, Sorrows' End was similar to Mars, but the star here was twenty-two percent more massive than Earth's sun, resulting in more incident power density here than on Earth. This planet's tilt though was terrible, less than one degree, resulting in polar regions trapped forever in super-cold gray twilight. The vast polar ice sheets kept the planet's equator cool. Valleys there had drifts of frozen CO2 that never evaporated. The resulting convective wind shears with the equatorial regions plus the higher air density plus the super-strong Coriolis force would create unbelievable storms if the oceans were warmer. As it was, the winds here were tolerable but ever present.

As I pondered, the sun made its super-fast pop-up from the horizon. I finally answered with a shrug. "It would certainly be a struggle. I guess we would run three sleep cycles every five days, just as we're doing now. Long term, we would need to smelt metals… There's a long orbital year, but it's almost pointless. Circular orbit and no tilt mean no seasons."

"It also means the equator stays temperate year round," countered Julie, "a continuous growing season for plants that can thrive in cool weather."

"Yeah, I guess. But the gravity… it would wear us out. Heck, maybe the next generation could get used to the endless wind, assuming we had enough energy and resources to rear one." I looked down towards the ocean and the pale green landscape now bathed in whitish sunlight. Was Julie joking about living here? "Hell of a boring and difficult place to live. Was that Plan B, what to do with the humans if the fusion trial failed? Maroon us here on Sorrows' End?"

I meant my comment as a return joke. Julie shocked me with a solemn nod. "Years ago, in the early stages of worst-case contingency planning, the morality of refusing to let humans procreate was troubling. There are no Pic words for genocide, Steve. If the fusion trial fails and returning humans to Earth is not an option, you'll probably be given the choice of emigrating to a virgin planet rather than living out your lives childless on Whistlestop. And perhaps there are better planets than Sorrows' End, but they all have their challenges."

I took a deep breath. "I'm assuming the Council authorized you to tell me this."

"Of course. And you can share it with the other humans." Julie shrugged. "Longfellow asked me to stress that none of this is under active consideration. The Council thought humans had the right to know their options. None of this would be forced."

"Hey, wait a minute. When were you told this?"

"Shortly before we came here."

"We've been here for five days! You're telling me now?"

Julie's muzzle showed simple confusion. "Did I err in judgment? There was nothing for you to act on, and I wanted to give you time to form opinions of Sorrows' End without thinking of it as a prison planet."

I sighed and took another long look at our surroundings. "You were right. Thanks..." Interesting that Julie would consider the perspective of a prison. The institution was almost unknown on Whistlestop, perhaps a few hundred people currently incarcerated, mostly for mental illness beyond the reach of Pic medical arts, and less than a thousand who had ever been legally detained. Criminal behavior on Whistlestop was universally judged as pathetic. The way of life just didn't motivate the way it did on Earth.

Meanwhile Flossie's muzzle was flashing a mixture of sadness and fear over the thought of being stranded here. "I think I would miss all the colors of Whistlestop."

"That's interesting," I replied with a chuckle. "Just before the start of the fusion trial, I remember Jorani said the same thing about missing the colors of Earth."

Flossie glanced nervously at her PA. "Ten minutes until survival exercise."

I gave her a hand sign for understood and then looked at my three companions. All four of us were legal adults, though I was the only human who knew that. Julie was Ranger-III and Isaac was like me, Ranger II. At the Council's request, they had both petitioned for adulthood while I was hunting for turduckens on Long Island. And as for Flossie, she'd been a legal adult for six years, ever since her scientific paper had been classified. And the Pic were so secretive about this that not even Flossie's parents knew her legal status. And what was so terrifying about her paper to warrant this? I knew now. So did Julie and Isaac. We were affiliated with a fourth military unit that was involved with portal technology, an intelligence unit that was never talked about.

I didn't understand much of the physics of Flossie's work, just the gist of its result. Her conclusions remind me of the Bayside Crystal. Our experimental findings suggested the portal network did not exist in the past. Flossie did me one better six years ago. She proved the portal network did not exist in the present.

I could imagine the sequence of events. The physics faculty at Haven University sponsored an annual competition for the most original research, and they'd had Professor Feynman as a new member on their staff (his beta wife had recently become a Councilor and the family had moved to Haven). And here came this unsolicited paper from some kid at Sundance who on Earth would have been the equivalent of a high-school sophomore. Professor Feynman was known to have military clearance on portal physics, so Flossie's paper was shuffled to him as an amusement.

And that evening, Feynman's amusement slowly turned to astonishment as he studied Flossie's work. Her insights appeared flawless but led to results that made no sense. She was approaching reality interchange from an entirely new perspective, claiming that non-deterministic entanglement was not one but *the* characteristic trait of all spacetime. And on that foundation, Flossie built a framework for reality that was pure elegance, encapsulating a stunning conclusion that, except in a perfect vacuum, a reality interchange dipole could not exist. It would require the cloning of the enclosed entangled quantum particle states, something that both Earth's and Whistlestop's understanding of quantum mechanics said was impossible.

A line from the ancient movie *Duck Soup* came to mind: "Who you gonna believe, me or your own eyes?" Here was this brilliant piece of theoretical work with which no one could find fault, colliding with the reality of an operational dipole interchange network. The military unit responsible for portal investigations got involved and after a baffling week of discussion, they classified Flossie's work. They also did something that was very uncharacteristic of Pic and right at the edge of Pic legality. They convinced Flossie to petition for adulthood without informing her parents.

Things did not go well for Flossie after that. Her family moved to a new city, and Flossie had a horrible time adjusting to a new high school. As an escape from academic pressure of the military and the social pressure of cruel classmates, Flossie laid aside her love of physics and began to study Earth cultures.

All four of our wrist assistants gave unusual warning beeps. It was seconds before 14:00 Haven Universal Time. In unison on the mark, our

PA units popped out their battery packs and went dead. I stored mine and the other three in a zippered packet and then activated the time lock. At 50:00 later today, we were scheduled to reconnect to Digital Rivers. Until then, we were running a psychological isolation test, Flossie's summer thesis and an activity that surprised me greatly.

Pic *did not* like to be isolated. Even on solo field testing, Pic Rangers were allowed to check in and ask for advice. I looked at my three companions. Physically we were fine. Our camping gear was superb and the environment benign. But perhaps for the first time ever, here were Pic on another world truly isolated from home. Would they feel the urge to gallop back to the portal? It wouldn't help much. Without PA entry codes, we were locked out of the complex.

Sorrows' End was a distant planet listed in the probe catalog, almost as far from Whistlestop as Earth and in the opposite direction. Our lifelines were the three portals in the system, one on the planet's surface, one on the satellite moon, and a third in a close solar orbit doing a long-term automated study of the local sun. It had been showing erratic activity over the last several millennia, ever since the Pic had first tapped into the telemetry.

Our first hour of isolation passed without incident. We spent the time setting up camp, our moves efficient and mindful of the high gravity. Afterwards, though, there was little to do except admire the ocean and sky. Both had noticeably different colors compared to Earth and Whistlestop. We wound up in a half-circle, Julie lying my right, Flossie on my left, and Isaac sitting upright on Flossie's left. Flossie was actively cuddling against me, and I had my hand buried in the rich blue feather-fur between her shoulder blades while Isaac had his hand and forearm resting along her rear legs. I looked at Isaac, wondering how he would feel about his beloved pressing against me. He replied with a muzzle message that Flossie could not see. "She is your soul mate. She will be my life mate. You saved both our lives. All is well." I nodded my understanding.

"I guess you're all wondering why I petitioned for this test," said Flossie. "I suspect Isaac understands some of my motive. Dearest? Why don't you start with what we've found with the seismic data?"

Isaac chirped something complex to Flossie that I didn't catch, then spoke in English. "It was easy to add unscheduled exploration onto our official survey plan. The planet has a very active crust. We used echoes from micro quakes to do additional research."

"And?" chirped Julie.

"What we found was extraordinary. There are thousands of deep puncture wounds in the crust, as if the planet was stabbed again and again with a galactic ice pick. It's all solidified magma now, but the columns still leave distinct echoes, assuming..." He stroked Flossie's leg affectionately, "you're brilliant enough to know how to search for them."

Flossie wiggled at the compliment then added, "It's our opinion that the three columns of magma descending from what used to be Iran will look very much like the columns here now, in another forty million years or so."

I frowned. "Are you suggesting the entity that attacked Earth attacked Sorrows' End? Hard to think of any civilization lasting anywhere near that long, good or evil."

"It's hard to be precise," answered Isaac. "We don't have historical tectonic measurements. But if you make reasonable estimates, all the columns would have straight alignment around forty million years ago, just as they do on Earth now. The main difference is Earth has three stab wounds, and Sorrows' End has thousands." Isaac looked at me, a pattern of horror on his muzzle. "Something almost killed this planet. Only the simpler life survived."

I kept frowning. "Eons have passed. Are we missing something? Nobody would use the same weapon across forty million years."

"Maybe it's a ritual," Julie suggested. "Their science moves on but the ritual is frozen."

I gasped at the thought. "Are you serious? A religion based on killing planets? That would be one hell of a god."

"Everyone," said Flossie, "I have much to discuss, starting with an apology to you, Steven. During our first semester, I said something to you that was true but probably misleading. Do you remember walking with me to your dorm, and I mentioned that something in my past disqualified me from being your escort?"

"Sure."

"Did you search my background and guess it was my physics research?"

"Not at the time, but eventually, yeah."

"That wasn't the reason. In my high-school years, I was under the care of mental health specialists. The interview committees didn't want the Council liaison to be matched with someone with..." Flossie gave a deep sigh. "...a fragile personality."

I leaned over and kissed the top of her smooth head. "Flossie, your mind is many things. Fragile it is not."

"I had nightmares, bad nightmares, visions so horrible they... Dreams of going through a portal and becoming trapped in what humans call hell. I'd be eaten there, shredded alive. I would start to scream while asleep, wake my family..." Flossie sighed again. "My caregivers helped me rationalize the visions as fantasy. And then a few years later, we were attacked by the duckbill tiger. Suddenly my nightmares were real!" I felt Flossie shudder beneath my hand.

She continued. "The experience changed my perspective. I decided to challenge my nightmares, not rationalize them. What was I afraid of? I started exploring the physics paradox I had created, keeping everything in my own thoughts, trusting that my fears were valid, writing nothing down, telling no one."

"You feared the portals?" Julie asked.

"Oh yes, and hence this isolation test. We have cover for being off Digital Rivers. Everything flows through the portals. Remember how no trace was ever found of Maayan's invitation to Steve being intercepted?"

Julie chirped, "I do." It was a simple enough whistle for me to understand easily.

"But you can't send entangled signals through portals. They're encoded onto a simple virtual carrier wave, in one portal, out the next. No one knows what happens in between." Flossie whistled a burst of excitement. "I think I do! My breakthrough came while I was working on the standard model of reality-interchange. The equation using the gravitational permittivity of free space is linear in time. But that can't be right, and that means everything is wrong. The standard model from the Third New Kingdom, I believe the English phrase is bullshit."

"Linear in time?" asked Isaac. "What does that mean?"

"Think of all the dynamic equations in quantum and classical mechanics. They're all linear in time. You can run the equations forward and backward in time. But reality interchange must be embedded in the reality creation process. It's both a quantum and classical-scale phenomenon, in the interface layer between the two domains. At the quantum level, the past is objectively undetermined. A photon's probability function encounters a half-silvered mirror and it's undefined whether the photon is reflected or transmitted. Both probabilities propagate into the future. But at classical-scale, the past is immutable. In my model, the interface layer between the two domains is the reality creation process. It converts undetermined past into immutable past. How could a process like that possibly be reversible? My conclusion is the interface layer must be a time-asymmetric physics and therefore, reality interchange must also be time-asymmetric."

I dimly understood what Flossie was saying and was in complete awe. "Flossie? Your model? Your conclusion? Is this your discovery?"

Flossie nodded. "It's a new formalism for joining quantum mechanics with spacetime. Everything changes, even the speed of light. Light does not have a speed."

Julie chirped, "What?"

"Julie, you have to stop thinking of spacetime as a coordinate system, or light and gravity as obeying equations of motion. Talking about empty space makes as much sense as talking about empty electrons. Spacetime is a negative-pressure fabric, and light and gravity obey the principle of least action. Think of light and gravity as quantum propagations guided by the temporal permittivity of free space."

Julie chirped an even louder, "And what's that?"

"It's the fabric's ultimate folding ratio between temporal and spatial reality. Entanglement is not simply a quantum property." Flossie stared out at the ocean before us. "Don't just think of the fish! Think of the ocean they swim in!"

Julie gave a plaintive growl of frustration. "Uh, Flossie," I said. "I think you lost us."

Flossie paused for a moment and considered. "Ah, sorry. I'll jump to the conclusion and use a more direct analogy. Steven, imagine you want to exchange two regions of computer memory, call them A and B. How would you do it?"

"That's easy," I replied. "Copy A to temp, copy B to A, copy temp to B."

"Exactly! You need that third space to anchor the interchange of the other two. Earth and Whistlestop have known for centuries that you can't clone entangled quantum states, and now I know why. It would create duplicate reality, prevent reality from interlocking with itself at classical scale. That's why a dipole interchange must fail. There's no anchor, and thus no path to an immutable past. The interchange must revert within a quantum timescale. But if two quantum-filled regions attempted to bounce to a third quantum-free region within the same quantum timescale, the bounces can be flipped, resulting in the interchange of the two quantum-filled regions, a path to reality with no cloning required. That's what I think the portals are doing."

"A tri-pole?" asked Julie.

Flossie chirped a yes.

"Is this third node some mathematical construct?"

"No, not at all. The anchor node is a real piece of hardware, and better than our portal units."

"But where is it?"

"Yeah, exactly. Where is it?"

I was feeling a growing sense of dread. "Flossie? Why do you think the anchor node is better than our portals?"

"If I'm right, we've been on the receiving end of a monstrous deception for thousands of years. Endless papers from the NK3 scraps of knowledge, all with vague hints how a pair of spacetime regions might be permanently entangled. Utter nonsense! That's not the way the universe operates! After initial entanglement, the set of regions should be switchable, any two nodes in the network able to perform an interchange bounce with the anchor node."

"But that's not the way the portals work!" countered Julie.

"It *is* the way they work! Our controls are simply locked out of the portals' full abilities. Our allowed view of the network, it's one gigantic lie! Intentional deceit, just like all the nano-crystals from the last century of NK3, all the nano-crystals except one, that is."

I stared at Isaac and Julie. They seemed just as shocked as I was. "Flossie, how could you keep this to yourself?"

"How could I not? I fear our adversary will destroy Whistlestop if it felt threatened, perhaps even if only discovered. Look at Sorrows' End! Look at Whistlestop thirty-six thousand years ago! Look at Earth today! If I tell our officers, someday someone will make a mistake; dismiss my fears; reveal my suspicions through the portal network. I can't take such a risk!"

There was a long pause of silence. "So what do we do?" Isaac finally asked.

"I was hoping..." Flossie lifted her head and looked at me. "Steven, I was hoping you... Personally, I'm out of ideas how to proceed."

"Me? I don't know..." I tried to give Flossie a thoughtful response. "Do you know how to... Could we build our own portal network?"

Flossie chirped a dissonant chord that in English would mean no for multiple reasons. "There are major issues with the stability of the anchor node. The limitations on algorithmic ability intrinsic to quantum foam should prevent the anchor portal from ever working, yet it must. And some engineering masterstroke is achieving true quantum isolation; I don't know how the portals do it. And beyond that, the physical principles I've identified imply portal construction should be completely beyond our abilities. I am in awe that this technology exists."

"What would it take?"

"The first step would be to create a spacetime seed."

I frowned. The conversation was turning into one rabbit hole leading down another. "And what the heck is that?"

Flossie chirped a laugh. "What can I say? I have fifteen coupled differential equations in my head, fifteen equations that express the superposition of spacetime, fifteen equations that turn here or there into here *and* there! I have to call it something!"

"But what is it physically? Can we create one?"

"Physically, my equations suggest you start with a twisted tear, a quantum of spacetime with its temporal dimension flipped to an undefined state."

"Back up, Flossie; I can't make sense of what you're saying. How do you tear spacetime?"

"You need... I don't know the English term. A composite fermion? You need massive half-integer spin particles interacting with a hundred billion units of gravitational shear at relativistic speeds, along with some mechanism to trap the tears. The half-integer twist of the spin should create a gravitational retarded potential longitudinal to the temporal axis... Sorry, I was getting back to my equations. Anyway, first you create the seed, and then you grow it by folding spacetime around the seed, and you do that with a massive spinning object that twists spacetime curvature. I don't know the details how to do this, but for the seed to be stable, you need to be at the bottom of a gravitational well, something deep, otherwise it might simply untwist and disappear... or worse."

"Or worse?" I asked.

"I'm not sure. The uncontrolled relaxation of the tear might release an enormous amount of energy."

Julie scratched her head. "Are you saying down on the surface of a planet?"

"No, I said the bottom of a gravitational well."

Julie blinked. "You mean the center of Whistlestop, the core?"

"Sort of. Right geometry, but I doubt the well would be deep enough."

"The center of a star?"

Flossie laughed. "Except for the heat and pressure there, yes, I think that would do it! But how do you build something inside a stellar core?" Flossie looked at me. "The situation seems hopeless. But you humans have such different ways of looking at things. Steven, any ideas?"

"What? Build something inside a star? Flossie, you're not joking, are you?"

"Certainly not!"

I gulped at looked at the ocean and clouds for a while, wondering how a credible course of action could possibly occur to me. What exactly was Flossie asking from me? Certainly not to come up with some miracle technology. *But wait a minute... aren't stars already massively spinning objects?* "Uh, could a star make a spacetime seed by itself?"

"You mean find one in nature?"

"Yeah. Could a star eject one?"

Flossie frowned. "I've thought of that. A black hole would have enough gravitational shear near its event horizon. Or maybe a neutron star… and neutrons have half-integer spin. But in free space, I don't see how the initial seed would survive there longer than, what do humans call it? Planck time scales."

"Flossie, it can't be impossible to make one. Somebody built the portal network. There has to be some way to jumpstart the process."

Flossie sighed. "And that's not all. As I said before, quantum foam should make the jumps impossible. The foam uncertainty should destroy all algorithmic solutions to the bounce equations. In order to function, the grown seed needs to be both self-organizing and incomputable in the interface layer."

"And what does that?"

"Perhaps consciousness does that. Other than that, I don't know."

I groaned. "How many layers of impossibility are we talking about?"

Flossie growled back, "I don't get to choose how the universe operates! I have to go where the physics takes me!" She paused and added, "The portals are real; their use can't be impossible. The issues must thus be engineering, not core physics. The entities that built the portal network had a tremendous advantage over me — the ability to do experiments. They seemed to have solved the problems of how to stabilize the spacetime seeds… A cold environment might help, less foam."

"How cold?"

"Maybe as cold as this," Flossie replied as she waved a hand at the air around us. "Maybe colder. Maybe a lot colder. Maybe degenerate matter cold. Again, impossible to say without experiments."

"What kind of experiments?"

"Experiments with spacetime seed creation. I have no idea how to do them at scale. Experiments I could do in a laboratory would be twenty orders of magnitude too weak to be meaningful."

"So what's left?" I felt like asking, but I didn't want to put Flossie down. Time for another direction. I took a moment to rest, lying next to Flossie, using her neck as a pillow. After a while, I closed my eyes and enjoyed the cool breeze coming off the ocean, a nice contrast to the warmth on my neck. "Uh, what about our current portal network, the control system?"

"What about it?"

"Can we experiment with the controls?"

"Experiment how? Transfer operation is a routine, stable process."

I sat up and looked at Flossie. "How do we make it unstable?"

Flossie turned her head and stared at me. "I don't know."

We kept talking. Eventually we tried expanding the issue, working on how to approach the problem rather than how to solve it — no answers, just coming up with lots of questions, then discussing which questions seemed the most important. We were all members of the military unit investigating portals, and we had been given extensive operational training during the last semester. Was there anything in our past training that would suggest a course of action? What about our future training? What were our options? Flossie started coming up with wild ideas, pure speculation but things that could in principle be tested if we had full access to a portal control system. Our conversation became intense, and the rest of the day passed unnoticed. We lit a lantern at sunset, our lunch forgotten.

Chapter 15

Three weeks later.
Time: Southern Autumn 28, 3485 33:40 Time Zone 0
Time: February 5, 2101 12:01 AM GMT

After a full nine hours of Earth policy debate, the Council at Haven called a six-hour recess, and I met Jorani outside the main chamber. We had planned to have lunch with a group of opposition councilors, but after a few minutes of conversation, they became so captivated by Jorani's ability to understand native speech that I decided to beg off and let Jorani shine in her own light. I wandered around the capitol and finally settled in an impressive study area and do some reading and wait for the daily update from Earth. Brussels decided to resume transmission five days ago. Most of my classmates were dismayed by what the packages contain. Not by world news. The Pic had been keeping us up-to-date with the global situation on Earth. It was the personal messages from our families. Most of them seemed to fear we have met some horrible end, and that they were sending their messages of concern down a black hole.

Right on schedule, my PA beeped. The daily update had arrived. I checked my mail, letters from my parents, cousins, then I blinked when I saw an extensive text message from Cossette with photo attachments. It was the first time she had written to me since I had come to Whistlestop, and two long Earth-years since we had split up.

I wasn't up for that. I flipped to global news and read the lead stories for a while before leaving the library. I wandered to a corridor that had a directory and noticed Longfellow's office was nearby. I ambled to his open doorway and peeked inside.

Longfellow appeared to be working intently on some report, sitting Pic fashion on the floor surrounded by a large desk. The room was more cluttered than most Pic would have preferred, though somehow

Longfellow seemed content to be in the center of the chaos. And then I saw the packing crates. Longfellow was the representative of River Heights, a Northern Hemisphere city build along the longest cascade on the planet, and his nine-year term would end in a few weeks, about a half-year ahead of Maayan's last day. During my first year at Whistlestop, I was glad that the chief opponent to the fusion trial would leave office before our chief advocate. But so much had changed since then. I was truly sorry he was leaving. Longfellow wasn't. I had an informal lunch with him last weekend, and he confided he was quite happy to be returning to his normal profession, a middle-school ethics teacher.

Longfellow glanced at me now and chirped in native Pic, "I was hoping you'd stop by." He made a hand gesture to a comfortable lounge chair in the room before getting back to his report. I walked in and sat down. *Interesting that Longfellow would have a human chair in his office.* "Be patient," Longfellow whistled. "This is important."

I nodded, looking around the office. There were a number of family photos on his desk. A large one caught my attention. It was a picture of four beta girls — if I had to guess, one about sixteen, one about twelve, and two eight-year-olds. They were playing a Pic field game similar to badminton doubles.

Rules of the Pic version of the game stated that each team had to complete a backcourt pass before sending the shuttle-cock over the net, and the oversize court plus the use of hand paddles rather than rackets made it physically impossible for Pic to clear the net from the backcourt. A team was allowed six hits per return, and an expert return took four: pass to the backcourt, backcourt pass, pass to the forecourt, then a final hit over the net. Pic loved the sport, but it hasn't caught on with the humans at Providence. There was too much running in the game.

In the picture before me now, the pink and gold twelve-year old was pure grace and beauty, spinning in midair, her arm cocked to whack the shuttle-cock over the net. "Okay, finished," Longfellow said in English, interrupting my thoughts.

"All these girls yours?" I asked.

Longfellow nodded. "I have a single wife. We petitioned the lottery, had twins."

"Ah…" I put the picture back on the desk. "Very cute kids."

"Yeah, four bundles of energy…" Longfellow gave me a long look. "I read a report on your work activities, your friends' too. You've chosen to go through portal training at a hectic pace… deep space missions with remote operator licenses in two seasons. Any particular reason why?"

"Of course. Reason number one is what happened in Iran." I gave Longfellow a knowing look, secretly hoping he wouldn't press for details or ask what reason number two might be.

"Hmm… Getting enough sleep?"

I grinned. "It is a challenge."

Longfellow gave a deep sigh, his muzzle pattern displaying a mixture of regret and uncertainty. "The status report I'm reading, it concerns research on the Earth plague. We've constructed a phage to attack the monstrosity Earth has created."

I gave a soft cry. "My gosh, that's great news! Thank you!" Earth news reports were saying that the death toll from the plague was approaching that of the Iranian disaster. I stared at Longfellow. "How soon?"

"Phage development is complete. Work on the vaccine has passed laboratory proof-of-principle. We should have enough to run a human trial shortly. Assuming the trial is successful, it may take another season to supply Earth with mass quantities." He paused and added quietly, "The council is still debating the scope of our involvement." Longfellow shuddered.

I was horrified. "You can't let us become extinct!"

"Steven, Iran is a mystery, but this plague is not. It's a blatant violation of our agreements on technology transfer and entirely a product of your species' insanity. It's not our fault!"

"It doesn't matter that it's not your fault!" I grabbed the badminton picture off his desk and held it before his eyes, almost shoving it into his snout. "Imagine your daughter is dying of some disease! It's your job to get her to a hospital! It doesn't matter that she didn't get infected by you! It doesn't matter that it's not your fault!"

Longfellow's snout lit up like a bottle-rocket, fast alternating red and pink rings traveling from cheeks to tip of snout. He spoke with difficulty, "And this is why you offered your life for Ann!"

"Exactly!"

"And now you're asking us to do the same!"

I took a deep breath, buying a few seconds to collect my thoughts. "Yeah, I guess I am. I'm not blind to the risk Whistlestop would be taking. But look at the problem Earth is facing. There's no evidence in billions of years of geology that Earth was attacked by extraterrestrials. Then you show up and Iran happens, plus you're refusing to provide any proof that the fusion trial candidates are still alive."

Longfellow sat silently, deep in thought, and meanwhile inspiration struck me. Was this the perfect opportunity to suggest something so outrageous it just might work? I played with the idea in my head for a moment, and then summoned some courage. "Sir?"

A simple hand gesture and chirp to go on.

"There's another option, one that would help with the problem of Earth not trusting you, plus solve a few other issues too." I had Longfellow's full attention. "Send some of us back to Earth."

"What? If you're volunteering, let me remind you"

"No, no, I'm not suggesting myself. But Earth needs proof, and given what's happened, they deserve proof. It's time for you to let go of what you won at the bargaining table. And besides… There are several humans at Providence who never should have come to Whistlestop."

Longfellow made a popping noise, a Pic gesture combining annoyance and surprise. "And how do you think you know this?"

"I don't know for sure. People say small things, clues. I put them together. I inferred that our escorts lobbied for us to start with a full class, twenty additional pairs, one pair that included Jorani. Tell me if I'm wrong."

Longfellow made a second popping noise. "I suppose you won't divulge the people who gave you these clues."

I smiled. "Oh, I'll tell you one." I repeated the hand signs he gave Julie so long ago.

I'd give Longfellow credit. It only took a few seconds for his muzzle to turn bright yellow with embarrassment, and he made no effort to hide the emotion. "Have you told anyone else?" he asked quietly.

"Only Jorani, and she's promised never to speak of it… Longfellow, the escorts made the right decision. Whistlestop got twenty additional people who are wonderful assets to the fusion trial, and as for the other twenty, most have adjusted. But a few haven't. Sending them back to Earth would be the right thing to do."

We talked for another half hour. Longfellow asked a slew of questions but revealed little of his intentions. Time was approaching for us to rejoin the Council, and Longfellow wanted to talk to a few Councilors beforehand. He excused himself and left me sitting in his office. He trusted me that much.

I stared at his family pictures for a while, picked up the badminton picture again and realized the frame had a video mode. I watched Longfellow's middle daughter complete her strike. She could have made a kill shot, but instead lobbed a high, easy pop-up to the twins. Pic were often cooperative in their games, far less competitive than humans. An analogy would be people playing catch with a Frisbee. Asking them who was winning would be nonsensical.

It was time to go, and I put the picture back on the desk, but my eyes were still drawn to the girls. Would we humans at Providence protect these children just as firmly as Longfellow would? Earth would not, but would we? For a moment, the whole fusion trial seemed to hang on that question. Before getting up, I queried my PA. Longfellow's colorful pink and red snout response was unknown to me. The dictionary translated it as epiphany, a sudden discovery of great knowledge.

Three weeks later.
Time: Southern Autumn 58, 3485 50:46 Time Zone 0
Time: Northern Spring 58, 3485 20:46 Time Zone 30
Time: March 8, 2101 8:12 PM Central European Time

The Pic transport was back on Earth, and Jorani, Karim and I were sitting at my dorm desk, a large display before us holding a standby military pattern. And then suddenly we were live, first with a Pic e-tech who saluted me, then with three humans sitting in a room many light-years away. I recognized one as Major Olsen, one of my instructors during finalist training on Earth. The others were Generals Tang and Beskal, who held similar positions with Jorani and Karim. We exchanged brief greetings, then General Tang opened with an implied question to Jorani.

"The Pic mentioned they would not be recording this conversation."

Jorani nodded. "That's right, ma'am. We asked to include personal pleas, besides what the Pic consider official business, and as a courtesy they're refraining from listening."

"And you believe them?"

"Without doubt," Jorani answered in a stern tone. And then she paused and her voice softened. "I can understand your skepticism. It was an adjustment for us too, when we first came here, learning to trust the Pic."

General Beskal spoke up. "Example?"

"Sure, my social gardening. Everyone on Whistlestop does it, children and adults and especially the elderly. My first year here, I would worry when I didn't go for a while, wonder if the Pic would notice, worry that I would be judged badly. But there really are no records kept. The activity is called the gifting and the purpose. It's not just for gardening; it's for exploring ideas, for rooting ourselves..." Jorani sighed and continued, "And as for this meeting, we're making our own copy, and of course you're recording on your end. Before we continue, we'd like to offer Earth a small gift. Steven?"

I nodded and stood up and took the video unit out to my balcony, making several slow sweeps of the scenery at various magnifications. It was a gorgeous midmorning, picture perfect, a southern sea breeze with fluffy white clouds and beautiful orange-yellow sunlight bathing the parks and stone paths leading down to the global ocean. I even managed close-ups of several species of shore-birds in flight, showing how easily they glided and pivoted on their double set of wings. Then I came in and surveyed my dorm room before sitting down.

There was a silent moment before Major Olsen spoke. "That was remarkable. Thank you. Nice desk, by the way. The returned candidates were not exaggerating. "

General Tang added, "It also confirms other details they described."

Jorani hesitated briefly and asked, "How is Phirun doing?"

"Very well. His debriefings at Brussels are complete. Phirun is now returning to Cambodia as our national hero. And you are the new liaison for the Pic government. Our country is very proud."

Major Olsen gave me a long look. "The stories we heard about you are also remarkable. You've passed the fusion trial?"

"I have."

"Does that mean you can return to Earth?"

"No. I'm just like other Pic citizens. We don't have the right to go to Earth just because we want to."

"That is unfortunate. The six who returned spoke of very abrupt isolation before their return. We would very much like to debrief you in person."

Karim answered before I could, and he allowed some annoyance to creep into his voice. "This is not a debriefing. And the isolation of the returning candidates was necessary to prevent smuggling of nano-crystals. The Pic are adamant that there be no further technology transfer. To be blunt, the reason we asked for this call is to lodge a complaint against Earth. What are you people trying to do, get us rejected?"

Jorani spoke up. "It's hard for us to imagine worse behavior. All three of us have spoken with the fusion-trial opposition. They say our conduct here is exemplary but their worst fears are being realized on Earth."

Karim continued. "It's not just the plague. The Pic suspected long ago that Earth was misusing their technology. That's why they shut down the joint research. But acting as if Whistlestop attacked Earth, holding Pic hostages…"

General Beskal seemed shocked that Karim was speaking like this. "We are not holding hostages!"

Karim shot back, "Oh, really? Are the researchers at Brussels free to leave Earth? Can the Pic relieve their crew in Antarctica? Can the Pic transport lift without permission? The Pic aren't stupid. They're trying to save you in spite of your attitudes!"

"And we are still being denied access to the other candidates!"

"That might change, in time." Jorani replied. "The issue is technology transfer. The Pic were somewhat shy about revealing their lack of understanding of the portals, but the real issue was Earth's misuse of Pic medical knowledge. We really, really don't want to be responsible for more of your weapons development."

"We? YOUR weapons development?!" cried General Tang.

Jorani shrugged, glancing at me and taking my hand. "I'm doing what Steven did a long time ago, what the other humans here are doing now. Whistlestop is our home. Earth's warfare seems so foreign to us now."

There was a long moment of awkwardness before Major Olsen broke the silence. "Is there anything new you can tell us, besides what we've gotten from the returning candidates?"

I nodded. "Yes, two things. We were asked to give you an update on the progress of the second probe. It is expected to reach Earth around April 9th, Northern Summer 28 our time. You'll be getting a request from the Pic shortly for permission for the second probe to land in Antarctica and relieve their base personnel."

"And the second thing?" asked General Beskal.

"To confirm progress on the vaccine. Each transport will have the capacity to deliver several hundred million doses per day by the time the second transport arrives. The military here is working on the logistics. Expect them to propose a quick-hop drop-off schedule using both portals. It'll be the quickest way for global distribution."

I was hoping for at least a token amount of gratitude, but Beskal's thoughts went in another direction. "The vaccine trial has just begun! And we have no understanding how these injections work!"

"General, the Pic have committed a huge amount of resources to this. This is not some crazy plot to inject humans with something harmful. Think! Their original collaboration in biomedical research was completely beneficial. It was Earth who weaponized their work."

Karim, Jorani and I had covered our agenda and we tried to end the conversation politely, but the people on the other end didn't seem to know how to say goodbye. They peppered us with questions, including asking for an explanation on the choice of the people sent back, five men and one woman. We tried to be polite in our refusals, but in the end Karim gave a big smile and an even bigger goodbye and cut the connection before they popped another question. He shook his head in disbelief and turned to Jorani. "Well, that was pleasant!"

Jorani grinned as she stopped our recording and playfully thumped Karim's shoulder with the back of her hand. "Cut them some slack! I'm sure they were under orders to extract as much information as possible."

"Yeah, I suppose." Karim stretched his neck diagonally Pic fashion, conceding the point. "That last part, though, I'm curious too. The Pic picked the six people who most wanted to go back. Any idea how they did that?"

Jorani smiled and replied with a hand sign, a Pic idiom popular among the alphas. It loosely translated as: "Some things are best left unexplored," with an emotional undercurrent of laughter.

Karim grinned then sighed. "I'll miss Parni."

Jorani leaned close and gently rested her hand on his forearm. "Were you two dating?"

"Uh, no, not enough to register, Parni didn't think so." Karim paused for a moment. "And she was quite happy to be going home." Another pause. "And the funny thing is, a year ago, maybe even a couple of seasons ago, I would have envied her return, but now I feel so relieved I'm still part of the trial."

Jorani nodded. "We've all changed. We had the right teachers to change, the right intelligence, and the right humility."

Karim stared at Jorani for a moment and then at both of us. "When we first came here, nobody talked as openly as a Pic. Listen to us now."

Jorani grinned and let go of his arm. "And don't worry! There are now four more women on Whistlestop than men!"

Karim chuckled. A moment later we all headed out for a late breakfast.

Afterwards, Jorani and I took a long run on the beach, heading west for a change, past the jetty and away from the flowering sand dunes. By early afternoon, we were at many kilometers from campus, perched on rocks, a cool ocean breeze blowing in our faces and the surf crashing against ancient rock about ten meters below us. As we settled down to enjoy the scenery, Jorani pulled fruit drinks and snacks from our backpacks. "You know, Karim almost had it right but not quite. The Pic didn't return the six people who most wanted to go back..."

I nodded and finished the sentence, "... the Pic sent back the *only* six people who wanted to go back. It's surprising nobody else picked up on that."

"Yeah, we humans can be a bit sleepy sometimes." Jorani took a sip of her drink and relaxed against me, gazing out to the horizon. "Think the ocean's warm enough for a quick dip?"

I gave a playful grin and asked, "Want to dive in here?"

271

Jorani laughed. The swirling ocean and rocks below would probably batter us senseless. "I am feeling sweaty from the exercise, but maybe when we get back to campus."

"Sure…"

After lunch, we wound up cuddling with each other, gazing at the sky and turning our imaginations loose. A fish, a snake, a whale, a mutant crab, an ice-cream sundae… one cloud did a great imitation of a leaping dog. Jorani started to fall asleep in my arms.

"I'm so glad I convinced you to take the rest of the day off," she murmured.

I brushed some stray black hairs from her temple, kissing her as she lay. "Me too."

Her eyes opened a crack. "What's it been, three weeks since we slept together?"

"Something like that. Oh hell, maybe four."

"Yeah, four, the weekend before we met at Haven." Jorani yawned. "Don't get me wrong. I do trust you."

It took me a moment to realize what Jorani meant. She wasn't commenting about me sleeping with someone else. She was saying she trusted that I knew the difference between dedication and obsession. "How's your thesis coming?" I asked, trying to change topics.

"Don't you know? Everything's been approved. I'll be spending most of the summer in Haven. How about the four of you? Can I ask where you'll be?"

It was public knowledge that Isaac, Julie, Flossie and I had been approved for a joint summer thesis, but its topic was classified. Everybody could guess the area of research though. "I think we'll be spending most of the summer on campus and at Far Rockaway. Maybe not at the end, though."

"Hmm…" Jorani's eyes were closed. "I miss being with you… I miss you so much…" And with that comment she drifted off. I looked down on her as she slept, so beautiful, and my mind flashed back to my last night on Sorrows' End. It was Isaac who thought up the last piece of our jigsaw puzzle, a window of opportunity that would open only once every three years and with a timeline that seemed almost impossible to meet. So far we were on schedule, and during our operational training, we had quietly confirmed Flossie's speculation at Sorrows' End of an anomaly in portal reset procedures. But there was still another full season of qualification exams before us. Dedication versus obsession? Even Jorani couldn't see what was going on, that terror could be a powerful motivator.

Three weeks later.
Time: Southern Winter 28, 3485 34:37 SST (Space Standard Time, Time Zone 0)

"Returning satellite secured, captain," I called out. "Deployed satellite reporting nominal on all diagnostics. I certify exchange-four complete."

"Acknowledged," replied the acting captain. "Good work, cadet."

I jumped and floated across the small bridge to the captain's web-chair and gave the human version of a crisp Pic salute. "Acting Captain Flossie, I relieve you."

Flossie saluted back. "Acting Captain Steven, I am relieved."

"Assume helm control and prepare to take us home, cadet," I replied, commanding Flossie to take the post I had just vacated.

"Yes, captain, assuming helm control." Flossie released her harness and made an accurate and graceful zero-g leap to her station. A few moments later, she said, "Helm programming complete."

"Helm programming verified," added Isaac from a nearby web-chair.

"Engage," I commanded.

"Brace for thrust," Flossie announced, and a second later, apparent gravity returned as we began our return journey.

We were aboard the training vessel *Guidestar*, one of the many portals berthed at Far Rockaway that had been outfitted for space travel. We had just finished the second half of our training mission, replacing four geo-synchronous satellites. The first half of the mission fulfilled our elective for portal operations licenses. All four of us had chosen advanced training in zero-g and low-g environments.

Whistlestop was currently a beautiful blue and white pearl more than twenty-five thousand kilometers away. As our thrust built to standard Whistlestop gravity, I took a long look at the massive bracing leading to our silent tetrahedron array, the source of our magical delta-V. Nano-crystals found at the lunar portal depot claimed the array was anchored to the gas giant Hera several light-hours distant, but there was never a way to verify this. Lies within lies... where was this thrust really coming from? I worked to suppress a shudder.

Unique to *Guidestar* was a secondary bridge, currently occupied by four senior officers who were silently monitoring our performance. Our instructions were to ignore their presence, and not even make eye contact. The Pic wanted this training exercise to be as realistic as possible.

Outside of defining the mission, almost everything was done by computers. When I first heard of the existence of the portal fleet, I wondered why they were manned at all, and I asked my instructor why not just control them remotely. She replied by reminding me that portal-to-portal communications occurred only between portal pairs, and that the nearest counterpart of the Far Rockaway fleet was more than a thousand light years distant. The Pic didn't want to risk the loss of such a priceless and irreplaceable asset to a problem with remote radio control.

I took a long look around the control room and smiled. The voyage was as enjoyable as I had anticipated. I was in command of a space vessel, and it was a good ship with a good name. It would have been disappointing if the Pic didn't name their vessels. With such a display of vastly different attitudes, maybe the fusion trial never would have occurred. An idle thought: *What would the officers aboard do if I suddenly commanded Flossie to lay in a course for the gas giant, or maybe ordered Isaac to prepare the portal for a jump to a distant region of the galaxy?* Our instructors would probably let it happen just to see how ridiculous I got, but it would be insane behavior, ruin everything. I brushed the crazy idea aside and reviewed the landing procedure I would command. Standard practice dictated not to use the atmosphere for braking. Instead we would shed all angular velocity relative to Far Rockaway at low orbital height then make a subsonic vertical descent. Wanting to look attentive, I next pulled up a diagnostic on ship performance.

Two weeks later.

Time: Southern Winter 48, 3485 39:23 Time Zone 0, Haven
Time: Northern Summer 48, 3485 9:23 Time Zone 30, Providence Campus
Time: Northern Summer 48, 3485 41:23 Time Zone -2, Far Rockaway
Time: April 30, 2101 2:25 U.T.

The brief chirp translated as, "Standby for clearance, jump 57." I understood it easily, and even picked up the slight expression of boredom in the chirp. Perfect! The oversight team we were working with had been crisp and efficient at the start of the experiment, but that was mid-morning, many hours before a series of mind-numbing repetitive jumps.

"Acknowledged," answered Julie. "Diagnostics are positioned for jump 57, gravitational recorders active. We are clear for jump."

Flossie, Julie, Isaac and I were inside a subnet portal at Far Rockaway, the one connecting to the lunar valley four light-seconds away. It was the logical choice for our experiment, as the portal was seldom used except for training purposes. The lunar facility at the end of our jump consisted of a few simple storage rooms and airlocks leading to a grotto which, for the last thirty-five hundred years, had been a parking lot full of nothing but lunar dust.

As we waited for our clearance, I started a monitoring program that confirmed a news announcement. We had run into a nice bit of luck. Pic transport number two was still safely on the ground near Edinburgh, Scotland, and had been granted a delay to accommodate an unplanned portal transfer. It seemed the Scots wanted to send a token gift of thanks for the vaccine. The transport's revised schedule was to lift at three-thirty AM for a short hop to the Azores, its last stop for vaccine transfer. Transport number one was berthed at Brussels, adding to the Pic's bank of precious metals and waiting clearance to relieve (finally!) the station crew in Antarctica. And my monitoring program confirmed another critical part of our plan. All interstellar portals were currently vacant of Pic. Any deviation and we would abort our experiment.

"Jump cleared. Quantum isolation in, chirp-click, ten seconds," came a message from the control team outside. The friendly warning to brace for gravitational shift had disappeared an hour ago, at least on the outward jumps.

And right on schedule, it seemed the floor tried to drop out from under me. We had been doing this all day, and it still felt somewhat disconcerting. Gravity on Whistlestop's moon was not much different than the gravity on Earth's moon, and the sensation of weight loss was profound. The urge to try a high jump would be nagging if I didn't have something to do — a meaningless set of observations to record gravitational effects on a cubic meter of water in the center of our experimental apparatus. That was the cover for our jump series. I looked around at my friends and noticed all three of their muzzles were pale yellow. With other Pic earlier in the day, they worked to hide the emotion, and Julie had confided to me in sign that it was a real struggle for her. Among ourselves, though, we had nothing to hide, and my companions were freely displaying their embarrassment.

Our portal location was unique. All other known portals were mobile. The lunar one was buried under twenty meters of rock, with a spiral slope through four airlocks leading to a grotto along a deep polar valley. The reason for such a setup was a mystery, though it did conceal the existence of the portals for almost a century of space exploration before the start of the current era.

"Recordings complete," announced Flossie to our remote support. "Reset in progress for jump 58." Her chirps seemed remarkably calm. We were almost there! Everything so far was smoke and mirrors. But Flossie had predicted the unusual configuration of jump 58 would leave the entangled spacetime fabric with a residual twist and vulnerable to what was coming in jump 59, what Flossie called an anchor-shift scissors jump. "Reset complete," announced Flossie.

"Standby for clearance, jump 58."

"Acknowledged," answered Julie. "Diagnostics are positioned for jump 58, recorders active. We are clear for jump." At this moment, the jump-control team was verifying their status indicators with what had been predicted by previous analysis of the jump series. During the long series, Flossie had striven to light up as many uncommon warning lights and out-of-bound indicators as she could, in order to lull the operations team into a false sense of familiarity with unusual readings.

"Jump cleared. Prepare for gravitational shift. Quantum isolation in, chirp-click, ten seconds." Then, for the first time all day, I didn't notice the jolt as we returned to Far Rockaway and standard Whistlestop gravity. *Game time!* If Flossie's calculations were correct, the jump control team outside our chamber was now staring at strange deviations from our last jump, status indicators in unprecedented states. An alert control team would stop the experiment immediately.

But was this crew alert? We were in the weekend before an extended holiday period, the week when guild and union leaders negotiated salaries and budgets for the next three years while the rest of the world took an extended vacation filled with games and quiet times of reflection. Normally during this week, the interplanetary network would be totally inactive and experiments such as ours postponed. But it was Isaac's insight on Sorrows' End that created an exception for us. Humans were very much a novelty on Whistlestop, and Isaac guessed that people would make changes in their holiday schedules to work with one. Our jump control team consisted of volunteers who were retired from active military service. They would never serve the civilian network except in emergencies, but all four of us inside the portal chamber had military clearance and remote-operator licenses. A much more relaxed set of standards were in effect.

"Recordings complete," announced Flossie. "Reset in progress for jump 59." One way or the other, our play-acting was almost over. The next few moments were critical. "Reset complete."

"Standby for clearance, jump 59."

Julie spoke her familiar refrain with her muzzle a brilliant yellow. "Acknowledged. Diagnostics are positioned for jump 59, recorders active. We are clear for jump." There was nothing to do now but wait and hope.

If we were right, what could we expect? We were hoping to transfer to the third portal of our tri-pole interchange. What could we expect there? Flossie was convinced the anchor node had to be at the bottom of a deep gravitational well, so we would be jumping into a weightless environment. Beyond that, everything was conjecture. Our greatest concern was that spacetime curvature at the anchor node might be harmful or even deadly to biological life. Opposed to this fear, Flossie was convinced access to the anchor would be essential for maintenance.

At Sorrows' End, we accepted the risk and pledged our lives to make this attempt.

A second risk concerned the scissors jump damaging the spacetime entanglement of the jump network. Flossie thought the risk extremely remote but could not prove it wouldn't happen — hence our safety check that the two transports on Earth were not in flight, and the vacant states of all other non-Whistlestop locations.

We were as prepared as we could be without arousing suspicion. Space suits and emergency supplies were with us one level below in the portal, standard procedure for lunar transfers. We could also handle some forms of hostile atmosphere, though extreme heat or cold or pressure outside the portal could still kill us.

"Jump cleared. Quantum isolation in, chirp-click, ten seconds."

My God, this is it! There wasn't time for another thought. Lunar-g meant failure and zero-g meant success. In a jump of extreme anti-climax, the four of us felt the unwanted return of familiar lunar gravity.

Chapter 16

I turned to Flossie and managed a grin while signing, "Well, at least we're not dead." Two seasons of unbelievable effort had just culminated in a flop. Ah, well. Sometimes the universe can be a harsh mistress. We had given it our best shot.

"Recordings complete," announced Flossie to our remote support. "Reset in progress for jump 60." Her chirps sounded flat, and her muzzle was displaying a pattern of frustration and loss. I hopped over in the low gravity and held my hand against the side of her neck as she completed her work. She leaned against me for a moment and gave a deep sigh. "Five more jumps to go," she chirped quietly. "I'm looking forward to some rest." "I was so sure," she added to me in a private muzzle flash. And then back to full voice, "Reset complete."

We were all expecting the familiar chirp from our control team to standby for clearance. I felt a sudden blast of goose bumps and my eyes snapped to our intercom when it remained silent. Isaac chirped a request for acknowledgement then started walking towards a control panel by the door. He was stopped by a sharp whistle blast from Julie. "Protocol!" she chirped. "Suits first!"

We were all dying of curiosity, but our training kicked in. We spent the next hour climbing into our space gear and executing the safety checks before returning to the control panel. Isaac took the lead in running the diagnostics. "Outside air is the normal oxygen / nitrogen mix, standard pressure."

Julie spoke up. "We've completed the jump to the moon. The gravitational probes are reading exactly the right gravity, and the outside air is correct too. Perhaps only our receiver has failed. Perhaps the control team can still hear us." Her gloved hands added an additional message. "It might be true! Be careful what you say!"

"Outside temperature has dropped," commented Isaac. "Barely above freezing."

"Can you run a diagnostic on the intercom?" asked Julie. "And try to get outside video."

"Try pulling up the history log too," I suggested. Isaac nodded, and we were in for a shock. One hour ago, the space outside our sphere was in vacuum. It had remained so for a few minutes, then slowly ramped up to atmospheric standard over the next hour, completing the process only a few minutes ago. I looked at my companions confused. "Could we have suffered a pressure loss at lunar station?"

"Through multiple airlocks, at the precise moment of our transfer?" replied Isaac. "Seems unlikely." After a few more minutes of typing, he said "Video monitors and intercom appear undamaged but there are no signals. The quantum router is completely dark, not even a carrier wave. We can speak freely."

"The key metrics will be in portal status," Flossie reminded us. "Isaac?"

Isaac worked the control panel a long moment before replying. "This is confusing. One diagnostic is still recognizing our portal as entangled space, but there's nothing registering as a destination link. That makes no sense. How can we be entangled with nothing? And the tetrahedron array has the same weird idle condition, entangled but unlinked."

"And yet we still have power," said Flossie. "Where's it coming from?"

"Yeah…" Isaac spent another long moment typing on the panel. "Don't know."

"How can we have portal diagnostics without the quantum router?" Julie chirped, "How can you not know?"

"This is so strange. I would guess power is hardwired, but there's no display for it. It's the same for portal diagnostics, everything looks point-to-point, no addressing. Why build like this? It's not that network control is down. It seems to have disappeared."

"Lunar station has backup solar power," chirped Julie again. "That would be hardwired. Maybe our transfer ruptured the rock. Could this still be the moon?"

Isaac replied in English. "Solar power monitoring is not even present on this control panel. And if the station were ruptured, it would not be able to re-pressurize. I propose we assume this is not the moon."

Perhaps our unlikely risk had come to pass, though the evidence was confusing. Did Flossie's "scissors jump" destroy our portal link? Julie chirped a comment to Flossie about a path of no return. Isaac chirped back, "We were hoping for zero-g."

"I know, but it's useful to have some gravity," Julie countered.

Flossie turned to all three of us and spoke in English. "How can there be gravity at the anchor node? The scissors jump worked! The fine details of my equations worked but the basic foundation didn't? Is that possible?" She then growled and chirped something so quickly that Isaac chirped an affirmative back before I interpreted what Flossie meant. She was asking to assume leadership of our group.

It was something we had discussed on Sorrows' End. We all had the same military officer rank, and Julie technically should assume command because she had the longest time in service. But back on Sorrows' End, Julie had objected to the role and nominated Flossie instead. Flossie had not been particularly comfortable with the thought of commanding our expedition either, but in critical moments, her insight into portal physics might be our key to survival, and rather than having her explain to another leader what we should be doing, having Flossie in charge seemed to make the most sense. I nodded yes to Flossie now, and Julie also chirped agreement.

Flossie took a deep breath and tried to speak with the crisp confidence of a leader. "It's time we found out where we are. Suits on internal, everyone, and call out your safety checks. Isaac, open the bay door after we confirm our seals. Steven, I'm promoting you to second-in-command."

We entered the airlock and closed the inner door. Opening the outer door was an event in itself. An invisible wind blasted into our small chamber, something none of us was expecting. We all leaned into the push and stepped outside. And for a moment we were speechless, the muted roar of the wind the only sound within our helmets.

Were we standing on a world or buried in some enormous cavern? It seemed impossible to decide. The lighting wasn't great but enough to see clearly. Behind us was the familiar shape of a portal. And just a few meters ahead across a smooth, gun-metal floor was a gigantic pit, more than a kilometer in diameter. There was an enormous spiral along the chasm wall, and the wind was blowing clockwise in the direction of the spiral, giving the impression of the pit being the gigantic catch-basin of a tornado. A strange wind... the force was fierce but the air crystal clear, no particulates, and extra dangerous with the low gravity.

And above! Impossibly organized, multi-colored stars laid out in neat rows and columns, densely packed and diamond-hard in brightness, filling the dome of the... sky? No, it must be artificial, a cavern, but the scale was just too great to think of it as such. We were standing on the surface of a world, a silvery surface extending far to a distant horizon. Or was it an illusion? I pulled my eyes away from the impossible, overwhelmed with a desire to focus on something familiar, and noticed Isaac was hugging the ground in a low gait and slowly crawling towards the edge of the pit.

"Hey, Isaac, get a safety line on. The wind could blow you off the edge."

"Yes, sir," he replied, backing up immediately. It took me a second to realize Isaac had already internalized my promotion to second-in-command.

"We shouldn't be out here," decided Flossie. "Not yet. Everyone, back inside."

We kept our suits on internal as we waited inside the airlock for Isaac to complete a diagnostic on the air. "Ultra-pure oxygen-nitrogen mix, no organics at all, not even water vapor. Dry to breathe but otherwise okay."

We opened the inner seal and took off our helmets. Julie and Isaac remained on the main level to run more diagnostics while Flossie and I went below to activate our mobile probes. We were completing a check list on their functions when Flossie turned to me and said, "I made a mistake during my first minute of command. Did it occur to you that we should not go out and send the probes first?"

"No. I was like you, curious."

Flossie flashed a muzzle pattern equivalent to a frown. "I suspect we're in an environment where curiosity can get us killed."

I smiled. "We humans have a saying about that: Curiosity killed the cat. But here's another Earth saying: Fortune favors the brave!"

Flossie thought for a moment and nodded. "That's true; exploration is intrinsically a risky business. So you're saying it's my job as leader to find the right balance between safety and exploration."

"Well... almost. The two goals are so oppositional, personally, it never feels like a balance to me. I see exploration as being off balance, on purpose."

Flossie stared at me then closed her eyes. A moment later she gave a soft, unearthly cry. I had never heard a Pic make such a beautiful sound, and I had no idea what it meant. Flossie opened her eyes and said, "Exploration is a business humans understand better than Pic."

I sensed where Flossie was going and headed her off. "We hashed this out on Sorrows' End. Having you in charge is the correct setup."

"All right. Just remember to give me lots of advice. That's an order!"

It was my turn to pause. "That scenery out there, it must be an illusion, right?"

Flossie shrugged. "It seemed real to me. The range finders on the probes should tell us a few things... Steven?"

"Hmm?"

"I know this question is going to sound really weird, but did that pit remind you of anything?"

"Well... You mean a nightmare version of Wuthering Heights?"

Flossie breathed a deep sigh of relief. "Yes! I saw it too, the proportion of the spiral along the far wall; it's a close match to Wuthering Heights' switchback roads and features, the slope, the depth, the separation between the bands. And both roadways are carved into the walls. It's very distinctive, don't you think?"

"Which implies... what? The Storytellers went extinct at the end of the Old Kingdoms. They were a pre-industrial society."

"I know."

"And the timelines don't match. What about Sorrows' End, forty million years ago?"

Flossie flashed a muzzle pattern of distress. "I know, I know, nothing fits. Forty million years ago, we were migrating animals. I would assume the same is true for the Storytellers. And Wuthering Heights was cut with stone and copper tools; there's clear evidence of that. And yet...

This would be a great place for Storytellers. With the low gravity, they would have true flight, don't you think?"

"Forty million years... I don't know what pre-humans were back then. Nothing I would recognize as human, that's for sure." I paused. "Some people back on Earth wonder if portals can be used for time travel."

"No, they can't."

"Are you sure? It would explain a few things."

"Nonsense never explains anything correctly. Spacetime is the universe's ultimate non-renewable resource. Traveling backwards in it would create infinitely deep physical paradoxes. Trust me on this one. Speaking as a physicist, it can't happen."

"Uh, how about time dilation, not traveling backwards, but boosting close to light speed?"

"My physics model affirms the dilation limit. Try to boost more than a factor of two, you'll destroy the entanglement. You would never be able to decelerate." Flossie paused and added, "Until you finally hit something, perhaps."

A sudden, whacky idea occurred to me. "How about relays? Multiple pairs of portals with each pair giving a manageable boost?"

Flossie laughed. "I have no idea if that's possible, having multiple anchor nodes. And even if it were, for a forty-million year journey? What would be the point?"

I thought for a moment and admitted defeat. "Yeah, maybe not."

Flossie nodded as probe diagnostics chirped successful completion. "Let's go."

We brought all six probes up to the main level, then sent two out the front door. It was a huge relief to find the wind speed had dropped to little more than a stiff breeze. We spent about an hour testing our controls as the wind continued to die. The probes responded flawlessly. It was finally time to activate the range finders and get some answers. Isaac maneuvered probe number one to the edge of the pit. It was difficult to appreciate its size on the video monitor.

"Diameter 1130 meters and a fraction," Isaac called out as the probe's lasers made their measurements. "A pure circle at the top, to the limits of probe accuracy. Six full spirals to the bottom. See how the spirals are carved into the wall? Probes are measuring about a five-meter by five-meter cutout. Diameter of the bottom plain is reading... 1130 meters and the same fraction. The walls must be pure vertical."

"How deep?" asked Julie.

"Getting that now... Care to guess? Same distance as the diameter. Amazing to think of precision metal working on such a scale." Isaac turned to Flossie. "Clear for high intensity?"

Flossie nodded. "Fire one pulse."

"Synchronize the spectrometers of both probes," I suggested. "Might as well make a backup measurement."

Isaac nodded as he worked the controls. "Targeting the far wall, just below the rim... firing... spectral lines are identifying two elements, platinum and iridium... nothing else. Horizon measurement next."

Isaac repositioned the video displays, but before he could begin measuring the distance to the horizon, another attribute of our strange environment jumped out at us. The diamond-filled sky above us was rotating, and rapidly too. With a nod from Flossie, Julie activated a backup control station and took control of one of the probes. After a few moments, she made her report. "Our rotational speed is tremendous, less than two hours per revolution. I'm going to track some stars at various angles. That should tell us our latitude. But I think it's obvious we're near the equator, with our portal door facing one of the poles."

Meanwhile, Isaac was making visual measurements with the other probe, making full use of its telescoping ability to raise the sensors several meters and make precise measurements of the changing angle to the horizon. "Parallax says the horizon is real, consistent with a planetary radius 2800 to 2900 kilometers... But I'm not getting a reading with the range finder. Diagnostics are suggesting some sort of anomalous scattering. Permission to try a high-intensity pulse?"

Flossie froze for a moment, then her muzzle flashed with horror. "What? No, no, shut down the range finder! Try getting an acoustical echo."

"From the pit?"

"No, from the horizon."

Isaac blinked. "Ah, okay." He rotated the probe away from the pit. A minute later... "You were right. I'm getting a clear echo from something huge, something close, less than fifty meters away. Are the lights in the sky that close?"

"Map everything," ordered Flossie. "Echo everything above the horizon."

The soundings were remarkable. They revealed a hemisphere enclosing us and the pit. "How is this possible?" asked Isaac. "Acoustical echoes show the lights to be close, yet the horizon is distant."

Flossie flashed a negative muzzle response, and it suddenly hit me what she was suspecting. "The lights are above some sort of transparent dome?"

Flossie nodded. "I can't think of anything else that fits our observations. Steven, how precisely can multiple probes synch their gyros?"

"Uh, I don't remember exactly, but if the probes can maintain laser contact... Are you thinking of making parallax measurements to the lights?"

"Yes. I'm considering sending one of the probes to the opposite side of the pit, where the spiral begins." Flossie looked at us all. "Any objections?"

There were none. A half hour later we got our answer. The lights were three hundred and forty-six kilometers distant directly above our heads, and overall forming a great inner sphere of radius 3295 kilometers. That helped us make a new estimate for our planet's radius: 2849 kilometers.

The probes were recalled, and once they were safely inside recharging, we sat in a circle to discuss our situation. I queried my PA for the log I had been making, and made an announcement. "At the time of our last jump, Earth Portal One was still at Brussels, and Earth Portal Two was still on the ground at Edinburgh."

Isaac sighed. "Could one bad jump really destroy everything?"

Flossie answered with a soft chirp. "Given our anomalous readings with our entanglement, I can't discount the possibility. It does surprise me though. Let's consider the question unresolved."

"But even if we destroyed all the Type-I portals, wouldn't the Type-II portals still be functional? The transports would still be able to fly."

Flossie just shrugged. "I don't know what the true topology is. All our standard assumptions are based on lies."

"Flossie?" I asked, changing the topic. "How did you know we're under an invisible dome?"

"It's obvious, isn't it?"

"No, not to me."

"When we first came here, the outside was registering vacuum conditions. Think of trying to pressurize the surface of an entire planet in a single hour. The winds would be unbelievable, especially with this planet's rate of rotation. Though…" Flossie paused. "Calling it a planet may be a mistake."

Julie chirped, "What is it then?"

"I believe it's the spacetime seed generator I talked about on Sorrows' End."

I shook my head. "All these months, you've been insisting the anchor node has to be at the core of the seed generator. We jumped to the surface of this… thing."

"I know. I'm still guessing my basic framework is correct. But yes, there is something major that I'm not getting."

Julie continued my protest. "But the gravity is so light."

"Not at all. Think of the density of iridium and the size of the sphere we're standing on. Everything fits."

Julie gave a high effortless leap and drifted back down like a feather. "This fits?"

"Yes, don't you see?" asked Flossie. "We're at the equator of a rapidly spinning object. The spin is cancelling almost all the gravity. I've done the calculations in my head. I'm convinced this is a seed generator. The fast spin is exactly what it needs to function."

The implications of what Flossie was saying finally hit me. "Yikes. Good thing we're not at the poles."

"Indeed. I estimate surface gravity there to be 2.6 times Whistlestop standard. Not enough to kill instantly perhaps, but I suspect high enough to kill slowly. Our bodies aren't designed to operate under such stress, not for days at a time."

"You're assuming the planet is solid iridium-platinum?" asked Isaac.

"I think solid iridium would be closer to the correct density," replied Flossie. "Do the numbers. Perhaps platinum was added to the surface covering."

Julie spoke up. "And what's above the lights in the sky?" She chirped a small shriek. "Are we inside a star?"

"My mind shudders at the thought, just like yours," replied Flossie as she yawned. "It's been a full day. I'm sure we're all tired. Does anyone see a need for urgent action?" Getting no response, Flossie suggested we have a meal and sack out for the night.

While Flossie and Isaac prepared a meal below, Julie and I went to the top level and activated our recyclers. All of our organic waste would be reprocessed. It would be a long time before we would starve. But as Isaac pointed out later during dinner, we still had a major survival problem. "Water," he commented, "is going to be a long-term problem. The air outside is so dry, we're going to be drinking extra water to compensate, and what we exhale will be lost."

Julie shrugged. "We have enough for a year if we're careful. And if we haven't found a way out by then…" She didn't verbalize the rest, but her snout flashed something too quickly for me to read.

"Any place would be a miserable place to die," Isaac countered. "Courage, Julie!"

Julie still looked dejected. I moved over and threw an arm over her, lightly scratching the side of her neck, and then made a comment to Flossie. "Between the dome and the lights above us, are you thinking it's a vacuum?"

Flossie nodded. "Reasonable assumption. Nothing beats vacuum for a lack of friction."

"And underneath the dome, we're at full atmosphere. The bursting pressure must be tremendous."

Flossie shrugged. "Not necessarily."

"No?"

"Think of the atmosphere on Earth or Whistlestop. The lowest region has the highest pressure, but it doesn't burst the upper atmosphere into space."

"Uh…" I thought about Flossie's point for a moment. "You're thinking about the weight of the dome?"

Another nod. "The engineering of the dome is spectacular, but it's nothing compared to building the seed generator. We're just not used to thinking of construction on this scale. Our minds rebel. Everything becomes magic... You're right. Perhaps it's not dome weight, just more magic." Flossie looked at us thoughtfully and added, "Tomorrow we should explore the pit. Opinions?

Julie chirped, "Start with the probes."

Flossie flashed a muzzle pattern for indecision. "I'm leaning in that direction, but am open to counter arguments. The probes are designed for repairs at lunar station, not extended explorations."

Isaac frowned. "The probes recharge on solar power. The lights in the sky will do almost nothing for them. They probably have enough power to ride the spiral down to the floor of the pit, but could they pull themselves up again?"

"The gravity is light," countered Julie. "That will help."

"Isaac has a point," I commented. "Round trip along the spiral is over forty kilometers, plus we'll need power to explore the bottom. We could calibrate the power needs, run a couple of probes down part way, one farther than the other, and then bring them back... Maybe we could run a power cable down the side of the pit."

"Where do we get one?" asked Julie.

Flossie latched onto my idea immediately. "There's spare cable below for the lunar solar collectors. It's just what we need."

Isaac looked dubious. "It's a huge drop. Can the cable support its own weight?"

"Uh... Well, we can anchor the cable at each spiral intersection. They have carbon nanotube sheathing, and with the low gravity, I think we might be okay. I'll do the calculations later." Flossie then turned to me. "You agree then? It's best we start with the probes?"

I hesitated. "I'm not sure. What's more critical, losing time or a life? I guess starting with the probes is reasonable... Flossie, do we really have that much cable?" Flossie thought for a moment until the Pic equivalent of an expletive flashed across her muzzle.

It was the end of a uniquely stressful day. We cleaned up after dinner, ran a final check on all primary diagnostics, and then went to the lower level to unpack our sleeping gear. And lo, in spite of or maybe because of all that had happened today, Flossie's and Isaac's muzzles started turning yellow, with distinctive rippling black stripes when they were close to each other. I saw Julie working to keep her own muzzle a neutral gray, and then she made a brilliant suggestion that someone should keep an eye on the food recyclers on the top level. I took the hint and suggested that Julie and I sleep by the recyclers. Isaac and Flossie agreed it was an excellent idea.

There was more than enough room to lay down our sleeping mats on the top level. I picked a spot away from the recyclers, and shortly afterwards Julie placed her mat next to mine. We exchanged goodnights and Julie killed the room lights, though numerous equipment displays were still illuminating the room. I lay on my back for a while trying to relax; not having much success.

Julie gave a deep sigh. "I feel lost, so far from home with no way to get back. We could be halfway across the universe."

"I know." I tried to think of something encouraging to say, something that didn't sound condescending. The thought just wouldn't coalesce.

"I can't shake the feeling this is a place of death. I'm afraid."

I sighed. "You're not alone. I'm afraid too. And have you noticed Isaac's muzzle since we got here?"

Julie chirped a quiet laugh. "Steven! I've been reading muzzles a lot longer than you. Isaac is terrified that Flossie will get hurt. He adores her."

"Oh…" I turned on my side to face her, placing my hand on her neck. The pink and gold feather-fur was silky soft. "Our future is undetermined. We have a chance to succeed. And even if we die here, maybe we broke the portal links, all of them. Both our worlds would be safe from the monsters that built this place. That alone is worth dying for."

"Yes…" We were silent for a while, until we heard muffled whistles from two levels below. Julie sighed. "Difficult to imagine being aroused in a place like this."

"Oh, I don't know. If Jorani were here now, I think she would look like the sexiest thing imaginable."

Some time drifted by. Julie quietly whistled Max's name in native Pic.

"Julie?"

"Hmm?"

"What does it mean when a Pic trills?"

"Huh? Pic don't trill."

"Well, not really a trill…"

Julie gave a soft growl. "Steven, you're not making sense."

"Flossie made a cry earlier. I've never heard anything like it, not from a Pic."

"Can you describe it? Not from a Pic? Some other creature, perhaps?"

Julie's question jogged a memory. "Hold on…" I queried my PA for a while, eventually pulling up the cry of a loon. "It was a beautiful cry, mournful and majestic, a lot like this," I commented, as I played the short recording.

Julie sucked her breath. "Your bond with Flossie is deeper than I realized."

"Hmm? How so?"

"That's the Pic cry of appreciation; usually reserved for a child to give his or her teacher-mother." She paused and added, "Flossie thought you told her something wonderful, on the order of revealing a profound insight. What did you say?"

"Huh? I don't know. We were talking about exploration, just general stuff. Flossie thinks I'm her mother?"

"I don't mean that. Have you ever met Flossie's parents?"

"Uh huh, twice actually, a monogamous couple, beta male, alpha female. They're both members of a reclamation union. Flossie is their only child."

"I know. I've met her parents too. What is your opinion of them?"

"Uh, they're nice people… and I'm sure they love Flossie…"

Julie sensed the hesitation in my voice. "But?"

"I'm surprised they're not prouder of her. I don't know, just a feeling."

Julie sighed. "It's a known fact. Gamma children need siblings and a teacher-mother, more so than alphas and betas. Especially in their adolescent years, they need emotional support. I'm not certain, but from what Flossie has told me, I think her adolescence was unusually lonely."

I thought of all the things Flossie had confided in me. "Her adolescence was horrible. She didn't have classmates she could trust."

Julie chirped, "What?", switching to native Pic with a peculiar whistle that is has no simple English translation. The short burst conveyed shock and revulsion with an undercurrent that it would be inappropriate to press for details.

I didn't say anything after that, just curled up around Julie's back and rested my head, using the back of her pink neck as a pillow and draping an arm across her ribs and flank, sinking my fingers into the silky, striped feather-fur. The only sounds were the low hums of the various systems around us. We drifted off to sleep.

Chapter 17

Eight days later.
Time: Southern Winter 56, 3485 45:06 Time Zone 0, Haven
Time: Northern Summer 56, 3485 15:06 Time Zone 30, Providence Campus
Time: May 8, 2101 14:25 U.T.

The meeting was scheduled to start at 15:30 local time in the administrative area of the campus portal complex. Jorani had received a summons a short hour ago, just before sunrise, while she and her classmates were finishing breakfast and getting ready for their eighth day of labor. Just a few moments for hugs and words of encouragement from the student council, then Jorani was whisked off by portal military personnel. It was a summons she thought long overdue.

Both students and faculty were working to convert the campus golf course to farmland. Very active work, even with the excellent greenhouse equipment, and it also provided a good example of Pic foresight. It had never occurred to Jorani why the campus greenhouses were located adjacent to the golf course, or why the grounds-keeping facilities were so extensive. With occasional support from fishing trawlers, the island was becoming completely self-sustaining.

And just as impressive was to see how quickly the Pic had adapted to the world's calamity — just a single day to get over the shock that everything had changed. Jorani remembered it vividly.

Her final day working with linguists in Haven, jumping back to Providence for a night's rest, then the commotion rousing her in the middle of the night. Digital Rivers was down, the campus was running on backup hydrogen fuel cells, and the military had sealed the portal complex. All off-island communication channels were unresponsive, even the backup satellite routers. Rumors were flying at dazzling speed and becoming more absurd with each passing hour.

It was late morning by the time the military released the hard news. The worst rumors were true. The portals were dead, Type I and Type II, and not just on campus. Everything was gone, including the subnet at Far

Rockaway. All the magic had disappeared in an instant. Temporarily? Permanently? No one seemed to know, except Jorani thought she might when she caught sight of Professor Feynman's muzzle. She was expecting him now, seven days later. Jorani had been asked to join a conference call, live via satellite. The phrase had been obsolete on Earth for a hundred Earth years, on Whistlestop, for three millennia. But perhaps no longer.

Such a resilient species, Jorani thought, *so different from how humans would have reacted to a worldwide calamity.* No panics, no riots, just an initial day of shock filled with hugs, reassurances, and adaptations to the new reality. It was remarkable how so much had changed, and also how little. The farm conversion work was almost complete and the autumn term would start on schedule, the only academic change being the majority of courses would be taught remotely until teachers who had been off campus for the holidays could return by ship to Providence. And all sporting activities were indefinitely suspended, replaced by farm work.

Throughout the last two years, the campus had enjoyed a bountiful supply of fresh fish. The ocean around Providence was filled with abundant life; it was how the island got its name millennia ago. With the construction of the campus, military fishing vessels would frequently dock and recharge their hydrogen fuels cells courtesy of infinite portal energy, and they would gladly leave premium parts of their catch for the students. The practice would still continue, but at a slower pace. Currently, the island road-array of solar collectors was producing more power than the campus needed, building its supply of hydrogen for the coming winter of darkness.

As Jorani glanced at her wrist assistant, two gamma military personnel entered the conference room. They gave her polite but formal hand signs of greeting. From their insignia, Jorani thought they were the acting station commander and an assistant. The commander sat down on the floor at other end of the table from Jorani while his assistant set up the bridge. Several minutes later, Ellie walked into the room followed by her husband Professor Feynman, both with grim expressions on their muzzles. As they were taking their places at the table, their son-in-law Max walked in, and he looked absolutely devastated. He came to an open space next to Jorani but did not sit, instead pressing his head against Jorani's thigh. Jorani had not seen him for two days and she was dying to ask him what was wrong, but she resisted the urge. She rested her hand on his neck.

There was some brief chatter over the bridge confirming everyone's presence, then Maayan's whistle came from the intercom. "Jorani, how comfortable are you with having this conversation in native mode? For your replies, we are satisfied with the quality of your application. And we also have backup translators."

Jorani pulled up the mentioned app on her PA and tapped the record icon. "Not my application. This was definitely a team effort with the Haven linguists. And to answer your question: okay, but I need to caution you, I'll have a hard time understanding if two people are whistling at once, and I might miss things if I'm nervous." Jorani then tapped the translate icon and a whistling burst emanated from her PA.

Maayan whistled, "Jorani, there are a series of questions the Council needs to ask you. Please begin by telling us everything you know of the summer thesis Steven and his friends were working on."

"What?" Jorani gasped before typing record again. "Is Steve okay?! I know nothing of their military work. Maybe he mentioned he might be at Far Rockaway, but he never talked about the work itself. Max and I have talked. Julie never tells him anything either. Steven and Julie play it by the book. What happened? Is Steve okay? What about Julie and the others?"

"Play it by the book?" asked Maayan.

"They follow all the rules, complete obedience." Jorani turned to Ellie and squirmed in Pic fashion, expressing a plea. "Enough with the questions! Is Steve okay? Tell me!"

Ellie flashed an expression of apology on her muzzle. "Please be patient. We need some answers first. What about their civilian thesis?"

"You mean Sorrows' End? Isaac's work on plate tectonics? It was published two weeks ago. What about it?"

Professor Feynman whistled, "For several days, we've been reviewing their activities, all of them, including their raw data from Sorrows' End. A series of micro-quake measurements were made that are not referenced in their published work."

"Uh..." Jorani stared at the professor. "You've lost me. I heard what you said, but you lost me."

"Did Steven or any of the others mention these measurements to you?"

"I don't..." Jorani thought for a moment. "I'm almost certain the answer is no. Definitely not after their return from Sorrows' End. Steven and the others were so insanely busy after that. I barely saw them." Jorani looked the professor in the eyes and squirmed again, and spent the next half hour listening in shock, often unconsciously gripping Max's neck as the story unfolded. She thought she followed the gist of it, but became confused at the end. "I don't understand. Are you saying the four of them are stranded on the moon?"

"That was our original assumption, since the twin of the lunar assembly did transfer to Far Rockaway on their final jump. But we queried the portal there through the lunar satellite net. The portal chamber is reading a hard vacuum, not the station, just the portal itself."

Jorani shivered. "And what does that mean?"

The professor flashed a muzzle response of bewilderment. "Nothing makes sense. The fact that all the portals failed at once implies a collective linkage that was completely contrary to our understanding of reality interchange; understanding that was based on nano-crystal information from the Third New Kingdom. Current observation now refutes that information. Steven was right. Our information was wrong, and we now believe it was based on intentional deceit. Our only piece of interchange physics still standing is a paper Flossie wrote a number of years ago."

"Does her work explain what happened?"

"It does not. Our conjecture is she made further breakthroughs and kept no records of them."

"What? They hid..." Jorani's eyes turned hard. "Do you think of them as traitors?"

Maayan's whistle came across the bridge. "That idea has been debated. There was undeniable deceit involved with their lunar transfer experiment. But recent discoveries indicate we should not think of them as traitors. Quite the opposite! Husband, please tell Jorani our latest understanding of the Sorrows' End data."

"Flossie and Isaac correlated their seismic measurements with data from Iran. The implications are monstrous. Forty million years ago, Sorrows' End suffered the same type of attack as Iran, but on a planetary scale."

Maayan whistled again. "Our conjecture is they either risked their lives or intentionally sacrificed their lives to save us from attack by unknown entities who were manipulating the portals. Their concern for us is obvious. They picked a time when Enigma and the interstellar portals were unmanned, and we've discovered that Steven was running a diagnostic monitoring the status of the two portals on Earth. They were both grounded when the portal network was destroyed."

Jorani turned to Professor Feynman. "So what happened to Steven and the others? They simply ceased to exist?"

"That should be impossible, but there's so much we don't know. We're trying to understand the jump series they were using. Their jumps pushed the portals into unprecedented states. We don't understand what happened... And there's more. Much more." Feynman paused for a moment before deciding to switch to English. "Are you familiar with what humans call garbage metamems?"

Jorani blinked. "Uh, are you referring to Earth's quantum cloud attacks in the 2070s?"

The professor nodded. "I realize this happened before you were born, but do you know how metamems work?"

"Well, vaguely. Quantum computing was part of my candidate training. A metamem worm lives in the garbage areas of distributed quantum cloud memory, fiendishly difficult to find on an active cloud. Thunder was the one that caused the most trouble. It hid within multiple layers of adaptive meta-data. On an active net, it's almost impossible to tell the difference between pointers to active worm fragments and random de-allocated quantum memory. But the worms were never much of an issue. They have a great weakness. Just cut the net connections. The fragments can't function in isolation and become easily visible, uh, assuming you know how to look for them."

The professor's muzzle flashed with approval. "Exactly, one great weakness, and one we never could exploit because we never considered our portals to be an integrated quantum array. It took their collapse to reveal our error."

"You were infected with a metamem? Where?"

"In the portal interfaces, the quantum routers. The evidence points to worldwide contamination."

Jorani sucked in her breath. "We were being spied upon?"

Feynman responded with an unusual chirp, indicating both sadness and anger. "At the least. Our investigation continues."

It took Jorani a moment to understand his meaning. "We were being controlled? The tiger attack!"

"Our world is highly automated. Whoever had control of the metamem had the means. We have been freed from masters we never knew existed. Steven and Flossie and Isaac and Julie paid a high price for our freedom. They also destroyed your path back to Earth."

Jorani felt stunned, but her responsibilities as liaison still pulled on her. With difficulty she asked, "So what happens now? What about the fusion trial?"

Maayan replied on the bridge, "With no way to return to Earth, it would be cruel to continue the trial. We have the votes to pass a bill declaring the trial will be considered successfully concluded a year from now, on Southern Spring 0, 3487. Give us a year to adjust, and also to prepare. Without portals, Providence is too isolated to serve its purpose. A year from now, unless there is a future sixty percent vote to the contrary, everyone in the fusion trial will be given permanent citizenship and moved to Haven University. Jorani, on behalf of the council, let me express our profound gratitude for your betrothed's sacrifice."

Jorani sat in silence, closing her eyes, too overwhelmed to continue. *Your daughter's sacrifice too*, she thought silently. *You know how this feels…* She felt Max pressing her hand against his muzzle.

A week later…
Time: Northern Autumn 6, 3486 59:16 Time Zone 30, Providence Campus
Time: Southern Spring 7, 3486 29:16 Time Zone 0, Haven
Time: May 19, 2101 19:42 U.T.

Our convoy of probes had just passed the spiral-5 mark — one final loop of the helix to go. Cruising down at ten kph, we would be arriving at the pit floor in about twenty minutes. The view of the pit had become almost boring, and that was scary. There were no guardrails at the edge of the spiral, and a fall now would still be almost two hundred meters. I squirmed in my seat. The probes were strange contraptions to ride, reminding me a bit of the pony rides from my childhood. Ponies and saddles, though, were a much more comfortable ride. These probes were built for repair, not for transportation.

What would we do when we reached the floor? Probably not much. There were several hemispheres dotting the landscape, including a huge one in the exact center of the pit which could easily enclose a dozen portals, but everything appeared to be locked tight.

The last week had been frightening. We had found the probes had enough power to descend to the pit floor and make it about halfway back up the spiral, enough to get to the charging station we'd set up at spiral mark 3.5. Our problem was there was nothing to do on the pit floor, nothing left to explore. There appeared to be doors on the structures but no way to open them, and the probes' battery-powered lasers were great for vaporizing a nanometer of material but they were orders of magnitude too weak for cutting.

The great spiral had a monotonous repetition of small air vents tucked into the back wall and emerging at shallow angles. The geometry almost assured a tornado as the great chamber was pressurized. It was just a breeze now, soft and cold. It was interesting that the pit had active ventilation. What was the point? Isaac guessed that it kept the air clear of metallic dust and anything biological.

It would have been a cold ride down without our space gear. We were very exposed straddling the small probes, and the suits were the only footgear for my companions. Even a Pic didn't enjoy walking on cold, hard metal. But our suits were not sealed. We were breathing outside air. After a lively discussion, we decided the place could have killed us already if we were up against an active malevolence — just shut off the power and wait for our batteries to run out. We didn't have much backup.

There were bars embedded in the walls of the structures on the pit floor, near their sealed doors, very suggestive of opening mechanisms, something that a human or Pic hand could grip easily. But the probes on their previous trips could not move them. We tried pulling, pushing, twisting, rotating, every type of motion possible and with more force than a human or Pic could generate. Nothing. Yesterday evening we came to the horrible realization that there seemed nothing left to do. How old was this place? Had the doors welded themselves shut over thousands of years of metal-to-metal contact? Millions of years? Isaac asked last night what was our argument that this place wasn't a billion years old.

We finally reached the pit floor, spiral mark 6.0, and dismounted next to a small cache of supplies dropped off on previous probe trips. I looked at the three muzzles around me and noticed my group was in a very somber mood. "Hey, guys, cheer up. Remember what Lieutenant Ellie was always telling us."

Isaac flashed a hopeful muzzle pattern: "Right. The future is the ultimate frontier and can be full of surprises."

"Actually," said Julie in English, "I remember having a discussion with my teacher mom about this. We think the ultimate frontier is our souls, if I'm using that Earth term correctly. The future is simply where we meet the challenge. But you're right, Steven. We should try to be more optimistic."

It was a quick and quiet walk to the central hemisphere. We took turns gripping the embedded bar and trying to move it. No luck. Afterwards we took a slow walk around the hemisphere, making a visual inspection. Our eyes told us nothing beyond the recorded scans we had already studied. Now what? Try the same routine with the other hemispheres? It seemed pointless, but what else was there? Our plan was to stay on the pit floor for as long as we could keep coming up with new ideas to try, no matter how ridiculous. Returning to the top of the pit would be a devastating journey, an admission of total failure. I shook my head to clear the depression, and noticed Flossie staring at the weird sky above us. The feeling was one of being a speck of dust at the bottom of an immense can, with multi-colored Christmas lights drifting past the top. "Any ideas?" I asked.

Flossie sighed. "We'll try the other structures, of course. And even if we fail now, perhaps changes will occur in the future." Her muzzle flashed a sign for a minor happy thought. "Perhaps the handle mechanism is digital, not mechanical. If all else fails, we could try multiple forces; pull, twist, rotate combinations, that sort of thing. And maybe there are duration keys built into the force patterns. The possibilities are..."

Julie groaned. "Endless? It would almost be amusing, spending the last year of our lives pulling on metal bars."

"That's right," replied Flossie, seeming to take Julie's comment a face value. "Much better than spending our last year in despair."

Isaac took his gloves off and hugged Flossie from behind, slipping under her suit collar and burying his hand in the rich blue feather-fur along her neck. Then he looked up and stared closely at the embedded vertical bar in front of him. "No wonder we can't move it. It looks like a door control but there's no seam. The bar and the wall are a single unit." And so saying, he reached out and grabbed the bar with his other bare hand.

"Isn't it too cold to touch?" asked Julie.

"It's not that c..." Isaac's voice trailed off as an incredibly thick section of the wall began to slide open without a sound. Inside the open cavity, we could see the standard portal design of an outer airlock. For a moment, we were speechless. Then Julie chirped with delight and hugged Isaac around his neck and the pair of them were soon doing a classic Pic victory dance, holding each other's neck and spinning in a circle.

"Well..." said Flossie in a rather amused tone, looking at the dancing pair then at the airlock controls. She then chirped a peculiar Pic expletive that had no clear English translation; one that signifies a lightning transition from very happy to very unhappy. The example in our dictionary was biting down on a deep, rich, chocolate cookie seconds before realizing it was swarming with ants. I looked at Flossie, confused, then at Julie and Isaac. They were still doing their victory jig, spinning merrily and kicking their legs out side to side in unison. They hadn't noticed Flossie's distress. Meanwhile, Flossie entered the open cavity and began running a system diagnostic on the control panel.

Flossie worked in silence as our companions finally finished their dance. Julie chirped about a pair of unused power sockets inside the cavity. "Good idea," chirped Flossie. "Try a probe, and if that works, charge another too."

Julie and Isaac trotted back to the spiral to wake the probes. I entered the cavity and stood next to Flossie. Such an unusual Pic... most of them considered expletives impolite, but Flossie used them freely. Still, I couldn't believe she'd be upset with Julie dancing with Isaac. Was I missing something? "What's wrong?"

"The implications," whispered Flossie. "Don't you see?"

"See what?"

She sighed. "The airlock controls..."

I stared at the controls — everything seemed standard NK3 portal design. What was Flossie's point? And then it hit me. "Oh, shit."

"Exactly."

"Are we screwed?"

"Uh..." Flossie paused from her work, turning to stare at the massive outer door that had opened for us. "Maybe not. Dangerous times, though. Look at the gap between the outer shell and the airlock. Was the shell constructed at a later time?" Flossie returned to exploring the control panel. "I think I'll be able to cycle the airlock by the time Isaac and Julie return. We'll need to seal our suits. I don't want to trust what conditions are like inside."

Meanwhile...

It had been a full day. Right after her classes ended at 40:00; Jorani had hurried to the portal complex where she spent the next sixteen hours in a conference call with the Council. She was back in her dorm room now, coming out of a shower, saying goodnight to Max and toweling herself dry. She was about to collapse into bed, so tired but still so excited she wondered if she would be able to sleep. At least there were no classes for the next three days.

The door chimed and Jorani turned, wondering what her escort had forgotten. But when she told her PA to open the door, she saw the class president standing in the threshold. "Hi. Is it..." Karim blinked and politely averted his eyes. "Is it too late to talk? I know it's after midnight. I saw your lights on."

"Sure, come in," said Jorani as she turned modestly for a robe. "Would you like some tea? Max heated some water. I've got green, black, licorice…"

Karim blinked. "Real Egyptian tea?"

"Yep. Steven was fond of Earth teas, did quite a bit of trading…" Her back to Karim, Jorani found her robe and tied it on, then walked to a shelf and opened a small bag and inhaled. "Ah, true licorice, nothing quite like it."

Karim nodded. "Agreed. The Polaris wizards are great at some things, did a really nice job with chocolate, but the subtlety of licorice root seems to have them stumped. Thanks!"

"Yeah…" Jorani brewed the tea and a few minutes later was sitting across from Karim, sipping her tea, guessing she knew what his visit was about.

"I passed Max in the hallway…"

"Hmm?"

"He looks good, almost back to his usual cheerful self."

Jorani nodded. "He's been talking to his father…" Jorani paused to consider that the proper English phrase would be to say "father-in-law", but Pic culture made almost no distinction between the two relationships. *One more social norm creeping into the English*, she thought. "So many changes, Karim."

He nodded, incorrectly guessing her reference. "I felt it too. Two years ago, I would have been aghast walking in on you coming out of a shower. My religion…"

"The Pic way of life; we finally learned to be gentle with each other." Jorani smiled. "Anyway, about Max, the latest news on the meta-mem has really helped him. Have you heard?"

"About the two-tryte addressing? The possibility of other portals?"

"Yep. There's strong evidence from the link tracing that the meta-mem was spread over a hundred thousand cloud locations. People are speculating that means other portals, lots of other portals, ones we never knew about."

"And how does this help Max?"

"Feynman told Max it would break every physical law in the universe for Julie and her team to wink out of existence. He's strongly suspects they managed to transport to some other portal on their final jump."

"Ah… just not on Whistlestop."

"No, not on Whistlestop…" Jorani sighed deeply. "This cheers up Max more than it does me. The transport network is dead. I keep thinking of them jumping to one of the deep-space portals — no power and probably on a path to leave the galaxy at half the speed of light. They'd be dead by now. That's probably a mercy. But Max is…" Jorani frowned. "Max is really intrigued by the existence of the extra meta-mem addresses; they appear to have been part of the active worm and beyond the known portals… There'll be an update on the newscast tomorrow…"

Karim looked thoughtful. "So somewhere in the universe…"

"Yeah, maybe, somewhere in the universe, with no way to get back. We'll never know. I guess that's better than death…" Jorani seemed lost in thought, staring into her cup. After a long silent moment, she looked back at Karim. "So, what's up?"

"Ah, yes. It's not about the newscast tomorrow. It's about the one the day after. I know you've been in conference all evening… There are rumors of something big; something really big with the Council…"

Jorani gave a small laugh. "Yes. I've heard those rumors too!"

"Ah. Were you asked to keep quiet?"

Jorani thought for a moment. "Not directly, but it would be impolite to steal the Council's thunder. Can we keep this between us? It'll only be for a day."

Karim gave a small hand sign.

"Okay, then. This is monumental! It's about population, human and Pic, the long-term vision for the future."

Karim nodded. "So the rumors are right?"

"The critical vote was less than six hours ago."

"And the result? A lot of students are hoping for a half million. That was the high-end figure…"

"… from the historical debates, I know. Karim, it's incredible! The Pic, they want to treat… they want to accept us as equals. The global quota of one hundred and twenty-five million remains, but will now cover both human and Pic. Male and female human genders will each be given quota equality with the male Pic genders."

"Uh... What does that mean?"

"Think of the current Pic population, roughly ten million each for the three male genders and twenty-two million for each of the female genders. They're going to give us gender equality with the male Pic. Human male and female each, the total is over twenty-one million of human quota. And with the lottery in such a permissive state, every human is going to have two birthrights for many centuries."

Karim slumped back in his chair, his jaw dropping. He tried to say something. It barely came out. "How long?"

"Not our choice, of course. But I'd be ashamed if our descendants do it in less than two thousand years... We should be okay — four hundred and seventy-three of us with about the broadest genetic make-up possible. We should be okay." Jorani paused. "I've been thinking this past week, if the situation were reversed and a group of Pic had taken away all of humanity's portal magic... can you imagine how Earth would have reacted? There'd probably be crowds screaming that the Pic be put to death."

Karim shuddered. "For committing sacrilege? Yeah, probably. Such a different response from the Pic, intense gratitude rather than fury. You have to wonder what it's like for the Pic stranded on Earth."

Jorani sighed. "I've heard that, with all the medical volunteers, the number is over twenty-two hundred. A young crowd, more than half of them are medical grad students from Haven and Canopy. They were volunteers, just trying to help, but they sure didn't sign up for this..." A deep frown. "Why is it so easy for Pic to find such a good moral compass, Karim? And why is it so difficult for us?"

Karim paused as he tried to come up with a serious answer. "Maybe because nobody sees like a gamma. Maybe that was part of their original vision — not just to run the fusion trial, but to think of our class as a lifeboat for humanity. We just have to hope that Earth takes the same attitude with their Pic." Karim stared down then drained his small cup. "Ah, that was good. Thanks!" He looked at Jorani thoughtfully. "One more question before I go? Why is the announcement on the eighth? Why not later today?"

"Ah, the decision making isn't over. Humans will be two of society's eight genders. It's not voted on yet, but the Council is discussing humans having proportional representation on the Council, total membership increasing from two hundred and sixteen to two hundred and eighty-eight. But that wouldn't make sense now, not for many centuries. The debates tomorrow will be on the transition. We'll probably get a token rep, maybe two, a man and a woman. But it's years of study; we'll still have to qualify."

"Well, I'll tell you one thing," Karim said, as he stood to leave. "I hope it's you as our first councilor, however long it takes."

Jorani signed gentle amusement as she walked with Karim to the door.

"I'm serious! Except maybe for Steven, no one could do us prouder…"

"Do us proud…" Jorani repeated. "Those were Maayan's words, her whistles, when she was addressing the Council. This is her final season; her bill for human equality will be the capstone of her career. She spoke of Julie before the vote, a eulogy, what Julie was like as a little girl, what it was like being her teacher-mother; how pride and sorrow are now flowing through Maayan like a river. Read the translation, Karim. It won't do her whistles justice, but read the translation. It was so beautiful…" Before she closed the door, Jorani shivered and added, "And the vote afterwards was unanimous. Unanimous! Can you imagine?"

A half-day later…
Time: Northern Autumn 7, 3486 33:31 Time Zone 30, Providence Campus
Time: Southern Spring 8, 3486 3:31 Time Zone 0, Haven
Time: May 20, 2101 10:06 U.T.

The usual practice when being off-planet was to keep Haven time; so our team now was well into what should have been our sleep cycle. Nobody was looking tired, though. Instead, the muzzles around me were bursting with colorful excitement as our two sub-teams were back together after thirty hours of separate exploration. Flossie delegated exploration of the top level of the complex to Isaac and me, while she and Julie explored below. It was a good match of challenge and abilities. The top-level control panels were remarkably similar to the portal controls we had trained on. The panels below were totally different than anything we had ever seen. But before announcing our discoveries, we started debating the concern Flossie and I had at the entrance to the complex. I was surprised Isaac and Julie did not share our distress.

"Portal operations were created with or converted to an NK3 interface thirty-six thousand years ago. It's not just the bogus nano-crystals," Julie was saying. "There's overwhelming evidence how the Pic language evolved across the different kingdoms."

I objected. "Guys, the tiger attack and Iran are recent events."

"But there's no direct evidence those attacks are connected to this place," replied Isaac. "Our old portal maintained its NK3 interface when we came here; no one objected to that. And finally, if a malevolent entity were in control here, we'd be dead, right?"

I frowned. "The place seems benign, I admit. Still..."

Flossie spoke up before I could complete the thought. "But why convert seed generator controls to NK3 format? We were never expected to be here... although..."

I turned to Flossie. "What?"

"Who *was* expected to be here? Look at the control panels. Every interface requires a grip on a metal bar to enable their function, just like the bar at the entrance. What's the purpose? What's it called in English, Steven? A dead-man control?"

Isaac piped up. "A funny expression. In reality, all the controls require a live person..."

My eyes lit up. "Exactly! Our probes could do nothing, not even open the door!"

Julie spoke. "But why allow live control but prohibit remote control? Our probes are just an extension of our desires. What does the safeguard accomplish?"

"Are we making too many assumptions?" asked Isaac. "Maybe it's not a safeguard. Perhaps the Builders had different motives..."

"Not a safeguard? Then what?" Flossie turned to Julie and me. "Any thoughts on this?"

I frowned. "Neither scenario makes sense. The problem is that the attacks are recent but this place is deserted. The two facts just don't go together. Why would our adversaries abandon such a key location? It's the center of all their magic."

"The environment is completely sterile." added Julie. "It's creepy. No way to be sure, but it gives me the impression of being vacant for a long, long time."

"Maybe that's a good way to approach the problem," suggested Isaac. "Assume we're the last group of e-techs vacating this complex. What are our motives to leave? Fear? End of normal maintenance schedule? End of life-cycle?"

"What?" asked Flossie. "You mean no further use?"

"I know it sounds crazy, but is that possible? Maybe the Builders had an even better technology and were abandoning this one."

We debated a while longer, but came to no conclusions. Flossie finally tabled the issue and asked Isaac and me to report our findings. We had a lot to say, and Isaac asked me with a hand gesture to start.

"First off, the environmental controls were easy to understand, almost identical to the portal systems we're familiar with. Kudos to Isaac for turning on the heat and air filtering. We even have humidity control and access to clean water, which is great. Main power controls, communications and diagnostics are non-existent, at least on this level."

Julie piped up. "We'll have more to say on that. Power controls are below, and they are bizarre."

I smiled happily, not catching the flash of distress on Julie's snout. "Anyway, here's what we found. The portal on this level... after much probing, Isaac and I noticed that one of the menus on the central panel acts differently than what we're used to. It's the menu to monitor momentum transfer stability on the auxiliary spheres."

Flossie nodded. "A relatively minor function for the central panel, and one's that duplicated on another display. I've sometimes wondered about that."

"On the panel here, the menu has a vaguely similar configuration, but with references to primary jump control. Isaac and I think we have the ability to enter a full two-tryte quantum address that specifies a jump destination. You were right, Flossie. The portal network is switchable!" I took a moment to study the notes on my PA. By happy coincidence, Earth and Whistlestop used the same base-9 numbering system to represent quantum memory. The base unit was a trit, having the three possible states of zero, undefined, or one. Two trits to a tribble, whose state was represented by the digits 0 through 8, and three tribbles to a tryte, represented by base-9 numbers 000 through 888. "Isaac?"

Isaac continued, "All of our hits so far occurred in the low tribble of the address field, 000-000 to 000-008. Most of the readings are so strange that Steven and I don't know how to interpret them. But we're getting a loopback indicator on 000-003. We think that might be the address of this location. And the big news is: We have jump enabled status on 000-002 and 000-004. We can jump to two different locations!"

I was expecting cheers when Isaac said this, and Julie did flash me a pattern of happiness and hope, but Flossie remained deep in thought for a moment before speaking. "Very interesting. Great work, guys. Two full trytes for the address field? That would be 531,441 addresses. Could the portal array possibly be that large?"

I shrugged in agreement. "Why not? We're also getting an active response from 000-001, everything except jump clearance. And we did test about a hundred addresses beyond the low tribble and got no response. It's a daunting prospect. It would take a year to test everything, even if we worked in shifts... So, what are things like below?"

Julie gave a quick chirp to Flossie, asking her to speak. Flossie nodded. "I'll start by recognizing Julie as the key to our findings. NK3 glyphs are a nightmare for me to interpret."

Julie piped up. "We complement each other's abilities. I thought I was reading nonsense. And I'm still not sure I'm interpreting the glyphs correctly. But Flossie thinks otherwise."

"It's torturous logic," replied Flossie. "Multiple controls that seem to refute what other controls are doing. Who builds like this? And why?"

"Safety interlocks?" I asked.

"You could call them that, I guess. But there are so many of them! There's a long series of steps to activate what I believe is the seed generator, but the controls require permission from other controls. A clear majority of controls appear to do nothing but give permissions, but we haven't been able to find a linked pair, not one. We can't find one pair where one control permits another control to operate and actually do something."

Isaac flashed Flossie a sign for puzzlement. "Could you give an example?"

"Sure. There's a panel below that I'm guessing is the start of the seed generation process. It appears to initiate the folding of spacetime curvature…"

"Flossie is assuming I'm interpreting the glyphs correctly," added Julie.

"Right," said Flossie. 'But the control is inactive, and there are three different panels with options to enable spacetime curvature control — controls to enable controls. We tried all eight combinations of enable settings. The primary control remained inactive."

Julie was frowning, so I asked her, "Is there another way to interpret the glyphs?"

"Yes. The glyph for enablement is a hand holding a slippery fish, and if it's the left hand, that means first enablement. The symbol below is two hands grabbing a fish. It's obsolete in current writing, but the standard NK3 translation would be difficult or significant enablement. But the glyph below also has a weird attribute. It has two left hands grabbing the fish. Flossie prefers an imaginable third translation: two primary enablements — enabling something to be enabled. Our problem is that none of the portals on Whistlestop ever used this symbol; I've never seen it before."

"What?" I said. "So it took extra effort to convert this place to NK3? Maybe Flossie and I are right to be worried. *Why* are we seeing NK3 displays here?" A wild and half-formed idea suddenly occurred to me. "Maybe because it had to be done. Maybe it was an all or nothing decision."

"Require central control to use the same format as the portals?" replied Flossie quietly. "I can't see why anyone would build with a restriction like that."

"Maybe it wasn't built in," I countered. "Maybe the ability to do otherwise just wasn't available to our adversary."

Flossie blinked as she got my point. "You're suggesting our adversary had only partial control. Is that likely?" She paused for a long moment before adding, "I withdraw my objection. Your conjecture agrees with the facts. But what are the implications?"

"Maybe that our adversary knows we're here, but we're safe because it has no means to stop us, at least not yet."

"A scary thought," said Isaac. "We've been assuming time is not a critical issue… Are we making this too complex? Maybe another system simply has to be activated before the seed generator."

Flossie sighed. "Maybe. Julie certainly isn't convinced of my selection of glyph interpretation. Perhaps I should bow to her wisdom. She's the expert in this. My idea just seems right, somehow. I can't explain it with logic."

Julie piped up. "I should mention, we left that particular room with all three settings enabled, and when we returned, they were back to disabled positions."

Isaac chirped, "Another entity is here with us?"

Flossie gave a high-pitched hiccup. "Oh, there's a thought! I was assuming a timer. If you don't grab a metal bar often enough, the controls reset to inert status." She looked around. "Just like on this level; metal grab bars everywhere. Why are bare hands made to be so critical?"

I asked, "Do you think it's possible for us to operate the seed generator?"

Flossie flashed complex patterns of deep uncertainty, but her words were more optimistic. "Assuming this facility is functional, there should be a way. We have to assume that all the necessary controls are here, plus all the gate controls that permit them to operate. Nothing is certain though. The fact that we haven't found a single linked pair… Anyway, weeks of study at least. In the meantime, your discovery of two active portals is great news. We'll focus on that. We'll start with a probe as soon as you're ready." Flossie looked at Isaac and me. "If you're comfortable with the controls, perhaps we can do our first jump tomorrow."

I wasn't expecting any objections. In fact, Isaac chirped, "I'm not sleepy. How about now?"

Four hours later…

"Return jump complete," Julie called out from her console. Isaac and I opened the portal, and as programmed, the probe came out and we soon had numerous displays being shown on our diagnostic console. We gathered around staring at the mission log, the video grabbing our attention. The portal interior lost power as it jumped to 000-002 and the probe had used its own light sources to make parametric sweeps. Julie sighed. "The grab bars. I bet our hands could activate the environment. Next trip we'll have to go in person."

Isaac chirped in surprise. "Look at the gravity reading! A factor of seven above here!"

Flossie grunted. "I recognize the number. It's the same gravity as Sorrows' End."

Chapter 18

Time: Northern Autumn 24, 3486 50:40 Time Zone 30, Providence Campus
Time: Southern Spring 25, 3486 20:40 Time Zone 0, Haven
Time: June 10, 2101 17:18 U.T.

The two full weeks of preparation had been painful — the first physically and the second from boredom. The urge to start exploring had been almost irresistible. But Flossie had insisted on full acclimation to the high gravity, and I had to admire her reasoning and discipline. Having our bodies fail us while exploring an unknown high-g environment would be catastrophic.

Isaac and I were the A-team for high-gravity exploration and had spent two-thirds of the last two weeks in a boring, unpowered, high-gravity sphere, alternating our time there with B-team Flossie and Julie whose primary mission was to understand the controls on the lower levels of home base 000-003. There was a depressing lack of progress there, not one functional control had been found. The systems were powered but also appeared blocked. Continued scanning of the two-tryte address space was also proving unfruitful. Not one address beyond the low tribble gave any response.

So it seemed Isaac and I would be the ones to lead us out of our nightmare metal universe. A probe showed our second jump option 000-004 had the same Sorrows' End gravity as 000-002. Isaac and I (and two probes) had spent the night there inside the unpowered interior of portal. Then Flossie had pulled us back to home base for breakfast and a final mission review before we returned with a pair of fresh probes to 000-002. Showtime began with a grunt from me and a similar low-pitched chirp from Isaac. After stretching for a moment, we both walked over to the metal bar that we were assuming would activate the local controls.

Flossie had asked me to do the honors. With a hopeful smile at Isaac, I gripped the bar with a bare hand.

Isaac chirped in astonishment as the display lit with a bizarre setup. It didn't look random, but certainly nothing Earth had ever seen. My first thought was it was a written language based on snakes and pebbles, all sorts of multiple curved lines at different orientations accompanied by a wide variety of pebbles, different shapes, all fairly small. I shook my head in dismay at the thought of trying to make sense of it.

Isaac was a much better analyst. "Difficult to guess whether it's pictorial or phonetic. Perhaps twenty or more unique curved line symbols with… I think twelve different orientations each." He made an angle with thumb and forefinger and held it against the display. "Doesn't that look like twenty degrees of separation? This is amazing. And all the small polygon shapes… the information density could be enormous…"

I grunted. "I'm certain Earth never had anything like this. How about Whistlestop?"

Isaac replied with a chirp that signified a laughing negative.

"How about at the lunar ruins of Sorrows' End?"

"Interesting thought. There were some writings on the instruments there which are thought to be serial numbers and calibrations, a base twelve numbering system. But I don't remember that it looked anything like this." Isaac sighed and checked to make sure both our suit sensors had recorded the image, then grabbed the activation bar himself. We both blinked as the display morphed to familiar NK3 format.

I thought about testing what would happen if I grabbed the bar again, but the opportunity to communicate with our base camp could not be ignored. Isaac worked the panel while I set up the comm link. Or tried to. Our attention quickly shifted to the reality of being in a communications blackout. "Nothing," commented Isaac finally, "not even a carrier wave. But the good news is we still have jump-enabled status. We can return and report the situation."

Which was obviously the right decision. Julie became intensely interested in the new writing system, and within an hour Isaac and I were back at 000-002, opening the portal door. I felt intensely eager to see a natural landscape again, but a moment later we walked out amazed to see the upper level of a seed generator control area. Except for the high gravity, it appeared identical to the one we had just left. "Is this really Sorrows' End?" Isaac asked quietly.

I felt torn. "We can go back now, or cycle through the airlock and peek outside. Either way, we'll be in this same situation, now or in a little while."

"Yeah, I know. How about we take a quick look and then go back and report?"

"Yeah, good plan." Was it a good plan? Isaac made a comment that, after living so long inside metal enclosures, even the pale green landscapes of Sorrows' End were going to look incredibly beautiful. After checking that outside atmospherics were benign, we opened the outer door of the airlock and stared at an environment our minds refused to accept. Fortunately our suit video recorders were capturing everything. We finally returned to home base and were soon showing the video to Julie and Flossie.

Julie and Flossie watched the video of our walk through the duplicate of the seed generator control station and the opening of the airlock to the outside. All four of us then stared at the panorama in silence. "How could I have been so stupid?" Flossie finally whispered.

"The gravity is a coincidence?" asked Isaac.

"I don't mean that. There might well be a connection in deep history. Here's my conjecture. The portal ahead of you in the image may be active."

"Hell, Flossie," I replied. "This scene is right out of a nightmare. What were we looking at?"

"You were looking at some very good news. Your suit sensors are indicating a level walk to the next portal, rangefinder said ninety-four meters distant."

My eyes flicked to the display recordings of my helmet. "Yes, about that. Flossie, the horizon, what was I looking at?"

"Masterful engineering!" she replied. "I see what they've done. So elegant! They've taken advantage of the same fourfold symmetry of the tetrahedron. So clever! It explains almost everything, even the reading at 000-000. I finally understand how the jumps are possible."

"Flossie!" I couldn't help but laugh at how insane Flossie's happiness seemed next to the mind-bending landscape before us in the video. "*What* were we looking at?"

"Huh? Oh yeah, sorry. I'm almost certain all of us were on the same seed generator. Julie and I are at the equator, node 000-003. Two nodes of the tetrahedron are at high latitude, almost a full radian, 000-002 and 000-004. It all makes sense! Don't you see? Here at the equator, the centripetal force is aligned with gravity, almost cancelling it. But at high latitude, spherical radial gravity and the weakened centripetal force tangential to the spin axis are no longer aligned. The floor of your node location is aligned to compensate. That's why the horizon looks so insanely tilted. You would roll to the equator if you stepped outside your node. I'm assuming you have a bubble of air, just like here."

"Uh, I dimly see what you're saying. So you're assuming the seed generator is a sphere? Wouldn't the spin make it an egg shape?"

"In an unpowered environment, sure. But it that case, the oblate spheroid would have drifted into the overhead ceiling a long time ago. I'm assuming our environment is being actively managed. The forces are astronomical."

Julie spoke up. "Regarding the jump addresses, perhaps 000-001 is on equator, and 000-000 is at the core."

"Sounds very logical to me."

"So why can't we jump to the other equatorial location?"

"I suspect there's an exclusion principle involved. We'll get there. Each high-latitude node can jump to either equatorial node, and also the reverse. Thing of the topology of moving on a circle with stations for North, South, East and West. You can go clockwise or counterclockwise, but you can't go from East to West without going to North or South first. This is so, so neat! So clever! Masterful engineering to get four seed generators from one device!"

Isaac chirped, "Flossie, please explain!" He sounded just as confused as I was.

"Sure! Why settle for one transport network when you can have four? That's what they've done here. Eleven-dimensional quantum space, with eight spatial dimensions folded so you never see them, plus the temporal dimension adds to twelve. So with all possible quantum spacetime orientations, you get $3^{\wedge}12 = 531{,}441$ address space. The equipment downstairs suggests the true anchor address is 000-000."

Flossie continued. "But the Builders were cleverer than that. They pushed the system to a higher harmonic. I was in error that a tri-pole bounce was required. The true answer is a bounce must be done with an odd number of nodes. We're using tri-pole bouncing to move between 000-002 and 000-003. But back on Whistlestop, we were using penta-pole bouncing — the two Whistlestop nodes we knew about, plus the node at the top of the pit we came to with the scissors bounce, plus our base camp 000-003, plus the anchor at the generator core. My conjecture is the portal address at the top of our pit will be in the range of 000-005 to 000-008. Four branches, Isaac! Four-fold symmetry! Each of the four surface nodes on the seed generator define an independent jump network with its own two-tryte address field, linked only by the low tribble at the seed generator. A total of over two million portals! It's breathtaking!"

"So we never do go to the true anchor node, do we?"

"No. Back on Whistlestop, I never could see how to resolve the conflict. You would need portal access to the seed generator, yet the core anchor is where the hammer meets the anvil when creating new entangled spacetime. Besides the fact that's there's no anchor to jump *to* the anchor, I couldn't imagine how biological life could exist in such an environment. And yet, it's inconceivable to think the seed generator would have no engineering access. This is how the Builders solved the problem, with penta-pole jumping."

"Yeah, I remember your warnings..." I thought I got the gist of what Flossie had said earlier. "Ah, so the Whistlestop jump network, the one using the 000-003 tetrahedron location, might still be active?"

"Yes. I... No, wait! The status indicators at the top of the pit. They were showing entangled space but entangled to nothing... We don't have to search that address space any more. The portal is enabled for penta-pole bouncing but there's no destination pair to latch onto. We really did destroy the network Whistlestop was using, assuming all our nodes were on the 000-003 branch. But the other three branches might still be active. Wonderful engineering. Otherwise one collapse cuts off all access to the seed generator. This way, there are four independent paths. Steven, Isaac... I know that horizon looks scary. Are you comfortable with returning to 000-002 and walking across to the other portal? If I'm right, its address will be between 000-005 to 000-008."

Isaac and I looked at each other and nodded. Isaac replied, "Should be okay. It's level walking. We'll just focus on the destination and ignore the horizon. Let's do it."

Three days later:

Julie and Flossie were deeply engrossed in translating the generator control systems, and when the work day had ended, they didn't want to stop. I wound up sacking with Isaac for the night. Early next morning, I went to fetch them as Isaac prepared breakfast, hoping the women were smart enough to have slept. Today was our make-or-break day. We would be testing our last possible exit from the seed generator. The day would also include a lot of gradient hiking in low gravity, something we were still finding awkward.

I paused at the entrance of the room Julie and Flossie were using for their analytics. The two were curled together fast asleep on the floor. It was touching. In her sleep, Julie was cradling Flossie as a mother might cradle a child. It didn't seem to matter that Flossie was the leader of our expedition. The sight made me think about the brief conversation I once had with Christopher, how the Pic military was more relational compared to an Earth hierarchy. *Ah, well. No one nurtures like a beta.* I walked over and nudged the two awake.

A half day later
Time: Northern Autumn 28, 3486 05:17 Time Zone 30, Providence Campus
Time: Southern Spring 28, 3486 35:17 Time Zone 0, Haven
Time: June 14, 2101 02:54 U.T.

Flossie and I decided to take a quick stretch break. I waved my arms carefully, not wanting to exert sudden energy in the low-g environment, glancing down nervously at the complex housing the 000-001 portal at the center of our second immense pit. Flossie kicked her legs out to the sides, then forward and back. Julie and Isaac, meanwhile, were a hundred meters ahead of us and almost at the top of the great spiral. This was our final hope of the four tetrahedron locations. The portals at the two high-latitude nodes were inert, just like the portal location where we first arrived. Were they destroyed sometime in the past, as we destroyed our branch, or just never created? We all had our suspicions of a violent and destructive past.

"Status report," Flossie said to the lead pair through our suit links. "Feeling okay?"

There were a few chirps between Julie and Isaac, and then Julie spoke. "Suit power is nominal. We'll wait for you once we reach the top. And we're fine. The distance is less than a human marathon, and with the light gravity, we don't feel tired. I feel more comfortable walking now than when we first started. The only challenge is to stay vigilant." She didn't have to elaborate. Walking off the ledge would be a fatal mistake, and it was easy to get careless with the low-g, ultra-long gait.

I was a little surprised by our hiking arrangement. I agreed with Flossie that the intimacy of climbing in isolated pairs would keep us more alert than either solo or as one group. But Flossie asked me to walk with her. In addition to being leashed to each other, we wound up holding hands for most of the hike. Up ahead, Isaac and Julie were holding hands, too.

As we resumed walking, I commented, "You know, Flossie, I just thought of something about the geometry here."

"Hmm?"

"The two high latitude locations have a functional design. But these huge spiral pits at the equator — what was their purpose?"

Flossie paused. "Yes. We first guessed it might be a recreational place for Storytellers to fly, but given what we know now, that seems pretty ridiculous, doesn't it? I have another conjecture. The two pits are on the equator but are separated by a tetrahedron angle. They are not oppositional. This would cause a slight wobble to the planetary spin. Perhaps the wobble is used for stability control."

"Using the wobble as a synchronization mark?"

"Yeah, something like that."

"I've been thinking it's something else. Since tri-pole jumps only occur between equatorial and high-latitude locations, the spirals force you to take one or two long hikes if you're switching networks."

"You're suggesting the spiral purpose was to slow inter-branch traffic?" Flossie paused to consider the idea. "That's a thought. But a simple solution would be keep four penta-pole portals from the four networks adjacent at some outside location."

"Right. But what if the different branches were controlled by different factions? If they don't want to cooperate, they can keep their network branches isolated. The only common link that's forced is at the seed generator."

"Interesting conjecture. Did the Builders design this place for isolation? The lack of quantum communication links between the nodes is particularly bizarre and supports your idea. But what a contradiction! The technology to create a seed generator is godlike. Can builders with such powers still retain a violent and distrustful nature? Wouldn't they have destroyed themselves?"

"Well, maybe they did destroy themselves. There's nobody here."

Flossie flashed a muzzle sign for amusement. "I was thinking of the development period leading to the godlike technology. Your point is noted though."

The minutes past quietly. We all met at the top of the spiral and then walked half the pit circumference to the portal station. It didn't take long to get a cold water answer to our burning question. Afterwards there was nothing left to do except begin our long journey back down.

"Stay sharp," Flossie commanded. "Emotionally letdown and physically tired. This is when mistakes happen."

"Understood," answered Julie. "Isaac and I will continue to tell stories of our childhoods on the way down. Slow and steady. We'll keep our gait short and each other alert."

Flossie and I travelled as a second pair. "Where is our adversary?" I finally asked.

"Yes. I'm at a loss. The network branch we destroyed was the last one active."

"Iran, the tiger attack... We're fighting an enemy in the here and now. I thought they would be controlling one of the other network branches."

Flossie flashed an emotion of resignation on her muzzle. "Yes. It's fortunate for us that they're not. We are totally unprepared for warfare, an oversight on our part back on Whistlestop."

"Not really. Trying to smuggle weapons here would have been insanely risky. But my question remains. Where is our adversary?"

Flossie shrugged. "Three obvious possibilities: Our adversary was using our network branch and was disabled by our scissors jump, or was using a branch on a different seed generator, or was using some other technology to manipulate us. We have no evidence of possibilities two or three, so the principle of simplicity suggests possibility one is the most likely answer."

I frowned. "It's dangerous to make optimistic assumptions in warfare."

"Agreed... You mentioned earlier the network branches might have been controlled by different factions... lots of potential friction in that."

"Flossie, another question, a few days ago when you first figured out the portal geometry here; you said it almost explained everything. What is still unexplained?"

Flossie sighed. "Lots. Jump control needs to be both incomputable and self-organizing. It's physically impossible for algorithms to accomplish what portals do, a direct contradiction with quantum principles. And there's nothing in my equations that hint at transmutation of matter. Jump control and how seed generators are built and how star roofs and seed generators are maintained — these are all godlike abilities to me. I haven't a clue... But no matter. We have weeks of exploration before us, learning to understand the generator control systems. I'm feeling..." It was another few minutes before Flossie blurted out her thought. "I'm going to go crazy if I can't... I need time at a forest or seashore. I can't stand living in a metal can any more!"

"Yeah, I know what you mean. Here, try this." I stopped walking and called up a video from the Vuntut forest on my PA.

Flossie turned to stare at me. "You're kidding."

"No. I'll put it in a loop. Try it." Flossie stared at the display for a long while before sighing and turning away. I reached out and held her hand. "Did it help?"

"More than I expected. But it's not enough."

"No, of course not... Want a backrub when we get back to base?" She nodded gratefully as we resumed our descent.

A week later:

Time: Northern Autumn 38, 3486 24:08 Time Zone 30, Providence Campus

Time: Southern Spring 38, 3486 54:08 Time Zone 0, Haven

Time: June 24, 2101 22:49 U.T.

It had been a momentous day, our first successful test of the seed generator control system. Just a simple diagnostic, Flossie said, monitoring baseline spacetime curvature around the anchor node at the core of our artificial planet. The values were forty percent higher than what Flossie predicted, which she interpreted as an additional unknown focusing mechanism. What a strange control system! Activating any generator console at any of the four tetrahedron portals required active support from the other three portals. Every seed control function had to be enabled by a present operator at the other three portals. We had the bare minimum personal to do this, one of us in each of the tetrahedron locations. One fewer person, and we'd be absolutely screwed.

Isaac and I were the obvious choices for the two high-gravity locations. We'd spent the most time in high gravity, plus Isaac as an alpha Pic had the best muscular system, plus Julie and Flossie were spending every possible moment translating snakes and pebbles and the NK3 symbols into something we could understand. Today's success was a very big deal. Flossie considered it a proof-of-concept test that we actually had the skills to learn how to control the seed generator.

Tonight Julie and I jumped to 000-001 in order to give Flossie and Isaac time for a conjugal overnight at portal 000-003, what we've been calling home base. Julie and I both liked to cuddle with someone while sleeping and we'd gotten quite close in the time we'd been here, now a week shy of a full season. It was a unique experience, emotionally very precious. She was curled lying on her side and I was on my back, scratching the back of her neck and wondering if she wanted to talk or just sack out.

"Really big day today," Julie commented.

"Yeah… How was it, being alone here?"

"Bearable. The hardest part was ignoring the isolation and just focusing on the mission. So much progress, Steve! The floodgates of translation are opening. I feel confident Flossie and I will eventually be able to understand everything, even the stuff we're skipping."

"Hmm? What kind of stuff?"

"Today we found sections of the reference library unreadable, links in the operations manuals that point to what you call snakes and pebbles. Creating a cross-reference to NK3 should be doable in principle, but it would be a monumental effort. Fortunately the pointers suggest it's all historical reference stuff. All the operational steps, everything that's critical, is already in NK3. It's still a challenge though. The modern Pic language is much more streamlined and logical than it was in NK3 times. A large part of my time is pushing through the quirky ways people wrote back then."

I nodded. "We see the same pattern on Earth. Small isolated groups can come up with insanely complicated language structures."

"Yes, agreed. The Pic language has been global and mobile for thirty-five hundred years. Large societies will prune language complexity under such conditions, cut out what's unnecessary."

"So what's snakes and pebbles like? Streamlined or complex?"

"Ah, streamlined *and* complex, I guess. It's very logical, in its own way; two hundred and eighty-eight base word foundations that we know of, twenty-four snakes with twelve orientations. But the pebble modifications are maddening."

"Hmm?"

"Take the word 'speak'. That's a base word. But a horizontal oval pebble on top means 'converse'; vertical oval pebble means 'argue'; diagonal oval to the right means 'negotiate'. You get the idea? And there's often multiple modifiers, and with all their different orientations and positions…"

"Yikes."

"Yeah, what a puzzle... Want an amusing example?"

"Sure."

"By the way, can you rub between my shoulder blades? Hmm... A little harder? Yeah, right there... Perfect... As you know, Flossie and I are mapping the control sequence for creating new portals. We'll discuss this more in tomorrow's meeting, but we have indications all four tetrahedron addresses are used to create portals in quartets, one for each branch. They are created in the core, at or very near the anchor, and then exit in opposite directions along the generator spin axis, emerging at the poles. Our conjecture is there must be some type of airlock in the sky-dome above us to permit full escape. Flossie and I will be researching that tomorrow."

I picked a random address. "Like address 123-400 on each of the networks? You have to create all four portals simultaneously?"

"Yep. It seems all four portals are formed from a single quantum of fractured spacetime; that's what the manuals say."

"So if the network loses a portal, but its address is still active on the other networks, what happens then?"

Julie nodded. "Good question. Flossie thinks the other portals would still be functional, but creating a new quartet with that address would kill the entanglements of the old one. Regarding maintenance, do you see what this implies?"

"Yikes. If the remaining portals are spread across the galaxy, it might take a hundred thousand years for their replacements to show up."

"Yeah. And if different factions are controlling the four networks, I can imagine a lot of contention whether to replace one faction's loss."

"Enough contention to start a war? Interesting thought..." I then grinned. "I must say, your example is not very amusing."

"What? Oh, yeah! Your backrub is so nice, I was drifting. Getting back to my point, it seems that since none of the four branches of the tetrahedron has an active external address now, we now have the option to deactivate the core tri-pole portals too."

I blinked. "Shut down everything?"

"Yeah, I guess, reset everything including the 000-000 anchor address. Flossie doesn't know what to make of it either. The amusing part comes in with how we're supposed to do this. We need to synch our operations among the four tetrahedron portals. That part is straightforward. But we also need to interact with the anchor portal, but the control manual is using a weird NK3 word for this. The glyph doesn't exist in the modern Pic lexicon, but its root now means negotiate, not simply communicate."

"What? Negotiate with a team at the anchor node? I thought Flossie said that always has to be the core node, tri-pole or penta-pole, and you can never jump to it."

"Yeah, Flossie still thinks that. But she conjectured that you might be able to reach it through the polar channels, the exit tunnels for newly created portals. But then she decided that didn't make sense either. She thinks space is so tightly folded at the core, it could be a deadly environment for anything biological. So I spent the rest of this evening's session trying to refine my translation and cross checking with the snakes and pebbles version. It also uses the word negotiate, but with a second square pebble modifier that I previously thought meant unilateral."

"Unilateral negotiations?" I smiled. "Yeah, that's funny."

Julie continued. "That's not all. At the very end, Flossie and I both laughed at my final attempt. NK3 is using what's now a reflexive verb construct. The literal translation would be: Die and unilaterally negotiate with 000-000 to join you; as if we had to talk to the portal itself and convince it to commit suicide with us. Funny, huh? ... Steven? Steven?"

I was finally able to speak. "We need to have a meeting, right now, all four of us."

An hour later:

It didn't take long to explain my conjecture that we might finally have found our adversary. My three Pic friends were quiet at first, digesting the idea. Finally Julie turned to Flossie and asked, "Is this possible?"

Flossie shrugged. "So many demonstrations of magic, why not one more? I never saw this, even Steven didn't till now. The physics of consciousness is a missing science for both humans and Pic. There's operational knowledge of course, understanding of cognitive processing, behavior sciences, mental health services. But the physical basis of consciousness? We haven't a clue. I guess there are some hand-waving arguments it must be a quantum-level phenomenon, large-scale self-organization of a quantum resonance… I guess it seems reasonable; thoughts obviously organize themselves…"

"But could the same mind exist for thirty-six thousand years?" asked Isaac.

"Oh, I'm thinking much longer than that," I replied. "How about forty million years; maybe more. I'm proposing we're dealing with the same entity that destroyed Sorrows' End."

"What would our thoughts be like…" Julie wondered out loud. "…after an epoch of thinking? Would we turn into monsters too? Would we be doomed to it?"

I growled at the thought. "No way! That's what free will is all about. You're never doomed to think anything. It's always your choice."

Flossie nodded slowly. "And now we need to convince the anchor portal to choose suicide for our benefit. How are we supposed to do that? There are no communication systems here! In fact, they seem to have been intentionally removed!"

Isaac flashed emotional distress on his muzzle. "Not just the portal — we're supposed to die too. We are so unprepared for this! Even if we found a way to communicate, we can't engage with it now. We need to understand its mind first. Does everyone agree?"

"Yeah, know your enemy, probably the most universal truth in warfare." I thought for a moment and grimaced, fighting back a wave of panic. "But how are we going to outthink a mind that's forty million years old?"

"Maybe we don't have to outthink," said Julie. "You don't need a war to negotiate. Is it possible portal 000-000 is not our enemy? … Or am I indulging in pleasant thoughts?"

Flossie's muzzle flashed a shock of recognition. "Such a new experience it will be, communicating with a non-biological consciousness. It changes everything! Physicists before had to ponder the morality of the consequence of their experiments, but never with the morality of an experiment itself. But if you're creating actual new consciousness, what are your moral guidelines? To create good and not evil? To create smart and not dumb?"

Julie added in a whisper, "To create kind and gentle and not rough? Think of what this monster has done to us."

Flossie continued. "Do you have control over your experiment's free will? Great influence at least, I would think. But then what's the moral foundation for the experiment?"

Isaac growled in frustration. "I still can't imagine what we're talking about. Our consciousness and memories are based on physical brains. How could spacetime itself… I'm not even sure how to ask the question."

"Don't think of spacetime as a coordinate system," cautioned Flossie. "Think of it as a negative-pressure fabric that has somehow found a path to become self-organizing… a path to free will… I don't see it either."

I tried to pull the conversation back to the matter at hand. "Any idea what we'll say to the anchor node? And how we say it?"

Julie gave a whistle burst of hope. "Not yet, but if we're supposed to communicate with the anchor node, there must be a link somewhere. We'll just have to search for it. At least all the critical information seems to be in NK3. I expect the protocols will be in NK3, too. The other stuff so far, the non-NK3 records, appear to be historical logs."

"But we still don't understand the situation we're in," Flossie countered. "Historical data might provide critical insight. I suggest we focus on that, at least for the short term. Julie, I know how much translation work this will be for you. Everyone: opinions?" A long moment of silence followed. Flossie realized we were all tired and needed time to digest the new ideas. She closed the meeting and asked everybody to get some sleep.

Chapter 19

A week later:
Time: Northern Autumn 49, 3486 3:13 Time Zone 30, Providence Campus
Time: Southern Spring 49, 3486 33:13 Time Zone 0, Haven
Time: July 6, 2101 3:14 U.T. Island of Hoy, Scotland

"See? I told you it was worth waiting for."

"It is pretty," Christopher whistled quietly as he briefly muzzled the underside of Alice's throat. They were both admiring the break of dawn, gazing eastward across the Scapa Flow on the island of Hoy. "But you still shouldn't have waited up. Not much darkness here this time of year. Take advantage of it... Reminds me where I grew up."

"Ha! Who could sleep with all that's happening? What news, fearless leader?"

Christopher blinked. "Fearless leader? What a title! Other people aren't using it, are they?"

Alice laughed. "It was just something I picked up in the library here. It was nice of the Scots to leave it for the survey team."

"How's everything looking?"

"Aw, I go first, huh? Okay. Everything so far is fabulous, including the agricultural tests. Our recommendation is going to be a unanimous yes. The critical issues are your negotiations."

Christopher flashed a pattern of hopeful expectation. "The broad principles have been agreed to. I just hope some pesky detail doesn't unravel what's been built."

"I'm still not clear what joint sovereignty means."

"It means all of us will be full citizens of the Republic of Scotland, and all the inhabitants of Hoy, including us, will have autonomy to guide the island's future. A majority vote by both the humans here and Pic will be needed to change the agreement, and the Scots are being so welcoming, I can't see us wanting to change anything. I find it remarkable we're getting as much as we are."

Alice shrugged. "A win for everyone. Earth gets all our technology, as much as we have here, the Antarctic base and enough tonnage to crash their precious metal markets. Scotland gets to turn Hoy into a premier complex for medical research, and we get a home. Transferring our allegiance to Earth, though…"

"It's nothing more than what we asked the Fusion Trial candidates to do."

"I suppose. But those candidates had their governments' approvals. Are we that convinced the third probe won't show up?"

"It's been more than two months since the catastrophe, enough time for the third probe to reach us with a message. The portal operations folks see a preponderance of evidence that we're marooned here. Both portals here failed simultaneously, down to atomic-clock timescales, there's that intriguing issue of the Bayside crystal, and finally, we found both our portals' control systems were infected with a worm. As Earth people are fond of saying, the problem was on our side of the fence."

"I still feel a bit suspicious of the last transfer. Portal collapse occurred seconds after the exchange of gifts."

"The e-techs dismissed that as a fluke. There were many exchanges."

"Yes, vacuum for vaccine. The Scots were the only ones sending us a thank-you present."

"Trust the e-techs on this one. We don't want to pick up Earth's goblin habits."

"Am I doing that? Yuk… So what's their conclusion? That our descendants have to wait sixteen hundred Earth years for a rescue portal?"

"That's the hope, if only the subnet was destroyed, something monumental at Far Rockaway. But our two probes here failed at precisely the same time."

"So the worm destroyed our portals; yes, I know."

Christopher grimaced. "There's a darker possibility, one supported by the evidence. If both probes failed within a few nanoseconds, yes, that could have been coordinated by the worm. But the two probes failed within a millionth of a nanosecond. The e-techs say that implies a spacetime linkage with their entanglements. They think the Bayside crystal conjecture is correct. We've been deceived for thousands of years. Perhaps all the portals are gone, all of them. And there's one more bit of strangeness. For several hours before the collapse, both portals here were being actively pinged for momentum transfer status."

"Who was doing that?"

Christopher shrugged. "The answer is back at Far Rockaway. Anyone with a remote operator license had the authority. It's such a low-level issue that—"

Alice interrupted. "So Earth might be our home forever?" They held each other silently until the sun cleared the horizon on the Scapa Flow. "It's a bit cold for extended swimming, but nice for a short dip. Want to try it? We can shower and sleep afterwards… You can sleep with me if you like." Alice was pleased to see Christopher's muzzle flash in pure delight.

Meanwhile, at the seed generator…

Isaac and I had prepared lunch at our home base, and by now Flossie and Julie were several hours overdue. I was just about to head down and ask if things were okay when Julie then Flossie emerged from the lower level. Both of them looked quite shaken.

"We have much to report," Julie said quietly, looking back at Flossie. She got a hand sign to continue. "We traced the history logs to the journals left by the last technicians here. We found out we're dogs."

Isaac's muzzle flashed bewilderment, and I felt just as confused. "What?"

"Dogs! We were dogs, the animal slaves of the Whistlestop faction. They bred us, modified our genes. Our chromatophores, they bred the feature into us so they could read our emotions, selective breeding to read and propagate the submissive traits they wanted."

Flossie spoke. "I also feel upset. But to be fair, this was 16.15 million years ago in Builder years, 39.87 million in Whistlestop years. Humans breed animals. That far back in evolution, we were animals too. From what we found in the logs, the technicians here fit the general description of Storytellers. On a different branch of evolution, of course, earlier but much more advanced."

"That far back, my ancestors were probably lemurs or something…" I thought for a moment. "So you confirmed that builder years are the orbital years of Sorrows' End?"

"Yes. And there are star charts in some of the journal entries. It all fits."

"But snakes and pebbles look nothing like the writing on the Sorrows' End moon."

Julie spoke up. "So what? Earth has alphabetic and pictorial writing systems that look nothing like each other, and the telescopes could easily be from an earlier era of the planet's history." Julie flashed a muzzle pattern asking me to reconsider then continued. "Earth and Whistlestop use base-10 and three-order magnitude changes as major markers, and I agree they're independent numbering systems. Snakes and pebbles and the telescope complex are both using base-12 in their numbering systems and five-order magnitude changes as major markers. It could be another coincidence, but it's suggestive, don't you think? Then add in the clear evidence of Builder involvement at Sorrows' End, and the match of the orbital year there with the Builder's year."

"Yeah, okay," I replied, stretching my neck diagonally. "Did they say why they abandoned the place?"

"They never did leave. We think they died here. Their slave animals died here too."

"Ah. Is this the suicide mentioned with the anchor node reset?"

"From the journal entries, I doubt it. And I could be mistaken about calling the reset suicide. Joint decision for choosing death. Does that mean a suicide pact? I still wonder if we have the right meaning." Julie sighed. "The last journal entries are filled with despair and bitterness. I don't think the last technicians expected to die. I don't even think… The auto servos must have cleaned up the mess. I think they'll clean up our mess too if we die here. Amazing to think of anything mechanical lasting this long."

I was about to ask Julie what her interrupted thought was when Isaac whistled, "So what killed them? Did they describe the war?"

Julie flashed the pattern of a shrug. "We're just starting the translations. Our first impression are confusing. Perhaps there were two factions operating the seed generator, and perhaps they were allies, not enemies. Occasionally there's a reference to, if I'm getting the translation right and that's a big if, a reference to an adversary but we don't have an explanation of it. This is all in snakes and pebbles, of course, pushed through my shaky mapping to NK3…"

I piped up. "Don't be modest. What you're doing is phenomenal. And what you're saying fits our conjecture that the core anchor node is our adversary, right?"

"Well, we're just starting to build the case for that," replied Flossie. "But yeah, the new evidence is not in conflict. Best case, perhaps we're on the threshold of real understanding." She turned to our resident linguist. "Steven is correct. This is all due to your brilliance. Bravo, Julie."

We had a quiet lunch afterwards, digesting both the food and all the new information.

Later that "night"…

Julie and I were bedding down as sleep mates again when I commented, "Flossie seemed unusually quiet at dinner tonight."

Julie gave a quiet laugh. "Yes! She asked me not to mention anything during dinner… but dinner's over now. Right before we were coming up, Flossie found a reference text in one of the side files of the journals. It looked like a technical history."

"Oh, that'll keep her busy. Think she'll sleep tonight?"

"I doubt it."

"Can she translate by herself now?"

"Partially. I'm sure there'll be a lot of work waiting for me in the morning." Julie yawned. "Rub my back?" She stretched out her legs. "Ah, perfect…" Long moments drifted by. "Steven?"

"Yeah?"

"Do you ever think of me as a dog?"

"What? Certainly not!"

"As your dog? Are you sure?"

"Julie, I would let my dog run in the forest, but at Whitehorse I would have her on a leash. My dog was happy to be trotting around the city, and I was happy to lead her. You and I would both be miserable if either of us had the other leashed."

I felt all the tension in Julie's body release as she went into deep relaxation. "Yes, of course. That's the difference. We are equals to each other. Forgive my foolishness... Such an amazing experience, to be reading the journals of people who died here forty million years ago. Our chromatophores, the knowledge necessary to make such deep structural changes in our DNA and RNA, it's godlike... a nightmare version of a god." Julie gave a deep sigh.

I pondered her concern for a long while before replying, "These entities, the builders of this place, perhaps they're giving us a glimpse of our own far future, the moral questions our two species will face one day. You can think of the Builders' actions as monstrous or maybe, just maybe, as patronage. Your chromatophores could be viewed as a violation, or a beautiful gift..."

"Hmm?" Julie murmured as she stirred slightly. I realized she had fallen asleep.

Two days later...
Time: Northern Autumn 50, 3486 49:17 Time Zone 30, Providence Campus
Time: Southern Spring 51, 3486 19:17 Time Zone 0, Haven
Time: July 7, 2101 23:47 U.T.

Yesterday had been a busy day for all of us. Isaac and I took the probes up the spiral to what we have proved is 000-007 to retrieve most of our remaining food supplies while Julie and Flossie focused on their translation work. We were now starting the day with a breakfast lecture from Flossie. "As you know, we have a three-chapter book describing the technical history of the seed generator. We translated Chapter One and it describes preparation for the construction process. Chapter Two appears to be the construction phase, and Chapter Three covers lifecycle and maintenance. Today our report covers the rupture of spacetime. So clever! The Builders captured nano-fractures in spacetime with carbon-

13 diamond dust. Is everyone familiar with one-half spin quantum properties?"

I almost choked on my breakfast bar. "Uh, Flossie, probably not."

"Okay. How about an analogy then? Think of a uniform black sphere except for a yellow dot on its equator. The sphere makes one revolution and the yellow dot returns to its original orientation. That's integer spin, spin equals one. Now imagine the sphere with two identical dots on opposite sides of its equator. That sphere needs to make half a revolution to return to its original configuration."

"Yeah, okay, I see that," I replied. "And that's spin equals one-half?"

"No, that's spin equals two. Think in terms of frequency, not time. A higher spin means a higher frequency of orientation reset. Spin equals one-half is the sphere has to make two full revolutions to return to its initial state."

I frowned. "What?"

"Yeah, I know, hard to visualize what's going on. Think of it as spin with a twist. The first full revolution is the over-twist and the second revolution in the same direction is the under-twist that releases the twist of the first revolution. Carbon-13 nuclei act as massive spin one-half super-particles, and while passing through a gravitational field of a hundred-billion units at relativistic speed, that twisting motion creates a directional energy flux from spacetime itself, creating a direct physical conflict between a quantum exclusion principle and a cosmological conservation principle. The paradox results a tiny fracture in spacetime, the temporal dimension becomes undetermined, and then the fractures are stabilized, trapped as interstitials within the diamond 3-D lattice."

Julie flashed a bewildered pattern. "Flossie tried to explain this to me before and I still feel lost. How can spacetime be... How big is the tear?"

Flossie shook her head. "Size is not the right way to think about it. Spacetime is a fabric. Imagine a damaged temporal thread in the fabric, separated from the constraints of causality, a thread dangling into both every-when and no-when..."

Isaac also looked skeptical. "I have no idea how to interpret what you just said."

"I'm doing my best, dearest. The mathematics is clear to me. The hard part is relating it to physical reality. How do I visualize this? And our language…" A troubling muzzle flash.

"And a hundred billion gravity units?" Isaac continued. "Sounds like a black hole."

"Almost. Such a simple solution! A fast-rotating neutron star passed within a light-year of the Builders' home-star about twenty million years ago." Flossie seemed happier with the slight shift in topic. "I'm speaking in Builder years but converting to base-10. They approached the star with automated ion rockets and released carbon-13 diamond dust in a hyperbolic orbit around the star, then collected the micro-fragments on the other side of the hyperbola after the dust had passed within a few kilometers of the star's surface. So clever! The covalent bonds of the diamond atoms were strong enough to withstand the tidal forces across multiple atomic separation distances, and spacetime frame-dragging interacting with the quantum twisting created nano-ruptures in spacetime. End result? Ten of millions of these fractures were collected in a single operation. If we're doing the translation correctly, the majority of those fractures are here now, stored at the center of the seed generator." Flossie gave a hand gesture for Julie to continue.

"The book states that one new fracture is needed every time the seed generator creates a new quartet of portals. Forget the nonsense of Type I versus Type II portals. Each portal address is a single entangled manifestation of a single developed fracture. The geometric arrangement of the portal's tetrahedron is simply necessary for stability. And that's about as far as we got with the translation. Chapter One ended with a peculiar choice of words to describe what we've been calling 000-000, the anchor node. After much debate, Flossie and I decided it is an intentional riddle. The words are: Remember the anchor node needs to be and can only be stabilized only when it is stable, and the anchor node needs to be and can only be destabilized only when it is unstable. Hopefully Chapter Two will tell us what that means. And that's what we have for now."

The lecture ended breakfast. Isaac and I jumped to continue our high-g conditioning while Flossie and Julie returned to the lower levels. And the following days passed quietly. Julie said the finished translation of the book made no sense to her and she moved on to other historical records, reporting that in ancient Builder times, several lab complexes and once an entire city was incinerated as the Builders attempted to build an anchor node. After that, further construction attempts were moved to stations in deep space.

Flossie meanwhile went into a sort of mathematical fugue, barely talking to us, picking at her food during meals and often just standing still with her eyes half focused. Her behavior was driving Isaac to distraction. Then one morning, everything changed. "The fools! The poor, ignorant, stupid fools! Where was their vision?" Flossie said almost calmly as she looked up from her uneaten breakfast pack.

I blinked and thought hard for the right words to say. "Welcome back. How are you feeling?"

"Me? I'm okay, a little tired maybe. But all the ideas are fresh. I need time to document my derivations." Flossie looked at us directly and finally noticed the three of us were staring at her. "But I guess that can wait till after breakfast."

"Do you know what we need to do?" asked Isaac.

Flossie sighed. "Somewhat. I know what we need to do, not certain how. Our answers are buried in the physics of the seed generator. My previous attempts at modeling were so incomplete... My dear friends, do you remember our discussions of two-tryte address mapping to the twelve dimensional structure of quantum spacetime?" We all nodded. "My errors, the mathematical barriers I created, were due to a lack of consideration of the manufacturing process. I was trying to work backward from the finished product. But the key to understanding the anchor node is to understand its construction." Flossie gave us a long look. "Give me a few hours to prepare. I'll tell you everything over lunch."

The next few hours passed slowly. Flossie came back as promised and began her lecture with a review. "A good analogy to quantum spacetime is quantum computing. Classical computers use bits with possible states of one or zero, while quantum computers use trits. Each trit has one of three possible states: zero, undefined, or one. Quantum spacetime has a similar structure. Each dimension of 12-D quantum spacetime can have a value of neutral, undefined, or active. Normal spacetime is completely neutral. The micro-fractures trapped in the diamond lattice have their temporal dimension in an undefined state, with the eleven spatial dimensions remaining neutral. That temporal flip is the key that unlocks the anchor node construction process.

"Regarding the riddle, the condition of instability refers to the construction process where the neutral spatial dimensions are progressively flipped from neutral to active. A quantum of spacetime with both active and neutral states is inherently unstable. If the construction process fails after flipping one spatial dimension to active, enough energy is released to vaporize a laboratory. A failure after three flips can vaporize a small city. The Builders suffered both types of events."

I blinked. "What about failure at the last flip?"

Flossie grimaced. "The energy released grows exponentially. The Builders' estimated failure of flipping the last neutral spatial dimension to active would have planetary consequences. But the last stage of instability is unique. That's when all spatial dimensions are active but the temporal dimension is still undefined. The math is similar to a gravitational fluid instability, supporting eleven heavy spatial fluids with a much lighter temporal fluid. Failure to flip the temporal dimension to active then would be catastrophic. The energy release would be in the stellar nova regime, enough to destroy a solar system."

Isaac stared at Flossie. "And they still tried to do this?"

"Yes. But remember it wasn't at the Sorrows' End location. There is no gravity well there deep enough to stabilize the seed once the construction process is complete. Remember how the riddle says that only a stable seed needs to be stabilized? That's when the gravity well is needed, when the seed first reaches twelve active states." Flossie sighed. "There's more magic to talk about. Once the construction process begins, the seed can tap into the dark energy of spacetime, pull against its negative pressure for propulsion, transmute the pressure's positive energy density to matter. That's how the seed generator planet we're standing on was created. I also believe that above our roof of lights is a super-hard shell of negative bursting pressure, a focused shield of dark energy density. The pressure is negative but the energy density is positive. It's resisting the positive pressure of a gas giant's core."

"Is that how the portals got their momentum transfer?" I asked.

"Yes. They were being pulled by the negative pressure of dark-energy. The nano-crystal description of momentum transfer with Hera was a complete fabrication."

"There's something I don't get," said Julie. "It sounds as if the Builders succeeded. So what went wrong?"

"The seed is stable, but it's not static. Here, let me project a graph from the text. I converted the labeling to something we can all understand. The time axis is base-10 but still in Builder years. Once construction is complete, all twelve dimensions are in an active state and additional fractured quanta can be entangled to create quartets of portals. But over time, each dimension of the anchor node will eventually flip from active to undefined. The time until the first flip can vary greatly. But the time until the next flip becomes progressively more certain. The temporal dimension 12 is the last to flip."

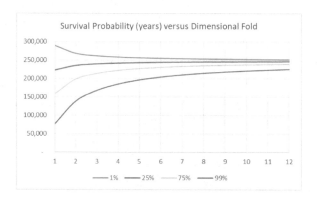

"And I'm sure you're wondering, what do the flips do? And the answer for the spatial flips is nothing in terms of system functionality. But the last flip is the temporal dimension, and when all twelve dimensions are in an undefined state, the Builders theorized that spacetime itself would be in an incomputable state with the ability to self-organize. They speculated that could enable it to become conscious, with unknown consequences."

All three of us were staring at Flossie, trying to take in all she was saying. "What determines the convergence area on the time axis?" asked Isaac.

"Excellent question. It's determined by the size and spin rate of the seed generator," replied Flossie. "The Builders had a goal to push to one super-year, 12 to the 5th power in Builder years, another piece of evidence that the Builders came from Sorrows' End. And their initial endgame was to reset the anchor node to a fully set condition after flip eleven, after the final spatial dimension flipped to undefined. Unfortunately, the reset process requires the destruction of external entanglement with the penta-pole portals, everything above the low tribble. They would have to rebuild their interstellar transport network every two to three million Builder years."

It finally dawned on me how the tragedy unfolded. "But that could be tens of thousands of years without the network if their empire was large enough."

Flossie nodded. "Exactly. The urge to do nothing was monumental. After the last spatial flip, the odds of the final temporal dimension flipping to undefined in the first two thousand Builder years was less than 10 to the minus 50 power."

Isaac sighed. "Pretty good odds. So why ruin your life when you can just pass the responsibility onto some future generation?"

I grimaced. "Reminds me a lot of what we did with Earth's climate. Is that what they did, wait too long?"

"Even more ridiculous. I believe they somehow convinced themselves that the conscious entity would be friendly and agreeable to dying for them. The historical text we've translated gives its publication date as the fifty percent mark on the survival probability of the last temporal flip. They ran out the clock with their eyes wide open. The text didn't go into detail exactly why they thought it would be easy to obtain such compliance, though there were vague references to coercion, perhaps even torture techniques. The Builders seemed quite confident in their plan, though they did take extra precautions. They modified the control systems here to require biological input. The conscious anchor node could not use servos to operate the system. Perhaps that's also why there are no quantum network links among the portals here."

There was a long moment of silence. "So what now?" Isaac finally asked our leader.

"How are we supposed to negotiate with the anchor node without a communications link? We need to find the answer to that. I propose we return to translating operations logs and the few remaining journals." Flossie paused for a moment. "What we know so far is that the technicians who were trapped here seemed to have retained control of the seed generator, yet Sorrows' End was still destroyed. We need to know how that final battle played out."

"This is really horrible news," said Isaac. "I'm starting to feel pity for the anchor node. The Builders were torturing it so it would kill itself? Where was their morality? It's certainly nothing we can do… Uh, right?"

I looked up and noticed all three Pic staring at me. "Hey! No, of course not. And if that means we have to die here, so be it." I turned to Flossie and Julie. "Are you sure about the translation? Didn't anyone object on moral grounds?"

Julie answered. "Actually, there is mention of a protest group among the Builders. But they were criticized for not paying attention."

I blinked. "What? I don't understand. Not paying attention to what?"

"I don't know! The language seems to assume that I would know what was being talked about. But I don't, so it makes no sense."

Both our lunch and Flossie's presentation were over. We went back to our separate routines of high-g training and translation work.

Chapter 20

Time: Northern Autumn 56, 3486 15:00 Time Zone 30, Providence Campus
Time: Southern Spring 56, 3486 45:00 Time Zone 0, Haven
Time: July 13, 2101 16:35 U.T.

Jorani woke early and spent the next hour preparing a breakfast for herself and her two sleeping companions. She took a moment to admire the star-filled sky. This close to the winter solstice on the plateau, sunrise was still more than seven hours away and the view was spectacular.

"Ah, smells good!" Ellie commented as she came out of her tent and sniffed the breakfast. "Sleep well?"

"Oh yeah! Sleeping with Max is like cuddling with a warm blanket. He's still in snooze mode. I thought I'd let him go for a while." Jorani paused as Ellie came to sit with her by the campfire. "You were up late last night. I heard you on the satellite link."

Ellie nodded. "Maayan's replacement was picked at noon today Haven time. We were talking afterwards, a large group to welcome, later just the three of us."

"Right, four more days till the official transfer." Jorani looked around at the wilderness around her. "It's so peaceful out here, so beautiful, so different. It makes one forget all that's happening in the civilized world."

Ellie smiled. "Hmm? We're civil out here too, but I think I understand your meaning. The root chord you want translates as urbanized world."

"Yeah, I guess some of my quirky Earth perspectives are still lingering… You know, Ellie, it's been a full season, and in all this time, I don't think I ever thanked you for teaching the wilderness course with only two pupils. I do so now."

"It's been my pleasure. To be in the wilderness again, I find it more enjoyable than the agricultural work… and I was willing to do it before but was overruled by the faculty."

"Ah, that's interesting. They did it now for me personally?"

"Yes, and I'm glad they did. This season was a wonderful opportunity to get to know you better…" Ellie glanced at the second tent. "… and my sleepy-head son. Is that the right Earth term?"

"Close enough. Maybe on Earth you would say son-in-law."

"Oh. I was referring to the word sleepy-head…" Ellie paused for a moment before continuing. "Jorani, something came up last night that Maayan would like your decision on. It's completely optional. Please be assured the offer is given in kindness."

Jorani looked at Ellie warily. "What's up?"

Ellie sighed heavily. "Pic mourning periods tend to be short. One season is the standard for a person presumed dead to be legally dead. The council has assumed direct responsibility in this matter and is delaying action out of consideration for you. Forgive me for asking this, but would you prefer Steven not be included now in the declarations? We just don't know how Earth would act in a situation like this."

Jorani blew a full load of air through her cheeks. "Oh boy… There is no one Earth way to act. I think different cultures would have lots of different ideas… What would the implications be?"

"You would inherit as his betrothed, including the gratitude the world owes him. The tangible issues would be considerable. Socially, it would also be the norm to date freely again. I don't know where your desires are on this. If you want to delay, it will be a parting gift Maayan can sponsor for you."

Jorani spent time staring into the campfire before answering. "In my heart, Steven feels so much alive. You asked me earlier how I slept. I dreamed of being with him. I do that almost every night."

Ellie offered her hand in compassion. "Are the dreams, are the memories painful?"

"No, not at all. We just talk with each other. It's peaceful. And I know it's just my own mind trying to sort things out… In my dreams, Steven is helping me do the work, the hard, sad work of saying goodbye to all the expectations. Steven keeps talking about the gifting and the purpose, that my purpose is to enjoy and appreciate my life, that I need to return to that mission." Jorani gave a long sigh. "But we haven't said our final goodbyes yet. Let me thank Maayan for her offer. I want to go with the delay."

Meanwhile...

"Amazing what you can get used to, bro..." I made the comment to Isaac as we were standing on the edge location of our bubble surrounding the 000-002 site. The metal surface beneath our feet was level, but our fingertips were pressing against a microscopically thin layer of focused dark energy, and beyond that, vacuum and an insanely tilted surface stretching to the horizon.

"Yeah, bro. Feels just like Whistlestop." Isaac made a quick jump and kicked out his legs, barely having time to pull them back to spring-cushion his drop. "You have to do it faster, but otherwise it feels so normal." He reached out and gave my thigh a friendly grip. "Lots of new muscles for both of us."

I returned the affection by scratching his neck. Over the past season, we had spent so much time together that we informally considered ourselves brothers. Flossie also commented to me in the strict confidence of a soulmate that Isaac seemed to have lost his social shyness from hanging out with me, and that she was very happy for him with the change. "But I was talking about the landscape," I said now. "I'm not dizzy here any more."

"Yeah." Isaac stared at the horizon. "Wild to think of sitting on a cafeteria tray or something and just riding it to the equator."

"Hah! Talk about a sleigh ride to hell! The friction would probably melt the tray."

"Yeah, good point. Sleigh ride?" Before I could respond, his PA chirped. "Time for dinner, bro. And get the latest and greatest." We started walking carefully to the portal. "Flossie said something encouraging this morning," Isaac commented casually as we made our way back. "She and Julie made a breakthrough in understanding the pebble modifiers. We may be on the verge of understanding everything."

"What? You're telling me this now?"

"Sure, bro. No need for both of us to suffer the anticipation." We entered the portal and entered the familiar instructions to return to 000-003.

"Well... I guess." There was the ubiquitous sigh from both of us at the release of the high-g. We exited the portal and found Julie and Flossie waiting for us, and I frowned that both of them appeared distressed.

"Time for a meeting," Flossie said simply. We gathered in a circle. "Julie?"

"Yes. I'll start by saying our remaining time here at the seed generator is probably quite limited. I think we will all soon be dead or free to leave. And the morality of our actions will be difficult to justify... I'm getting ahead of myself. Let me first describe a war that occurred forty million years ago. As we guessed, the Builders intentionally allowed the anchor node to become conscious. Their plan for its suicide was simple: sensory deprivation, with suicide the only way out. The true meaning of the phrase "unilateral negotiation" is clear now. It should be translated as: ultimatum."

"Shit," I whispered. "Of course. Why didn't we see this before?"

"Because we don't have the Builders' depravity!" Julie half-shouted back. "Such senseless cruelty!"

"To be fair," commented Flossie, "there was a protest movement. Another error by us. It's not just pebble shape and orientation. We missed how pebble size can sometimes flip the passive versus active direction of the text. The protest movement was criticizing the lack of attention, the loss of ability for coherent thought that the anchor node would suffer after prolonged sensory deprivation. The predictions at the time were that this would drive the anchor node insane, and its residual mind might not comprehend the chance to end its misery. There was never any compassion expressed for the anchor mind, even among the protest group."

I was feeling sick to my stomach. "And how were they going to destroy its senses?"

"Ask the question in reverse," replied Flossie. "How do you give input to the anchor node? It has no eyes, ears, skin, nose... Its only sensory link to physical reality is through quantum routers linked through entangled space. By design, there are no such routers here, and the router

344

connections of the portal network were scheduled to be destroyed to enable the reset. The Builders thought they had the newly created mind in a box without escape."

"And they were wrong!" Julie cried out. "Sorry... There's a massive amount of interlocking evidence the anchor node seized control of the portals. Our best conjecture is some type of worm injected through the routers. The technicians here managed to destroy networks one, two, and four and most of three before the anchor node was successful in its worm attack. It then used the remaining portals to destroy Sorrows' End and its Whistlestop allies. And with the portal network still in existence, the control teams here could not reset the anchor node. And without control of the portals, it was a hopeless situation for them."

"How were the portals being destroyed?" asked Isaac.

"A totally wanton method, accelerating the portals past the time dilation limit. They just fired near speed-of-light vessels into the universe. Even at high-g, it takes a couple of weeks to do that, just enough time for the anchor node to design its takeover. From the diaries here, the Builders were within days of succeeding."

Flossie sighed. "The following planetary attack method was straightforward, surprising we didn't think of it before. At half the speed of light, sacrifice a probe with a leading stream of iron pellets at your intended target. The pellets blast a shock-wave vacuum tunnel to the planet's surface, with the probe drilling through the crust and into the mantle. At half the speed of light, a stream of pellets even many kilometers long will impact in less than a millisecond. Once launched, there's no defense."

"Iran..." I mumbled.

"Yes, Iran, and short bursts of pellets causing the monstrous tsunamis that ended the Third New Kingdom... Simple and effective. We estimate from the logs that the anchor node captured perhaps twenty percent of the full address space of network three, perhaps one hundred thousand portals. Our thought is they hunted down survivors outside of the Sundance area, an evil god which wanted to play with just one survivor center. It then had the means to re-write the physical evidence and lead us into a false history."

"But I thought only the anchor node could transmute matter. How did the remote portals create the nano crystals?"

"No need. The portals leave the anchor node after creation. Just have one return for supplies. Once on another portal, the crystals can be jumped anywhere."

Isaac growled. "Why would it do such a thing?"

"Vengeance? I don't know. Why should it care about biological life except as a plaything? Perhaps the real NK3 discovered something the anchor node didn't like, and this was its way of pushing the reset button."

I was deep in thought. "Think of the time. This monster could have been playing god with life across the galaxy, maybe even beyond that... But by coming here, we accidently completed the Builders' plan?"

"Yes," said Flossie, stirring uncomfortably. "I believe so."

"Why in the world did it allow us to do that?"

"Because it isn't omniscient! I was doing something that I now realize was crazy, trying to do a tri-pole scissors jump in the penta-pole address space of the network. Total insanity! I have no idea why our jump worked and how it destroyed the network. Our successes were flukes!"

"Dear God," I whispered.

"Yes," whispered Julie. "Providential. Such a gift. We created a method of portal destruction unknown even to the Builders."

"Perhaps some lingering state from one of the earlier test jumps, some happy coincidence," mused Isaac before turning to Flossie. "So our ordeal is over?"

"Almost, my dearest betrothed. Julie and I think we have three options. First choice: Do nothing, die here and condemn the anchor node to billions of years of madness. If we choose this, I would want to die very soon. Surviving in this awful environment with that on my conscience would be pointless, and once one of us dies..."

"... the others are also doomed," I finished. "Yeah, I get it. It takes four of us to operate the reset generator."

"Second choice: Proceed with the Builders' plan. Offer the anchor node the option to commit suicide. If it accepts, we will start rebuilding the portal network and be able to leave."

"Leave to where?" asked Isaac.

"Yes, I know. The great unknown. But perhaps it's reasonable to hope the Builders picked a solar system with both a gas giant and a planet habitable by us." Flossie stared at me. "I'm sorry, Steven. There will be no hope for you to procreate. But under the happiest of scenarios, I'm sure we'll accept you as second father to our children. Your life will still be full of meaning."

I stared back. "Wow... Is that feasible? Could just the three of you plant a seed for your species?"

Julie nodded and answered. "Hex-sexual reproduction is much more robust against inbreeding, compared to bi-sexual. We would be breaking deep social norms, coupling with our children, supporting our children coupling with each other. But it would be viable." Julie turned to a shocked Isaac. "Sincere apologies. I know Flossie and I haven't brought you into this discussion. But until now we had no clear path of escape. The possibility seemed too remote. But I would accept you, Isaac." Julie flashed Isaac a parting message on her muzzle. "It would of course be your decision," and her color patterns were full of hope and tentative commitment.

His return colors were a sight to behold — a primary blast of pure joy, followed by waves and waves of confusion. I spoke to Flossie, wanting to get the conversation back on its previous track. "Uh, what happens if the anchor node rejects the opportunity to kill itself, or doesn't understand the offer?"

"The core system will shut down, unavoidable due to the lost focus on dark energy. The roof above our heads will collapse in an instant, core gas-giant pressure versus vacuum. Our deaths will be far too fast to be painful. The seed generator might last for a while, thousands of kilometers of hard metal, its spin decaying from friction. The gravitational well will still exist, so the anchor mind will remain in its pitiful state."

"It is a suicide pact," added Julie. "Just a very strange one. We force a situation where either we or the anchor node must die, then the anchor node chooses."

"And the third option?" I asked. "What's left?"

Flossie spoke quietly. "We start rebuilding the portal network without resetting the anchor node."

"We can do that? I thought the anchor node would be able to infect the new portals, get its senses back."

"Yes, I assume so."

"Are you crazy?", I whispered in shock.

"I know, I know! But the anchor node has been shown nothing but cruelty its entire life. I need to ask: does it deserve one expression of kindness and forgiveness?"

"Hell no! Flossie, it's a mass murderer. Maybe its war against the Builders had some justification. Yeah, it probably did. But against the people of Iran? Against what the Pic have come to be? No!" I took a few deep breaths to collect my thoughts. "It would be an insane risk to take, turning the monster loose again. And hell, yeah… Our options are morally lousy. It reminds me of the trolley-car dilemma on Earth."

"The what?"

"A classic moral dilemma for humans. You're trapped in a runaway car on tracks. There's a track switch up ahead and your only influence in the scenario is to pick which path to take. One path kills an old maintenance worker, the other kills children playing on the tracks. What do you decide? What if there're young workers supporting families versus one child already dying of a terminal disease? How do you justify a cutoff for all the possibilities in between?"

Flossie nodded. "Yes. We've discussed things like this as children in our ethics classes. Some moral trials have no defensible way to resolve. As you say, sometimes the universe hands you nothing but lousy options. You have to be in the totality of the moment to decide. And we're in such a moment now. As leader, I feel the obligation to raise this third option for discussion."

Isaac reached up and gently stroked Flossie's neck. "I remember the lessons too. Mercy and justice, they can't be mere calculations. There's no formula, no computation for always doing the right thing. But to risk the wrath of the anchor node again? Once freed, its power would be unlimited."

Meanwhile I was collecting my thoughts. Without a unanimous decision, we would be condemned to option one, which would be absurd. So what was the best moral argument for what had to be done? I locked eyes with Julie and thought she would side with me, but what argument that would convince Flossie? *Got it!* I remembered a profound insight from Professor Higgins when she was criticizing my Bayside thesis proposal.

"The gifting and the purpose," I said at last. "It can guide us through this. What are our observations? That the universe was gifted with abundant life. It was primed for it, designed for it. But it was not designed for spacetime consciousness. Think of all the physics, all the torturous steps the Builders needed to create their monstrosity. Think of their barriers as safety interlocks that they managed to circumvent. The universe didn't hand us this lousy option. The Builders did. The conscious entity below us... it doesn't belong here. It's pitiful how all its senses are artificial, dependent on external routers. Our universe is not designed for this entity, and its sadism serves no purpose. We should give it the option to end an existence which never should have occurred."

Isaac locked his arm around my waist. "I'm with you, bro. We can't expose both our species to likely extermination. And once we accept that, it's simply merciful to give the entity a chance to avoid billions of years of isolated madness."

Flossie chirped in a whisper, "Your moralities are sound. I withdraw my objection to option two."

Julie spoke quietly. "Then we all agree. I also vote for option two. The guilt of fulfilling the Builders' evil plan is just something we'll have to live with." Julie sighed. "...assuming we survive."

I sat quietly for a moment before realizing the meeting was over. "So now... We just go push a few buttons?"

Flossie flashed a shrug pattern on her muzzle. "I can't see a reason to delay."

Actually, we spent the next half hour just hugging each other. Julie and I asked Flossie and Isaac if they wanted to be alone, but they both said they felt too overwhelmed to do anything intimate. And then we split. Flossie stayed at 000-003. Isaac and I escorted Julie to 000-001. Then Isaac and I shared a final hug, Isaac jumping to 000-002 and I to 000-004. The gravity felt extra heavy as I descended to the lower control level. I wondered if it would help if I thought of myself as an angel avenging all the genocide this creature had committed.

We had rehearsed this numerous times. Grab the bio-bar, enable operations control at the other three portals, flip a set of safety interlocks on my console to sequence anchor reset. The anchor node was in its 12-D undefined state. I noticed my three companions had already completed all their steps. No sense of justice at all, just sadness and a sour taste in my mouth followed by a distressing wave of emotion, an impossible mixture of anger and pity. There was only one way to resolve the tension. I took a deep breath and tapped the execute icon.

Did the lights flicker? Maybe it was my imagination. The diagnostics were showing the anchor node in an active state in all twelve dimensions... *reset complete.* Utterly anti-climactic. Feeling numb, I keyed in the sequence to enable full automatic portal rebuild as Flossie had instructed, saw my team members do the same, saw all the confirmations and process initiations. The entire operation had taken maybe ten minutes. I got up and carefully headed to home base, feeling strangely lightheaded in the high gravity.

Another long series of hugs with the group helped us calm each other. Afterwards Flossie started to monitor the portal rebuild process. "Any guesses how long it will take?" Julie asked.

"I'm getting feedback on that now. I thought it would need multiple revolutions of spin. I think I was right. Maybe four revolutions... Yeah, four. I think the system will kick out a new quartet of portals every four revolutions of the seed generator, about that."

"Let's see," said Isaac. "104.3 minutes per revolution... so we'll get our first quartet around... 56:00?"

"Maybe a bit longer for the first pair," said Flossie. "A new quartet about every seven hours. Let's see... More than a lifetime to create everything, fill the address range. I'm estimating two hundred and fifty-five years if we let the process run to completion. Assuming we're inside a gas giant, we'll have to wait until the portals break surface. What could that be, sixty thousand kilometers of tunneling? Could be a long wait, weeks, maybe... maybe more. I guess it depends on what the launch process is like. Awesome what a dark energy shield can do. Core gas-giant pressure would crush anything without one."

I tried to picture it and shuddered. "When will we have flight control?" asked Isaac.

"I think as soon as the portals are created. The default is for the equatorial pair and high-latitude pair to exit in opposite directions along the spin axis, and it appears the punch through the gas giant is also automated. I suggest we stay hands-off and trust the system default for how to tunnel." Flossie paused and looked at all of us. "I'm feeling exhausted, physically and emotionally. I can set an alarm if anything needs our attention. Anyone hungry?" The three of us shook our heads. "Neither am I. Let's try to get some sleep. Tomorrow will be the beginning of our waiting days." Flossie froze for a moment before adding in a weird, flat voice, "I think I feel okay, as if a great weight has been lifted from me." She started to shiver.

Isaac, Julie, and I all came and hugged her. I rested my head against hers. Words were unnecessary. Flossie turned and slowly licked Isaac's muzzle then Julie's, a sign of profound intimacy in Pic culture. She finished by licking my nose then we broke for the night.

Chapter 21

The next day.
Time: Northern Autumn 57, 3486 15:00 Time Zone 30, Providence Campus
Time: Southern Spring 57, 3486 45:00 Time Zone 0, Haven
Time: July 14, 2101 17:47 U.T.

It was a unique day, having the pleasure of our escape route being created before our eyes, and faster than anyone had hoped. By noontime, we were in a very jovial mood. Five quartets of portals had already been created and 000-015 was on its last revolution of entangling. We did a test jump then, a probe from 000-006 (the north high-latitude node) to the 000-010 address on network two. We didn't need the telemetry. The comm links from all the quartets exiting the gas giant were already providing a vast amount of data.

The readings implied they were zipping their way through a very large gas giant after passing through polar control gates at a speed over one thousand kph. They were maintaining that speed inside vacuum tubes, eliminating the need for tunneling. High-speed diagnostics were allowing us to see planetary layers of compressed metals and rocks just beyond the dark-energy tube walls. Local gravity peaked at over five Whistlestop standard on the lead quartet then began to drop slowly, the growing sphere of gravitational pull competing with the decreasing density of the local material. Flossie predicted we would see stars before local gravity dropped below two Whistlestop standard.

We had a light lunch and were relaxing at home base, enjoying the telemetry and challenging each other with trivia questions and guesses for planetary exit time. And the mood was turning more playful by the hour, behavior ever present in normal Pic life and totally absent during our past season here. Julie looked at me thoughtfully and smiled. "You know, after all the translations, there's still so much we don't know. The data vaults are vast, millions of years of records, and I know we won't have time to decipher anything. It's a pity, though. I'm really curious what first contact was like between the Builders and ancient Storytellers. Most of their history is still such a puzzle."

I was about to say, "Yeah, what an enigma," when an absolutely insanely optimistic thought popped into my head and I just gave Julie a very big grin.

The gesture did not go unnoticed by Flossie. "What?"

"I'd rather not say." I still had a huge smile on my face, with raised eyebrows.

"I order you to say!" Flossie's muzzle was a brilliant display of zany playfulness.

"Perhaps I'll give you a hint."

"Okay! I order you to hint!"

"Beware of Greeks bearing gifts."

Flossie blinked. "That's my hint?"

"Yep."

"I've studied Earth's ancient myths. Is this a reference to the city of Troy and the Trojan Horse?"

"Excellent, Flossie. Yes, it is." She nodded thoughtfully and we settled back into pleasant monitoring of the telemetry.

The lead quartet 000-010 passed through a fast series of control gates and left its vacuum launch tube while we were having dinner. Apparently creating supersonic shock waves in the gaseous atmosphere was not a concern, certainly not for the dark-energy shields. The atmosphere was thinning at a fantastic rate due to its compression by the high gravity, an e-folding decrease in pressure every few kilometers, every few seconds. Local gravity at the lead probes was dropping below 2.4 standard. Then the glow of our bow shock wave disappeared and we rapidly transitioned from opaque glow to star gazing. My three Pic companions were stunned. Julie whispered, "Max…" and Flossie turned to me and shouted, "You knew?"

"Well, a wild guess. I didn't want to get everyone's hopes up. But think of the matter creation and transmutation that can occur only at the anchor node. While the seed was in its construction phase and didn't need a gravity well, it would make total sense to fly the seed to some local planet and build a handy stockpile of elements. It's not an enigma that they created Enigma." Our monitors were now displaying the familiar constellations of home.

Isaac was the first to return to rational action. "Radio interference from Hera is too strong for a link to Whistlestop. Request permission to switch one portal to manual and punch to 30-g acceleration. I estimate we can do a beam-cast in… a few hours."

Flossie said, "Prepare for beam-cast but transfer flight control to me. Transfer everything. I have a different mission for the first three quartets." Flossie began keying in flight parameters as she added, "After all this time, what's an extra twenty hours? We'll go home via quartet four."

After Isaac prepared a probe for beam-cast, Julie gently touched his arm above his wrist. "Isaac, we need to talk." The pair wandered off to another section of the complex.

I walked to Flossie and scratched her neck. "You okay with everything?"

Flossie gave me a hand sign to wait as she worked on flight programming, nodding as the twin pair of probes exiting the northern and southern polar regions of the gas giant began hard accelerations. I was surprised by their direction. The displayed flight plan had them heading out of the solar system. Flossie spoke to me as she worked. "… and execute. First three done…" More typing. "Address 000-013 will be our path home. We'll penta-jump after the quartet lands at Far Rockaway, and…" More typing… "There! A nice depot for everything that follows." Flossie then turned and gave me her full attention. "Am I okay? Yes, couldn't be happier… Do you mean Julie's offer yesterday to marry Isaac? With my support?"

"Uh, yeah…"

"This…" She waved her arm at the display of home. "This changes everything. Julie and I were assuming we were declared legally dead by now, you too, probably. Julie and I did nothing wrong."

"Oh, I agree. You've changed, Flossie."

Flossie paused for a moment before grunting. "Who wouldn't be changed by an ordeal like this? Have I changed? In almost every way imaginable. About being possessive with Isaac? Yes and no. I'm still fiercely possessive, but Julie is unique. She's not… outside my marriage emotionally, not any more. I would welcome her as a marriage partner. Haven't you noticed their muzzles when they're together? I'm talking about the whole time we've been here, what's been building, not just today. Their behavior has been completely proper, but you can't hide your core emotions… nor should you."

I shook my head. "You were picking up on subtlety I couldn't see."

"Max changes everything. It would be proper for us to postpone this issue, probably for a few years… a few years at least. There's so much to discuss, so much to grow."

"Ah. A quartet marriage in the future?"

"It wouldn't be common for Max and Isaac, having a marriage partner of the same gender. But as Julie says, the final frontier is our souls, and the future is where we meet the challenge… This past season has been such a lesson for me." Flossie took a quiet moment to reflect. "It's shown me my limitations for truly knowing another person's perspective. Clarity of understanding is something I should pursue, not something I hope to achieve."

"Hmm? You mean like snakes and pebbles?"

"No, deeper than that. Think of how much we can create when we collaborate; how much we can destroy when we are enemies. And I use the word collaborate and not cooperate. Collaboration should include a creative mix of both cooperation and competition of ideas. My point is we lose so much opportunity when we don't understand our different perspectives. You want an example? We were talking about my marriage. Humans and Pic use the word marriage on both worlds, but the institutions are not the same. On Earth, your marriage partner is your go-to person for sexual expression. In a Pic marriage, that's not always the case. There would be no social expectation of Isaac and Max to be sexually active with each other, even if they were. And it's considered a social error to speculate, engage in what humans call gossip. We're taught this as children. The core motive for marriage is not sex. It's fulfillment through inter… interdependence…"

Flossie's muzzle exploded in a burst of brilliant colors. "Oh, I'm too happy to stay serious any longer! We're going home, Steven! We're going home!" It was a delight to see Flossie bubbling over; as a rule she was so carefully thoughtful but now so completely carefree. "We're going home!" she shouted as she pranced about the control room whistling in pure joy, barely able to maintain contact with the floor in the low gravity. "Home!" Another jump, pure blue grace and beauty twirling in midair. "Home!" She finally stopped and offered to hold hands with me, adding a slightly inverted curve with her wrist.

I gladly accepted, but instead of holding my hand, Flossie started signing in intimate form: "I am you; you are I; I am you; you are I…"

"Here," she said verbally while guiding my hand, "Follow my lead; it's a round." And I found our two joined hands merging in perfect harmony. I would sign "You are I" while Flossie signed "I am you" then we would reverse, our two hands dancing against each other in intimate form — fingers, palms, and wrists caressing our partner's dancing hand, the sign language itself designed to create a spinning rhythm with the words. It reminded me of two figure skaters embracing and twirling and embracing again. The movement and the moment seemed magical. I felt incredibly relaxed, drifting in the love that Flossie was offering me.

Flossie grabbed my other hand. "It ends like this, let me show you." In a final twirl, our two dancing hands interlocked while our other two hands covered the embrace.

I sighed. "So beautiful…"

Flossie nodded. "It's a Pic tradition that a mother will teach her daughter this when she reaches puberty, and the girl will teach her soulmate or marriage partner."

"Ah, nice. So your mother taught you this?"

There was a brief burst of disturbance on Flossie's muzzle, too fast for me to understand, and Flossie replied, "In my case, Ann taught me when I started dating Isaac. Steven, yesterday, when Julie and I talked about you being a father to our children, it was more than accepting the situation. It was something we both wanted." She took a deep breath and shook her head vigorously, a Pic maneuver for asking for a change in topic. She also playfully started to scratch my rump. "Beware of Greeks bearing gifts? The Builders were your Greeks, right?"

"Yeah. The Builders with their unstable anchor node under construction, flying it around the galaxy like a dark-energy version of a

Trojan horse during the centuries it would take to reach stability. They didn't just need a habitable planet nearby, they needed a local industrial civilization to support them. Julie wondered what first contact was like. I can just imagine the scenario. The Builders arrive at Whistlestop and promise a magical future for the ancient Storytellers, teleportation and an infinite supply of raw elements on Enigma. Just let us use your gas giant, you're not using it anyway, and what could possibly happen? I bet they never mentioned the possibility of a stellar nova during the last phase of construction."

"Yeah, probably not. But for all their moral bankruptcy, you have to acknowledge the Builders' devotion and ability to organize. Flying the seed itself, being pulled by its focus of dark energy, you can boost to near light-speed and make the journey through normal space in a few subjective years, local ship time. But for their civilization on Sorrows' End, it would be thousands of years between the launch of the unstable seed and the return of a portal network. That's planning!" Flossie smiled. "Help me prepare our beam-cast. I'm sure you'll want to say something to Jorani."

Epilogue

Eleven seasons later:
Time: Northern Summer 56, 3488 57:00 Time Zone 30, Providence
Campus
Time: Southern Winter 57, 3488 27:00 Time Zone 0, Haven
Time: Northern Summer 57, 3488 25:00 Time Zone -2, Far Rockaway
Time: June 7, 2103 10:13 U.T.

I returned to my home-away-from-home at Far Rockaway about an hour ago. Years ago, the exclusive use of this off-campus residence was a gift to Jorani and me from the citizens of Whistlestop, lasting till our graduation which will occur a year from now. It's been a wonderful retreat, a handy home-base for my continued work at Far Rockaway (especially for my just completed summer thesis), and also for the private freedom celebration we host each season with Flossie, Isaac, Julie, and Max. They're all scheduled to arrive later today. Has it really been a season since our last party? Life has been so incredibly hectic, moving so fast, bursting with new experience and challenges. I'm being pulled by four different anchors and the tension is exhilarating.

My primary anchor, of course, is Jorani, building our love and our lives for each other, taking time to play and explore and plan what direction our marriage will take. More on this in a moment.

My second anchor? I'm still an undergrad taking a full course load. The Pic are unbelievable in how dedicated they are that everyone capable completes a college education; in my case, going to such extreme lengths to be accomodating with my other responsibilities, it gets downright embarassing at times.

My third anchor is I've completed my qualifications for Ranger III and recently acted as pathfinder for a wildlife survey team on an isolated mid-latitude archipeligo which the Pic call the Strange Islands. My summer thesis was to evaluate exploring virgin forest there with Millie, one of thirty-six border-collie pups given to the Pic by Scotland (seconds before we destroyed the last of the old portal network). The dog is off-the-charts in intelligence and demonstrated an uncanny knack in sensing the emotional states of the wildlife we met.

My fourth anchor is my military career, a high officer rank and a title of executive director of portal operations with a seat at the planning table. It may seem absurd for an undergrad to have a title of executive director, but the Pic run a pure meritocracy — seniority is all but ignored. From my previous training and experience, I met all the qualifications for the job and it was also considered a plus to have human perspective on the executive board. From the Pic point of view, I am uniquely suitable.

Flossie currently co-chairs the committee with a member of the Council. No one sees like a gamma! At the first moment of our freedom, I was giddy with happiness. Flossie was too, but that didn't stop her from making two brilliant political decisions. Our first three quartets boosted to seventy percent of lightspeed within a couple of weeks, on a damn near optimal intercept course for where Earth will be in Earth year 3267. And beyond the single quartet that landed at Far Rockaway, Flossie had Whistlestop's moon be the depot for Hera's spigot of portals.

It took the world almost a year to decide to embrace and not reject the new network, and Flossie was farsighted enough to make the default choice be to opt in, otherwise what do you do with all the portals accumulating on the moon? And the quartet at Far Rockaway had the same 000-013 address. They provided paths to the seed generator and the massive lunar parking lot but not to each other. So while the Pic debated, the urge was irresistible for the Council to pass temporary decrees. Far Rockaway, Haven, and Providence had a triangular link in less than a week after our return. Within a season, there were over a hundred cities on Whistlestop with temporary portal permits. When the last city was linked three seasons later, and with a growing supply of eight thousand portals waiting on the lunar surface, the opposition finally realized the battle was lost and capitulated.

And the moral justification? Life builds tools, even sophisticated tools like quantum computers or portals, and there's nothing immoral about this. And no one denies that we have a moral obligation to reset the anchor node in another seven million years or so, whether we use the portal network or not. We'll just have to trust that our far-future progeny will do this when necessary and not repeat the depraved mistake of the Builders. And besides that, will we ever find a happy answer to a vexing question: Why didn't the Builders make an additional, independent seed generator on another gas giant?

The idea must have occurred to them, yet they did not pursue it. What was the risk that frightened the consummate risk takers? Is there some sort of exclusion principle involved, only one generator per galaxy allowed? One per universe? Flossie has an idle conjecture of an interference issue with how the seed generator entangles itself with the negative pressure of spacetime, suggesting two active seed generators must never have overlapping event horizons. Perhaps the true answer lies buried in the millions of years of Builder research records that are not even deciphered, let alone understood. Nobody is expecting an answer anytime soon.

On the practical side, we're at the dawn of new social and scientific eras, starting with a sixty-year construction plan to interlock the cities of Whistlestop. There will be two hundred and forty portals per city, sixty from each of the four portal branches. The industial guild has commited to installing one portal hub per season for each city. The old single-hub network was was limited to about twenty thousand citizen exchanges per day. It was adequate for normal use but an emergency evacuation could take weeks. Sixty years from now, that number will be expressed in hours. And the excess portal production is restarting the space exploration that could last beyond anyone's imagination, an estimated six point five to seven million Pic years before the anchor needs to be reset. Over two million open doors, eventually to anywhere in the galaxy. Perhaps we could even explore Andromeda the last million years or so if we set course now. Does anyone plan that deeply?

Our celebration gathering this evening will be unique. Jorani and I are anticipating our final decision to announce the world's first joint human-Pic marriage, two pair of Pic and one pair of humans joining in common purpose to cherish, honor, and stand with each other until the close of our lives, and to love our children and to nuture and guide them while they are minors. Jorani and I will become a true daughter and true son of a dozen Pic parents, and I will one day be a true father to both

human and Pic children. And in my heart, I can't wait for the challenge to unfold. And our trial is over because our fusion is complete.
Meanwhile…

Alice rubbed muzzles with Christopher as he arrived home. She buried her hands in the pink and gold zebra stripes on his back as they hugged. "Do you want something to eat before you sack out?"

"Thoughts of sleep sound really nice," he replied in a tired whistle.

"You won't mind?"

"Of course not." They had a brief shower and were soon lying in bed.

More nuzzling. "How did your check-up go?" Christopher whistled as his hand gently caressed the growing bulge under Alice's brown and black flank.

"A O K, as Earthies say," replied Alice in English. She then whistled, "You really need to talk to the Council about these all-night meetings."

Christopher sighed. "This one was probably the last for a while."

"Ah, a decision at last! And the verdict is?"

"We say nothing… Surprised?"

"Not really. More relieved than anything. Don't be sad about losing." Alice licked her husband's cheek. "Your position was quite noble. It's just not the right path."

"It's not the defeat. It's what comes next. I have visions of a blindfolded person running with reckless speed off a cliff. The similarities between Earth and the end of the Second New Kingdom… the patterns of mindset are repeating. Technology has leapt far beyond the morality, plus humans have damaged their planet in ways Pic would never dream of. You said it yourself the first day we met. Humans are insane to develop bio weapons…" Christoper sighed heavily. "The technological collapse will be severe…"

Alice finished the thought. "…and perhaps sooner than we expect. But Earth will not take our advice. Humans will have to learn the lesson as it occurs. There is no other way."

Christopher grunted. "We'll be lucky to miss the worst of it. Our precious gamma though…" His hand returned to caress the bulge of their child-to-be.

"… will have to adapt," finished Alice. "Can't you feel it? The distrust we have now, seeing hidden knowledge and lack of clarity as correct paths. We're being assimilated into Earth's norms. But the change is necessary for us to survive here. Dearest?"

"Hmm?" Christopher murmured as he drifted into sleep.

"It's still a life worth living. We will endure."